ISLAND
OF
DEAD GODS

ISLAND
OF
DEAD GODS

VERENA MAHLOW

atmosphere press

To Alan and Konstantin, my two beloved males of the species!

I can't thank you enough for supporting me in every possible way. Also thank you, Carolyn, and thank you, Dana, for reading and reviewing whole drafts in different stages. Thank you, Blake, for your professional encouragement, and thank you, Barbara, for your as professional edit and review. Thank you, Linguee and my old dog-eared dictionary, for eliminating my occasional linguistic doubts. Thank you, Ibiza, for being the magic motivator. And thank you, Nick, Bryce, Viannah, Cameron, Kelleen, and Matthew, for making this book happen.

I decided to tell this story because it keeps haunting me. But be aware: it is dangerous—for everyone involved. And the whole dilemma, I'm afraid, is just starting to show.

~Philine Mann

It's a pandemic of global proportions.

~UN General Assembly

Villa Éscorpion, Ibiza, March 9th, 2019

It is not true that trouble shared is trouble halved. Your pain will always be yours alone, whether it hurt only you, or three others, or millions. And it doesn't matter if you tried to resist or learned to live with it or if you were courageous or a coward.

"Coward" was the last word Amanda thought when the cyanide, traveling to her insides on a gulp of French champagne, started a fire. First it burned her tongue, her gullet, and when the poison hit her gastric acids, things really got wild. Membrane, tissue, nerve fibers, muscles were slashed like paper in a shredder, flinging her body in crazy spasms. The pain seemed to last forever. It only died down when seagulls announced the new day Amanda would no longer have to face.

Rosenda, the housekeeper, discovered her employer in one of the lounge chairs at the swimming pool. The first thing she noticed was Amanda's smooth, rosy complexion. Rosenda frowned. So she's done it too instead of growing old the way Mother Nature intended. Isn't this supposed to be a woman's world now? Does she really think this can be a solution to the problem? To him?

What Rosenda did not know was that Amanda's rejuvenated face only reflected the oxygenating effect of the cyanide. When, after multiple repetitions of "Good morning, ma'am" the closed eyes still wouldn't open, it dawned on Rosenda that no plastic surgeon had worked here, but *Moth*, the God of Death.

LAST TRIP TO IBIZA

CHAPTER 1

Departure had been delayed to almost midnight. For the umpteenth time, the ferry's loudspeakers emitted the old resistance song and last year's summer hit, "Bella Ciao." Philine—or Phil, as she preferred to be called—hummed along, "One morning I woke up / and there was the invader..." but after a while, the words felt like punches. When the engines finally fired up and drowned out the music, people cheered as if they hadn't counted on departure anymore.

From the upper deck, Phil watched the ritual of Spanish farewells: passengers throwing rolls of toilet paper at the people below on the dock. As the *Balearia* ferry pulled out to sea, the travelers kept the end pieces grasped while the ones staying behind tried to catch the rolls. Some paper dropped into the water, but most spanned between the hands of the people on board and those on the dock like a metaphorical bond. It blew in the wind, unrolled, stretched, still connected. Only when the ship left the harbor did it tear apart.

For a moment, Phil wished she also held such a piece of paper in her hand, but then she thought, why? It was toilet paper. Silly symbolism. Her connection had already torn. She should accept it. She did accept it, and she would manage on her own. She patted down her reddish curls, damp in the drizzle and writhing around her head like Medusa's snakes. She would.

The waves line-danced towards the open sea; the ferry stomped along. Seagulls accompanied her, screeching something like, "That's it that's it." Phil massaged her ears until the words disappeared and only seagull cries were left. When the lights of Barcelona had sunk into the night, she went below deck.

In the dormitory cabin, the crying of overexcited babies competed with TV noise, and a stale smell of food and sweat hung in the air. The only empty seat Phil could find was in a row of three. At the window lounged a blonde woman in a black leather coat with a profile like Charlize Theron. She focused on her smartphone, an intense expression on her heavily made-up face. An elderly lady sat towards the aisle reading a pulp novel. When Phil climbed across her, she accidentally pushed the book out of the hand of the lady, who reacted with a remarkable expletive, "*Ay! Hostia puta.*"

"Sorry." Phil fished for the book and was rewarded with such a mischievous grin she felt like giving the woman a hug. But she only smiled back, "*lo siento, señora,*" slipped off her boots and, with her toes, arranged them side by side under her seat, so none of them would get lost alone. She rolled her green sweater into a pillow and closed her eyes.

When she opened them again, Phil's first thought was that she should have paid for a plane ticket. As if a few more debts would have made much difference now. She often had sleeping problems, but this night in the dormitory cabin had been like sleep deprivation-torture. The air below deck had intensified to near suffocation, passengers competed in a snoring match, especially the elderly lady at Phil's side, and her *butaca* proved to be the most un-ergonomic sleeping chair on Earth.

But now, golden morning light fell through the portholes,

and on the horizon Ibiza appeared—*la Isla Blanca*. Phil's tiredness was replaced by giddy anticipation, as always, when she got close to her favorite island. The approaching coastline, the sandy beaches, the gentle hills over jagged cliffs where hotels and mansions jostled with modest farmhouses for the best sites by the sea—she loved it. As she loved her house, the charming old *finca*, three whitewashed stone squares that made two bedrooms and a *sala* with a kitchen, an unreliable shower and a roof leaking in two spots when the rain fell and the island winds howled. A house full of imperfections, but gentle like a rugged old friend.

It used to belong to Phil's great-aunt Charlotte, who in the Seventies dropped out of her affluent German existence to become a hippie and live in accordance with nature. Charlotte spent the rest of her life on the island she called magic. When she died at ninety-seven, Phil could hardly believe she was the lucky one to inherit the *finca*.

"Because you're a kind of hippie too," her cousin Felicitas, who got a whole townhouse in Frankfurt from Aunt Charlotte, had snapped. What she probably meant by "hippie" was that Phil was leading her life with no ring on her finger, a single mother in a freelance-job with no more than basic pension rights and no plans to change this. Which, in Phil's opinion, didn't have much to do with being a hippie. Her life was the result of a myriad of factors: reflections, reflexes, wrong decisions, right decisions, pure coincidences. Usually, she felt quite comfortable in it. Although not lately.

Phil's excitement was replaced by a heavy heart—but she'd better not dwell on the past. Instead she would have to act now, and everything would change. She would lose her beloved *finca*, the home she had dreamed about moving to full-time as soon as her son was through school and she could afford it. Now she never would. Because she was broke. Bankrupt. Alone. She had twelve days to solve the problem.

Phil struggled out of the uncomfortable *butaca* and fished

for her boots. The elderly lady had already left, but to Phil's left, the hand of the blonde woman was dangling from the armrest. It was a beautiful, strong hand, a hand one wanted to shake. No nail polish on the long-limbed fingers, no ring but a heavy silver bracelet that wound around the wrist like a snake. The hand's owner was sound asleep, regardless of the stale air, the narrowness and, again, the brutal noise. Her made-up face, contrasting strangely with the authentic hand, rested in the ghastly chair's cushion, protected by a cocoon of bleached hair.

Phil's lashes, almost invisible in their natural state, longed for mascara, her curls screamed for a comb and her teeth for a brush. But as the restrooms reeked of un-flushed things and seasickness, she decided to postpone her restoration.

CHAPTER 2

In Dallas, Texas, the sun rose seven hours later. The moment Adam opened his eyes, he knew he had made a mistake. Again. Damn booze. But after the daylong meeting in which Major General Anita C. Peyton had briefed him and his fellow investigators on the crisis, everyone needed a drink. Never before had they been confronted with so many voiced concerns, complaints, denouncements, and rumors concerning the armed forces. Adam, who had quit military police to become an independent contractor, knew that a hell of work lay ahead of them.

Not that evening, though. Adam had ordered another round.

When his colleague Lori from nearby Fort Worth sat down close to him, knees touching, and reminded him of how special their relationship had been, he was tackling margarita number four. And his rational brain had already begun to shut down.

Now it was morning, and Adam cursed himself for restarting an affair that had never been a relationship. Lori was searching his crumpled sheets for her lost real-hair eyelashes while her accusations beat down on him like cold rain.

"I'm very sorry," he said, genuinely sad, "I know I'm an egomaniac and incapable of a relationship. You mentioned that before."

Why in the world did it mean so much to Lori to leave her hairbrush in his bathroom? As if she wanted to stake a claim or leave a red dot on an object meaning "Sold." Did she not need her hairbrush at home?

"And that's it, right?"

"Look, we both said it'd be for the best..."

Lori was fuming. "Fuck you!"

Adam was relieved when the phone in the hallway rang. He closed the door behind him and picked up.

"Hello?"

Immediately his ears were attacked by a foreign voice full of rolling Rs. Adam heard "Amanda Scherer... Ibiza." Then he understood he had a policeman on the line, an Inspector Dziri, with heartbreaking information.

The phone in his hand, Adam stood petrified as Lori came storming, carrying with her a fanfare of new accusations. When she saw his face, she choked off the bitching.

"My sister died," Adam said.

Lori took him into her arms, pressed herself against him as if to seize the opportunity. Adam leaned against her warm body, wishing he would never have to move, or speak, or think again. Wishing he could just cling to her and trust and love. But this chapter was closed for him.

He softly pulled Lori's hands apart. "I´m sorry," he said, "but I need to be alone now."

Amanda's letter arrived the same morning, after a week in transit from Ibiza to Dallas. Hasty words, sputtered out in her tiny handwriting, a spidery scrawl, as if she had been shaking while writing:

Dear Adam,

It's been such a long time since we talked. You may say I'm responsible for this silence as I am the big sister and did nothing to change it, and you are right. But I never knew how to breach it. What to say. I will always remember the look in your eyes when Dad took off with you. Over 40 years ago, can you imagine? People are so cruel. When you came back, I knew we had another chance as Adam and Amanda. Remember how we used to say I have an extra syllable because I am the older one? Please forgive me, Adam, that I was not able to take this chance. I was already too screwed up then, trapped in my illusions. A friend of mine calls himself "Nobody," and this is me as well, reduced to nothing and nobody, betrayed, humiliated, effaced. Everything in my life has gone wrong. Oh, Adam, I miss you so much. Please, let's try one more time, I beg you, let's talk. But if something happened to me, know that I have always, always missed you.

Love, Amanda

CHAPTER 3

In the ferry's cafeteria, TVs were flickering in every corner. On the blurred screens, a newscaster threw out word cascades in rapid Spanish. Phil ordered a coffee and sat down by the big panorama window.

Someone asked, "May I?"

Without waiting for an answer, the blonde woman who had slept next to Phil placed a steaming cup on the table. She dropped in a chair and took a hearty bite from a croissant. Her unbuttoned leather coat, tight around her shoulders, revealed a camouflage t-shirt showing her cleavage.

She sipped her coffee. "Black. Strong. Doesn't get better."

Phil flashed her a smile. "That's true."

"Check." The blonde held up one hand for high five, the way Anton and his teenage friends welcomed each other. "I'm Tamar Stettin."

"Ahm. Philine Mann. Phil." Half-heartedly, Phil tapped against the palm. "Hi, Tamara."

"Tamar. Old Testament." The woman giggled and started chatting as if Phil were an old friend. She was coming from Frankfurt after dumping her boyfriend who, she said, had hung on to her like a damn leech. Suffocating. She needed her freedom. And couldn't wait to be back in Ibiza, her home.

"And you? Vacationing? You're damn early."

Phil made a face. "I wish." Like a blow, it hit her that this was actually the first time she'd traveled to Ibiza on her own, without Anton. She explained that she was coming to sell her house... as she needed the money badly, she added, infected by Tamar's frankness.

"What happened?"

"Oh, family shit." She wouldn't go so far as to reveal her drama to a stranger.

"Bloody hell, I know. Fucked-up finances can surely spoil a girl's mood."

"True again."

Phil was rewarded with a wide grin. "So... find someone to marry and let him take care of it."

"That's the plan. Know someone, tall, dark, handsome, tons of money?"

"Well, let me think. I could..." Tamar obviously didn't get sarcasm.

"Forget it. I'd rather sell a kidney. Or, for now, my house."

"Right. You'll work it out just fine. Just get the max out of it."

"That's what I hope."

"And you can." Tamar leaned close to Phil, conspiratorially, "Because today is your lucky day, believe it or not."

"Rather not."

"You should! Because you met me."

"Okay...?"

"What you need is someone you can trust. Who gets the best deal for you. And I know exactly the one."

Before Phil could react, Tamar had pulled out her phone and was already speaking. "Hey. Back in the fast lane? That's the right attitude. Listen, I've got someone for you..."

Moments later, Phil had an 11 a.m. appointment with an agent called Jorg Scherer, Mr. Big Shot in real estate, as Tamar boasted, on Ibiza and all of the Balearic Islands. Phil typed the address of TAB Real Estate in a *Villa Éscorpion* into her phone.

"Thanks... so much."

Awkwardly, she crossed both arms in front of her, a little overwhelmed. She would not even have time to drop off her bag and say hi to Doro. But she should be grateful for Tamar's helpfulness. Mr. Scherer might spare her a lot of running around, looking for a competent realtor on her own. The countdown was ticking.

"You can trust Scherer, he is the best," Tamar spoke as if she could read Phil's mind. A crease appeared between her eyes. "Even though life is not all too easy for him these days." She gently massaged the crease away and echoed Phil, "Family shit. But what can I say..." She grinned in her previous unconcerned way, "Hell is empty, and all the devils are here. Shakespeare."

Shakespeare? Literary quotes were about the last thing Phil would have expected to run across these painted lips. Proved one should not be prejudiced.

Tamar finished her coffee and pulled out a card. "Here, dear. Call if you need anything else. I know everything and everyone on Ibiza."

Phil started to thank her again, but suddenly Tamar's attention was distracted. She stared at a TV screen where the *telenoticias matinales* had begun.

This morning's big news was about someone called Kai Maurer, a name Phil recognized right away. He had been flying from the Spanish mainland to Ibiza when his single-engine aircraft went into a spin above *S'Espalmador* just north off the Ibizan coast. It brushed the tiny island's watchtower and crashed into the sea, killing the man.

Police boats bobbed across the screen. Underneath a helicopter's belly was a coffin attached to long ropes. A reporter wondered into his microphone: Why had Maurer, a pilot with longstanding expertise, not been able to safely bring down the plane? Especially as the Cirrus DC SR22 was standard-equipped with a rescue parachute. Why didn't Maurer push the right button?

"No loss for humanity, the scumbag," Phil heard Tamar mutter.

"You know him?"

"I told you, I know everyone on Ibiza." Tamar's face suddenly bore a fierce expression. "This was Maurer. *The* Maurer. The ALPHA Insurance-jerk..."

"Right."

ALPHA Insurance, Phil knew, had been involved in a public scandal about their executives' incentive trips to an Italian brothel. Kai Maurer had organized these trips and was caught trying to tax-deduct them. As one of the legal interpreters, Phil had been sworn in at the court hearings to translate the testimonies of two underage prostitutes. A job she didn't like to remember, as Maurer got away with a ridiculously low fine. It also had been Phil's last job as legal interpreter before she lost her license. Bankrupt people didn't qualify for this task.

She finished her coffee, ready to get out.

On the upper deck, passengers watched the harbor approach—and for a moment, Phil's excitement was back. Ibiza was so beautiful. A fairy island. And the air! She wished she could ask someone who knew about atmospheres, what exactly the Mediterranean air consisted of; what mixture of oxygen, nitrogen, and hydrogen made this special cuvée of smooth and aromatic, salty and sweet?

A flock of seagulls came floating towards the ferry like a welcoming committee. Behind them, the morning sun shared the sky with a fading moon. Brother and sister, *el sol* and *la luna*. Both equal.

"Magic," someone mumbled. Aunt Charlotte's word still rang true.

The vessel passed the peninsula of Talamanca with its hotels and discotheques and the few remaining farms and fishing huts that had survived the boost of tourism. Here, the magic got a bit lost, but it was back when the ferry entered the harbor, and the island's capital, *Ibiza ciudad,* appeared. The historic old town, an assembly of whitewashed cubic houses stacked on top of each other like toy blocks with which giant children play. Above them the fortification of Dalt Vila, the upper town, surrounded by massive stone walls. Like a *memento mori* they perpetuated the memory of all the foreign troops that, over the millennia, had invaded Ibiza: the Phoenicians and Carthaginians, Romans, Arabs, Vandals, and pirates. By building walls, watchtowers and perfecting the art of catapulting stones, the locals had protected themselves against the intruders. Only in the age of mass tourism had these effective methods gone out of style.

When a siren song of "ahs" and "ohs" drove the passengers to the ship's bow, Phil stayed behind. With one hand she grabbed the lucky charms dangling from her leather strapped necklace: a golden creole that used to be an earring, its double lost. A moonstone Phil had bought for its supposedly calming effect. A little brass owl for wisdom, a birthday gift from her best friend Doro. A green tourmaline. And the coin with an image of the Virgin, the only thing Phil had ever received from her father, the unintentional sperm donor, the priest.

CHAPTER 4

Adam spent hours convincing the Major General that he needed a week off. Yes, he was fully aware of the time pressure concerning his latest case—a high-ranking military man with a history of racist and sexist remarks—and he would not neglect it. But his only sister had died in Spain.

His boss only conceded when Adam promised that another skilled investigator, Lori Cummings from Fort Worth, would substitute for him. Then it took him an extended dinner at Urbano Café to convince Lori that he needed her more in Dallas than on Ibiza where she wanted to hold his hand at Amanda's funeral. Lori now called him "honey" and wouldn't stop talking about the dangers of withdrawing into his shell and the healing power of reaching out. Adam knew she meant well, even wished he could reach out to her. But his whole being yearned to be left alone.

The next morning, he acquainted Lori with the case of the highly decorated colonel and his as highly compromising quotes in social media. When Lori wondered, "Fake news or truth?" Adam knew she was intrigued.

He barely caught the 4:15 p.m. flight to Frankfurt where, the following morning, he would change planes to Ibiza. As the

American Airlines jet crossed the Atlantic, Adam was not able to shut down his brain for even one moment. Again and again he read Amanda's letter until he knew it by heart. The despair in her words caused him almost physical pain. How could it have happened that he and his sister had drifted so far apart? The loss of their closeness as children—*Amanda and Adam*—had been the result of their parents' bitter divorce. But why had they done nothing as grown-ups to reconnect? Even when Adam returned to Wiesbaden, Germany, where Amanda was still living at the time, they didn't find a way back to each other.

Adam sighed hard. Why had he been so distracted by a woman he thought he loved? Why didn't he turn to Amanda instead and talk to her? About their pain. The trauma of their separation. Once, Amanda had been the closest person in Adam's life. And now, she was dead.

After landing, Adam called his brother-in-law and announced his visit, but rejected Scherer's offer to stay in his villa. He rented a car, a Spanish brand called SEAT, and asked the rental agent in broken Spanish about a nearby hotel.

The young woman crushed a paper cup and threw it into a trashcan down the hallway. A perfect throw. Her English was perfect too.

"Most of our hotels are still closed this week," she said. "The onslaught has yet to start. But you're lucky, the Esperanza is open. It even offers the best view to Es Vedrà."

"Es what?"

"*Vedrà*. The magic rock on the west coast rising to an altitude of 1,300 feet," she explained in a tour guide-voice, "the third most magnetic spot on Earth. Home of the sirens that tried to lure Ulysses..." She stopped, realizing that Adam wasn't interested in tales. "I'll call for you. Single or double room?"

"I am alone."

After the young woman completed the call, she opened a map of the island. "You go to San José, see here. Turn left towards Es Cubells, left again and straight to Cala Cabo. At the next turn is the sign: Hostal Esperanza."

"Thank you. I appreciate that. Let me return the favor..."

... and get you a fresh cup of coffee, he meant to say.

But the woman interrupted him. In a serene yet slightly disdainful tone, she thanked him and added, "I don't do this merely—how do you say—as a favor to you. The hotel belongs to my husband's cousin."

Did she think he tried to make a pass at her? Blushing was new to Adam. Yet he decided against a clarification, said "thanks" one more time, and left.

Under an immaculate blue sky, Adam passed the brine basins of Ses Salines where sea salt had been extracted for three thousand years with the archaic methods of the Phoenicians and heaped up to a glittering white mountain. Then there were pine woods, orchards, cliffs, beautiful bays. Not so beautiful, however, those monstrous hotels squatting the cliffs. Adam drove on, turned left, took another turn and stopped the car. And there was the rock that must be *Es Vedrà*.

A breathtaking sight: an age-old chunk of condensed matter sitting in the sea as if a scornful god had thrown it down from the universe. A rock from another age of the world. A singular cloud veiled its peak. To its side, a smaller island stretched out like a sunbathing lizard. For a while, Adam didn't move. Then he drove on.

The cul-de-sac track ended in front of the Hostal Esperanza, a two-storied white building with a patio claiming the whole front. The second floor was framed by a balcony with eight wooden doors. The roof of fired tiles was protected by an enormous umbrella pine that called for hugging and stretching out in the white and red striped lounge chairs underneath it. In contrast to the monster hotels Adam had passed, the Esperanza had a sweet, old-world charm.

In the hotel's parking lot was another SEAT rental car with open doors. When Adam came to a halt, he saw a chubby man helping an as chubby woman out of the passenger seat. Only she clung to it with both hands.

"Now, come on," the man said. "Pull yourself together."

My fellow Americans, Adam smirked.

The woman stared at the horizon, the rock, her eyes terror-stricken. "I wanna go home," she whined.

"Enough now, woman. You're making a fool of yourself. You've got to stop taking those pills."

That worked. The woman gave up and was dragged out of the car. The blonde hair on her neck was drenched in sweat; the jacket of her beige traveling suit had dark spots under the armpits.

The man nodded at Adam. "Hi, there. Please do excuse my wife. After the long trip, she is a bit... exhausted."

He rolled his eyes, but jovially as if to say *Women!* and shook Adam's hand. "Mr. and Mrs. Ezra Huber from St. George, Utah."

"Adam Ryan. Dallas, Texas."

"Say good day, Trudy."

The woman ignored Adam's hand. "Hi. Who's that?"

Trudy pointed at the hotel. A young man with long hair had appeared on the patio, wearing a loose, white shirt above faded jeans. Something like hope was in her voice. "He looks just like the Archangel Gabriel."

In fact, the man had the face of a Renaissance angel and his shirt fluttered behind him as if hiding wings. From close-up, though, he showed to be not quite so young; his dark curls were partially streaked. Adam grinned. Archangel Gabriel with a gray sting.

"Announcer to the Virgin that she had conceived." Trudy folded her hands.

"Trudy," Ezra hissed.

Gabriel put on a professional smile and raised his hands as if to bless them. His English had a charming melodic accent. "*Bienvenidos* to Hostal Esperanza, Mrs. and Mr. Huber. And Mr. Ryan, I assume. I'm your host, Lluis Romero."

Adam said hello and took his luggage out of the trunk: a travel bag, his laptop, and the garment bag with his best black suit. The suit for Amanda's funeral.

Lluis led his guests to the patio. On a table lay two keys attached to big wooden numbers. Trudy wanted to grab one, but when Ezra darted her a warning glance, her hand petrified in motion.

"You may be hungry after the long travel." Lluis pointed to some plates containing bread, olives, a whitish cream. "This is *pan y aioli,* a specialty of our island. And may I offer you a drink? Coffee, tea, beer, a glass of wine?"

Adam sat down. "A beer would be cool."

Ezra plopped down opposite him. "If I may have some good, godly water."

Now Trudy did snatch one of the keys from the table and disappeared into the hotel.

Again, Ezra rolled his eyes. "Chemical imbalance," he explained.

CHAPTER 5

Phil did not rent a car but a Vespa, which was cheaper but a means of transportation she had never maneuvered in her life. First it stuttered maniacally, then sped up in wild leaps, almost throwing her off the seat. It was like taming a wild horse. On the back was only an elastic band to keep her carry-all, so Phil had to stop twice to gather it out of the ditch. Much to the amusement of some passing drivers who leaned out of their car windows and tried to flirt, "*Hóla, guapa.*" Some asked if she needed help. When one wannabe good Samaritan kept driving next to her at low speed, Phil took a turn to the village of Jésus.

She entered a café. It wouldn't hurt to have another coffee and one of those sweet pastries called *enseimadas*. Unhealthy but delicious. She was so tired.

Only two other guests sat at the bar, middle-aged tourists reeking of alcohol and frustrated testosterone. One was complaining about how many overpriced drinks it had taken to grope the *señorita* of last night.

"Well, hello there," he reacted to Phil's glare.

She suppressed the impulse to throw her coffee into his

face and finished it instead. But when she got up, she accidentally stepped on his foot. A quite primitive reaction as well, yet adequate. The guy shrieked, and Phil left. It was close to eleven, the time of her appointment with real estate agent Scherer.

A few kilometers from the town that, in the local vernacular, was named Santa Eulària des Riu, Phil made a turn off the main road. A sign with the name Vila Éscorpion led her up a steep trail lined with cypress trees. The scooter, huffing and puffing, barely made it to a semicircle framed by a whitewashed wall.

The figure of a scorpion punched in a metal gate showed Phil that she had reached her destination. She rang the bell above the nameplate TAB Real Estate Ibiza. The eye of a security camera seemed to contemplate whether to allow her in or not. A moment later, a silent mechanism moved the gate.

Under a pergola of rambling honeysuckle was a large silver vehicle with a winged letter "B" on the hood. Phil didn't know anything about cars, but this one looked like it belonged to the Queen. She followed the terracotta tiled path through a garden full of rockroses, oleander, and bougainvillea with their flamboyant but illusory blooms. A cactus hedge separated the path from a swimming pool surrounded by elegant loungers under matching sun umbrellas. Palm trees swayed in the breeze. Behind them, a panorama unfolded, which, even on this island with its thousand magnificent views, was breathtaking. The cerulean sky arched across the sea and, to the south, the islands Espalmador and Formentera.

The man who appeared, however, didn't match this perfection. His suit was rumpled, his hair an unruly comb-over, his face ghostly white. His eyes were bloodshot as if he had spent the night drinking. Or just hadn't had enough sleep. Welcome to the club, Phil thought.

"Mr. Scherer?"

"Welcome, Miss... ha... Mann." He pulled her hand to his lips, slobbering all over it. When he turned to lead the way, Phil hastily wiped it on a curtain.

The villa inside was as impressive as the yard. From the entrance hall, a wide brass-and-glass staircase led to the upper floor. To the right was a large parlor with two luxurious couches, a huge fireplace and a well-equipped bar. To the left, a Persian rug led to Scherer's office.

Its walls were covered with awards: Real Estate Agent of the Year, Top Selling Agent of the Balearic Islands, No. 1 on Ibiza. A framed caricature displayed Scherer as "Re d'Ibiza," the king with a ponytail, scepter, and crown. The most striking piece, however, was a small clay figure in an alcove. It depicted a stout, bow-legged creature that seemed to jump at the viewer, challenging him with his incredibly over-sized penis held in one hand.

Scherer sat down in a throne-like desk chair. He rubbed his eyes, fiddled with a crackling package, withdrew a pill and swallowed it without water.

"Mr. Scherer?"

For a moment, the realtor stared at Phil as if wondering who the hell she was. Then he seemed to get it. Or the pill took effect. He sat straight up.

"All right, Miss Mann, let's get to business. But first, thank you for choosing TAB Real Estate. A smart choice, if I may say so. Our customers around the world confirm we are the best."

Definitely at bragging. "Thank you."

"So you want to sell?"

"Right, actually I..." Phil swallowed the rest. No need to explain her reasons. The realtor didn't seem interested either.

"You are the only legal owner of the *finca?* Good, that makes things easy."

He entered Phil's name in his customer file, copied the land register plan she had brought and the *éscritura* proving her ownership.

26

"I'm in kind of a hurry to sell." Nervously, Phil added, "But ... I should mention that the *finca* is not in top condition."

Scherer waved this aside. "Zero *problemo*. On Ibiza, you can sell any shack. Meaning I can. When can I come by? Three p.m.?"

Today? Well, they had to be fast. But...

"Tomorrow, sorry. Or better the day after..."

"*Mañana, mañana.*" Scherer sighed. "Why, when the clock is ticking?"

"Excuse me?"

"We need to be on the market before the season starts."

"Tomorrow afternoon then."

"As you wish, Miss... Mann."

"Could you... I mean do you have an idea what the sale might bring? I mean how much, roughly?"

Phil hoped to make a profit of, maybe, a hundred fifty thousand. After all this was Ibiza, one of the world's holiday hotspots...

Scherer studied the documents. "Two eighty, at least, I'd say, probably three."

"Thousand?" Phil was baffled. "Three hundred thousand?"

Her surprise amused Scherer. Now, he was entirely in his element. "Dear Miss Mann, of course thousand. If the house had a view to the sea, we'd add another fifty. Thousand."

"Wow, I hadn't thought... There is a view, from the roof."

"Well, dear, great. But unfortunately, those dimwits from historical heritage are pretty rigid when it comes to turning an old roof into a sun terrace..."

A rant against building regulations whooshed by Phil's ears. Three hundred thousand! She had expected, as worst-case scenario, to be negotiated down to one twenty or thirty. Three hundred thousand was music to her ears. A symphony.

When Scherer was finished ranting, Phil agreed to show him the house at three p.m. the next day and exchanged an almost heartfelt handshake. Someone who brought such good news could not be *completely* unlikable. The phrase *pecunia non olet*—money doesn't stink—popped into her head.

Scherer walked her back to the gate, and Phil stoically endured another hand kiss. But suddenly he winced as if she had stung him and dropped her hand.

"Those goddamn crazy..."

Now Phil saw it too: the wall surrounding the estate that had beamed in immaculate white upon her arrival, had, in the meantime, been spray-painted with gigantic red graffiti. *Tu, lleno de toda maldad, hijo del diablo, enemigo de toda justicia.* You, full of malice, son of the devil, enemy of all justice. An Old Testament threat? Sounded like it. The letters dripped like blood down the wall. Someone seemed to dislike agent Scherer even more than Phil.

CHAPTER 6

Adam stretched out on his bed and briefly nodded off; then his restlessness returned. Amanda stood in front of his eyes, little Amanda, the day she had a wisdom tooth pulled. Holding Adam's hand, she had marched bravely into the dentist's waiting room. But when her name was called, she turned into a maniac—cried, howled, clawed her fingernails into his arm, her whole being helplessly exposed to the pain she anticipated. Adam remembered his parents discussing general anesthesia with the doctor who was afraid she might bite him.

Physical pain had always been Amanda's biggest fear. Since Adam had learned that his sister died from cyanide poisoning, a conviction kept growing in him: someone like Amanda would not expose herself to the agony of this poison. Not voluntarily.

He took a shower and dressed in a fresh shirt. Without paying attention to the spectacular view, he hurried across the balcony. No soul was to be seen, the hotel drowned in silence. Even the big hall clock seemed to be ticking more softly. At the door, a cat lay sprawled out, playing dead. *Siesta* reigned, the quiet hours. Adam typed into his phone. The navigator would show him the way.

Above the entrance of the police headquarters, a Spanish flag hung limply as if it were also holding *siesta*. A security guard rocked a machine gun in his arms like a sleeping baby. Adam asked his colleague at the reception for Inspector Dziri and learned that *el comisário* would be back from *siesta* any minute.

Forty minutes later, Adam received a friendly wave. "*Ahora el comisário está a Su disposición.* Third door to the left, if you may."

Bartolo Dziri was a short man in his mid-to-late thirties sitting behind a desk, a mountain of files in front of him. Instead of a tie, he wore a paisley-printed scarf and a meticulously groomed mustache. His hair was held back by fancy sunglasses. For a policeman, he seemed extraordinarily fashionable, which struck Adam as somehow typically European.

Dziri jumped up, grabbed his hand and moved it back and forth like a beam pump. His English was heavily accented but, as most Ibizans' who have to deal with the many foreigners on the island, quite excellent.

"What a tragedy, Mr. Ryan, to lose a sister, especially this sad way. A sister in her prime...."

"*Comisário* Dziri, I don't believe she committed suicide."

Obviously shocked, the policeman dropped his hand and gave him a bewildered look, sank into his chair, pressed his fingertips together, cleared his throat. Adam sat down in a visitor's chair and waited. In his job as a criminal investigator he was familiar with the various reactions a suspicion, bluntly thrown into the ring, could cause. Dziri's impulse was to regain sovereignty. It wasn't a surprise. He knew why Adam had said those words.

"But, dear sir, what would make you think so?" he pretended anyway. "Of course, I understand that one refuses to believe a beloved person would..."

"Let's not beat around the bush." Adam pulled out his Special Agent badge and shoved it over to Dziri, "Especially as we are sort of colleagues, even though I left active military police duty. These days, I am investigating for the Pentagon's Sexual Assault Prevention and Response Office. SAPR."

If Dziri knew about the office, he didn't show it. "I see." He returned Adam's badge, playing it cool. "Big Brother."

"Colleague," Adam repeated.

Dziri again cleared his throat. "All right. I can assure you, esteemed Mr. Colleague, that my men and I as the officer in charge investigated thoroughly."

"I don't doubt that, Detective Dziri. But I have reasons..."

Adam hesitated, aware that Amanda's sensitivity to pain would not count as valid evidence of murder. "My sister sent me a letter just before she died..."

"Ah—that's why we haven't found a suicide note."

"No suicide note. An attempt to get back into contact. She was afraid something might happen to her. And she was depressed..."

Which might have been caused by or led to Amanda's wish to die. Of course, Adam could understand the skepticism in Dziri's eyes.

"Mr. Ryan, be sure that the exclusion of murder was our utmost priority. But there was nothing. No motive. No reported hostilities. No financial conflicts. Not the smallest snippet of foreign DNA. The estate where your sister died is supervised by motion cameras and a highly sensitive alarm system. Nobody tried to gain entry that night. The housekeeper, Rosenda Marí Torres, left hours before Mrs. Scherer's death around four o'clock in the morning. Her husband has an alibi for the night. Testified by a bunch of... gentlemen." Dziri tugged at his mustache as if to remind himself to watch his words. "We have absolutely no indication of a crime."

"What about the cyanide? Where would Amanda have gotten it from?"

"From a *farmacia* that closed down two years ago. A silver cleaner that is not sold anymore. Who knows how long it was sitting in your sister's house. Know what?"

Dziri rummaged through the files and handed him one. "Why don't you just look at the report yourself? I know, quite an unusual offer, but among colleagues... If you don't understand some of the Spanish, please ask."

His hand waved across the mountain of files. "Other than that... I must apologize. I have to finish a report. A plane crash right off our coast, one victim. The deceased was a top manager." Dziri cringed, "The pressure—you have no idea!"

But of course, Adam did. He read and, although he didn't have the best command of Spanish, understood that suicide as the cause of his sister's death had been confirmed; the death certificate stamped and signed. The authorities had already closed Amanda's file.

CHAPTER 7

Phil decided to stop one more time and parked the Vespa on the boardwalk of *Santa Eulalia*. Down in the shell-shaped bay, beach chairs had been set up, and some early tourists sunbathed in bikinis and Bermuda shorts while the locals still wore their winter coats. Phil passed her favorite sculpture, a pack of *Podencos Ibizencos,* Ibiza-hounds cast in bronze by the artist Andreu Moreno Torres. Strolling along the water-lined promenade, *Las Ramblas*, she passed a pink building with the nameplate *Insular—The German Weekly* that brought back memories. Once, Phil had worked for the magazine, translating essays on the history of the Pitiusas Islands.

Down the *ramblas* was an old café where no two chairs matched, and no concessions to tourism were made. It was called Toni Pep and hadn't changed one bit since Phil ordered her first *bocadillo con calamari* here. When the waiter regretted that calamari were out, it seemed almost symbolic to her. Sticking to just another coffee, she leafed through an older issue of the *Diario d'Ibiza*. That's when a bold headline struck her: "Cyanide in Champagne: Suicide." Phil gasped: here it was, the reason for agent Scherer's strange behavior. Not even a week ago, his wife—and surely "Mrs. S., the wife of a well-

33

known German realtor" was she—had been found dead.

Phil went through the article and learned that Mrs. S. took the poison late at night at the pool with a glass of champagne and died a slow, painful death while her husband was partying with friends. Had he not gotten so wasted, the grieved widower was quoted, he might have decided to swim a few rounds after coming home, which could have been his chance to save his beloved wife's life.

In Phil's mind, the pool with the fantastic view appeared, the palm trees, the chic loungers. Mrs. S. in one, surrounded by beauty, but desperate, with no alternative to death. Phil wished she had been nicer to Scherer.

She strolled back to her Vespa. How she would love to stretch out in the sand and let the sun soothe her tired face. But it didn't make sense to procrastinate. She had to face Doro, her friend who had been living in her house for the past months and now would have to leave.

Phil had known Doro for a quarter-century, since her first day at university when she tried to find her orientation class. Well-organized, with a map of the campus, Doro showed her the way, and they became friends, even though they could not have been more different: Phil studied rather laxly, got by with waitressing and translation jobs, graduated, and received her Master's Degree late, and only became established as a court interpreter at the age of thirty. Doro finished her M.A. on the French Revolution in record time, switched from Robespierre's "one man, one vote" suffrage to the Suffragettes and, right after her Ph.D., landed a job in her faculty, specializing in historical gender studies. But she and Phil never lost touch.

Doro had also been there when Phil lost their home.

The day the ATM swallowed her bankcard, she had still been in denial. After all, a cousin was family. Close. For Phil, besides her son Anton, as close as family could get, as her own single mother, a classical soprano, had missed most of her childhood touring the opera houses of the world. Phil had grown up with the cousin like a sister, so as adults it made sense to buy the duplex together. And in all the years that followed, Phil paid off her part of the mortgage, month after month, and never worried about who had signed the papers and who hadn't.

Because of trust. Trust, which counselors and self-help books label a positive quality, and Phil at that time did too.

Until Felicitas stopped paying her part. If it was her idea or if her new husband was behind it, could only be guessed. "No big deal, only on paper," she had said when they bought the house together and only Phil signed as creditor. But then it became a big deal, ending with the legally binding act: "What's on paper is what counts." Leaving Phil as the only one screwed.

Because of trust, her world crashed. She lost her part of the duplex to the bank, and the guy from customer service gave her a week to clear her account. Phil had to realize she had only one chance left to get back on her feet. She talked the banker into two weeks, bid forever farewell to her deceitful relatives and transferred her last savings, set aside for her son's education, into a new account. Then she paid for Anton's student exchange in England and booked a trip to Ibiza for herself. Not to stretch out in the sun and lick her wounds, though, but to sell her last belonging of value, Aunt Charlotte's gift. The house they had baptized Can Philanton, Phil's and Anton's house. The house they loved.

Phil had ordered a pizza for Anton, a glass of wine for herself, and explained that it had to be done. That even the *finca* was just a material thing. That someday their luck would return. The reaction of the fifteen-year-old surprised her. Instead of complaining, he said that when he was through school, he would make a shitload of money and buy Can Philanton back. Phil had started to sob, and in typical teenage embarrassment, Anton said, "Come on, Mom, not your fault, right?"

Right. Phil blew her nose, took a deep breath and thought about the real horrors of this world. To live under a dictator. In fascism. To be oppressed by a man. To have cancer. Not to have Anton. Misery was only relative.

When Doro heard about the disaster, she was there. Without hesitation, she offered Phil and Anton to stay in her spacious loft above the old city of Mainz, and moved into the remote Ibizan *finca* herself. Doro even made it look as if Phil did her a favor, not vice versa, as she had just taken a sabbatical to write her postdoctoral thesis on the *Dea Caelestis* who had been worshipped in most ancient civilizations. For her research on Goddess cults in the Mediterranean, Doro said, living on Ibiza was perfect.

Two weeks ago, when Phil had to make this heartbreaking call to announce that she would have to sell the *finca*, Doro had also been sweet. She consoled Phil, even though she was the one who would lose the roof over her head. "Don't you worry about me," said Doro, the best, the most altruistic friend on earth. No one had to feel like a motherless child with a friend like Doro.

But tomorrow, the loud-mouthed realtor would show up and disrupt her studious peace. How would Doro react now that it was happening for real? Phil had no idea. Until she had one: if Scherer really managed to sell the house for those high numbers, she would soon have a lot of money. Which meant she could ease Doro's eviction by offering to bear the costs of a rental for a while, for as long as she needed! That was it! The world brightened up.

A melodic *bing* announced a text message on Phil's phone. The words, "Arrived, cool here, kiss," made her even happier.

When she had booked Anton's trip to England under the condition that he'd text her on a daily basis, he had complained, "Mom. I'm almost sixteen!"

"Exactly," she had answered. "Sex, drugs, alcohol. That's why daily. Not negotiable."

The scooter chugged towards the western coast. In San José, Phil turned into a narrow road that meandered through the countryside. Not for the first time, she experienced a typical Ibizan phenomenon—the deeper one delved into the island, the bigger it seemed to grow, much larger than the forty kilometers between its two furthest apart points. Just like the fake giant Mr. Tur Tur in the children's book *Jim Button* that Phil had once read to Anton, only the other way around: an illusionary tiny Morrowland sprawling out with ever new lengths, depths and widths. Fields stretched out while being crossed, hills grew overnight, unexpected canyons blocked one's way. A Land of Oz, providing endless adventures.

The scooter puffed by an assembly of trash cans where two wild *Podencos*, offspring of one of the oldest dog breeds on earth, concentrated on sniffing the scattered trash until, far out in the field, a rabbit dared to leave its hole. Immediately they leaped up to hunt. Phil had read that Cleopatra, on her way to marry Caesar in Rome, gave the first *Podencos* as gifts to the hospitable Ibizans to help them fight the frequent rabbit plagues. Maybe a legend. Fact was that the long-legged dogs with the high-set ears of the Egyptian god Anubis adjusted well to living on the island and were adored even in art.

Phil turned into a dirt track, avoiding potholes and rocks. Idyllic farms lined her way, dogs barked, chickens fluttered about. Peasant women in black dresses, faces framed by straw hats, worked in the fields.

Finally, Phil laid eyes on Can Philanton, her last earthly possession. How thrilled she was to see Doro again. She bet they would chat far into the night, catch up on everything they had missed in the last months. They would cook together, drink too much wine and share a hangover the following day.

"Mother Nature is a bitch," Doro once wisecracked after one of those nights. "Unfair right down to the liver."

They both had roared with laughter.

And here it was, the *finca* with its blue-framed windows and white walls, its paint flaking off again. An ancient carob tree shaded the house with branches that over time had assumed the most extraordinary shapes. Behind it, a hedge of cacti formed an impenetrable wall.

Phil steered her Vespa through the open gate and parked it next to the old draw well where a tin bucket sat on the edge as usual. But why these plastic canisters? Was the cistern empty so the shower didn't work? Hadn't Doro got hold of the water supplier? Well, Phil knew how to deal with the local *mañana* attitude.

She approached the house, wondering in a whiff of melancholy: What would realtor Scherer's first impression of it be? Would he see a shabby old shack? Or a cozy home? She pulled herself together. It was only a house. A thing.

In the front yard, Greek gladiolus showed early pink buds, the yellow broom shrub was in full blossom, the grape hyacinth had turned blue. Can Philanton, the name Anton had painted on the wall, was already fading. The crooked bench below it leaned far to the left.

Strange how deserted everything looked. Phil pushed the door open. Inside, it was dark, the shutters still closed. A strange smell hung in the air. When Phil's eyes got used to the dark, she realized that it also looked bad. Really bad.

True, the *finca* had never been a flagship of household perfection. But Phil always kept it clean, even when the damp sea air tore plaster from the walls, or rain dripped through the roof. Doro was pretty tidy, too. When she was surrounded by the occasional chaos, it consisted of her papers. But this?

The *sala* had gone to ruin: the earthen floor was a mess of sand, trash, and ashes that had fallen out of the fireplace. Ashes also covered the furniture. Empty bottles, food cans, and plastic bags with the imprint of old Catalina's grocery store heaped up on the kitchen counter. The sink, full of dirty dishes, was a mosquito resort. Phil tried to switch on the lamp, but nothing happened. The kerosene lamp on the mantelpiece she kept filled in case of a power outage was bone-dry.

What in the world? Phil opened the door to Anton's room. At least here everything looked like it was supposed to: Her son's drawings and posters on the walls, his collection of shells and bizarrely formed rocks on the shelves. In Phil's bedroom, a musty smell hung in the air. On her bed lay a tattered blanket reeking of sweat and dirty sheets. Empty wine bottles clustered on the nightstand. The clothing rack was empty, but on the floor lay a pile that Phil moved with the tip of her boot: baggy, torn pants, a man's flannel shirt...

Phil hurried back into the *sala*. Where was Doro? Where were her books, papers, her laptop? On the shelves were only Phil's own books and her ukulele covered in dust. A hodgepodge of as dusty glasses could not have been used for ages. Certainly not to drink wine of all those bottles. Some chicken bones were rotting on the floor. Doro didn't eat meat.

What the hell was going on here? Phil tried not to panic. Her phone was clinging with one last bar of contact to the outer world. She pushed Doro's number. "The person you called is not available..." said an automated voice.

Phil heard her own heartbeat. What had happened?

Everything looked as if Doro had packed up and left, and someone else had taken over. What should Phil do? Call police? But there must be an explanation. No reason to overreact. Maybe Doro had gone on a research trip and allowed someone to stay here during her absence. Not unimaginable. Suddenly Phil wondered if she had even talked to Doro about the precise day of her arrival. The last weeks seemed like a blur; she couldn't be sure. She did remember saying that she would come as soon as possible. After she bought her ticket, she hadn't been able to reach Doro but had thought nothing of it. In Ibiza's boondocks, phone reception could still not be taken for granted. Phil had left a voicemail, but Doro might not have gotten it. So, maybe she invited a friend over, unaware of Phil's arrival today...

But a messy, alcoholic, probably male friend? Doro? Unimaginable. Doro didn't have male friends.

A squatter? Phil remembered reading about a foreigner's *finca* that had been invaded by a homeless family. But that house had stood empty for years...

At least she had to dispose of the rotting bones. With trembling fingers, Phil opened the pantry by the front door to get the brush and dustpan out.

And there she discovered something after all that belonged to Doro: Hidden behind broom, mop and vacuum cleaner was her backpack, a worn leather thing Phil would have recognized among hundreds. For twenty-five years it had been dangling from Doro's shoulder. Why was it sitting in the pantry as the only proof of her existence? Phil tried to call again. Nothing. Only her phone died off.

What about the key? With growing unease, Phil searched the sooty *sabena* beam above the fireplace. On its backside was the nail where the house key should be hanging. Phil ran her fingers across the nail. Nothing! Shit.

But she needed the key. She had to lock the house. She also had to postpone her appointment with Scherer. No, she couldn't; only eleven days to sell. She had to clean the house. Phil's thoughts jumped in all directions. She wouldn't find a moment of sleep in an unlocked house.

Maybe the other hiding place. The gate. As those old keys weigh a ton, Phil sometimes left hers in a gap between the bricks of the fence post, behind a piece of loose mortar. But had she even told Doro about this spot? Phil went back out to the gate and closed the right wing to reach the post.

That's when she discovered the rabbit's cut-off head.

It stood impaled on the iron peak above the gate's hinge and stared at her with horrified dead eyes between its shriveled rabbit ears. Its flews displayed a last sardonic grin while meeting death.

With a scream, Phil jumped back, right onto the headless body of the rabbit, recklessly discarded. Its once carefree paws writhed as if still begging to be spared. Phil screamed again and jumped back. What was this? Not a dead rabbit hunted down by dogs. Or men. The animal's head looked like something in a horror movie. Like a decapitation, a ghastly ritual. Blood had painted the fence post in a black lacquer being attacked by a squadron of flies.

With all willpower, Phil resisted the instinct to run. The key. Without the key she was lost. If it was sitting in the usual gap, it would be right underneath the rabbit's head. Right in the blood. Phil took a little branch and with utmost reluctance started to poke where the key might be. Nothing. Only the branch got stuck in something tough, and all of the sudden the rabbit's head moved forward. Some final, already viscous blood poured out of the shredded artery. With a sickening smack, a bloody lump hit the ground right next to Phil's boot.

That was it. She was done.

She raced back to the *finca*, grabbed her bag, spontaneously also Doro's backpack and fled to her Vespa. The scooter extended her panic by two misfires, but finally started to move.

Only when she reached the road she could breathe again. With screeching brakes, she stopped at the grocery store run by a middle-aged woman everyone called "Old Catalina." When Phil stormed in, Catalina was building little pyramids of apples. She jumped in surprise.

"Police," Phil shouted. "Catalina, please call one-one-two."

Half an hour later, Phil's panic had turned into frustration. The policeman on the line had told her that a messy place was no reason for alarm. Like a father to a querulous girl, he talked to her. The cut-off rabbit's head? Probably a joke. A catfight. A pissed-off neighbor. Nothing they could do as rabbits weren't a protected species. To report her friend missing? This friend was grown-up, right? Nothing they could do for the next twenty-four hours. In a patronizing voice, the man suggested that Phil should calm down.

CHAPTER 8

Tamar tried to keep the corners of her mouth raised. Nothing made one look older than a grumpy face. But right now she had a hard time smiling.

Seriously, did she not deserve to rest up a bit? First, all the fuss with her ex, Rob the moron, then the stressful job. Even Tamar was only human. The last day in particular had been pure hell. When she had come home to the resort, preparations for the new season were in full swing. So same procedure as every time: her mother Jezebel kissed her cheek, said "Well done, Tami," and went back to her chore. Of course without mentioning money. As frugally as Jezebel lived, it never occurred to her that her daughter might expect a little extra cash for executing her extra orders. No matter how much Tamar worked for everybody's benefit, it was one grand a month for her as for the others, and that was it.

In former times, Tamar had been proud that Jezebel trusted her the most. Tamar, the crown princess, right hand of the island's queen. But those times were over since Anat had appeared. Maybe she should confront her. Maybe Anat could make sure she got a decent pay. If someone deserved it, right?

The problem was how to get a hold of Anat. Once again

she was embodying "our Lady of Great Recluse," as Tamar cynically called it. Gone to the rock to meditate, Jezebel corrected her. While she and Tamar did all the work.

The *thing* was burning a hole in her pocket, but Tamar knew she couldn't cash it yet. However, she needed money. Now. Because she was thirty-seven. And too smart to buy this crap about the "transience of youth and magnificence of age," the "improving with age like fine wine" baloney. Every wrinkle tells a story of your life? Bullshit! For Tamar every wrinkle was a defeat. She would never become one of those women one constantly ran into on Ibiza—slim and trim thanks to workouts and diets, with thinning hair and wrinkled skin. Women men whistled at from behind, but turned quiet when looking into their faces. Bad enough to imagine...

That's why Tamar needed money. Money for the little shots of poison injected into her cheeks to stop the aging process until she'd be ready to let go. Until her vanity would be gone. Tamar knew the time would come—but not yet.

Immediately after lunch, Jezebel had assigned her new tasks: pick up the new programs at the print shop. Collect the laundry. Turn in the broken laptop. Drive to the airport to pick up the guests from India. Close down the market stall. Jezebel would give her cash, and as usual, Tamar would not insist on invoices including sales taxes. A good deal for everyone, mainly for herself as she would deduct an appropriate fee for her services. Tamar hated to scrape money together this way. But what could she do?

In the afternoon, she was happy again. Jezebel hadn't wondered why the laundry, print, and electronics shops were much more expensive than last time. Also picking up the Indian guests at the airport turned out to be worthwhile. The girl only stared into space with tormented eyes, an expression Tamar had often pitied on new arrivals. But the older woman in her golden sari had been quite chatty. After arriving, she passed Tamar a 200 euro bill and declined when she pretended to search for change. Tamar had thanked her as nonchalantly as if getting a 200 euro tip was no big deal. Inwardly she had cheered: now she could call the dermatologist.

Tamar checked her cell phone: two voicemails. "Hi Tamar, this is Phil. Philine, calling from Catalina's. Sorry, but I already have to ask for your help. There is a problem with my house, and I need a bed for the night. A cheap hotel, if you know one. My phone is just charging. Please call me back."

The girl from the ferry. A cool cat, with her red curls, those enormous eyes and the matching green sweater. But Tamar could really do without the financial troubles Phil had mentioned. Stupid girl, pretty enough—but probably too proud to put her assets to use.

The second voicemail sounded desperate. "Tamar, *please* call me back."

Tamar did, and an utterly relieved Phil told her a confusing story about her friend who had disappeared with her key and police who wouldn't look into it.

Hysteria was not cool. As Tamar still had to go to San Carlos to close down the resort's market stall, they could meet there in an hour.

"Relax. A friend of mine owns a *pension* that is super cheap. I make sure you get the locals' rate."

CHAPTER 9

The so-called hippie market, situated in the back yard of the restaurant Las Dalias, is a genuine institution in Ibiza. Phil had visited it a few times with Anton and loved it. Only now, the rabbit head stood in front of her eyes. Who in the world would decapitate a rabbit and put its head on her fence? Definitely not Doro who didn't even eat meat for her love of animals. But who then? And why?

The uncertainty was agonizing. Again and again, Phil called her again and again without success. She tried to comfort herself: Doro wasn't a girl one had to worry about. She was a tough, no-nonsense woman. Maybe she had offended someone. She could be quite blunt at times. And the offended had put the rabbit there for revenge? Quite drastic.

Or the rabbit had nothing to do with Doro's disappearance. Maybe Phil's plan to sell the *finca* had pissed her off after all, so she left? Not unthinkable. Phil knew that Doro could lose her temper. Once she had disputed with her professor over a historical fact or fake and thrown his book out of the window with a curse.

Phil tried to calm down. Surely, Doro would call soon, apologize, and explain where she was. And give a damn good explanation for the mess. But then: the rabbit head! What explanation could there possibly be for it?

The rhythm of drums welcomed Phil to the valley of Sant Carles de Peralta, as the sign read in Eivissenc. She passed the line of rental cars, parked the scooter in front of Las Dalias and grabbed her stuff and Doro's backpack. How she longed to get rid of it all and take a shower. And sleep!

The hippie market was even more colorful, chaotic and cacophonous than the last times she had visited. A wild cluster of stalls with everything one might want but never needed. Hand-made, -knitted, -woven and -sewn, stacks of pottery, traditional Ibizan embroidery, handcrafted jewelry, leather-skinned acoustic drums, hash and shisha pipes.

Soon, Phil discovered the stall Tamar had described. Under its night-blue canopy glittered a firmament of tacked-on stars. Heavy-perfumed incense sticks were lit in spite of the sunshine. Two large posters served as sidewalls. One depicted the twelve moon phases of the year; the other showed an antique female bust. It had been discovered in a local cave and was said to represent Tanit, the Phoenician goddess who some 2,500 years ago migrated from the Levantine to the Mediterranean coast. Tanit's face was captivating, a mysterious Semitic beauty with heavy eyelids and voluptuous curls. On her lips lay the hint of a smile.

On the counter, the goddess's face appeared on smaller busts, brooches, and ear studs. There were also heavy silver bracelets like the one Tamar had worn, and matching choker necklaces. A row of paperbacks signposted as "Can Follet-Studies." Phil remembered that Tamar's card bore the same address: Can Follet.

Two women puzzled over some glass vials containing a reddish soil.

"Seriously?" said one, "mud for thirty-nine euros?"

The salesgirl behind the counter looked like a mix of Wonder Woman and street fighter in tight leather pants, a bustier, metal belt, bracers, and a crown in her ash blonde hair. "No ordinary soil," she explained, her voice soft with a nasal accent. "This is *terra sancta*."

"Terra what? Looks like mud to me."

"*Sancta*. Sacred soil. Don't you know about it, girls?"

The women's irritation was met by an affectionate smile. They shrugged, which the salesgirl took as interest, giving them a lecture on the red earth of Ibiza, known to be sacred because no poisonous animal could survive on it.

"Even though we have the ideal climate for scorpions and such. In the 70s, some foreign hippies brought their poisonous pet-snakes along. They all died."

"Seriously?" One of the women was impressed.

The other was skeptical. "Well, pets die. Like everyone else."

"But already the antique geographer Pomponious Mela pointed out that no venomous creature was ever born or could propagate on Ibiza. Also, Plinius wrote that the soil of Ebesus—as the Romans called Ibiza—banishes them. The Romans always carried *terra sancta* on them when they went to war and scattered it around their tents to be safe from nightly attacks. That's the truth, girls."

Now, both women were fascinated. The more convinced one chose a vial in form of a heart. The other picked a spiral shape. "Guess it can't hurt."

From behind, someone bumped into Phil. A chubby woman, pushing her way through the crowd like a steamroller. She looked like a bloated Doris Day of the later years, a dapper appearance from her beige suit to her sensible heels. But she emanated a hectic rush. Her eyes twitched like a rabbit on the run.

"Amy," she addressed the salesgirl, "Heavens, here you are."

The salesgirl made a step back. "What the hell are you doing here?"

"Honey, your father and I have come to bring you home. What's this you're wearing?"

The way she talked echoed the girl's speech, soft American lingo full of glottal stops and omitted consonants.

Amy stepped back. "Mom, you know I've made up my mind."

"But Daddy won't accept it. We will make it easy for you, I promise. But you've got to change..."

"No way, I told you, Mom."

"But you have to. Amy, come home with us. Please. If you only repent..."

Amy's answer came like a gunshot, "Forget it."

The dispute started to attract the attention of the tourists browsing the stall. They gawked, sensation-seeking.

"The Scripture says you will be forgiven if you repent with all your heart. Your father is also willing to forgive you."

"Oh, really, Trudy?" Amy's voice turned contemptuous. "Guess what—I couldn't care less."

Tears were running down the mother's cheeks now, but someone giggled. Phil grabbed a brochure from the counter and pretended to study it.

"He only wants to save you, Amy. It's your duty as daughter," the sobs mixed with shrillness, "You are obliged to obey."

"Leave me alone, Trudy. I found my home."

"No, child, you belong to us. If you repent, all will be good again."

Phil couldn't bear it any longer. How pitiful the mother, how needlessly harsh the daughter. Her face in the brochure, she fled behind a tree and leaned against its reliable trunk.

The brochure offered a seminar titled "The Naked Truth." In the beginning of times, Phil read, skin and nothing else was considered the primeval robe of goddesses. *Only at the turning point of time, nakedness became eroticized...*

"Cool, right?" sounded Tamar's voice. "History is one big domino effect."

What? But whatever—happy that Tamar had shown up as promised, Phil gave her a hug. It was cordially returned.

"I already talked to my friend Lluis, and he does have a room for you. A great deal: sixty euros. Normally it's double that price."

Phil had to swallow, but surely sixty euros was a bargain on Ibiza, even off-season. Besides, with a little luck, her financial problems would soon be solved.

"Thanks, I really appreciate it."

Tamar pulled Phil back to the stall with the blue canopy. The market was drawing to a close. The vendors had started to wrap up their merchandise.

"I'll do the cash-up, then let's go for a drink before I take you to your bed."

"Great. And..." Suddenly, Phil realized that the *enseimada* had been her only meal all day.

Tamar obviously read her thoughts. "And we both need a bite."

"Yours will be on me then."

"Deal."

Amy was also busy clearing up her stall. There was no more trace of her mother and none of the recent agitation in the salesgirl's face. She gave Tamar the booklet with the day's listed sales and a pouch with money. Tamar recounted and pointed at Phil. "That's Phil, by the way. Amaryl."

Amaryl? "Hi."

The girl in her Wonder Woman outfit made the peace sign. "Hi. And bye."

"I'm pretty sure Doro must eventually have shown up at Can Follet," Phil said when she and Tamar were sitting in front of the Bar Anita in San Carlos. On the narrow sidewalk, their wooden chairs stood so close to the road that every time a car passed, they instinctively pulled back their feet. But out here, the evening sun still warmed them. The bar inside was bustling with people. With its history as the first hippie bar on the island, Bar Anita was never lacking customers.

They had ordered white wine and *tapas* that were so tasty Phil thought she would never stop eating. Tamar had just told her about her home, a holiday resort and seminar center specializing in gender studies. Her mother managed it; Tamar was her assistant.

"Doro is writing a book about the history of female culture, so I'm sure...."

Tamar was distracted. "Sorry, what? Check this guy over there. Cute, right?"

Phil shrugged. To her, the guy who sat three tables down the sidewalk looked like a human hamster with too tight pants and butt fat transferred to his cheeks.

"I bet Doro looked into your seminars."

"I still don't know her, but all right. I'll ask around."

Tamar sounded impatient. What did she care about Phil's vanished friend? But when Phil mentioned the rabbit head, she gained interest.

"What in the world?" She giggled, delightfully thrilled. "That's sick."

"Exactly. If I only knew where Doro is."

"She probably met a guy." Tamar couldn't understand Phil's anxiety. "The police are right—they have better things to do than search for every girl that goes screwing around for a while."

"But Doro isn't like that."

Phil took the check to pay at the register. Three women in apron dresses, playing cards with a priest in cassock, were the only locals among visitors: sunburned two-week tourists for whom the Ibizans had invented the hilarious term *los roast beefs*. Also some *residentes*, foreigners who lived or had vacation homes here, who carried straw bags and slapped the waiters' shoulders to show they belonged. Last, the notorious old hippies who at some point had been swept onto the island like driftwood. They all called themselves artist or philosopher, liked to engage the tourists in a conversation to get a free drink out of them and despised them as intruders when it didn't work.

When Tamar was done exchanging telephone numbers with the hamster guy, they drove back to Las Dalias and lifted the scooter onto her red pickup truck. On the road, Phil talked about Amy and her desperate mother.

"Her parents are here? Fuck."

Tamar told Phil Amy's story. When living in a missionary house in Barcelona where the Latter-Days Saints had sent her to convince Catalan Catholics of the Mormon belief, Amy realized that she had only gone on the mission to escape her parents. That she didn't believe in their religion of extraterrestrials, magic underwear and suppressed women. "One day she took the little money these temple twits allowed her to live on and bought a ticket to Ibiza."

"Courageous."

"Yep. And here she found us and turned into Amaryl, happy to live in freedom. But I guess at Christmas she got sentimental and called her mother."

"I felt a bit sorry for her."

Tamar shrugged. "It's a woman's own damn fault to subject herself to a man who still thinks he can rule. Lluis said two Mormons checked in his hotel. Probably Amaryl's parents. If Can Follet wasn't booked out, you'd have to come with me."

"Thanks," Phil grinned, "but I'm not really in danger."

They fell quiet and Phil's mind was back with Doro. Why hadn't she called yet? And the house. Phil's stomach fluttered when she thought about the mess and Scherer and the little time she had left...

The road passed olive and almond trees dozing in their groves, ploughed red soil and pinewoods. On the coast, big hotel complexes took over, maybe built overnight by the efficient *familiá,* one of the ancient spirits the Ibizans believed in. They reached Hostal Esperanza where Lluis welcomed Phil offering her a sprig of rosemary, saying this was Ibiza's perfume. She felt her cheeks blush. Stupid.

"Thank you—also thanks for the room. I already dreaded having to check in one of those monster hotels."

"I know!" Lluis reacted with unexpected fervor. "I hate them too. When I grew up, the coastal meadows were full of orchids. Now these criminals pave over the whole island with these awful buildings."

Guess she had opened a can of worms. Phil made a sympathetic face.

"Suddenly we even have snakes here, which was never heard of before. They kill our local lizards and threaten the biodiversity. But what can we do?" Lluis sighed, "A lot of our folks make a living off the monsters."

"Well, I am happy to be here. Excuse me for a minute."

Phil's room offered a grandiose view across the sea. She took a shower, changed into a fresh dress and checked her face in the mirror. The scooter-ride had already brought some color to her cheeks and the freckles back on her nose. She applied lip gloss and went out on the balcony.

In the sunset, Es Vedrà—the rock where Odysseus, the smartest of all men according to the Iliad, was said to have wrecked his ship, lured by the sirens' songs—glittered like a diamond.

Back down on the patio, the charming Lluis handed Phil a glass of wine. Tamar stayed for one too and told Phil how to get to Can Follet. Her mother had named it after another familiar spirit, the *follet* who could move as fast as the wind and change his appearance in a heartbeat. "When you have a *follet* in your house, you have made it," Tamar said. For her mother, this had proven to be true.

Phil's eyes fell on a man leaning against the balustrade, his back towards them. She did not see more than broad shoulders, a strong neck, and the back of a head with brownish, graying hair. But what she saw was enough to start an alarm bell in her. As if he heard the shrill noise, the man turned around.

CHAPTER 10

It was him, no doubt. Phil's head spun. She felt like standing in front of an abyss, she and him on opposite sides. One more step and she would fall. Years dissolved and catapulted this one night back into the now. This one scene. First Phil had tried to simply delete it from her mind, in vain, of course. Then she had analyzed it to shreds, chewed it up in her mind until only a blurry, semantic mush remained. And something dull in her heart. My heart stone, she called it with bitter irony when she still thought about it. Others have kidney or gall stones; she had a heart stone and learned to live with it. After all these years, it had stopped aching. Time, the great healer. But when Adam suddenly appeared in front of Phil, time proved to have only covered things up. The stone started to move.

"Phil."

Instinctively, Phil made a step backwards. Adam. His whole six feet something. His slightly slanted eyes like a wolf's. The dimple in his chin. The hair above his temples now had silvery strands. He had grown older, of course, after all these years; she had too. But he was undeniably Adam. Adam, the American, the Texan, the cowboy, big love, huge mistake.

"You are in Ibiza?" Adam whispered coarsely.

Phil tried hard to pull herself together. "Obviously, I am," she answered, aiming for a nonchalant tone as if her life depended on it. Only she didn't succeed. The "I am" squeaked. "What in the world are you doing here?"

Later, she couldn't remember what followed. She didn't know if or what Adam had answered. She only recalled Tamar's stretched "heeyy" while she poked Phil with her elbow, asking something. Who the cool dude was or something. Then turning her back to Phil. Blocking her off with her broad shoulders. Leaning towards Adam. Saying something in the same throaty voice she had used to lure the hamster guy.

Adam looked across Tamar's head, into Phil's eyes. "Incredible. Phil."

Thus forced to acknowledge Phil's presence again, Tamar asked, "You know each other? How come?" She leaned even closer to Adam. "I am Tamar, stranger. Tamar Stettin. Is it your first vacation on Ibiza? A glass of wine?"

"More wine, Phil?" Lluis filled up her glass. Only now she realized she had finished a whole glass without even tasting it.

"Adam Ryan," Adam said, somewhat confused. "No, thanks. Yes, first time, but not for vacation."

"Business then. Nice."

Tamar struck a model pose, one hand on her hip, her chest pushed forward, chin a bit down, eyes up to Adam. In any other situation, Phil would have sneered at the cliché. She wished she could just walk away. But her feet wouldn't move.

Besides, to leave now would be childish. She was just surprised to run into Adam after all these years. A bit shocked, maybe, a completely normal reaction. Phil forced her expression into neutral and courageously looked at him.

Tamar interfered, "What now? How do you guys know each other?"

"From the past," Phil said a nanosecond before Adam echoed, "The past."

Then both sputtered words: Ages ago. A summer in Mainz. In court because of the G.I. who had smashed someone's skull at the wine fest. Phil the legal interpreter. Adam the military cop, witnessing. Then two days later at said wine fest. They just ran into each other...

Adam's wolf eyes met Phil's and blinked as if they couldn't be trusted.

Composure, she commanded herself. Behave like a grown-up, Philine. Only to rattle on, "What business does a U.S. cop have on Ibiza? Another misbehaving G.I.?"

"A cop? Interesting." Tamar offered Adam a plate with *pan y aioli* as if she were the hostess. He shook his head.

"I'm no longer in the military. Or a cop." Adam swallowed hard. Something in his face changed. "My sister died, that's why I'm here."

His words had the effect of a sudden volcanic eruption. Lava flooded Phil, petrifying her. "Vesuvius, 79 A.D." raced through her mind. She had the strangest selective brain in the world. Shit, she helplessly thought.

Tamar was the first to recover. "Oh Adam, I'm so sorry. How insensitive of... us. If there is anything I can do. *Anything.*"

"My condolences," Lluis said.

"Shit," was also the only word Phil managed to say. She remembered a sister of Adam's, his only one, he had said, so she must be the one dead. Once, after Phil had been dating Adam for about a month, this sister had dropped him off at her door; a lady in an elegant dress who didn't take off her sunglasses when she gave Phil a lax handshake. "I'm Amanda, nice to meet you," she said, checked her watch and left.

Later, Adam told Phil about this standoffish seeming sister. How close they had been as kids. How they got separated when his father was transferred from Wiesbaden to Fort Hood, and their German mother couldn't imagine moving to a Texan Army base. Adam's father never mentioned her again and never allowed Adam to talk about her, not even after his visits in school breaks, little Adam alone on the eleven-hour flight. When he grew older, the General subtly made sure these visits became less and less frequent by offering Adam exciting alternatives: surfing camps in summer, skiing trips in winter. When Adam was thirty, his mother died, and he and Amanda grew even further apart.

Years ago, Phil had taken him into her arms, empathizing with the lost boy in the soul of the man. She understood why he was so cautious when it came to feelings. To speaking about feelings. To her, he had only mentioned love once, after that night when it was too late. "I love you, Phil," he had whispered on voicemail. And all she could do was push *Delete* and cry her eyes out some more.

Phil made a spontaneous step towards Adam and dropped her arms. "Oh, shit," she repeated.

He nodded and asked Lluis for the key to his room.

"See you, Adam, okay?" In spite of the situation, Tamar's words contained an unmistakable seductive offer.

What a day this had been. In spite of her exhaustion, Phil tossed and turned in bed. First the strange encounter with Scherer. Learning about his wife's suicide. The messy *finca*, Doro's disappearance, the rabbit head. Now Adam and his dead sister. Out of more than seven billion people on this planet: Adam.

Phil gave up and opened the fridge with the bottle she had so far resisted. Not one of those tiny minibar bottles, but 0.75 liters of cold *Viña Sol*. She was well aware she'd had enough to drink. She didn't care, though, yearning for a merciful alcoholic mist to billow up in her mind and force her to sleep.

Instead, after a couple of sips, Adam was back in her head, their magic three-months-relationship that ended in one horrible night. How would their life be today, had Adam not forgotten their date then, boozing in a pub while she waited for him, with her homemade meal, like a stupid *hausfrau*. Had he just stayed away, not shown up at two o'clock in the morning. Had Phil not woken up and looked out of the window when this girl threw her arms around Adam and kissed him on the mouth.

His reaction? Phil didn't know, as she had jumped back in shock. When he came up, everything got worse. Adam was drunk and Phil stone-cold sober. And jealous. She welcomed him with accusations; he denied and told her to leave him alone. Neither of them made a step toward each other. They fought until everything escalated. Until his hand met her cheek, and the catastrophe took its course. Phil kicked Adam out, and he slammed the door so violently shut the frame shook. Words by the author Peter Hoeg, stored in Phil's eclectic brain, described it best: *He left in a state of seething, pent-up, livid, profane rage.*

Adam was also in bed, but it felt like trying to sleep in a burning house. Amazing what the shock of running into someone from a former, lost life could trigger. Quite a new experience. Adam's eyes ached.

How unreal to travel more than three thousand miles to bury Amanda and run into, out of all people, Phil? How fucking absurd. Phil with her red curls, her startling green eyes, the tiny freckles on her nose. The woman who once evoked such strong, almost frightening, emotions in him. The only woman he had ever wanted to share a life with. Until he screwed up.

The girl who had tried to pick him up that night never meant anything. She only gave him a ride, only tried to kiss him. Adam had been drunk, longing for Phil's arms, *her* kisses. He had hummed Leonard Cohen—*already touched her perfect body with his mind.* But instead of Phil, a wild shrew confronted him, who had marked him as the enemy when he was still longing for her. A furious hellcat, against whose attacks he defended by raising his hand himself. Not really slapping her, just not resisting his hand's involuntary movement. He immediately regretted it, immediately told her he was sorry, apologized like crazy. Only to be dumped like a bad cliché: the bully who would never be forgiven for hitting a woman.

He had been shocked by himself. Still was. He never would have thought he had *this* in him: violence. To be correct: one stupid, drunk slap. Nothing more. But nothing in his life had he ever regretted more.

With that, Phil and he were over, and he knew he would never love again. Probably for the better, Adam had tried to convince himself in helpless frustration. Life was much easier without strong feelings. What good had ever come from surrendering oneself to another person but the world's biggest dramas and tragedies.

Usually Adam could fall asleep on command. For a long time he stared into the dark, then switched the bedside lamp back on. His MacBook was sitting on the desk, but he felt too exhausted to get up. In search of another distraction, he leafed through a folder lying on the nightstand. It contained all sorts of information on Ibiza: schedules of the ferries to Formentera, Mallorca, Barcelona, restaurant-flyers, an invite to a full moon party. Some magazines in different languages. A German one showed an aerial view of Ibiza with the headline: "Spring Awakening on the Island of Scorpio." Thanks to his mother, Adam could read the article. It claimed that no scorpion could survive on the *holy grounds* of Ibiza, yet the island was assigned to the Zodiac sign of Scorpio. *This highly unusual combination nurtures a creative as well as latently dangerous atmosphere.* Although Adam understood the words, they didn't make any sense to him, but at least got him mercifully drowsy. Over a chapter that dealt with ancient medicine based on astrology, regarding Scorpio as the Melothesic equivalent of the genitals, he fell asleep.

Adam, who hardly ever dreamed, was standing in an

ocean swarmed by scorpions. But no matter how hard he tried, he couldn't reach the shore.

CHAPTER 11

The following morning, Adam sped through the lobby without stopping at the breakfast buffet. He would have a coffee somewhere on the road.

An hour later he was standing in front of his brother-in-law's mansion. A red pick-up truck was parked in front. Next to it was the van of a painting company. A guy was busy covering a huge graffito on the wall with a telescopic paint roller. "*del diablo...*," Adam read before the words disappeared under the new white coat. In the carport behind the open gate, a silver sedan was parked, a Bentley Mulsanne, Adam knew. An automatic watering system sprayed the yard's plants with a swooshing noise that didn't drown a voice. German. His brother-in-law. Adam stopped at an open French door, from where Scherer's words spilled out in the yard.

"You've got to get me a new maid. Holy crap, I'm drowning in dirt."

"True, man, you are," a woman purred in a timbre that somehow sounded familiar to Adam. "But don't worry, I'll find someone. If the price is right."

"I'll pay whatever is needed."

Adam heard Scherer clear his throat. "Even more important: The party..."

"Again—no worries. I've got everything under control."

"I think we'll have to cancel."

The woman reacted with an incredulous shriek. "You can't be serious. The RSVPs are in, all reservations have been confirmed. You *so* cannot do that."

"I'm *mourning*. They have to respect that."

"What should they respect? You never even introduced them to your wife. She had nothing to do with it all. Plus, you don't have to party along."

"How in the world could I not..."

"Nobody would understand if you botched up their plans. Let alone ours..."

Adam made a step closer to the door. The glass pane vaguely mirrored a big head with tousled gray hair. Scherer.

"I'm not their slave."

"You committed to them. That's an obligation. If you don't stick to it, they will find someone else. You are not the only realtor on the island. But they made *you* big. And in a heartbeat, they could crush you."

Mirrored in the glass, Adam saw Scherer slouch down on the armrest of a chair. "Well—okay then," he muttered. "But you have to leave now. My brother-in-law will show up any minute. Do fix us some coffee first, all right? How could the damn maid just leave like that?"

He added a curse in German Adam didn't understand. But the woman was outraged, "How dare you!"

Adam had to know with whom Scherer was talking. He stepped in. "The brother-in-law has arrived."

Scherer was startled, "Adam."

But Adam stared at the woman. It was the blonde sex bomb from Hostal Esperanza. She was on her way out but turned back to him, again coming too close. "Adam. I should have figured your sister was Amanda."

"What are you doing here?"

"Miss Stettin works for me," Scherer said hastily, "Adam, man."

"But not as his maid. They tend to flee. You know what he called his former housekeeper? *Küchenschabe*, cockroach." With a malicious grin towards Scherer, "Obviously he doesn't know that roaches are super-intelligent creatures."

With both hands, Scherer swiped the air as if trying to erase her. "Tamar!"

"They've been around for hundreds of millions of years. The ultimate masters of survival." Tamar clapped a hand to her mouth, "Sorry, Adam, I don't mean to be rude. But..." Pointing at Scherer, "To call Rosenda a cockroach." She opened the door, "I know, boss, coffee," and excited with grace.

Scherer needed a second to recover. Then, ignoring Adam's outstretched hand, he embraced him like a long-lost friend.

"Man," he said, "what a fucking disaster."

Adam felt a nerve on his temple twitch. "Jorg. What now is so disastrous?"

"What? Amanda is dead."

"True. A real fucking disaster. Could almost ruin a party."

Scherer ignored that too. "Adam. How shall I live?" His chin trembled. "Twenty-five years. This fall we planned to celebrate our silver wedding. And now..." His voice broke.

Adam watched him closely. If his brother-in-law was pretending, he must be a damn talented actor. His tears were real, his grief seemed genuine. But a party? Amanda's words, deploring a false, loveless life, resonated just as clearly in Adam's mind.

"How could she do that to me?" Scherer whined.

Adam took a deep breath. "I can't believe that Amanda took her own life."

Again Scherer's reaction surprised him.

"Exactly," he howled, "that's what I can't get into my head. She was so afraid of pain. The smallest shit freaked her out. And she knew what cyanide would do to her. She constantly watched crime series. It's so out of character. Why didn't she just leave me? People do that all the time, right? But cyanide?"

"So you discussed splitting up?"

Scherer went to a sideboard. Ice cubes fell into a glass. When he turned back, he had a drink in his hand.

"I didn't. I was married, *basta*," he raised his glass to Adam. "You too?"

"I'd rather wait for the coffee."

Scherer took a deep pull. "I don't understand Amanda. Has everything, gets everything, spends my money however she wants—and suddenly nothing and no-one is good enough for her anymore."

"What does that mean?"

"Hell if I know. She is... was over fifty. Menopause?" Scherer seemed to realize how disrespectful this sounded and tried to qualify, "It's a fact, right, that hormones run wild with women of a certain age."

Tamar reappeared in the door carrying a tray with two cups. She threw Adam a sympathetic glance. "Isn't he lovely? Sugar? Milk?"

"Thanks, black. What kind of work do you actually do for him?"

Both pretended Scherer didn't exist.

"Event planning. Organization. A little secretarial work, part time."

She placed the second coffee cup in front of Scherer. "Seriously, boss, cognac in the morning?"

"You know very well—just leave me alone."

"Right, he's mourning." Tamar winked at Adam and made a curtsy for Scherer. "Bye, my poor grieving boss. See you tomorrow."

"Just go," Scherer gasped. "And don't forget the maid."

"I never forget anything. See you, Adam, okay?"

When she had left the room, Scherer poured himself another glass. His coffee remained untouched.

"I am mourning," he confirmed. "That's why I drink, and yes, a bit too much. I just can't understand why Amanda would do something like this."

"Maybe she was lonely," Adam suggested.

"Possibly, as she didn't care for her husband anymore. And her only brother had turned his back on her, like, years ago."

Adam felt the blood rushing to his cheeks. But then Scherer added he didn't think Amanda had felt alone as she'd had a whole bunch of girlfriends.

"Like you?" The words escaped Adam involuntarily.

Scherer glared at him, perplexed. "What is this supposed to mean?"

"Did you cheat on your wife?"

Adam watched his brother-in-law closely. In reaction to his blunt words, Scherer's face showed confusion, but no sign of nervousness or bad conscience. He merely seemed to think about Adam's words, sat down on the arm of a couch and rubbed his sore eyes. Then he got furious.

"Now listen to me, my friend," he said icily. "If you think you can show up in my house and say my wife killed herself because I occasionally may have had something going on the side, you are dead fucking wrong."

"How can you be so sure?"

When Scherer only shrugged, Adam carried on, "Then allow me a different question. What would divorce have meant for you? Financially. Did you and Amanda have a prenup?"

Scherer jumped up again. Something clinked, his drink spilled. On the way down, his glass took along some framed photographs from the coffee table and smashed on the tiles. Scherer took a pillow from the couch, kneeled down, and tried clumsily to sweep glass splinters and liquid to a pile. Adam put the frames back on the table.

One held a wedding picture. A much younger Scherer and Amanda, his arm around her waist. Adam saw himself, smiling. Between him and Amanda was his mother; his father had not shown up for the occasion. On Scherer's side was his family, a bunch of plain Germans, all looking somewhat alike but for a skinny, surly faced boy on the outer edge of the picture. Adam couldn't remember the name of the punkish teenager, Scherer's son from a former relationship.

With difficulty, Scherer got back up. "I hope you are aware, Adam," he said with forced calmness, "that I do not have to submit myself to your interrogation. Nevertheless, here is one more private detail: no, Amanda and I did not have a prenup. Had we split, both would have received half of my fortune, more than enough for Amanda, okay for me. And it wouldn't have taken me long to make up for my losses. I'm a hardworking guy. It would also have meant something like... relief, to no longer be treated like shit."

Adam pulled Amanda's letter out. "Fact is, Amanda was desperate. Read the last sentence."

Scherer turned his back to him, read the whole letter and pushed it back into Adam's hand. "Seriously? You show up and imply I killed my wife? How the fuck dare you?" Outraged, he pointed at the door. "Out of all—good brother. *Get out!*"

CHAPTER 12

Phil longed for a coffee. At the same time, she was nervous about running into Adam again. But to her relief, only one couple sat on the patio behind plates loaded with food. Phil recognized Amy's mother Trudy, who didn't react to her "Good morning."

But the man with Trudy smacked his lips, "Hi there," and checked Phil out from top to bottom. Something edible, probably egg yolk, clung to his chin.

Phil chose a table behind the man and opened the newspaper she had picked up in the lobby. The top news was the plane crash off the coast in which Kai Maurer had met his death. The "scumbag" in Tamar's pitiless words.

A waitress appeared with a pot of coffee and foaming hot milk, and encouraged Phil to help herself at the buffet. She waved a "Good morning" to Lluis who was sweeping the stairs, his cell phone pinned between shoulder and ear. Focused on his call, he didn't reply.

Phil tried to think rationally. This afternoon she would have to present a clean, good-smelling house to the real estate agent. She had ten days left. Maybe Doro really had forgotten about her arrival. She had been in the house, the backpack proved it. Probably, Phil's call to police had been an over-re-action. Hysterical. But the mess, the rabbit...? Were there any cleaning supplies in the pantry? Along with—why the hell *there?*—Doro's backpack?

Phil's heart was heavy. She didn't remember seeing any detergents. Maybe Doro had used them up and not found the time to buy new ones, her head in her project. And lived in such a mess? Doro? And then the ...

No matter what, Phil needed to be pro-active. After break-fast she would drive back to the *finca* and roll up her sleeves. Maybe Doro had returned by then, and they could clean up together. They had until three p.m. They also needed to get rid of the rabbit head. The mere thought made Phil gag.

Lluis had finished his call and came towards her. He placed the broom in front of him like a gun. His face was tense.

"Hi," he said brusquely, "Tamar says you want Scherer to sell your house?"

Surprised by his tone, Phil frowned, "Good morning. Yes. But it isn't so much a question of want but need."

At the other table, the American woman rummaged through her purse. "Stop it, Trudy," the man said.

"But Scherer, *por díos!*" Shaking his head, Lluis picked up his broom and obviously meant to leave without further ex-planation.

"Wait a moment." Phil grabbed his sleeve. "Why *por dios* shouldn't I?"

Lluis's handsome face was distorted by revulsion. At the same time, he tried to smile, which made him look like an an-gry Punch puppet that couldn't delete the carved grin from its face.

"Sorry, Phil. It's just—nothing to do with you."

"Come on now. What's wrong with Scherer?"

Lluis sighed, "Nothing, really. *Au contraire.*"

With the broom, he pointed towards the giant hotels to the right of the Esperanza, blocking the view over the sea. A squad of house painters on scaffolds were sprucing up the monsters' flaking coats.

"Scherer and his likes are only doing us good. They build these cozy hotels wherever they can purchase a piece of land. They generously equip them with as many rooms as possible, so everybody can experience the authentic Ibiza-feeling. They hire half of Andalusia to work here for the summer. People like Scherer are the cornerstones of our community. Pardon my cynicism."

"I totally get it. But..."

"I shouldn't talk so much."

Phil could well understand how awful it must be for a dyed-in-the-wool Ibizan like Lluis to watch the beautiful coasts be turned into concrete jungles. But weren't there environmental laws? Politicians who cared about their island? And how the hell could *she* prevent anything by not selling her house? The only result would be her own financial disaster.

Before Phil could start her pleas, a voice behind her said, "So you know Scherer personally, Lluis?"

Weird feeling when your neck hair literally starts standing on end. Adam.

"He wants to buy me out too. I'm so sorry about Amanda."

Behind her, Phil heard Adam draw a hasty breath, and it hit her like a hammer blow: Scherer's wife who had killed herself, A.S., was Adam's sister. Amanda. Of course. Horrified, she turned to him, but Adam was focused on Lluis.

"You knew Amanda."

"Not very well, but yes. She tried to bring Scherer to his senses. In vain, of course. Shortly before her death, she turned publicly against him."

"What exactly happened?"

Adam's eagerness swept away any restraint on Lluis's part. "Scherer," he almost spat the name, "wants everything on Ibiza under his control. As he offers good money, some people are happy to deal with him."

Phil received a glance she bravely withstood.

"He is even targeting Es Vedrà. We know he has presented a concrete offer to the Council. Which, of course, is absurd. I mean, selling Es Vedrà?"

He pointed at the rock, towering over the sea in a veil of clouds.

Adam didn't understand. "Why would this be so absurd?"

"Because Es Vedrà is a sacred place. It may mean nothing to you, but..." Lluis hesitated, but his newfound trust outweighed his reserve, "we Ibizans are still subject to ancient beliefs and rituals. Tradition, for example, obliges us boys in our sixteenth year to row out to Es Vedrà. It's our initiation. We stay on the rock until we have hunted a young billy goat, no matter how cold the nights, if in a storm or under the burning sun. When we have caught the goat, we cut his throat and taste his blood. Then we can go home and call ourselves men."

Phil's mouth fell open. Strange? What about barbaric? Horrendous?

Adam was as perplexed. "And—this ritual was important to my sister?"

Lluis weighed his head, "I'm not sure if Amanda was familiar with it. But when the Balearic Ministry of the Environment sent snipers to the rock to kill all the goats, your sister took part in our protest march. A journalist recognized her as Scherer's wife, and she spoke out against him and supported our cause."

"The goat hunt," Phil gasped, "seriously?"

Lluis gave her an irritated look. "To keep Vedrà from being sold."

"Wait a minute," Adam said, "the Ministry of the Environment sent snipers to kill the goats so *you* couldn't kill them?"

"Right. They claimed the goat population had gotten too large and grazed off endemic plants, destroying the flora. As if they cared about plants."

"So you're saying they just want to keep you guys off the

rock?"

"Right. We think the Ministry has been bribed. Once they got rid of the goats and us, Scherer appealed to the *Consell Insular* for the permit to sell the rock. His arguments: a wealthy American client, a big nature conservationist, would safeguard and protect the island much better than we, the ignorant locals."

"When exactly did that happen?"

"The goats were killed in February, the demonstration was March 1st, the same evening the interview with Amanda was on TV. The 3rd it appeared in print, in *El Pais*. Amanda takes a decisive stand against Scherer's plans."

"And not even a week later she is dead." Adam brushed his hair back in a gesture still familiar to Phil. Then she realized what he had alluded to.

"What? Adam! You are not seriously saying..."

He didn't pay attention to her. "Can *you* imagine, Lluis, that my sister took her own life?"

Lluis thought about it. "I didn't know Amanda all too well, mostly from the protest group's meetings. At the march she seemed agitated, fully committed to the cause. Not like somebody who would give up, go home, and..."

"... kill herself."

Lluis nodded.

"People have murdered for lesser motives," Adam said grimly.

"I have recorded the TV report. If you want to see it."

The two passed by Phil as if she was invisible, leaving her flabbergasted. Did these guys really mean to say that Scherer, the only person who could help her solve her financial problems, get a new home for Anton—that this person was a murderer? Phil shuddered. No way. More probable was that Adam and Lluis both spun some kind of sailor's yarn for two different reasons. Adam couldn't accept his sister's suicide. Lluis hated Scherer. Phil reasoned with herself: had there been the slightest suspicion of murder, police would be investigating Scherer. And the newspaper would have mentioned it, instead of merely pointing out his solid alibi. Enough! Phil forced her thoughts back to the day's tasks. She would drive to her house and clean up. Praying that Doro was back.

Adam followed Lluis behind the reception desk and through an office into his private salon. A flat-screen TV sat on a built-in shelf stacked with albums and magazines. Lluis searched the recordings until he found the march.

The camera eye opened on the street sign "Plaza d'Espanya" and moved over a sky full of flags and banners: *Es Vedrà pertenece a nosostros, NO a los invasores, NO a los megaproyectos.* Es Vedrà belongs to us, Not to the invaders, No to the mega-projects. One banner, held by two young girls, pled in English: "Es Vedrà is our island's heart. You don't sell a heart."

A reporter rattled lightning-fast Spanish into his microphone and put it under the noses of some protesters. Then the camera eye caught Amanda. Adam heard himself utter a strange grunt.

Fifteen years ago, his sister had been of rather conservative appearance. "Jackie O.," Phil had joked after meeting Amanda once. The woman on TV, however, in her flowered dress and poncho, looked more like one of those aged hippies who populate Ibiza. Her gray-streaked hair was bundled up to a messy bun. Around her wrist, formerly adorned by only a *Panthère* by Cartier watch, jingled a collection of bracelets.

Adam gasped when the camera focused on Amanda's face. Her eyes shone so vividly it seemed impossible they were forever closed now. Radiating a fierce determination, she explained to the reporter she would do whatever it took to prevent the selling of Es Vedrà, even if someone got hurt. Because it was a sin like the goat-slaughter, a crime. That's all she had to say.

"If it hurt your husband?" the reporter tried anyway, but Amanda had already disappeared in the crowd. He explained that the husband of this courageous woman was the mastermind behind the plan to sell Es Vedrà. Behind him, the protesters whistled and jeered.

Adam needed a moment, before he asked Lluis to rewind the recording until Amanda was back on screen. In silent grief, he gave his sister a final farewell and took a number of iPhone photos. Lluis waited respectfully.

Adam cleared his throat. "Do you know who Amanda was with?"

Lluis shrugged, "I can't really say. I met Amanda only in the *Initiativa Es Vedrà* that had been founded after the killing of the goats. All kinds of people came together there: locals, residents, animal-rights activists, even tourists. Amanda usually sat with a group of women who talked English and German."

"Do you know someone by the name of Nobody? A friend of Amanda's?"

"That's Otto Niemer, called Ninguno. Meaning *Nobody* in Spanish. One of the folks that came to Ibiza in the Seventies to live a free life, and ended up just more or less surviving. Wait."

He brought the recording back on screen. Only now, Adam paid attention to the man next to Amanda. A frail, elderly man, his sparse hair in a ponytail, his back stooped, his eyes bleary.

"This is Ninguno," Lluis said, "Nobody."

Adam felt his heart bang against his ribs. He also took a few pictures of the man. "Where can I reach him?"

"Well, Ninguno doesn't have a fixed address. He's doing odd jobs, mostly gardening, for some *residentes*. But if you call a certain *tienda*, the shop's owner, Catalina, will pass the message to Ninguno, and if he feels like it, he'll call back."

Lluis gave Adam the number and address of Old Catalina, and Adam thanked him for being such a help. One last time he looked into his sister's eyes—and stopped short. He pointed at one of the protesters, a tall person with a black cap pulled down to her eyes.

"Who is this woman?"

Surprised by Adam's excitement, Lluis focused on the screen. "Sure that's a woman? I don't know her. Or him?"

Adam took a picture of the person. Lluis was right, the long limbs and rather coarse features could also belong to a man. Not easy to judge from merely the semi-profile under the cap. Still, he was almost sure.

CHAPTER 13

The horizon was a gray wall of clouds; the sun was about to give up fighting. When Phil rode her Vespa across the island, it turned dark as if nightfall was already close.

Phil stopped again at Old Catalina's tiny store that carried the assortment of a supermarket on its overloaded shelves. While she collected her cleaning supplies, Catalina gave her opinion about Doro.

"Don't worry, *querida*. I bet she met a man and forgot about you. Hormones."

"Maybe," Phil said, but she thought: Never! "And the messed-up house?"

Catalina shrugged. *"L'amor vuelve loco a todos."*

Love makes everyone crazy? Not Doro. Doro was rational, reliable...

Catalina changed the subject to Anton, the *niño precioso*, and frowned over the still-missing father figure in his life, definitely more worried about Phil's status as a single mother than about Doro. Maybe Phil had overreacted.

The plastic bag dangling from her arm, she restarted the scooter. When she turned off the road into the dirt track to her *finca*, the sun suddenly rose again...

...But no, it wasn't the sun. It was a glaring, unreal light blazing from the far end of the track, accompanied by strange, hissing sounds as if hell had opened its gates. An unnatural heat stifled the atmosphere. Phil cranked up the gas pedal, raced up to her house and couldn't believe her eyes.

She moved right towards a gigantic fire. The rabbit head on her gate's hinge had lost its ears and eyes; empty caves stared at her. No fur was left, only charred bone. The dried blood on the post, however, seemed to flow again.

Behind the gate, the flames were devouring Phil's house.

In a safe distance, yet close enough to enjoy the inferno, was a group of gawkers. An ambulance with rhythmically blinking lights and a fire truck in the yard. Phil blindly dropped the Vespa and started to run. A firefighter in full gear grabbed her arm, warning her to stay away.

Phil tried to shake him off. "That's my house, *mi casa.*"

But it didn't make sense to get closer to the fire. She froze in the heat.

"*Lo siento,*" the fireman gently dropped her arm, "*es peligroso*"—dangerous.

His colleagues unreeled water hoses and directed them at the flames that came bursting through the charred ribs of the roof. The strong jets triggered fireworks, sparks flew, window panes burst. The entrance door unhinged and crashed into the front yard, fuming bitter smoke. The lopsided bench made a jump as if trying to escape and collapsed in a shower of sparks. The flames hissed when the water jets hit them but didn't give up, flickering anew, unexpectedly, everywhere. Bushes and branches ignited. Only the stout carob tree still managed to withstand and received life-saving aid when one of the firemen directed his jet on it.

In the blinking lights, the gawkers looked like zombies, silently watching the elements fight. When the water had finally won, one of the firemen switched on a huge flashlight. For a moment, its light radiated across the scene like a disco laser.

He put a breathing mask on and entered what was left of Can Philanton. Someone in the same gear followed him.

Minutes stretched, bursting with tension, until they came back out. One lifted his hands in a helpless gesture. "One fatality," he said, "we need a hearse."

And the whole world stopped breathing. No bird dared to chirp. Phil was paralyzed. Until someone next to her said "Oh, fuck," and in her brain hell broke loose. She cried out, wanted to run, fell down to her knees, struggled up and was caught in someone's grip. Someone who wouldn't let go as much as she fought against him.

"Doro," Phil yelled, "Doro!"

Voices buzzed around her, praying, murmuring, sobbing. Something dripped on her hand, her tears. Her hand still held the plastic bag with the cleaning supplies. She shook it off, recognizing the arm that held her. Adam's arm.

"Doro?" she heard him ask. "Why in the world..."

What did he want here? "Doro lived in my house," she said flatly, "my friend, Dorothea." She heard him gasp in horror.

"*Your* house? What are you talking about?"

Strange question.

And suddenly Phil could think of nothing more than her house. After losing the flat in Mainz, the only place in the world she still could call home. And now it was gone too, leaving her with no place to lay her head. Out on the streets, Anton and her. Still, it was easier to think "homeless" than "Doro."

"*The* Dorothea?" Adam asked.

He had met Doro in those months with Phil and, Phil knew, he couldn't stand her. She made a brusque step away from him.

Two police cars and a hearse arrived. Uniformed men pushed back the gawkers, Phil and Adam included, shut off the yard with barrier tape, and set up huge lamps. In their harsh light, the ruin of Can Philanton looked like a bizarre film set. Phil saw herself standing there, saw the policemen, Adam, and suddenly didn't feel anything anymore. Everything in her was numb as if she had been given a narcotic drug. She heard Adam say, "Calm down, okay?" and thought, why, as she *was* completely still. Watching a movie in which two men carried a zinc coffin into a ruin and back out and loaded it into a hearse. A movie Phil couldn't relate to.

A short man in a striped suit appeared behind the barrier tape which a policeman lifted, so he could walk through without having to bend his head.

"*Comisário* Dziri," he said. "Señora, you are the owner of the property?"

"Yes," Phil said while Adam made a step forward, "Inspector."

"Mr. Ryan?" Confused, the inspector looked from Adam to Phil.

"My house," she said. "Yes, it—was my house."

"Okay." Dziri's attention turned back to Phil. Politely, he asked for her ID and studied it before handing the ID to the man in uniform.

"Very sorry for your loss, Mrs. Mann. So can you tell me who the person in your house was?"

The person? With this question, Phil's shock-induced numbness was gone. A tremor took over, the name Doro rattling against her chest. Desperately, Phil tried to explain that her friend had been living in the *finca* for about six months. That she herself had come to the island to sell the house. That she had not met Doro and immediately knew something was wrong. That Doro must have come back, and... Phil gasped.

"And now this," Her teeth shattered. "How could this happen?"

"Looks like your friend knocked over the petroleum lamp. Maybe trying to light a cigarette."

"No way. She didn't smoke."

Whenever Phil had dared to light a cigarette in her presence, Doro indignantly waved off the smoke. No one had welcomed the ban on smoking in public places as much as she.

"Interesting." The inspector rocked on his feet like a child that couldn't stand still. "Very interesting. Maybe it was only supposed to look this way."

"What?" Phil gasped. "What do you mean by that?"

The policeman didn't respond, but turned to Adam. "Mr. Ryan. And what, if I may ask, are you doing here, esteemed Mr. Colleague?"

How come they knew each other?

"I happened to be down the road when I noticed the fire. I didn't know it was Phil's—Mrs. Mann's house. I ran into her last night in the Hostal Esperanza. We know each other—we knew each other in the past."

"So you," the policeman turned back to Phil, "planned to sell this house?"

"Yes, and?"

Dziri took one of his whiskers between his fingertips and rotated it as if trying to open a can, while anger rushed through the emotional chaos in Phil. An almost agreeable feeling because it was so tangible. Was she expected to justify herself again for not wanting but having to sell her house? The painful fact popped into her mind, "As if there even was a house left to sell."

"Correct. No old house left." The inspector sounded rather complacent. "Only a beautifully located property and an automatic reconstruction permit without restrictions from the historic preservation authorities."

Phil swallowed hard. "What are you insinuating?"

"Inspector Dziri," Adam said, "are you insinuating that Phil, the owner, burned down her own house? With her friend in it? Ridiculous."

A tortured tone escaped Phil's mouth while the inspector lifted both hands in a guileless gesture of *what do I know.*

"My apologies. But you must know that we, on this island, have quite some experience with these kinds of *accidents*. Ever so often a defective fireplace blows up a house, a burning cigarette is forgotten, a knocked-over oil lamp sets the place on fire—and boom, building restrictions are gone with it. To have a human being burn to death, however, is a first time for me. Well, must not have been planned."

Unable to find words, Phil shook her head while Adam reacted even more angrily. "With all due respect to your experiences, Inspector, you can't suspect Mrs. Mann to have set the fire just because it's such a convenient theory." To Phil he said, "You don't have to put up with this."

"I..." I don't need you to defend me, Phil thought, but only repeated helplessly, "You suspect me of setting the fire just because it's convenient?"

Dziri rotated his shoulders back. "*Lo siento, señora* Mann. I'm only trying to consider all options. That's what police work is about, right? So, if you don't mind telling me where..." He looked into his notebook. "Where you were today between eleven a.m. and one p.m.?"

To Adam he said, "The fire cannot have started earlier. Not before eleven, if it sparked off on its own, not before one if it was accelerated."

So now she was even suspected of dealing with a fire accelerant? How insane. In Phil's head numbers ran amok. Between eleven and one? No idea.

"Guess I was at the hotel or already on my way here. I must have left around noon..."

Adam jumped in, "At eleven-thirty, I ran into Phil Mann on the patio of the Hostal Esperanza. She was having breakfast. Her scooter was parked in the yard. The hotel's manager can also testify to this. This would be Lluis..." To Phil who listened open-mouthed, he asked, "What's his last name?"

"Romero."

"Right. We talked for a while. Then I accompanied Mr.

Romero inside, and shortly after, Phil followed in. She went upstairs. I heard her open her door."

Right. After Adam and Lluis had left her standing there, Phil had one more coffee, then went to her room to brush her teeth and put on a warmer sweater.

"How could you have *heard* it was me?" she asked Adam.

He pointed at her feet, clad in the old cowboy boots bought decades ago, repaired a hundred times, polished a thousand times and dearly beloved.

"These boots sound—recognizable."

"What?"

"She left the house about a quarter to one, on the Vespa. So, Dziri, do the math: At highest speed, it would have taken her about half an hour to get here which, following your assumptions, was after the fire had broken out."

Now listen to that. Adam Ryan, defender of the damsel in distress. But she didn't need him. Now, Phil remembered that the clock in the lobby had shown twelve-thirty when she came back downstairs. She clarified the time and added that she had also stopped at Old Catalina's *tienda*, as Catalina surely could testify.

"All right then." Dziri scribbled something in his notebook. "So we have this settled—for *now*." He stressed the last word.

He straightened his back and slid one hand into his jacket as if imitating Napoleon. "Goodbye, Madame Mann. And sorry to say: as your house is placed under seal, you positively can't sell it now. Also, as long as we don't know what happened here, please do not leave our island."

CHAPTER 14

Phil ran to her scooter. Impossible to look back at her lost home. Somehow, she made it back to the Esperanza and climbed up to her room like a remote-controlled doll.

Once the door closed behind her, she collapsed on the bed, and the big tremor started for a new round. For hours Phil lay there, shaking, sobbing, curled up like a desperate embryo. Pictures flashed through her head in wild confusion. Doro, the fire, the *finca*, Adam, all things destroyed, life wasted, dead.

Phil's brain just couldn't accept the truth: her best friend Doro was dead. The one person in the world besides Anton who had her trust. Dead. Doro dead.

But how on earth could this have happened? Doro did not smoke. And Phil remembered now that she had picked up the kerosene lamp on the mantelpiece and it had been bone-dry. How then could it have started the fire? And why shouldn't Doro have made it out if the fire had started somewhere else in the house? These few meters from anywhere to the door? Had she been unconscious? Incapacitated? Had the fire been intentionally set?

Phil sat up with a jolt. Had Doro been murdered? As ab-surd as it sounded—a fire in the small house she could not have run from sounded just as insane.

Phil's eyes fell on Doro's backpack, and she lifted it on the bed. She had to do something. Didn't her parents have to be informed? Did police know where they lived? Phil knew that Doro had not been close to her family. Nevertheless. But where did her parents actually live? Maybe there was an address book somewhere.

The backpack was stuffed with papers. Phil pulled one after the other out without finding anything personal. Only essays and documents in different languages, ordered from libraries and historical institutes. *"La Déesse* TNT," "The Triadic Goddess", "Virgil's Legend of Dido," "Cults in Ancient Iberia", "Molk - *Menschenopfer"* and so on. Extracts from Phoenician history, pages over pages commented in Doro's handwriting. Numbered chapters under the header line "Dea Caelestis," identifying them as part of the book she had been working on. Files labeled with mysterious initials.

One text seemed complete. It was titled "Elisha's Voyage," the story of a Phoenician queen. With an entourage of eighty men and maidens and the crown jewels of Tyros, she had fled across the sea after her brother had seized power and tried to kill her.

Phil was strangely fascinated by the text, which also had to do with Ibiza:

Returning seafarers had told Queen Elisha about the magical island where the celestials resided and only a few humans. This island they would be heading to first and bring offerings to the Goddess so she would assign Queen Elisha the right place for her new empire. Elisha would burn a molk, dedicated to the threefold moon and evoking the ancient law of the Great Mother. Elisha would also pray and fast, imploring the world's return to the dignified balance in which sun and moon, female and male principle, would reunite again.

It was on Ibiza that Elisha, the ousted queen of Tyros, descendant of Jezebel the Blonde and Princess Europa, met her destiny. It led her to the North African coast, the land of Nubia, where, under protection of the black empresses, the Heavenly Mother still reigned. There, Elisha founded Quart Hadash, the "New City," which later would be called Carthage. As her patron goddess, the queen kept worshipping Tanit, the mistress of snakes and all elements. As Tanit's heros, she chose Baal Hammon, master, at least, over the incense altar...

Phil stopped here, even though "Elisha's Voyage" went on for about ten more pages. The text read more like fiction than historical research, but Doro had always played with this subjective perspective in her scientific treatises. In her faculty, this idiosyncrasy had earned her the nickname "Fairy Aunt," as she once told Phil with some bitterness. "Because I dive into my subject," Doro had said, "I identify." Which, in her opinion, made her writing vivid and memorable, but not one bit less accurate.

Occasionally, when she kept talking on and on about her studies, Phil had teased her. "Are you done yet, Fairy Aunt, can we have a drink?" Then, Doro just grinned and pretended to strangle Phil with her bare hands. Oh, Doro.

When Phil opened an index card box, someone knocked on her door. Adam.

"Lluis prepared a paella for all his guests. He asked me to tell you."

Adam's wolf eyes examined Phil. His voice was coarse, "How do you feel? You look pretty—strung out."

"Thank you." Adam didn't seem as fresh as dew either. "Really, thanks, Adam, for trying—but I think I can't eat now."

"Oh, come on, Phil."

He looked at her with such genuine concern that it was impossible to make the one decisive step back into her room, close the door and be alone again.

So she stepped out.

On the patio, an enormous paella pan was set up. Lluis

gave Phil a gentle hug while muttering condolences into her neck. He hadn't known Dorothea, but could only imagine how cruel it was to lose a friend this way...

Adam headed for a table as far away as possible from the carefree laughter of the other guests. Lluis filled two plates each with a portion of paella Phil knew she could never eat. Then he was back with a bottle of Tempranillo and two glasses. She knew she could deal with wine.

Strange. How strange to sit here with Adam as if it was the most normal thing in the world. As if anything was normal anymore.

Phil cleared her throat. "So, why were you there, actually?"

Adam took a sip of wine first. "I was looking for someone called Ninguno. Amanda mentioned him in her last letter to me. Lluis told me I could reach him by calling this grocery store. I drove there instead to talk to the owner."

"Old Catalina."

"Right. She last saw Ninguno the day after Amanda's death. He bought booze and made a call, she said. And that he was a complete wreck."

"Maybe he can tell you why Amanda died," Phil muttered.

"That's what I hope. From the shop's parking lot, I saw the fire."

The fire in which Doro's life had ended. Phil's mind still rejected it.

She saw a nerve twitch in Adam's temple and wondered if he was thinking the same. About Doro. After the breakup, Doro had accompanied Phil to his apartment to return his belongings from her place. Phil would have preferred to just leave his stuff in front of the door, but she needed the translation she had been working on, which he had promised to print out for her.

At the door, Phil had been overcome by the situation and fled. And Doro collected not only the translation paper but all things she recognized as Phil's. She also returned the key Adam had given to Phil and requested Phil's key back from him. Back in the car, Doro seemed to find satisfaction in Adam's "self-righteous bitch" that followed her down the stairs.

"Proves what kind of a guy he is," she said.

When Adam called Phil to apologize, he still had the nerve to maintain that Doro had infected her with what he called her pathological hatred of men. Phil had answered by slamming down the phone.

By now, all other guests had left for the bars and discotheques in the city. Night invaded the island, pitch-black like a mourning veil. Es Vedrà stood almost invisible in the dark sea.

Adam poured more wine while Phil rolled a cigarette. In their times together, he had smoked Cuban cigarillos, Montecristos, which he could legally purchase in Germany but not in the States. Both of them had barely touched their food. As Phil wasn't able to talk about Doro, she asked Adam about Amanda.

"Police say it was suicide, but I don't believe it."

Phil searched her brain for some consoling words, but could only think of a lame question. "Why not?"

"Because of the cyanide. Amanda was extremely afraid of pain. She would have swallowed every damn sleeping pill in the world. But never cyanide."

"Adam, do you seriously believe your brother-in-law murdered her?"

"Let's say, it's a possibility."

Adam showed Phil Amanda's letter. She *had* wanted to see him again. And then this, "If something happens to me..." Her words did contain a fear, a premonition, no hint at suicide. Phil could understand Adam's suspicion. But Scherer had a solid alibi, and there was no other evidence. Phil quoted the newspaper.

Adam waved it away. "That night, Jorg was at a party which he admits involved heavy drinking. His alibi was provided by a bunch of wasted buddies who probably wouldn't have noticed if he had left for a while and returned. Also: if one is meticulous enough to not leave traces, none may ever be found. I don't maintain Jorg murdered Amanda. But I don't believe she committed suicide."

Phil grabbed her glass. "Nor do I believe Doro's death was an accident."

Adam raised his eyebrows but didn't look surprised. Phil suspected his detective nose had already picked up the smell. She shuddered. Adam's reaction brought the possibility of murder even closer.

"There is something else," he said.

"W... what?" The one syllable trembled so much Phil bit her lips.

"Lluis showed me the recording of this protest march Amanda had joined. Standing behind her was Dorothea. I'm sure it was her."

"What are you saying?"

Adam took his iPhone and showed Phil the photo he had taken from Lluis's TV screen. Without doubt it was Doro. Phil wiped her eyes. Adam's hand moved towards hers but pulled back again.

He cleared his throat. "Lluis said Amanda was with other women who talked English and German. She and Dorothea must have known each other. I think it's very possible that their deaths are connected."

But what in the world could a rich, neurotic American housewife have in common with a German gender studies researcher who lived for her work and socialized with only a handful of people?

"That both were there," Phil reasoned, "may have been co-incidental. I mean, it was a public protest. Lots of people gathered there."

But two of them were dead. Both studied the photo. Amanda with this enormous liveliness in her eyes. Doro, tall and dark, right behind her.

"I don't believe in such coincidences," Adam said.

For a while they just sat there, lost in their own thoughts. Phil almost jumped when Lluis approached with a new bottle of wine and a glass for himself.

"Adam, I asked around. Ninguno also worked for the Scherers. Gardening and such. Rosenda, the housekeeper, said he showed up at Villa Éscorpion the day after Amanda's death, completely freaked out."

"What did he say?"

"He needed to talk to Scherer who wasn't home at this time, though. Rosenda was just packing her things. After what happened, she quit her job."

"Okay. How can I reach her?"

Lluis had already written the address and telephone number on a paper. "Rosenda also went to these meetings. I saw her a couple of times."

"You're a great help, Lluis. Thanks, man."

Phil took a sip of wine. How almost—comforting it felt to sit here with Lluis and, yes, also Adam, instead of going crazy alone in her room. When she tried to put her feeling into words, Lluis patted her arm. "But you really should eat. Some chicken soup?"

Right then, her smartphone, lying on the table, started to play the melody of "What's Up?" The name *Anton* lit the display. Phil turned the phone off, well aware that Lluis's as well as Adam's eyes had followed her movement.

Should she explain? Hell, no.

"Thank you, Lluis, but I really can't eat now. I'll just finish my wine."

After a while they got up. Lluis said good night and kissed Phil on both cheeks while Adam already turned to the stairs. She followed him up.

"Thanks again, Adam," she said to his back when she was at her door.

He didn't turn back. "'Night. Hope you get some sleep."

"You, too. Good night."

But even to think about sleep was absurd. Phil called back Anton who sounded so happy with his adventures in England, she knew she would only tell him her bad news after his return. She smacked a volley of kisses into the phone and let her son go.

When she pulled the blanket off her bed, something dropped to the floor—the index card-box she had taken out of Doro's backpack. A bunch of cards, labeled in her meticulous handwriting, scattered all over the floor. Phil picked them up and tried to refile them. There were quotes and notes, cryptic numbers and abbreviations, but it was hard to judge which sources they referred to. Which old Roman said, "Remember all the regulations our forebears installed to undermine the freedom of women...?" The same Cato who kept insisting that Carthage must be destroyed? Another fragment, however—"If not with love, then with violence..." Phil recognized right away. She had written her Master's thesis about its author Claire Goll comparing the bilingual versions of her work. In World War I, the Jewish writer had called European women for open rebellion against male war mongering. It touched Phil that Doro included "her" author—had included, she painfully corrected herself.

But to which file section did the words *Anath, Anat of the dance, powerful, violent, agile, assim. Astarte/Tanit* belong? Or the drawing of the so-called Tanit-sign, a triangle with a crossbeam on top, balancing a circle like a stylized head? It was a hopeless task—as if it still mattered. Hit again by almost unbearable grief, Phil gave up, and in the random order she held them, stuffed the cards back into the box. Only to discover a crumpled paper that didn't seem to belong there. She unfolded it. It was a list of unusual names: *Elisha, Veive, Usha, Proserpina, Tamar, Yse, Amanda.* Only the name Amanda was crossed out with fine ball pen lines. What did this mean?

For one thing—that Adam was right. Here was proof that Amanda and Doro had known each other. But why was Amanda's name crossed out? Because she was dead? And who were the other women? What did the ancient Phoenician queen Elisha have to do with them? And why was Tamar's name on the list? Hadn't she insisted she didn't know Doro?

Phil pulled the only remaining item out of Doro's bag, an empty file folder. Under its metal clip were only some scraps of paper, indicating that its content had not merely been taken, but torn out. Its cover was labeled with some initials in the handwriting she knew so well. It read, *J. S. (TAB)*. Phil's heart skipped a beat. Her doubts about Adam's suspicion were wiped away. Doro had opened a file on Jorg Scherer. And now it was gone.

CHAPTER 15

Phil could hardly wait to show Adam what she had discovered, but to knock at his door as early as sunrise didn't seem appropriate. So she forced herself to be patient, took a long shower and finally unpacked her bag. The sight of Doro's backpack re-evoked torturing images: Doro dead. The fire. The coffin. The *finca*. What would happen now? Would she ever be able to sell the burned-out ruin? Through Scherer, who possibly had murdered his wife? What if she didn't have money for the bank in, now, nine days? How long would the police keep the place sealed? Every new thought crashed against a new question.

When sun rays crawled through the window, Phil stuffed Doro's papers in the backpack, wondering what she should do with all the work material. Maybe it could be of use to one of Doro's fellow researchers. But was there even someone working in this specific field of interest, Goddesses? Phil could have cried at how unaffected the sun outside shone.

At nine o'clock, she knocked on Adam's door.

"Yes." A muffled voice.

Phil pushed the door handle down and peeked into the dimly lit room with the curtains still closed. Where was Adam?

She made a hesitant step in. The room seemed as empty as the unmade bed on which a strange, one-piece garment lay. A kind of male underwear, yellowed by the ages. A clicking noise told her that the door behind her had closed.

"Adam?"

The voice, no longer muffled, startled her. "Where the fuck have you been?"

The American, Ezra Huber, was doing pushups on the floor behind the bed, dressed in nothing but red boxer shorts. He was glistening with sweat.

"Oh sorry, I wanted—wrong room. Sorry."

Shit. She should've asked for Adam's room number instead of assuming it.

"Hey!" Huber jumped up. With a swing he was across the bed, shuffling the strange garment under the cover. "Wait a minute!"

"Sorry! Bye."

But the man blocked Phil's way in all of his half-nakedness. Now she could see that his plump appearance had nothing to do with being overweight. By size, Ezra Huber couldn't impress anybody, but his body was in top shape. His hairless torso gleamed like a water snake's skin.

He rubbed down his front with a towel and dropped it to the floor. "Not so fast, miss. What exactly do you want?"

His imperious tone alone! Without looking into his face, Phil guessed his disagreeable grin. "Wrong door," she said sharply, "my mistake. Sorry."

Huber grabbed her arm. She tensed all muscles, ready to fight him off.

"Wait," he said. "So you didn't come for Trudy? My wife?"

In one wild effort, Phil freed her arm, flung the door open and was out on the balcony. From this distance she was able to answer.

"What are you talking about? I don't even know your wife."

Now she realized the man was not grinning but pursing his lips. Or was this a worried expression?

"Maybe she's having breakfast. Or taking a walk."

"Bullshit," he barked, the shrill yap of a terrier.

Shrugging, Phil walked away while Huber yelped behind her, "If you see her, tell her to come back. Immediately. Hear what I'm saying..."

His door slammed shut.

"Yessir. Asshole," Phil muttered.

The same moment, another door opened and Adam peeked out. His hair was still tousled from sleep, but he was in jeans and t-shirt.

"Who? Why?"

Wordlessly, Phil motioned him to come with her. They sat down at a table on the porch, and she told him about Doro's backpack, the list of names that proved she and Amanda had indeed known each other, and Tamar's.

"Who works for my brother-in-law," said Adam and re-counted his encounter with Tamar in Scherer's house.

"She didn't tell me that when she made the contact for me."

"So you chose Scherer as agent because of Tamar?"

"Only because of her." Phil summarized how she met Tamar on the ferry and what had followed. Then she drew his attention to the folder.

"Look, this was also in Doro's backpack. J. S. must mean Jorg Scherer, as his company is "TAB Real Estate.""

"Damn!" Adam was electrified, "There we have a connec-tion."

"Exactly. Doro must have collected information on Scherer, a whole bunch of papers. But someone tore them out of the folder."

Adam had already discovered the paper scraps under the clip. "This can only mean Dorothea shared my suspicion about Scherer."

"Or the file had something to do with the purchase of Es Vedrà."

"Unlikely. The potential sale may be a tragedy for the Ibizans, but a strong enough motive to kill? Twice? I doubt it."

Phil's phone went off. A creepy feeling seized her when a name lit up.

"Tell him," Adam had read it, too. "Let's see how he reacts."

Scherer called to confirm their appointment at three, but Phil interrupted him and explained that she had nothing more to sell. When she said, "My house burned down," a new wave of desperation rolled over her. Even worse was "And someone died in the fire."

No reaction, so Phil added, "A very good friend of mine."

This had Scherer gasp, "What? Damn! You didn't mention someone was staying in the house."

What? Adam's lips moved silently; impossible to ignore what he wanted. She forced herself, "My friend—you may know her, Dorothea Bartholdy. She was also a friend of your wife."

Through the phone, Phil could virtually feel Scherer's frantic mind.

"I've no idea who my wife was hanging with. Bad enough it led to... this."

His voice broke while Phil and Adam exchanged a puzzled look. What, in Scherer's opinion, had led to what? But to explain was not the realtor's intention. He cleared his throat and soon enough, his coaxing business voice was back.

"Dear Mrs. Mann, these are unfortunate circumstances. Tragic. But cheer up, life goes on." Again, he cleared his throat. "At least, here's a little comfort: now we may work out a better deal for you."

Phil threw a stunned look at Adam, whose expression was mere disgust.

"What the hell are you saying, Mr. Scherer?"

"I know it's hard. But we must be realistic, Ms. Mann. Here's a fact: with the old shack gone, the bean counters of historical preservation will not be after us anymore either. So, I'd say, apart from the unfortunate victim we can almost deem ourselves lucky—no, of course not lucky, no way, I apologize, but we must see the positive in all things." Scherer's voice dripped like poisoned oil. "You do need the money, right? Badly, I can tell. And I'm sure your friend would have wished the most—the best for you. The best profit."

"How dare you..."

"Wait." Obviously, Scherer realized he had overdone it. "I'm totally aware how you're feeling right now. It's terrible to lose a friend. But fact is that I'm even more interested in your property without the old *finca* on it. Because now there's more flexibility in new construction. And more cash for you. Let's wait until the rebuilding permit is released, then we talk again. Deal?"

Phil swallowed hard. How could the man be so ruthless? Adam was right, Scherer would stop at nothing. He was totally indifferent to the death of a human being, as long as he could make a deal. Her finger went to the off-button.

"Wait. Hold on!" Scherer cried out as if he could see her. "Listen to me. Almost two thousand square meters, facing southwest, that's perfect. We can expand, build two floors, then we even have an ocean view. So I'd say four hundred, no less." He even chuckled a bit, "four hundred thousand, of course. I'd say, we officially go for three hundred, one hundred thousand cash in your pocket. The tax office doesn't need to know everything, right?"

So much money. Phil inhaled hard. But she knew the only acceptable reaction was to push the off button. She threw her phone on the table as if it radiated with Scherer's poison.

"That son of a bitch," Adam said.

They drank their tepid coffees. Phil nibbled at her croissant and put it back on her plate. Scherer had thoroughly spoiled her appetite.

"And now what?"

"Now," Adam said, "I must speak to Inspector Dziri."

"We."

He threw her a glance, "I'm not sure, Phil..."

But she interrupted him, mustering all her courage. "Adam, this is something that concerns both of us. I know there's the elephant of—our past in the room, but let's get over it, okay? We want to solve this, right? Both of us. You are a professional investigator. And I need you..." She felt her cheeks burning. "I mean, to investigate. And I can be of use because I speak Spanish and know the island. So if we work together, we have the best chance to find out why Doro and Amanda had to die. Okay?"

A few heartbeats later, Adam gave the tiniest of nods.

"Maybe you're right. We'll see."

ISLAND OF SCORPIO

CHAPTER 16

Today the inspector was wearing a checkered shirt in pink and green and a matching green tie, and his hair was styled back with excessive amounts of gel. He was talking to a policeman in uniform who greeted Phil and Adam with a vague nod, while Dziri welcomed them politely, gesturing towards the visitors' chairs. A panel on the wall behind him displayed a nautical chart, a graphic grid, and some pinned-on photos: the wreck of a small plane, a police boat, and the portrait of a man Phil knew. Kai Maurer, whose plane had dropped from the sky.

The case must put a lot of pressure on Bartolo Dziri. Despite his politeness, he was impatient. His answers, quick as pistol shots, were all dismissive.

That Amanda and Dorothea had known each other? Most of the *residentes* on Ibiza met at some point. That both of them had died in one week's time? *Señora* Scherer's suicide was verified, and he could not talk about the circumstances of *señora* Bartholdy's death as it concerned an ongoing investigation. That there was reason to suspect Scherer? They did not even know what papers had been in this folder. So there was no evidence to interpret them as suspicious.

Phil started to get annoyed. "When my house burned down," she said sharply, "you instantly suspected I started the fire. When I told Scherer about it, he immediately asked why I hadn't told him someone was living in the house. Strange reaction, don't you think?"

The inspector's expression was a blank canvas. Did *señora* Mann seriously believe this renowned realtor burned down a house he was asked to sell? Risk his reputation for a slightly bigger agency fee? Not all too convincing, Phil had to admit to herself.

Adam kept on trying. "What do you know about TAB Real Estate? Anything compromising? I bet you have something."

For an instant, the inspector blinked, maybe considering an honest answer. Then he said, "Nothing in the least. TAB is an honorable business that promotes the local economy with tax payments, jobs and projects our island profits from."

Phil rolled her eyes. Dziri talked like Lluis when she had asked him about Scherer. Only Lluis' words had been cynical.

"Projects like the sale of Es Vedrà?" Adam asked.

"Nothing has been decided yet. Dear Mr. Colleague, I'm afraid you are running down a dead-end street."

"I don't think so, Inspector. Do you know anything about this party Scherer organizes—so shortly after his wife's death?"

"I don't." But for an instant, something uncontrollable flashed up in Dziri's face. He grabbed his mustache, while the other policeman muttered something Phil struggled to understand.

Dziri turned to her. "*Señora* Mann," he said gently, "I promise you: as soon as we come up with new evidence concerning the fire and the—fatality, I will contact you immediately. Until then, my apologies, but I'm up to my ears in work. Thank you for coming. Ms. Mann, Mr. Ryan."

And the session was over. The door snapped shut behind them.

"*No te metas en berejenales,*" Phil said thoughtfully.

"Sorry?"

"An idiom of Arabic origin. That's what the other policeman said to Dziri. Meaning: don't get yourself into hot water."

Adam's hand spontaneously jerked as he opened the door, crashing it into the wall. The guard reflexively pointed his machine gun at him.

"Sorry." Adam pulled Phil down the stairs at her elbow. "You're sure?"

"I am an interpreter, remember? English, Italian, Spanish. French only if I have to."

"And what did Inspector Dziri answer?"

"*He aprendido la lección.* That he has learned his lesson. Concerning the TAB, you think?"

"That's what we have to find out."

They got in the car and headed west. It was time to do some straight talking to Tamar about Scherer and his company. She also owed Phil an explanation why Doro, whom she claimed she didn't know, had her name on a list.

Phil tried repeatedly to reach Tamar on her cell only to listen to the same stubborn *The person you called is not available...* But as, by now, they were only a few miles away from Can Follet, they decided to give it a try anyway.

Tamar's home was situated halfway down the bay of Cala d'Hort, from where the distance to Es Vedrà was the closest on the whole island. Adam followed a metal arrow into an unpaved track that ended at a barrier. Behind it was a massive, three-floor building; to the left a parking lot with a sign "Guests of C. F. only" and, to the right, a park area with a pool. It was enclosed by a wall of lush plants and fortified by a ten-foot-high fence that went all the way down into the bay, cutting the beach in half. Laughter and music ruled on its public side, exclusive quietude on the resort's.

In a guardhouse behind the barrier sat a striking-looking

woman with a towering beehive of hair, decorated with pearls and pins. When Phil and Adam approached, she smiled at Phil, "Welcome to Can Follet."

"Good afternoon," Adam said. "We would like to see Tamar Stettin."

The woman joined her hands in a triangular gesture, lifted her fingertips to her forehead, and slightly bowed to Phil. "Love to you. What brings you to us?"

"Tamar gave me this address. We need to talk to her."

The woman scrolled down a laptop in front of her, "I'm not sure if she is in. She has not logged out... but, well, it would be a miracle if for once she had thought about it. If you want, go in and look for her."

Now having to acknowledge Adam's presence, she gave him a minimalist smile. "Not you, sir. I'm sorry, but men are not allowed entry to Can Follet."

In the meantime, two security guards in uniform had appeared behind the bar: sturdy females with reflective sunglasses, combat boots, and belt holsters. They just stood there, legs apart, and watched. Phil pulled Adam aside.

"Okay, a resort" he said, "And they need security like the White House?"

"Maybe the FLOTUS is visiting."

As it was only a twenty-minute walk from Cala d'Hort to the Esperanza, they decided to meet again later in their hotel. While Phil would look for Tamar, Adan would try to contact Scherer's ex-housekeeper, Rosenda.

As soon as he was a few steps away, the metal bar jumped up.

"And in you go, my friend," the beehive woman said.

CHAPTER 17

In the crowded lobby, Phil's first impression was that she had landed in a Marvel comic book: a female circus of Black Widows, Scarlet Witches, Medusas, and She Hulks. A fantasy of shimmering sci-fi frocks, Egyptian-style robes over skin-tight leggings, headgear in dazzling forms, pink pussy hats. The sunlight falling through the open doors of a patio reflected on the plethora of jewelry: gold and silver bands across foreheads, metallic bracers around wrists, heavy belts, necklaces, and nose rings. The sea breeze triggered a crescendo of clinks and chinks, in sync with the women's moves. The scent of aromatic herbs and maybe weed lay in the air.

At the front desk, an impressive black woman with blue hair and a star tattooed around her right eye was absorbed in a crochet work. She definitely smelled of weed. To Phil's "Hi" she looked up and smiled out of dilated pupils.

"Love to you. I am Stella."

Phil asked for Tamar who, Stella said, might be in one of the classrooms down the hallway. With the same triangular gesture the gatekeeper had made—fingertips to forehead to heart—she sent her off.

Phil wiggled her way through a group of chatty teens in yoga gear and opened the first door. It led to an empty studio, lit by two huge TV screens. One showed a famous actress in a group of veiled women, the other a terribly beaten up female face with a broken nose and a terrified look in her eyes.

The next door led to a classroom. Women of all ages sat on big cushions and listened to a lecturer in harem pants and a shirt with the imprint "HERstory." Behind her was a panel with the words *Secret Notes of the Carmelite Francisco Palau, 1811–1877* and, underlined, *Nuestra Señora de las Virtudes.*

"Palau retreated as a hermit to Es Vedrà," the lecturer said, "and this transformed him forever. In the cave, he experienced ecstatic states and transitioned into a *woman,* the Goddess's daughter…"

No Tamar. Phil quietly closed the door and tried the next one. There, a class had just come to its end. The instructor, who was Amy or Amaryl, the market vendor and daughter of the American Mormons, closed her folder and announced a tea break. Her listeners, comfortably lounging on cushions spread across the room, knocked their fists on the floor to show their appreciation.

In front of Amy sat Trudy in her wrinkled travel suit. Her knees were pressed together, her whole body in such a clearly uncomfortable position that Phil's back ached from just look-ing at her. Among the other women in their fantasy costumes, Trudy looked like a beige bourgeois alien. She struggled pa-thetically to get up from her cushion. Amy helped her to her feet.

"Mom, you are way too stiff for your age. You have to lose some weight."

"I know, honey, I know. That's what your father keeps say-ing."

Trudy clumsily hugged her daughter, whose lecture must have enthused her.

"Amy, I had no idea! The imagination you've got. Amazing. You know, honey, that's why you have to attend BYU's crea-tive writing classes. Stephenie Meyer was a student, and see how successful she is with her *Twilight* novels. Maybe if you also add some vampires or zombies... I'm sure you and I together can convince your father to let you go. After all, the school is run by our fellow believers."

Amy looked at Trudy, utterly surprised. "You think 'Elisha's Voyage' is a novel? Didn't you listen? I swear, Mother, it's as if you've been brainwashed!"

"Yes, a novel." Trudy was confused, "What else?"

"Reality. Elisha's escape from Tyros is the authentic story of a queen, chased out of her empire by her brother who wanted the throne. That her existence has been denied through history by the Romans, Christians, by Elder *brothers* like Father, doesn't make her any less real. There was a time, Mother, when women were in charge. In heaven and on earth."

Trudy was perplexed. "But—God?"

Amy rolled her eyes. *Hopeless*, seemed to be written in them. Her hand slid under the chubby elbow. "Well, how should you know about this? Come on, Mom. Let's have something to eat, and I'll explain it to you."

But now Phil stepped forward. Since Amaryl had mentioned the name Elisha, she could barely hold back her excitement. Here she was, looking for Tamar, and whom did she find? Doro. At least a connection to her.

"The story," Phil said, "Elisha's Voyage. Doro wrote it. So she was here."

Amaryl frowned. "Who?"

"Dorothea Bartholdy, the historian. The author of 'Elisha's Voyage.'"

"Honestly, I have no idea who wrote down the facts. This must have been ages ago."

Phil's glimmer of hope faded. Quite possible, she thought, that Doro had used the Elisha text as secondary literature and not written it. Disappointed, she returned to her initial concern and asked for Tamar. No luck here either. Amaryl only remembered that she left Can Follet in the morning.

"Maybe Jezebel knows," she offered, "Tamar's mother. Come on, she's on the patio."

With Trudy shuffling behind them, Phil followed Amaryl back through the lobby, which now was empty apart from the crocheting Stella. Voices and the clattering of dishes could be heard in the distance. A delicious smell of baked goods hung in the air.

Phil turned to Trudy. "Oh, hey..."

"Mrs. Ezra Huber," Trudy emphasized.

"Your husband is looking for you, Mrs. Huber. He seemed a bit worried."

"My goodness, right." Trudy bit her lips as if caught in an improper act. Her voice trembled, "I know. I have to go."

She grabbed her daughter's arm, "And you, too, Amy. Please, honey, you have to come to your senses. I'll tell your father ..."

"Mom." Amaryl shook her off. "Tell him I'll stay here."

"But he won't accept this... never in his life."

Trudy started to sob. Dismayed, Stella put her crochet work down while Phil wished she had kept her mouth shut.

Stella came close, making cooing sounds, "Ssh—ssh, calm down, dear," while she threw Amaryl a pleading look. "Everything will be all right."

"Sorry." Amaryl turned back to her mother and gave her a hug. "You don't have to go back either," she said tenderly. "Stay with us, Mom."

Now it was Trudy who broke away. "Of course I have to. I'm his wife and swore obedience to him," she yelled hysterically, "as you must be obedient too! You will burn in hell if you don't!"

"Oh fuck, Mom."

Struggling to get away, Trudy dropped her purse, and its contents spilled all over the floor: a cloth handkerchief, an age-old lipstick, a plastic tube with blue pills, a child's wallet big enough only for coins. Phil helped Trudy collect the stuff, while Amaryl snatched the pill tube and read the label.

"Xanax," she hissed. "Mother! So you too."

Her voice almost spat into Phil's and Stella's faces. "My parents' church, you must know, doesn't allow their believers to drink alcohol or coffee. Let alone smoke a joint. But they don't mind these dumbasses poisoning themselves with this shit, getting addicted in a heartbeat. Because in their Bible pill popping doesn't violate the so-called wisdom of the word." She laughed out, furiously, "Isn't that fucking sick?"

"Amy, *language!*" Trudy sobbed. "Give them back."

Amaryl raised her fist with the tube high in the air. Her shorter mother couldn't reach it, as much as she tried.

"Stop it, Amaryl," Phil said, "please."

"What, me? Am I supposed to look away or what?" Amaryl raged. "Watch my mother turn into a fucking addict? Are you aware that my wonderful home state of Utah ranks highest of all U.S. states in the consumption of opioids? Anti-depressants are specially favored by Mormon women coping with their fate as mere breeding machines."

"Unbelievable, what you are saying," Trudy screeched.

Gently, Stella put an arm around her shoulder. "We can help you, dear. Amaryl is right. We know how to deal with this."

But Trudy shook her off too. Without insisting any longer to get her pills back, she grabbed her purse and ran out of the lobby wailing.

Silence. Feet shuffled. Stella went back behind her desk. When she passed Phil, she threw her a strange, worried look Phil could not interpret.

"Stella, do you know where Jezebel is?"

"Are you sure you want to see her?"

Well, yes, that's why she asked. But before Phil could answer, Amaryl cleared her throat and pointed at an open patio door.

"In the back. She'll be the one in the green dress."

The patio ran along the whole seaside of the building. When Phil stepped out, she realized the woman in green was sitting in an electric wheelchair. Snow white hair was sneaking out under her turban. Her arms were extremely muscular, her legs stick-thin, her face haggard. Still, and even though Jezebel didn't wear any make-up, there was an obvious resemblance to Tamar.

"Excuse me, ma'am," Phil said.

"Don't you madame me," the woman snapped. "What do you want?"

"Ahm, Tamar..."

But Jezebel interrupted her, waving her hands as if to chase off her words, "Oh shit. Will you excuse the bad-tempered hag?" She tapped her forehead. "Sorry, honey, I was just resting a bit. You know, we are in full swing with the new programs, the house is booked out, the big dinner has to be arranged and what else. But now of all times, my partner excels in absence and my daughter is busy with whomever instead of giving me a hand."

"Sorry. So Tamar's not here? Can you please tell her to call me when she gets back? I'm Phil."

"Sure, Phil. Whenever she shows up. Tamar's a damn butterfly, if you know what I mean."

Jezebel smiled and her former beauty appeared like the sun behind a cloud. She must have looked ravishing once.

"But please, dear, sit down. Is there anything I can help you with?"

Now, she sounded so genuinely nice and interested that Phil pulled a chair next to the wheelchair and told her everything: about meeting Tamar, her visit to Scherer, the messed-up *finca*, the fire, Doro's death and Amanda Scherer's questionable suicide. Only Phil didn't mention Adam.

Jezebel seemed genuinely shocked. "Oh dear, I'm so sorry.

To lose a friend in such a cruel manner."

"She was called Dorothea Bartholdy. Have you ever met her? Tamar must know her."

Again a disappointing head shake. "Doesn't ring a bell. I knew Amanda a bit; she came to our seminars for a while. But not so much lately. Guess we were too much for her."

"Too much?"

"Too free-spirited, you know. Too feminist. Too much involved in history, mythology. Some call it esoteric, some utter nonsense. We call it our heritage. To each her own, right?"

"Right."

Jezebel smiled. On the beach before them, a woman taught yoga to the group of girls Phil had passed in the hallway. They were just doing the "Downward Facing Dog" with their butts high up in the air.

Phil looked over to Es Vedrà, its massive presence lit from behind by the sun that stood just above the waterline. A memory crossed her mind. One summer when she and Anton visited Cala d'Hort, there had been boat excursions to the rock. An inventive fisherman had organized them and, as Anton figured out, made tons of money with the enchanted tourists. Anton was good at mathematics and considered taking over the business when he was old enough. "Only two boat tours a day, and we're rich," he said. When Phil asked him how he would get the Ibizan fisherman to team up with him, Anton had thought hard about it. "I will ask him to adopt me," was the solution he came up with.

"Do they still do these boat tours to Es Vedrà?" Phil asked Jezebel.

"They do, but only in summer. And only to look at the rock from the boats. Even this is insane." Jezebel's face darkened. "The authorities must prohibit this nonsense. They know that the bay is full of dangerous shallows and currents, and the few passages a boat can take are spiked with sharp rocks. Every so often a tourist even tries to reach the rock in his private boat.

Unaware of the danger." Jezebel hesitated, "Do you know the legend of Es Vedrà?"

When Phil shook her head, she started: "Then listen. Once upon a time, a splendid sailing ship coming from the Levantine coast tried to pass by Ibiza. Onboard was a group of rich youngsters from all parts of the Orient, a wedding party on their way to Carthage. But the ship came too close to Vedrà, and a tempest—or the rock's magnetism—smashed it against the cliffs. It sank, and with it all the precious gifts and most of the passengers. A few managed to swim ashore; they remained here and became *Ibizencos*."

Jezebel's voice was full of warning, "But all others drowned. Their spirits are bored in the underwater world, so they try to pull new people down for their entertainment. No one should underestimate Es Vedrà. Always be aware of this."

A little later, Phil walked up the coastal trail. She came by a restaurant called *Ca na Vergera* that a local fisherman and his wife had opened in the Sixties, serving the same dishes of paella and seafood first to the sailors arriving in their *llaüts* and later to a never-ending succession of tourists. Soon, the trail got steeper and steeper, passing some mansions with spacious gardens and huge walls between them. Then civilization gave in to loneliness, to scrub and boulders overgrown by small-blossomed orchids that had already grown here in the subtropics of the Tertiary. On the waterside, the trail turned treacherous where the winter rains had crumbled the edges and caused landslides, pulling whole bushes and trees into the depth. A perfectly awful route for someone with acrophobia.

Phil's thoughts went back to Jezebel, who didn't want anyone to set foot on Es Vedrà. It was too dangerous, she said. In fact, the rock *was* enormously steep, barren with no infrastructure, off the grid, not suited to be built upon. Nevertheless, Scherer went through all kinds of trouble to buy it. Why?

Phil's imagination ran wild. What if the realtor's plan had

something to do with the "legend" Jezebel had told her? Because it wasn't a legend? Because the precious wedding gifts from the sunken boat really existed? Could it be that Es Vedrà was a kind of Troy and Scherer a Schliemann who knew where to look for an ancient treasure? Quite a far-fetched idea; however, who knew...

No, Phil thought, this didn't make sense. Had there ever been the slightest notion of a treasure, these waters would be swarming with archaeologists, adventurers, treasure hunters. If they *knew* about it. But what if only Scherer did?

CHAPTER 18

When the doors of Can Follet had swallowed Phil, Adam called Rosenda Marí Torres. The former housekeeper of the Scherers had just started a new job in the household of a rich Russian and had no time to talk. But the next day, she suggested, after Amanda's burial, they could.

Adam thanked her—shocked, however, that Scherer had not even informed him about his sister's burial. But when he was back at the Esperanza, a black-framed envelope waited for him at the front desk. The card inside let him know that Amanda had been cremated. According to the deceased's wishes, her ashes would be handed over to the sea in Cala d'en Serra, next morning, at 9 a.m.

The door to Lluis's private wing opened and the hotel manager appeared and smiled, "Hello, Adam."

Behind him was Bartolo Dziri. "Mr. Ryan. Is *señora* Mann with you?"

"She'll be back soon."

Adam tried to push by. The way Inspector Dziri had brushed him and Phil off in the morning, like a couple of amateur detectives, was still a bit hard for him to digest. Even harder to swallow was that the policeman was clearly hiding something from them.

But Bartolo Dziri's attitude had changed. He now seemed sheepish, worried. "Okay," he said, "then I will wait for her. Mr. Ryan, could we have a word, please? Lluis, if you don't mind getting us some coffee."

"Sure."

Lluis disappeared, and Adam followed the inspector back out on the patio. They sat. Dziri kneaded his hands. Sheepish was the exact right term.

"So what is it, Inspector Dziri?"

The policeman uttered a dramatic sigh. "*Puta madre*, I must say..."

He was interrupted by Phil coming up the patio stairs.

"Any news, Inspector?" she asked breathlessly.

"News indeed," Dziri groaned. "Concerning the fire."

"What?" Phil dropped her purse and held onto the table with both hands.

Dziri made the face of a martyr. "Concerning the cause. We are sure now that the cause of the fire is spilled kerosene. In the *sala* of your house, *señora* Mann, on the wall, the floor and on what is left of the big chair. Forensics have found residues of it. Splashed kerosene all over."

"I'm sure there was no kerosene in my house." Her voice wavering in shock, Phil told the inspector about the dry oil lamp on the mantelpiece.

Her words provoked a new aria of laments. "*Eso es*, Madame, *eso es*. We found the lamp, at least what is left of it: cracked glass, half-melted metal. But no trace of kerosene, not the slightest. Which means..." Dziri paused.

"Yes." Adam bent forward.

"Well, we first raised the question if Ms. Bartholdy may have purchased the kerosene. Or you, Madame, just to exclude..." he gave a little cough, "so we asked around, but the only person who actually knows you and your friend is Old Catalina. She confirmed your alibi and said she hadn't seen

Ms. Bartholdy in months. Catalina suspected she must be shopping in the big *supermercados* now. Before, your friend came over to her *tienda* all the time. Catalina remembered her well, also because they talked about you, Ms. Mann, and..."

"Please, get to the point," Phil interrupted.

"Right. Your friend never bought any kerosene from Old Catalina. Neither in the other *tiendas* around. But someone brought it—no...!" Dziri wrung his hands. "...rather *threw* a bottle with burning kerosene right through the window. A kind of firebomb. We found it among splinters of the window-pane *in* the *sala*, not outside like the burst glass of the windows. And with reasonable certainty we can say this: someone aimed it directly at the chair in which, I'm afraid, the poor victim was sitting."

Phil hid her face in her hands. A moan crept through her fingers.

"Phil," Adam's hand reached out for her.

She fished for her purse. "Sorry. Excuse me."

"Phil." Adam got up, but she had already turned away.

"Please—later, okay."

She fled into the hotel. An instant later they saw her climb up the stairs to the balcony. A door opened and closed. Adam sank back into his chair.

Dziri cleared his voice. "Poor Ms. Mann. Both of you suspected it."

Adam threw him a furious glance. "But you didn't, right? You didn't suspect anything. Ridiculous." He tried to stay calm. "Why don't you tell me what so clearly stinks concerning Scherer and the TAB? Why did Dorothea open a file on them? I am convinced, Inspector, you are asking yourself the same questions."

"I'm asking myself a lot of things."

"But you are afraid to get into trouble again," The word popped in Adam's mind, *"berenjenales."*

After a moment, the inspector nodded. "This, indeed, is the

danger. I'm sure, Mr. Colleague, you understand that it doesn't make sense to attack respectable citizens, especially the ones who know the right people, with unfounded accusations. Without one-hundred-percent unshakable proof. Because to do so would bring some very clever attorneys into the game, impede my investigation and make me highly unpopular. Not only with the public prosecutor."

Adam's anger dissolved. He nodded, too. "Okay. I get it, Inspector."

"Thank you." Dziri stood up.

"One more thing. Tomorrow I'll talk to Rosenda, Scherer's ex-housekeeper. Who found my sister dead, as you know, and gave up her job the following day."

Dziri hid his eyes behind fashionable sunglasses. "I'm sure that's an excellent idea. Bye for now, Mr. Ryan, it was good seeing you."

"Bye, Inspector." Adam watched as the policeman drove off.

Indeed, now he did understand. How often had he as investigator run up against walls. Walls of opportunism, cowardice, pre-arrangements he couldn't prove. To bring down Scherer, Adam had to help Dziri crack the code.

CHAPTER 19

Adam was up early the next morning. He dressed in his black suit, had a coffee on the patio and went back up. Behind Phil's door, everything was silent; the curtains still closed. The sleeping pill Lluis had brought her late at night must have done the job.

Google maps guided him across the island to the far Northeast. The farther Adam drove, the lonelier it got. At a certain point, nothing suggested the "Party mile Ibiza" anymore, the image that had shaped the island's global reputation. Quiet pine woods and archaic ferns lined the road. Near the coast, even the pavement had resigned to nature's forces, eaten up by potholes big as craters. Adam parked his SEAT at the shoulder. According to Scherer's description it couldn't be much farther.

A few minutes later he arrived on top of a horseshoe-shaped bay with a sloping beach of gravel and coarse sand. The only signs of civilization were an abandoned wooden shack and a drab hotel ruin above the beach. And a rakish motor yacht that sat in the turquoise waters, its name in big enough letters to be read from this distance, "Apollon."

Three people were sitting in the sand with crossed legs:

Jorg Scherer, a woman with leathery tanned skin and a man in a blue-white uniform and a captain's hat lying at his side. In their middle was a clay urn wreathed with white roses. Scherer wore a black ribbon around the sleeve of his white suit. When Adam arrived, he only said, "Sit. Let's start."

Adam felt his throat contract. Inconceivable that this urn, looking like a Roman wine amphora, should contain his sister's ashes. The man in uniform started to give a speech about the late Amanda, longtime companion and beloved wife of Jorg, his good friend. On a trip to Ibiza ten years ago, the speaker said, Amanda became so infatuated with the White Island, her loving husband decided to open up a new branch of his company here. In one decade, both of them integrated in the local community in a remarkable way.

Adam was astonished to hear of all the philanthropic causes Amanda had been engaged in. Only recently he had learned about her involvement in this group protesting the sale of Es Vedrà—which, however, the speaker did not mention. For Scherer's sake, Adam guessed. Sad how little he had known his sister. Through the years, she had almost been deleted from his mind. And from his heart? No, Adam knew, not from his heart. There, a door had merely closed and reopened too late.

The speaker now reflected on Amanda's death, so painful and incomprehensible, a result of the merciless cosmic powers reigning over Ibiza. Adam felt an urge to protest but didn't, and the man went on about the forces bringing out the good and creative in people, but also the dark and destructive. His words reminded Adam of this article he had read. They didn't make sense to him, either.

The whole ceremony struck him as surreal, but Scherer and the woman sat in the sand as if in church, with bowed heads. Now, the preacher fantasized about "the eternal Ying and Yang," finding oneself and self-destruction. Two forces competing for Amanda's soul. Although she hadn't succeeded in balancing both, he said, only her material self had died, while in the universe her energetic being was forever alive.

Scherer listened with his eyes closed. Tears rolled down his cheeks. He did love Amanda, Adam suddenly knew. In some way, Scherer had really loved his wife, even if he was her murderer.

The speaker was done. He put on his captain's hat, handed the urn to Scherer, and picked up the wreath of white roses. In silence, they walked to a dinghy lying onshore. Adam and the woman got up as well. She mumbled something in Spanish, kissed her joined fingertips and made the sign of the cross.

"Rosenda?" Adam asked, while the captain shouted, "Coming, Mr. Ryan?"

"Yeah." To the woman, "You come along?"

"No, I wait here. You say goodbye to your sister, then we talk."

At high speed, the yacht speeded into the open sea. Adam and Scherer stood on deck, close enough their shoulders almost touched. Scherer's hands, clutching the urn, trembled. When they were out of the three-mile zone, the captain throttled the engine and joined them, the wreath of roses in his hand. For a while, all three just stood in silence.

Until the captain turned to Scherer, "Are you ready, bro?"

Without a word, Scherer opened the urn and tipped it over the railing. White ashes were lifted into the air, stood there like a sudden fog and gradually sank down onto the water. All that's left of a human being, Adam thought, of my sister. A white cloud evaporating, disappearing in a blink.

The wreath followed the ashes, merrily swaying on the waves. "*Adiós*, Amanda," the captain said and gave Scherer a hug. "My condolences, bro. Remember we are with you."

He returned to his wheelhouse and reeved up the engine.

Scherer leaned heavily against the railing. "Dammit, Amanda," he uttered between clenched teeth, "Why? Why, for fuck's sake? This is crazy."

Adam felt the urge to put his hand on his shoulder but didn't.

"We never talked much. Not about... us. Our relationship. I didn't need to talk, and for the first twenty years she seemed perfectly fine with it." Scherer sighed, grief-stricken, "Why it suddenly became a problem—I just don't get it."

Unexpectedly, Adam was touched by his brother-in-law's words. He knew the feeling. The women he had come more or less close to in the last years had also, at some point, complained about him not being communicative enough. They wanted to talk about their relationship, and he had nothing to say. Questions like "What are you thinking?" reliably triggered his flight instinct. Adam never understood why the women couldn't just wait and see what would happen. As if *he* knew. He and Scherer seemed to have more in common than he cared for.

"Jorg, I'm really sorry," he muttered.

"For what?" With sudden vehemence, Scherer faced him. "For your accusation that I killed Amanda or that she took her life because of me?" There was a kind of frenzy in his eyes, "What exactly are you sorry for?"

"That Amanda is dead. I'm trying to understand why, and I will find out."

"Right. Adam, the master detective." Scherer's voice dripped with sarcasm. He smashed his palm hard onto the ship's rail. "But again, I didn't have any reason to harm my wife. And something else I'll reveal to you: Amanda didn't give a shit if I occasionally shagged someone else."

"Is that so?" Sudden furor hit Adam. "And you expect me to believe this?"

"She spit it right into my face: 'Go screw who you want.' And that she... despised me. After all these years together. The only ones she was still interested in were her friends." Scherer gave a nasty laugh, "Who didn't even care enough to bid her farewell. Great friendship, don't you think?"

Adam didn't answer, overcome by a feeling of helpless-ness. How could he judge Scherer when he didn't know a thing about Amanda? Nothing about her friends, nothing but as-sumptions about her married life...

"Not even the fucking gardener bothered to show up," Scherer continued full of bitterness, "who also claimed to be her friend. I invited him when he called about some important shit he wanted to meet about." He punished the rail with an-other hard punch. "Money, I guess, now that he can't suck it out of Amanda anymore." Scherer wiped his sweaty forehead. "Well, he should have tried. Only the coward never showed up."

Meanwhile, the yacht had returned to the bay. The captain lowered the dinghy to bring Adam back ashore.

"Goodbye, Jorg."

His jaws grinding, Scherer stared across the sea. "Bye, ass-hole" were the last words Adam heard from him.

Rosenda was sitting in the shade of the wooden shack.

"*Mi más sincero pésame,*" she offered her condolences and switched to broken English. "Amanda was good woman. Good boss. But not happy."

"That's what I am thinking."

"Didn't want no more life."

Adam searched her face in surprise. "How would you know that?"

"*Era evidente,* obvious." Rosenda put her hand to her heart. "She so alone."

"What did she say to you?"

"Not speak." The hand pounded on her chest to show that she had felt it.

"What about her friends?"

"*Amigas? No,* Amanda always alone."

"Really? What about Dorothea? A German..."

"*Alemana?*" Rosenda seemed to ponder. "*No me acuerdo.*

Don't know."

"And Ninguno?"

Rosenda shrugged. "Don't know why he not here. He was friend."

"Why do you think he tried to contact Scherer after Amanda's death?"

She rubbed an index finger against her thumb. "*Dinero.* Amanda give money for garden work. And for food when no work. Ninguno always need money."

Adam fell quiet. If Scherer was right on this point—on what else? The story of Amanda's last times on earth, as it unfolded here, was devastating. A husband she despised. Who cheated on her and didn't talk to her. Some women who didn't really care about her. Only one friend, her gardener who tapped her for money but didn't bother to show up at this last ceremony for her. An absent brother. Her fearful personality. Reasons enough to despair?

But: "*If* something happens to me..." Amanda had written. Her vivacious face appeared in Adam's mind. With every fiber of his being, he knew she had not taken her own life.

But Rosenda insisted, "Amanda not wanted life. *Lo se*, is hard."

"Do you know of any problems with Scherer's company, the TAB?"

"Scherer!" Rosenda made a fist and shook it towards the yacht that was just leaving the bay. "Bad man. *El y toda la tertulia! Hijos del diablo.*" Her voice broke; she bit her lips and shot Adam a wary eye. "Don't know much. But has bad *amigos, el señor* Scherer."

"Who are these *amigos*? Please tell me what you know."

Rosenda avoided his eyes. "*No se nada. Lo siento.* I have to go."

She got up and patted sand from her skirt. Adam cursed himself for not speaking Spanish. Living in Dallas, with a forty percent Latino population, one really should.

CHAPTER 20

The sleeping pills Lluis had given Phil had knocked her out. But in the morning, her head felt clamped in a vise, her tongue like a dead mouse, and something was wrong with her usually excellent vision. With some effort, she staggered under the shower and let cold water patter over her. When her head was halfway clear, things changed: the shock of learning that Doro really had been murdered, turned into determination. Phil's first clear thought of the morning was: whoever did this to Doro will be held accountable.

Tamar still hadn't called back, so again, she dialed her number. She wouldn't give up, and if she had to try a hundred times...

A voice roared into her ear. "What else, man? For fuck's sake, stop it."

Tamar sounded so furious, Phil involuntarily jumped backwards.

"Got it, asshole?"

"It's Phil, Tamar. I need to talk to you."

Silence, deep breath, forced politeness, "Oh, aah—bummer, Phil, I really don't have the time now."

No. She would not be brushed off again. "Give me a sec,

okay?"

Tamar sighed impatiently. "What is it?"

"About my friend, Dorothea: I believe you knew her after all."

Tamar interrupted without suppressing her anger any longer. "What the fuck are you talking about? Damn, Phil, I said I don't know your Dorothea."

"I found this list in her backpack. Also with your name, Tamar."

"Is that so? Mine? I'm pretty sure there are more girls called Tamar."

Phil hadn't thought about that. "But..."

"Listen. I'm really sorry, but I have to cut you short. There is a gigantic problem I need to solve. Later, okay?" Tamar giggled artificially, smugly stressing the next word, "*Men*, you know."

"Doro is dead!" Phill yelled but Tamar had already hung up on her.

A little later, on the porch, Phil let her coffee go cold, absorbed in the laptop Lluis had lent her. Under the search term "Tamar, Ibiza," Google offered a pop singer called Tamar who once had vacationed in Ibiza, and a seminar, published in *Can Follet Studies,* under the title "The Prostitution of Tamar in Genesis 38 from the Matriarchal Perspective." A Tamar Stettin didn't appear anywhere on the web, neither did Jezebel. In the age of online transparency, this seemed quite odd, especially as Jezebel was the head of an international women's center. One entry led to a Can Follet intranet that required a password. There must be purpose behind keeping the names of instructors and guests private.

Phil looked up when she heard steps. Adam. Words were not needed to know where he had been—his black suit and somber face told it all.

"That must have been hard," she said. "I'm so sorry."

Adam dropped into a chair. "A corny sermon, an urn,

ashes spread on the high seas. Quick and—no, not easy."

Phil was aware how difficult it was for him to talk about it. But obviously, Adam tried to open up; his vulnerability started to shine through. Something new had built up between them: a connection oblivious of their screwed-up past. A kinship of shared grief.

But, as if this was too much for him, Adam cleared his throat.

"Rosenda is not willing to talk—even though I'm sure she has a lot to talk about." Restlessly, he got up and started to circle around the table, his hands behind his back. He had always been one of these people who could think best when in motion. He described what Inspector Dziri had insinuated the evening before: that he could not open up an investigation against Scherer as his hands were tied. If only Scherer's connection to the authorities were the reason or some further specific interests, they would have to find out.

"*We*," Adam said. "You're right, Phil, we have to get over our inglorious past and join forces. Everyone else here closes their eyes or doesn't want to talk. But nobody can deny us the right to ask questions. So let's do it our way, okay?"

Adam held his hand out. A little dizzy from his circling, Phil wondered for a moment where "their way" would take them. But all she could still do for Doro was to hunt down her killer. And Amanda's. She shook Adam's hand.

Now they needed a plan. To be free of a superior's orders might be an advantage, but they both knew it wouldn't work without inspector Dziri. They would have to get him in private and grill him until he spat out what he knew or assumed about Scherer and the TAB, but wasn't allowed to investigate.

"How can we catch him alone?" Adam thought aloud and a moment later had an idea. "I think you'd be better at this than me," he said with his first little grin for the day, which made Phil a little happy, too.

Meeting Dziri in private turned out to be a cinch. They drove into the city and Adam parked his car in a side street close to the police headquarters. When it was close to two, time of the sacred *siesta*, Phil took a deep breath and called the number of the police station's operator. She introduced herself and explained her "a bit embarrassing situation." That she was about to meet Bartolo Dziri for lunch, but had forgotten in which restaurant. That she didn't want to call Bartolo and ask, as he shouldn't think she was, even before their first... date, a *tontaina*, a nitwit. Because she wasn't; it had just slipped her mind. If the operator happened to know where Bartolo was going for lunch?

Adam grinned his second, now cynical, grin of the day, but to the operator, Phil's show was a hit. Dziri, he said, would probably go to Tia Maria, the bodega across from the police station. Definitely he would, as today was *paella* day. Excited, the operator gave Phil a detailed description of the chef's culinary talents. He was convinced: a date on paella day must mean Tia Maria. If not, Phil should dump Bartolo right away. Only a joke, he hastened to add, as his friend Bartolo was a man of outstanding qualities. He wished them all the best for the future.

Her ears ringing, Phil thanked him: "Don't tell him I forgot, okay?"

"Don't you worry, *Señorita. Adiós.*"

Phil turned to Adam with a smirk, "Someone doesn't seem to realize that the inspector is gay."

"He is?"

She rolled her eyes: so much for male power of observation.

CHAPTER 21

From the outside, the bodega Tia Maria was the most non-descript restaurant in the world: a flat-roofed concrete box, wrapped in the dust the cars and trucks whirled up to a constant dervish as they raced by. Inside, however, the dining hall showed class, with tables clothed in white linen, heavy silverware, and artistic photographs of Ibizan landscapes on the walls.

After only coffee and a microscopic piece of almond cake in the morning, Phil almost fainted from starvation. She and Adam sat down by a window from where they could keep an eye on the police station.

They didn't have to wait for long. When the waiter brought them the menus, Bartolo Dziri appeared in the entrance across the road. Today he was dressed in a blue-striped suit with a matching vest. The guard saluted him and was rewarded with an approving slap on the shoulder. Nodding, Dziri commanded his sunglasses to glide from his head onto his nose. One palm held against the traffic that obediently came to a halt, he crossed the road and entered the bodega.

"Now see who is here." Adam got up. "Hello, Inspector Dziri."

"Good day, Mr. Ryan. What a surprise to run into you." Dziri's words dripped with irony as he shook Adam's hand while winking at Phil. "And Ms Mann. So we are having a date, I hear."

Phil shrugged, playing it cool. "Men are such chatterboxes." Only her cheeks betrayed her and blushed.

Adam came to her aid. "We have to talk to you, all right?"

"That's what I figured."

But first, they would eat, the inspector insisted, because he wasn't able to function on an empty stomach. With an elegant gesture, he slid his Ray Bans back on his head and invited Phil and Adam to sit with him in his regular booth. A smiling woman appeared, whom Dziri introduced as *tia* Maria in person, the bodega's owner and chef. She greeted the *estimado comisário* and his guests cordially, signaling to a waiter who was on his way to another table but, to the snap of her fingers, ran in the kitchen and was back in a flash with *pan y aioli* and a carafe of white wine. Without asking for anyone's consent, he filled three glasses. Dziri finished half of his in one gulp and had the waiter refill it. Drinking alcohol while on duty didn't seem to be an issue for him.

"Ah, the dry air in the office. Drink, please, *salud, amor y dinero*. And let's eat. Will you allow me to order for you?"

They did, so Dziri gave Maria a lengthy description of his wishes. She beamed as if she'd never before listened to such a grandiose order.

"*Paella* day," he coquettishly winked at Phil, "as you know. Tia Maria makes the absolute best *Paella Valencia* on the island."

When the chef retreated, Dziri gave Adam a look of fake resignation. "So, you're determined to not let go."

"You bet." In precise words Adam summarized why he—*they*, he corrected himself—were convinced Amanda's and Dorothea's deaths were connected and had to do with Scherer and his company.

This time, the inspector abstained from giving quick, re-jecting comments. He dipped pieces of bread into the *aioli,* dabbed his mouth with his napkin, had more wine, sighed, frowned. When Adam mentioned Rosenda's allusions to Scherer's club, the *hijos del diablo* and, at the same time, her reluctance to open up to him, Dziri's sighs became even more profound.

"That's the problem. Nobody here wants to talk."

"Then you do it. Talk to us."

Dziri gave Adam a look as if he had asked him to jump off a cliff. "Let's make sure, just in case a tad of information left my mouth, it would have to remain *entre nous.* How do you say in your language: off the record. Agreed?"

"Take it for granted," Adam said while Phil lifted two fin-gers. "I swear."

They waited. But when Dziri, with an "okay, *vale,*" started to speak, Maria reappeared, pushing a serving trolley with a large metal pan. She placed the *paellera* on their table and stirred its contents lovingly.

"*Bom provech,*" she said in the local lingo. "Enjoy your meal."

In response, Dziri joined his fingertips on his lips, smacked a kiss and let it fly towards the chef. Phil couldn't help grin-ning. She wondered why Dziri had become a policeman and not an opera star. Maybe he couldn't sing. Dziri called Maria's attention to the sacrilege of the empty carafe, and when the glasses were refilled, there was no time for talking. All three were absorbed in the opulent mix of chicken, rabbit and veg-etables, rice in saffron and the most aromatic olive oil Phil had ever tasted. This paella really could make one forget all trou-bles and pains. For a while. When she had spiked the very last artichoke heart on her fork; when Dziri shoved his plate aside and again took his napkin to dab his lips, Adam was ready. "Go right ahead, Chief."

This seemed to flatter Dziri. He smiled graciously, but first had to fold the napkin, take another sip, hesitate a bit more. Finally, he started to talk.

Dziri admitted he had always shared Adam's suspicion that Scherer killed his wife. Of course he knew about Amanda's part in the protest march, her speaking out publicly against her husband's ridiculous plan to buy Es Vedrà on behalf of some shady client. But Scherer, the inspector continued, had an alibi for the time of Amanda's death, supplied by five witnesses. They swore Scherer hadn't left the party until a driver brought him back to his villa in the early morning, at which time Amanda had already been dead for hours. Maybe, Dziri shrugged, these witnesses lied. But there just wasn't enough to press charges against Scherer. Amanda's words "If something happens to me..." couldn't change this fact.

"The prosecutor wouldn't have it. And Scherer's attorneys would tear me to pieces and eat me alive."

Adam banged one open palm so hard on the table the glasses chinked.

"Sorry," he said to the guests around them who looked up in alarm and then lowered his voice, "So you're saying there's nothing we can do, Dziri. Why are we sitting here then? We need some straight talking from you or we're wasting our time. Come on, *Chief*," Adam added, remembering how Dziri could be lured.

The waiter brought three cups of highly welcomed coffee. When he had cleared the table, the inspector blurted out, "Because of the TAB."

"What do you know about them?"

"The TAB, as you know, is Scherer's real estate company, through which he is trying to buy up the whole island." Dziri jumped up, agitated. "But behind this company hides a dubious international men's club. I guess they chose Ibiza as their clubhouse because of our reputation of being so nice and tolerant."

Nice and tolerant? The ancient Ibizan stone slingers, the

honderos, who fought off invaders by throwing stones at them, came to Phil's mind.

Like a satellite, Dziri circled around a bar trolley that had miraculously appeared. He decided for a *Hierbas*, the famous Ibizan herb liqueur, held up the bottle invitingly and set it back when Phil and Adam declined.

"The TAB is not just your same old club where the boys hang out and get wasted," Dziri continued. "In fact, it is a secretive brotherhood with a network spanning all seven continents. The members are rich businessmen, media moguls, high-ranking economists, aristocrats, bankers, celebrities, and politicians. They want to be among themselves, they say, to find solutions for the world's problems without advertising the good they do. Like the Bilderberg Conference or Skull & Bones. You can believe this or not. I don't. Because if their intentions are honest, why keep them secret? Sure you guys don't want a digestif? Okay."

"Skull & Bones," Adam reflected, "a club of former Yale students. Both presidents Bush were members. Sworn to secrecy. Strange rituals. Known for nepotism, favoritism. Without them, someone like George W. would never have been president..." Adam thought about this, "Well, that's what we believed then."

"Exactly," Dziri agreed. "They all insist they keep out of the public for a *good* reason. In reality, they just don't want to be looked into and held responsible. The Chatman House Rule: no names mentioned. Think of the Bilderberg Conference, one of the most powerful clubs in the world. Today we know they triggered the 70s oil crisis to keep the U.S. dollar up and prevent economic growth in the so-called wrong countries. Did you know my family roots are in Algiers? But everyone who questions the Bilderbergers' intentions is called a conspiracy theorist. The TAB-Brothers are actually more generous as they open their doors not only to Westerners but everyone. As long as they are rich. And men."

Dziri nipped at this glass. "The acronym TAB," he kept on, "stands for *Tertulia des los Amigos de Bes*, brotherhood of the friends of Bes, an ancient god who has been worshipped on Ibiza since the early times. Some say even the name Ibiza goes back to him: *Eibossim*, island of Bes. The philosophy of his worshippers includes letting it all hang out. And I mean: All."

Two sets of eyes stared at him.

"Yep. While the Yale folks have a logo with a skull and bones to symbolize death and transformation, the TAB brothers are more... simplistic with their symbol, the figure of Bes. The guy's not a sight for a lady with his big..."

Dziri made an unmistakable gesture, and immediately Phil remembered the sculpture of the little man with his oversized penis in Scherer's office. When she described it, Adam got up and poured himself a schnapps after all. And one more for Dziri, who held up his glass.

"Okay. A club of males who worship their dicks. Nothing new under the sun." Can Follet popped into Phil's mind. "Women have their exclusive resorts too. So, apart from the fact that one may laugh or cry about these male, ahm, *dicks*— where is the illegality? Why would police be interested in them?"

"And first and foremost," Adam cut in, "what do they have to do with Amanda's and Dorothea's deaths?"

Dziri avoided a straight answer, "When you are as rich, powerful and well connected as the TAB, you think you're above the law. You live in a world without concern for the low life around you. That's where the TAB brothers live. And they are not satisfied with a little private island in the Saint Lawrence River like the Skull & Boners. They are determined to take over Ibiza. They bought who knows how many local politicians, so despite all former scandals, illegal permissions are issued again. To them. There is always someone willing to accept a bribe. That the *Consell Insular* didn't right away reject the idea to sell Es Vedrà is evidence enough."

Dziri lowered his voice, "And there is more. I'm talking about drug offenses, illegal prostitution, deprivation of liberty, rape..." Now he whispered, "and murder. Or let's phrase it differently: a few years ago, the death of a girl was linked to the TAB. Some suspected murder, especially me and my father, at that time the chief police commissioner."

Bitter cynicism had crept into Dziri's voice. "But while we were still investigating, the case was dropped. The prosecutor couldn't see a connection between the girl's death and the TAB, no matter how obvious the evidence we presented. Evidence that a girl had died after coming too close to the Brothers. Fantasies, the prosecutor called it, fabrications by the *comisários* Dziri, father and son who, as a result, became highly unpopular in the high places."

Phil's head spun: a secret brotherhood, bribery, drugs, another death, a girl, frustrated policemen. Seemed like out of a Dan Brown novel, not reality. What did Doro have to do with it all?

"A dead girl?" Adam asked, exasperated by Dziri's cumbersome ways. "What the hell, Chief!"

"Exactly, the girl." The policeman raised his index finger. "Yesterday, I searched the archives for the file about this girl that had caused problems for the TAB and later died under strange circumstances. Her name was Neves Niemer. She was the daughter of Otto Niemer. Ninguno."

Dziri enjoyed the effect his words had. Here it was, the connection that could not be mere coincidence, linking two, no, three cases of death to the TAB: Amanda, the wife of TAB brother Scherer. Doro who had known Amanda and started an investigation on Scherer. And now the daughter of Ninguno, Amanda's gardener and friend.

Adam urged Dziri to explain, but the inspector was not a friend of being rushed. "In order to understand the present, we have to dive into the past..."

"We get this. So what happened?"

The occurrence took place, Dziri said, when he had just been promoted to police inspector. "At twenty-seven, imagine. My father, the chief, was really proud of me, and my mother..."

"I'm forty-seven," Phil interrupted, "and wonder what will come first, menopause or you getting to the point."

Adam bellowed out a laugh while Dziri gasped and tried to speed up.

"One morning four years ago, Neves and another sixteen-year-old girl showed up at our headquarters..."

Barefoot and half-naked, they had run across half the island after spending a night in Can Salammbo, the clubhouse of the TAB. There they had worked as waitresses, until the Brothers invited them to join the party. The girls thought nothing of it, actually felt flattered. But the men forced heavy alcohol on them and put something in their drinks. Dizzy, half-conscious, they were tossed around like rag dolls and stripped of their clothes. And then, the girls said, several men raped them, while the others watched or didn't care. Only when the Brothers were completely drunk and the sedatives wore off, did they manage to escape.

Bartolo's father, Manuel, thought he could finally nail the TAB. Sure enough, medical exams determined sperm of different men and traces of Rohypnol in the girls' bodies. Such clear evidence. Until they showed up again at police with their fathers, one being Ninguno, and withdrew their report. The Dziris knew immediately that hush money had been paid. They told it to their faces, but nothing could convince them to return to the truth and file a complaint. Manuel was so frustrated he almost quit his job two years prior to retirement.

About a year later, Neves Niemer was found dead, a syringe needle in her arm. But although she only had this one puncture site on her body, even though her friends swore she never had gone beyond a joint, the prosecutor again didn't pursue criminal investigations. Only Ninguno started his decline into alcohol, probably guilt-ridden about his daughter's death.

"It stinks," Dziri said, "it stinks to high heaven."

Phil was outraged. "What in hell is wrong with this prosecutor?"

"Rumors have it he belongs to the TAB. But you'd better not say it aloud."

"What happened to the other girl?"

Dziri raised his thumb. "Right question, *señora*. Laura Ten Vaar soon moved back to the Netherlands with her family and was never seen again."

"You're right, Chief, it stinks," Adam said. "A swamp we have to drain. First step: we have to talk to Ninguno."

"Exactly."

"Then this Dutch family. It's worth the try to find them. Maybe they are ready to talk today, from this distance."

Collective agreement. The inspector ordered the waiter to charge his account with the whole check, refusing the others' request to split. When the extensive ritual of goodbyes with Maria was over, almost two hours had passed since he had gone for lunch. In no rush, he followed Phil and Adam out.

"Those Americans," Adam said, "the American members of the TAB. Do you have names?"

"I wish! As said, the brothers are a *secret* society, very hush-hush."

"What about the American who wants to buy Es Vedrà?"

"Scherer says he wants his name kept out of the public. Nothing we can do." But Dziri had an idea, "This wouldn't work for completed real estate deals. When you own property here, you have to be registered. Four years ago, I actually started to investigate on this aspect. Can Salammbo, I remember, was owned by an American."

The clubhouse of the *Tertulia de Bes*. This sounded promising.

"Okay, Chief," Adam said. "Bring me names, and I'll see what I can do. I have some contacts, you know."

Dziri beamed *"Vale, colega, muy bien."* Now that the story was out in the open, he was all fired up, a cop on a mission to law and order. "Finally," he shouted, "we will bring them to court, this gang of thugs."

Adam saw the need to curb his enthusiasm. "Slow down, Inspector, will you? At the moment we can't risk stirring up the hornet's nest. As you learned last time: if we don't proceed carefully, they will muzzle you again."

One could tell that the inspector would have preferred immediate arrests and handcuffing. But then, he didn't want to end up as frustrated as his father.

"Ah, yes, I know."

"We need concrete evidence or better—solid proof the prosecutor won't be able to reject again without severely compromising himself."

"You are totally right."

They exchanged goodbyes, but Phil still had a question burning her tongue. "Inspector, is there any news about Doro? Like what she was up to before her death?"

"Por desgracia, here, we're still in the dark." Dziri raised both hands. "We know that she contacted the *Oficina de Extranjeros,* the Foreigners registry office, last December and was given the form to complete her Residence Certificate as every foreigner who's been living here for three months has to do. Only your Doro never did and thus never got her *número de Identifación Extranjeros.* In the unlikely case that her application got lost, why didn't she come back and complain? If only to claim the benefits she as a resident would have been entitled to, like reduced airfares? That's strange, especially as she did go to the mainland several times. The name Dorothea Bartholdy appears on the passenger lists of two flights to Frankfurt in December and January, from where, both times, she returned four days later."

Dziri led his sunglasses slide down on his nose again. "In January, she went to Mallorca, and just three weeks ago to

Rome, Italy, where she stayed for a week. What she was up to? No idea!" Dramatically, he threw his hands in the air. "I swear, this Dorothea is like a phantom to me."

CHAPTER 22

Inspector Dziri returned to his office and Phil and Adam to the *hostal* where a number of new guests had arrived. Luggage was piled up in the lobby, the building buzzing like a beehive. A group of Danish tourists hung out on the patio, gobbling down wine. Some Swiss women who were only staying here because Can Follet was full, were excited about their upcoming hormone-yoga-class.

Two guys were holding hands while Lluis checked them in. The elder one smashed a golden credit card on the desk's counter like an ace. He looked like the archetypical American tourist in his shorts, sneakers, and a t-shirt with the print "Abs shaped by beer" over his huge belly. The younger one wore cowboy boots, a Stetson, and nothing but very short shorts.

Ezra Huber came storming into the lobby, followed by Trudy. He stopped short at the sight of the gay couple, his face twisting with repulsion. Forced to get in line behind them, his cheeks inflated like a blowfish sensing danger, then the air escaped with a high-pitched noise. The half-naked cowboy took it as a whistle of admiration and flashed a peroxide white-toothed smile at him.

"Well, howdy there."

"My key."

Huber snatched it out of Lluis's hand, made a step backwards and landed on Trudy's toes. "Ouch," she winced.

Huber didn't apologize. "Degenerate human trash," he rumbled, marching to the stairs. "Just like these dykes. Should have run them over, all of them."

Trudy followed him, panting, "Don't even say this. You don't want to end up in a Spanish jail, do you?"

"Shut your mouth, woman. We'll get Amy out of this Gomorrah. I'll sue these bitches, I'll have *them* thrown in jail. They kidnapped my daughter."

"Amy is of adult age," Trudy gasped with the tiniest trace of rebelliousness. "According to the law she can decide..."

"I'm her father. *I* am her law."

"But, Ezra..." Trudy's faint voice broke.

All the more clearly, Phil snapped, "And the world is a flat disc."

When she entered her room, she was still foaming with rage over Huber, but soon she was back in her own hell. What in the world should she do about money? There was no realistic way she could sell the ruin of her house, still sealed by police, in the remaining days. But she had less than two hundred euros left. She knew she could have asked Doro for a loan, but Doro was dead.

Doro. Another question was nagging at Phil after Dziri mentioned the trips to Frankfurt. Why hadn't Doro told her she was coming? Frankfurt was only half an hour away from Mainz. She probably had gone for a work reason; but still, wouldn't she have found the time for at least a drink with her old friend? Where had she slept? Her place was big enough to share, even with Phil and Anton in it. Four days, twice, without a call wasn't like Doro. And when Phil had called her, she never mentioned these trips. As if she had wanted to keep them secret. Why?

It didn't make sense. Phil sighed. But right now, there was

the other, the biggest problem: money. She had to get money. Where from? Her mother? No way. What she would do instead was contact her bank, explain the situation and beg for mercy and another extension. If necessary, she would even throw in what Scherer had said, that the lot without a house but a building permit would get her an even better deal. A crying shame to end up on the agent's level.

Glad it was past four p.m. and a Friday, too late to call the bank now, Phil postponed her worries and grabbed the scooter key. She had an idea where she might get information about the TAB, and it seemed too good to not give a try.

The accelerator depressed, Phil speeded down the road to Santa Eulalia. The city must be preparing for a party. The white-clad stalls along the *ramblas* had multiplied down to the bay, food trucks were being set up. In front of the *Podencos* sculpture, a man in a fancy uniform was trying to organize a mob of excited teenagers to a brass band formation.

Crossing the promenade to Passeig d'Alameda, Phil entered the pink building that accommodated the German magazine *Insular*. Her idea was to talk to the editor-in-chief, the best-informed guy on the island he had chosen as his home. If a pin dropped, Hans von Brolow would know the reason why, who was responsible and with what consequences, as long as it dropped on Ibiza. If someone could tell her about the TAB, it was Hans.

In the lobby behind a desk, a woman with grass-green hair was absorbed in a PC screen. She only looked up when Phil tapped a knuckle against the door frame. Immediately her face petrified. Two summers ago when Phil worked here as a translator, Nia's hair had been brown. She had gained quite a bit of weight.

"*Hóla*, Nia, how are you? Is Hans in?"

"Oh—you don't have an appointment, do you? I'm afraid he's busy."

Nia pretended to not remember Phil. Seriously? Two years ago, she had already been Hans's assistant, and how the hell could Phil have known that he was the kind of guy who would choke if he had to say "girlfriend." When Phil asked him about Nia's obvious jealousy, he called her an acquaintance who had followed him from Germany to Ibiza. Which he hadn't asked for.

"I'll just see for myself, okay? Don't bother."

Before Nia could save her data, Phil knocked at the door to Hans's office. To an indistinct "yeah," she pushed it open.

Hans von Brolow, the tallest man Phil had ever known, was sprawling behind his cluttered desk. In one hand he held a pen, in the other a writing pad; he still worked old school. A laptop seemed to be there for musical reasons alone, thundering an old Whitesnakes hit: *Like a drifter, I was born to walk alone...*

"... *and I made up my mind. I ain't wasting no more time...* Hi, Hans."

"Phil—really and truly?" Hans catapulted what he had in his hands onto the desk, pushed himself back and jumped up. His liana-like arms wrapped around Phil. The crown of her head barely reached his coastal arch.

"Phil, to see you again! It's been ages. Although you promised..."

Both had promised to keep in touch and known this wouldn't necessarily be the case. What they'd had was only an affair, a two-night-stand. Phil wiggled herself out of Hans's embrace.

"You're right—*mea culpa.*"

Hans stepped back and took her head in both hands like a crystal ball.

"What a joy to see you, honey. You look fantastic."

He positioned a quick kiss on her lips and let go. Phil patted down her hair.

"Thanks, Hans. All well with you?"

"Well—wait a minute."

Hans went to the door, called for Nia in quite a bossy voice to bring him a *Viña Sol* and two glasses. "Don't think I forgot that *blanco* is your poison, Phil. Look at you, you have not changed one bit... Thanks."

He took the bottle and glasses out of Nia's hands, thus sparing her from having to serve Phil. Long training in relation-balancing, she thought, amused.

He poured the wine. "Cheers!"

This day, Phil had wandered from one glass to the next, and again was holding one in her hand. Oh well, who cared... "Cheers."

"Life has meant well with you, dear."

"Well, I'm not so sure."

"Okay?" Abruptly, Hans turned serious. "So what brings you to me, Phil? You need work?"

"No, that's not it."

"Oh, good." Visibly relieved, he admitted that this would have been a bit of a problem. That these days he had to turn away people who had worked for him for years. The net kept ruining print media, not only the *Insular* was affected. Even the *New York Times* had to dismiss people. Hans von Brolow had never been shy of comparing himself with the big shots of his business.

"Less and less ads. If this goes on, I'll open up a craft brew pub."

Phil took a sip and explained that she had come to the island to sell her house but that it burned down. When she added, "And can you imagine, my best friend Doro died in the fire," Hans again took her in his arms and held her tight. His shirt was getting wet from her tears.

"Horrible. I'm so sorry," he muttered. Of course, he had heard about the fire that took someone's life. That it had to do with Phil shocked him.

"And it wasn't an accident."

"What are you saying?" Stunned, Hans dropped his arms.

Unable to go through the painful details again, Phil only said, "Someone threw a firebomb into my house."

"Oh my God."

"Before that, when I still had a house to sell, I contacted a real estate agent. Jorg Scherer. Know him?"

"Sure."

Had she imagined the involuntary hesitation?

"His wife also just died, suicide they say. She was a friend of Doro's. And he, Scherer, is connected with this men's club, the TAB..."

"Damn, girl!" Hans was alarmed, "Don't get involved with these folks."

He took a sip of wine and refilled his glass. Phil had barely touched hers.

"What do you mean? You're talking from experience?"

Hans dropped into his chair, folding his arms. Suddenly, there was a wall between them. Mistrust, maybe. Or fear.

"Yes," he finally said, "but it was me who made a mistake. A huge one."

"What did you do?"

"A bad thing that could have destroyed my reputation, the *Insular*, my life. Sort of did, actually. I fell prey to deceit."

"Deceit? How come? Hans, tell me. What's it got to do with the TAB? Maybe I'm in danger of being deceived too."

He hesitated. Dziri was right, nobody wanted to talk. But Phil wouldn't back off. "Hans, please. I swear I'll keep it confidential."

Maybe it was his good heart that wanted to keep her from making the same mistake. Hans leaned close to Phil.

About a year ago, he said, he got offered an article on the TAB, and of course he was interested. At this time, rumors about foul play in the club had gotten louder and louder.

"Rumors about exactly what?"

Hans shirked a concrete answer. "No one knew facts. Just

rumors. Until one day this girl shows up in my office. German, super cute. She tells me she knows a guy with a sensational inside story on the TAB. That she can make the contact."

Hans sighed pitifully. "I believe her, you know, women are my soft spot. And will be my downfall. She says the guy with the story, R. W., needs to remain incognito, but is willing to present facts. So I meet him, and indeed he seems to know what he is talking about. His story describes in great detail certain—ahm—meetings of the Brothers. Doesn't mention names, only initials, but some reveal who's behind them. The Italian G. G. with the dueling scar. The American L. Y. with the Cobra. There are only two of them on the island."

"Cobra? The snake?"

"The car. A super expensive sportster."

"What kind of meetings?" Involuntarily, Phil adopted Hans's staccato. "Orgies Berlusconi or Strauss-Kahn style?"

From what Dziri said about the incident with the two girls, this seemed probable and would provoke a huge scandal, even if the rape might never be proven.

Hans, however, backpedaled. "Sorry. I can only save my ass by keeping my mouth shut. What I can tell you is that the story was nothing but bullshit, an unproven, probably made-up farce."

"Of what?" But the more Phil tried to probe, the less Hans offered.

"You don't wanna know. Leave it to me being the stupid one who buys alleged whistle-blowing crap and puts it in print without checking the facts first. The moment it was out, hell broke loose." He shuddered at the memory. "Lawyers show up, requesting verified proof, threaten me with lawsuits and regress payments. And R. W.? Vanished into thin air. With all the facts and photos. When the issue was delivered, we immediately had to recollect it. Fortunately, only a few magazines had been sold at that point. We had to destroy every single copy, pay back the money for ads readers couldn't see and print a rectification instead. The money we burned! The clients we lost!"

"That sucks."

Phil could only imagine how Hans must feel, seeing what he had built up in years go down the drain. "And you have no idea who is this R. W.?"

"He wanted to stay incognito, as said."

"Did he mention any accusations of rape four years ago? Charges against the TAB that were dropped again? Did the name Neves Niemer come up?"

This time, Hans's denial seemed honest. He poured some more wine into Phil's still half-full glass and the rest in his own. With that, the bottle was empty.

Phil gave him a stern look. "So they muzzled you."

"Of course not."

Hans tried to look innocent but couldn't help a nervous flicker in his eyes.

He must have had proof, Phil thought. Hans would not have been a successful journalist for decades to amateurishly fall prey to undocumented assertions.

"You said R. W. had photos."

"No. I—may have said he *talked* about photos."

Now, Phil knew Hans was lying. His face told it too. What she read in it indeed seemed to be fear.

"They threatened you, right? You can tell me, Hans."

The flickering in his eyes stopped. For a moment Phil thought he would be honest, but he turned to stare out of the window. When his fingers combed through his hair, she knew the moment had passed. The gesture was too energetic.

"Nothing of the kind. I fell prey to a fucking deceit. I would have been brought to court had those lawyers not tempered justice with mercy. I even think Scherer advocated for me. He appreciates a German weekly on Ibiza."

He looked as embarrassed as the editor-of-chief of another German magazine, the widely circulated *Stern*, who'd had to admit that "Hitler's secret diaries" bought from a forger, were a gigantic scam.

"Can you show me the story R. W. wrote?"

"Man, Phil, what are you thinking? I absolutely cannot do that. I had to sign to not comment on the case and to destroy all false evidence. That was the requirement to let me off the hook."

"And the whole issue was destroyed?"

"Every single copy. And all online data deleted," Hans maintained.

As if this was even possible. Didn't he just say most copies had been recollected? So some must have been sold. Hans gave Phil a contrite smile. She was sure both of them understood the show. But his warning was stone serious.

"Phil. Don't you fall for gossip, like me. Super rich people are surrounded by a gossip-stirring aura, as they don't relate much to ordinary folk. You know, Scherer may not be the most agreeable person. But neither is he the most villainous. And definitely not a murderer. Okay?"

Phil felt urged to nod, which gave Hans huge relief. "All right. Now let's get over this and be happy about us meeting again."

He started to dig through the paper mess on his desk and fished out a folded card. "You still like the arts? Tonight, the Georgia O'Keeffe show opens in Galeria Cosmi. We are even invited to the after-show dinner. What do you say?"

The invite, in handwriting, read *Hans von Brolow and Nia Hoffmann*.

"Nia doesn't wanna go anyway," Hans said.

Phil wondered if Nia knew that too. "I'd love to, Hans, but..." In thoughts, she apologized to the potential one who might punish lies. "I already got a date."

"Too bad." Hans grabbed Phil by the shoulders. For a moment, she thought he wanted to kiss her again, but he only gave her a big, worried look. "Be careful, babe, promise me."

"Why?" As he wouldn't answer, "You are afraid, Hans. Still?"

His hands dropped from her shoulders. "Everyone should be, Phil. On this island there are... forces one shouldn't mess with."

"The TAB?"

Hans's mouth twitched. "Sure. The TAB."

But something about these three words didn't sound right. Phil felt crushed by the mountain of information Hans withheld from her. She gave him a goodbye peck and opened the door, behind which Nia pretended to not have listened.

"Off I am," Phil smiled falsely, "so you guys won't be late for the show."

"That's cool," Nia smiled back the exact same way.

CHAPTER 23

Inspector Dziri had spent the afternoon digging through files of land registry and now had the names of Americans who owned or had owned large properties on Ibiza. He called Adam, to whom two of the names rang a bell. One was Bud Winslow, a Texan radio host who had, however, passed away. The second name made alarms go off: Andrew Cruz. Like everyone who had to do with the military, Adam knew the man as one of the heroes of Operation Iraqi Freedom, a top-class military careerist who recently had been promoted to commander-in-chief. Cruz used to own villa Can Salammbo, the clubhouse of the TAB Brothers. Only two months ago it had been registered under a new name.

"And now, brace yourself." Dziri's voice thundered through the phone. "The new owner of Can Salammbo is no one but our good old buddy Jorg Scherer. Cruz, mind you, did not engage Scherer's services to sell his property on the market—no, he sold it directly to our man. And Scherer only had to pay the ridiculous amount of 800 thousand something euros for it."

"That's a ridiculous sum?" But Adam's heart started to beat faster.

"Considering that Cruz paid double that just two years ago."

"Damn. Then the question is why he was content with so much less."

"*Exacto, colega*. Especially as prices on Ibiza have constantly gone up, even in the recession. Who in their right mind would waive so much money?"

"Someone who doesn't want to be connected to the TAB."

"Exactly how I see it."

Adam thanked the inspector with a heartfelt "great work, Chief," and Dziri pretended not to be flattered. They agreed to get back in touch the next day. Until then, Adam said, he would try to gather information by his own means.

When Phil's Vespa pulled up, Adam was leaning against a pillar on the patio, watching her approach. She took off the helmet, and her curls tried to escape in all directions. A galaxy of freckles had taken over her nose and cheeks.

She raised her hand. "Hey, y'all."

Taken by surprise, Adam grinned, "Howdy there."

When they dated, Phil, always the language lover, had become obsessed with the Southwestern lingo and started to decorate her speech with terms like "lollygaggin'," "musta coulda" or "fixin' to." To Adam, those attempts at Texan twang sounded hilarious out of Phil's German mouth.

"Dang cool it is," she grinned back, and without warning, the words hit Adam like a blow. He took off his jacket and put it around Phil's shoulders. Only to realize the gesture made her instinctively go rigid. All she said was "thanks." She sat down on the balustrade and rolled a cigarette.

"Can I have one, too?"

"What happened to your Montecristos? Don't like them anymore?"

"You remember..." He swallowed the words. No way, he wouldn't go there

"I know, I need to get some. Sorry."

"That's not why I asked. I'll roll you as many as you want."

After a few drags, they exchanged their news. Adam repeated what Dziri had told him, and Phil summarized what Hans had said about R. W., the article about the TAB, their lawyers intimidating him, and her conviction that Hans hadn't told her the whole truth. Adam agreed. No halfway experienced journalist would publish such an explosive article without checking the facts first. R. W. must have shown him proof.

"And photos." Phil knew Hans had talked about pictures R. W. had shown him, not just promised to show.

"I think Hans is scared to death. By the way: Am I boring you?"

Adam just checked his watch for the third time since Phil had arrived.

He grinned his typical Adam grin. "Nope. That's one thing you never managed to do."

The reason he kept checking the time, he explained, was that he was expecting a call from Washington, D.C. With information about the TAB.

"You know I'm a private investigator now?"

Phil remembered he had mentioned that he quit the police force.

"Still working for the government, though, for an office called SAPR that deals with problems in the military. My job is to determine if an accusation someone raises against a member of the Forces holds up to open a case. Or if yet another commander tries to sweep a case of sexual harassment under the carpet."

"Wow. That means?"

Adam explained that he had a colleague in Texas who held excellent contacts to the information office of the Department of Defense. He asked her to inquire about U.S. citizens whose names might turn up in the context of the TAB.

Again, Adam checked his watch. Lori had promised to call back after lunch at two p.m., nine p.m. here. In seven minutes.

Phil followed him to his room. Only at the door it hit her how strange it was to be back in Adam's private world, where the faint scent of his aftershave was in the air. The same as sixteen years ago—but this could be just her imagination.

She shouldn't imagine things like that. Let the past be past.

Under the bed cover, the checkered leg of his pjs peeped out. A MacBook and a car magazine were lying on the nightstand. When Adam put his iPhone on the table, it immediately started to ring. Phil's finger dashed forward and pushed the speaker button. Adam frowned but didn't change it.

"It's Adam."

"Hey, baby." A stretched Texan *baybee*. Adam threw Phil a glance as if it was her fault.

"Hey. So what did you find out?"

"What about 'hello, dear Lori,' for starters, or 'I miss you, Lori, and thank you for calling'?"

"Thanks, Lori, for calling back."

"You're such a jerk. Only getting in touch because you want information."

Adam so obviously wished to turn the speaker off, he looked tortured. But Phil mouthed "Don't." Grudgingly, he acceded.

"Lori," he said, "stop it, will ya? So what do we know about the TAB?"

"Damn, you *are* a jerk," the far away Lori hissed. She cleared her throat and suddenly sounded like an automated voice, "Yessir, I looked into the matter. My contact man Andy McCullen identified the TAB as an innocent ticket broker in Manhattan. There is also a PR firm in South Carolina, named after its founder Theodore A. Bush. None of them exclusively for men or clubs."

"Have you tried the whole name: *Tertulia de los Amigos de Bes*?"

"Yessir."

"And?"

"No *amigos*, my friend," Lori's voice dripped with cynicism, "nowhere any amigos in sight."

Adam scratched his head. He seemed to have forgotten Phil's presence now.

"Come on, Lori, don't give me this crap. The TAB is a global affair, tons of stinking rich men. We've got to have *something* on them." He let the cat out of the bag, "For instance on Colonel Andrew Cruz."

Through the phone, they could hear Lori take a sharp breath. "What now does the commander have to do with this club?"

"Why don't you mention his name to McCullen?"

"The hell I will."

"Lori. What exactly is the problem?"

Lori was dead serious now, "Listen to me, Adam. Not half an hour after I typed 'TAB' into the inquiry form and sent it to Andy at the information office, I got a call from Major Donald Kearns. You know him, I'm sure. Sits right under the Major General and longs to be in her position. He urged me to make you understand that neither he nor anyone else in the Office has ever heard of this men's club. No information whatsoever. And that I 'must stop digging up dirt.'"

"'Digging up dirt.' Those were Kearns's words?"

"Exactly those. So stop it, Adam, will ya? Or you'll get yourself into trouble again. And deep shit this time."

"All right. Thank you, Lori. Man, you have been very helpful. See ya, okay."

"What the hell?" Lori got hectic. "Hey babe, wait a minute..."

Adam put the phone into the pocket of his jeans.

"At least it was worth a try..." Phil couldn't help grinning, "*baybee*."

He ignored her smirk. "Absolutely it was. When the Office warns me not to muckrake, it can only mean that someone has a lot of muck to hide."

CHAPTER 24

The question was how to get their hands on the muck. The next morning, Phil and Adam came back together for breakfast. Phil felt completely wrung out as she hadn't slept. Images of Doro's charred remains stood in front of her eyes as soon as she closed them. In reality, she had never seen Doro's corpse. That it had been sent to Mallorca for autopsy made her death even more unreal, more ungraspable. Phil wondered if she would have to identify the body at some point. She had no idea how a situation like this was usually handled.

Adam hadn't slept much, either. He had written down all pieces of information they had so far and tried to make sense of them. Now, he pushed their breakfast plates aside and rolled out the paper. Phil studied it thoroughly. Adam knew he wouldn't have to point out the one striking detail.

The name Tamar really did appear everywhere. There was her connection to Scherer, which meant she must have known Amanda and probably the TAB brothers as well. "Event planning/assistance", Adam had written in the margin, as this, in Tamar's own words, was the job she did for Scherer. So probably she also planned or assisted in organizing the events for the TAB. Tamar's and Amanda's paths crossed again in Can

Follet where the latter, according to Jezebel, had taken some classes. Then, Tamar's name appeared on Doro's list, and even though she wouldn't admit to knowing Doro, it was unlikely. Tamar was sitting in the center of the whole affair, like a spider in a big, ominous web. If anyone could tell them what was behind Scherer and the TAB, it was she.

How could they get her to open up? While at first glance, Tamar seemed candid and chatty, the typical Ibiza-party girl, there was something diffuse about her. Ask her a question, and she'd refuse to listen or pretend to not understand. Ultimately, she was elusive, slippery as an eel. And when pushed, as Phil had experienced, she could get aggressive. How should they gain her confidence? Make her spill the beans? In Phil's eyes, there was only one option.

"We have to be patient, yet persuasive," Adam said. "One of the main aspects of investigating is resistance. It's always there. Until it breaks."

But patience was not Phil's forte. She explained that the next step was up to him. As hot as Tamar seemed to think Adam was, he would have to coax her.

"One of the main aspects of persuasion," she tried to sound matter-of-factly, "is enticement. You have to lure her into opening up."

"Wow, best plan ever."

Phil made a modest face. "I do have my moments."

Adam swallowed what was on the tip of his tongue. In fact, he knew she was right, and he already had an idea: he pointed to a notice board on the wall where Lluis posted the field trips he organized every Saturday for his guests. Today's excursion was a hike up to Cueva D'es Cuieram, an ancient place of worship to the Phoenician goddess Tanit, followed by a visit to the archeological museum of Ibiza. The tour guide's name was Tamar Stettin.

"So, Phil," he asked casually, "why don't you come along?"

"Me? No way." Phil's curls flew up in rejection.

"Coward. I bet you'd be interested."

When she was back in her room to grab her jacket, Phil was still shocked by how little time it had taken Adam to talk her into it.

All guests of the Hostal Esperanza seemed to be taking part in the tour, even the Hubers. In the bus, Phil spontaneously sat down next to Trudy, who was curled up against a window. To Phil's "Good morning," she uttered a flat "Hi." Adam sat down next to Ezra in the opposite row.

The very last one to arrive was Tamar. She was wearing tight pink overalls, the front zipper pulled down to the last possible tooth before her breasts would fall out. Her hair was teased up to a stylish bun, her face made up as for a party. To Phil, she offered a wink. A vague smile was meant for all, but the kiss she blew was for Adam alone.

Trudy muttered, "Gosh"—exactly what Phil thought.

Lluis introduced Tamar to the people who hadn't had the pleasure yet. She slipped a headset with mouthpiece on her head, and now looked like an entertainer of a holiday club who made tourists do things they would later regret like dance the chicken dance or sing karaoke. Clapping her hands for attention, Tamar explained they would take the *camís,* the old country roads winding through the backlands. Only there they would experience the authentic Ibiza.

She was right. Leaving the herds of rental cars on the congested artery, they drove through a stunning landscape of peaceful isolation. The fields were divided by ancient dry walls, the hills were terraced orchards. The farther north they drove, the lonelier it got. Orange groves and meadows full of gnarled olive trees gave in to pine woods and huge algarroba trees. Soon they were in the green hills of *Es Amunts*. Among the few other vehicles on the road, mostly tractors, the bus looked like a spaceship. For some miles, it even had to crawl behind a donkey cart loaded with branches. When the bus finally managed to pass, the peasant steering the cart waved, a big smile all over his weather-beaten face. Out of the corner of her eye, Phil saw Trudy unconsciously return the smile.

Above the bay of San Vicente, the bus left the *camí* and climbed up a serpentine track that got narrower with every curve. From the safety of a high branch, a hoopoe with his surreal-looking headgear watched them pass by. Goldfinches kept flashing by the windows as if showing off their skills.

Finally, the bus came to a halt, and the group got out. The air was filled with the birds chirping, and the ground seemed to move with lizards that must never have had painful encounters with a human foot. Real natives, the *lagartijas*, Lluis explained, that had lived on the islands long before the first men. A pink sign pointed up the incline to Cueva D'es Cuieram.

The trail up was lined by pine trees. Only a double roped rail separated it from the precipice. Ever so often, they had to wiggle around large pieces of rock that must have fallen off the mountain in a storm. Phil noticed how nimbly Ezra Huber hiked up the steep hill, despite his body mass. Without running out of breath, he even whistled a little tune.

"Smelling sex and candy," Tamar joined in and winked at Ezra, who abruptly stopped his whistling and blushed. Trudy behind him huffed and puffed.

The trail ended on a plateau. It was framed by petrified tree trunks and a row of handmade rock formations, round stones heaped on top of each other like little totem poles. Towards the sea, the view was wide open, the precipice seemingly bottomless, pine trees way below. Above, flocks of birds elegantly circled the skies. Lluis pointed out an Eleonora falcon, an especially rare species.

On the mountainside, between massive boulders, a dark, trapezoidal form opened up: the entrance to the cave, Cueva D'es Cuieram. It was secured by a black gate with a padlock. Through the bars they could see a depiction of the well-known bust of Tanit, leaning against the rock wall.

Lluis explained that the cave, discovered in 1907, was not fully explored yet, as parts of it had collapsed. Still, hundreds of terracotta artifacts had been found here as well as a gold treasure of unknown origin. The cave used to be open to the public at certain hours but had been locked for safety after last winter's storms.

"So, friends, that's it," Lluis said. "Enjoy the view, peek into the cave, and we'll be off to the archeological museum where you get to see the artifacts..."

"Nonsense, Lluis," Tamar interrupted. She inspected the gate's hinges that were strangely twisted, as though worked on with a chisel or axe, grabbed two bars and pushed with all her strength. The hinges came loose.

"Will you give me a hand, Adam?"

"Adam!" But before Lluis could object, the crowd was around Tamar, excited to enter the cave. Only Trudy stayed back and fiercely grabbed Ezra's arm. He shook her off and stepped up to help Adam push the gate open.

Tamar gave him a smile, "That's my man."

Phil glanced at Lluis who seemed furious, yet couldn't but follow his group. They entered a low vestibule. On the right, Tanit watched them with spooky eyes. With her painted white face and flaming red hair, this plaster bust of the Goddess looked a bit cheap, like a made-in-China replica of the historical find. The group passed by the collapsed entrance to a cave room filled with crumbled rocks. The opposite wall, coated with verdigris and burn marks, opened up to the actual cult-side. A square slab of rock that must have fallen from the cave's ceiling, constituted the altar of the erstwhile sanctuary. However—erstwhile?

Leaning against a big scented candle, framed by a wreath of fresh leaves and blossoms, was another depiction of the goddess. A postcard-size photograph of the genuine bust with the words *Tanit la poderosa* underneath, it mirrored the original's charisma. A strip of daylight fell through an opening in the cave's dome, spotlighting it. The candle's perfume fought against a stench of something rotten. Around it, the altar was packed with more burned candles, incense sticks and tons of contemporary devotional objects: plastic and brass jewelry, figurines, yellowed photos of stern-looking people, a notebook bound in silver. One of the Danish tourists unabashedly opened it.

"Wow, look. All requests to the Goddess Tanit. For health, happiness, a child, for ... Lluis, what does this mean? Is that Spanish?"

Reluctantly, Lluis stepped close. "Eivissenc, our dialect. It means rain."

"The *Ibizencos* still worship Tanit?" How did this go together with Catholicism? There was a church, it seemed to Phil, in even the tiniest Ibizan village.

"Yes, Phil, they have been praying to the Goddess for thousands of years." Tamar's voice came from the cave's depth. "And never gave her up. Dear Lluis just doesn't like to admit it."

"A few backward peasants still do it," Lluis relativized, "They make the sign of the Cross and at the same time take care that the ancient spirits feel well in their house. Or pray to Tanit. Whatever they think may help."

Phil wished Doro could be here with her now. How she would enjoy hearing that people still had a connection to the ancient beliefs. What fodder for her Dea Caelestis book. Well, she surely had heard about the Tanit cult. Oh, Doro.

"People here have a saying," Lluis continued, *"Tanit o Jesus es iqual.* For them it doesn't matter which God it is as long as he answers their prayers."

"Goddess." Tamar could be heard out of the dark, "And *she.*"

"So what?" Lluis didn't try to hide his annoyance any

longer. "He *or* she. Our problem isn't the backward locals and their customs but the people who come and think they can take everything over. In the wake of tourism, so many esoteric nuts have settled on Ibiza that we can hardly master them anymore."

"Master them, Lluis?" Tamar appeared, a mischievous look on her face.

Lluis addressed the group. "Indeed, that's a huge problem. One example: some years ago, a group of squatter-hippies who claimed to worship Tanit kept the Cueva D'es Cuieram downright occupied. They just took it over to execute their rituals here that are as authentic as plastic beads. They got drunk, took drugs or whatever and freaked out. Their screaming could be heard down in San Vicente. It was only a matter of time until a self-acclaimed Tanit priestess on speed fell over the cliff and got critically injured. She's in a wheelchair now. After this, the cave was closed for a long time, not even accessible to the locals who had nothing to do with the accident."

Lluis glared at Tamar who tried to stare him down. How odd, Phil thought. These two claimed to be friends yet were constantly at each other's throats. She looked up to the cave's vaulted ceiling. From there, the slab of stone must have crashed down. Lluis was right; they shouldn't be here.

But now, some visitors had walked around the altar to the back of the cave. Excited voices called for Lluis, but Tamar stepped up.

"What in the world is this?"

On a flat stone, behind a curtain of burnt-down candles, was a cold hearth. On it lay a rabbit. Phil shuddered. Another dead rabbit! Its body was partly charred, partly left to rot. The biting sweet odor of decay emanated from it.

Tamar looked at it with undisguised awe. "A *molkmor*. An animal sacrifice to receive the Goddess's mercy. Because it's no longer permissible to sacrifice humans. Too bad, one sometimes may think... Just kidding."

"They are really serious about this, aren't they," someone said.

"We are leaving. Now," Lluis commanded.

At that very moment, a scream whipped through the cave.

Trudy had stayed at the Tanit altar, obviously fascinated. Only when Ezra whistled her to his side, she started to feel her way along the wall towards him and ended up in front of a niche full of rocks. And screamed.

On top of the piled-up rocks on a tray was another kind of altar, like a persiflage of the Tanit sanctuary. A damn vulgar persiflage. No candles but half-puffed cigars were lined up around the centerpiece, brandy bottles, a pile of shrink-wrapped—Phil stepped closer—indeed—condoms. Some erected rubber dildos, postcards of naked pin-up girls and the page of a porn magazine with an enormous female butt.

"Aargh," someone said, "where are we?"

Then there was the centerpiece, a clay statuette. A bigger version of the figure Phil by now knew all too well: Bes, the little god with his gigantic penis.

Trudy let out another shriek. "What... what... who...."

Ezra grabbed her arm. "None of your business, woman. Out now."

And like a slaughterhouse cow, Trudy allowed her husband to drag her off.

Phil took a closer look at the figure she had first seen in Scherer's office. Bes's eyes bulged as if he suffered from an overactive thyroid gland. His thick lips were distorted to a devious grin. Around his neck were countless amulets and charms, around his hips a scrap of fur, held together by a metal snake-belt. Its front gapped wide open and displayed his huge leathery penis.

Phil hadn't noticed Adam step up next to her. She almost jumped when he asked, "So this is the—god you guys talked about?"

"That's right." Lluis coughed nervously, "this is Bes, the

magi, the pygmy who eradicated the snakes, companion of Tanit, benefactor of the ladies."

"Yuck," escaped Phil's mouth.

CHAPTER 25

On their way back to the bus, Phil walked behind Lluis, who was in an intense conversation with Tamar. He tried to keep his voice down, but his fury could clearly be discerned. Phil perked up her ears.

"...out of your mind," she understood. "This is not a game, Tamar. You keep messing around like this, you'll be sorry."

Tamar laughed, "You are such a coward, Lluisino. You keep your boring low profile if you need to, but that's not me."

She playfully boxed his arm, stopped short and waited for Phil to pass her, looking at someone farther back. When Phil turned her head a minute later, Tamar was holding Adam's arm, talking as if she wanted to sell him something. Phil stepped up to Lluis and got right to the point.

"So, Lluis, what kind of war is going on between you and Tamar?"

"Well," Lluis's face was still red from anger. He searched for an appropriate answer, "No war, I assure you. Tamar isn't a bad person. She can be the greatest friend."

"I believe that. She's really sweet..."

... just not to you, Phil did not add.

"But she has been brought up in the belief that there are

no rules in the world that apply to her. That she can do whatever she wants. I mean, I'm not talking about her breaking the law, but social rules."

Lluis had decided to open up to Phil. "In a way that's typical for the offspring of the early hippies. They arrived in the 70s to lead a free life, away from the burdens of bourgeoisie. 'Anti-authoritarian' was the slogan their kids grew up with, and sometimes it only meant that the parents didn't feel like wasting time on guidance and education. Instead of teaching their children ethical and social behavior, they wanted to be rid of all tasks. But the downside of freedom is self-indulgence. And recklessness. As a kid, Tamar was left alone way too often by her mother, who told her that she was a divine feminine spirit and only needed to listen to herself to know what to do. So what Tamar learned was to overrate her abilities. And allow herself all liberties."

"What about her father?"

"No idea. She never talked about him." Lluis sighed. "As kids, Tamar and I were very close. She often came to my house when her mother was out with some guy and, once again, had forgotten to put food on the table. Now, in her eyes, I'm the narrow-minded bourgeois who worries too much. But I'm only reasonable. She really exaggerates this cult of—how shall I call it?—superior femininity."

Lluis looked as if he couldn't hurt a fly. But Phil remembered this other cult he had talked about, the goat hunt on Es Vedrà. To her, cutting a goat's throat in order to prove one's masculinity didn't sound all that reasonable either.

Then everyone was in the bus and waiting when, at last, Adam and Tamar arrived. Adam threw Phil a stressed glance but allowed Tamar to pull him into the front row. She turned her headset back on and explained that they would now drive into Ibiza City. Whoever wanted could visit the archeological museum where all the historical finds of Cueva D'es Cuieram were displayed. The others could go sightseeing, shopping or have lunch in the city. In three hours, they all had to be back at the bus.

Phil, who had admired the Phoenician terracottas and other treasures on several occasions, decided to go for a walk. She wondered what Adam was up to. He and Tamar had been the first to leave the bus. Good, she reminded herself. After all, he was on a mission.

Phil left the upper town through the Portal de Ses Taules, a vaulted passage flanked by two life-size statues of the Roman goddess Juno and her warrior that somehow in the course of history had lost their marble heads. She crossed the draw-bridge and strolled through a maze of alleys to Passeig Vara del Rey. The boulevard used to be a hell of noise and traffic jams, but when it was declared a pedestrian zone, things calmed down to a vivid city pulse. Behind it was Plaça del Parque, a tranquil square lined by old trees, restaurants, and cafés.

Courageously, Phil approached an ATM, inserted her debit card, and selected the choice of 200 euros. She knew what she did was a gamble. If no miracle had happened or some royal-ties for a republished translation had been transferred to her account, there could hardly be a cent left. Would the machine swallow this card, too? Hallelujah! The ATM granted her clem-ency and spit out ten 20-euro bills. A coffee was what she needed now.

Phil approached a café and immediately registered Tamar on its terrace. Her blonde hair shone, her eyes were hidden behind huge sunglasses, her pink overalls seemed ready to burst. Among the tourists in their shorts and sandals she looked like a movie star. A diva surrounded by fans. Opposite her sat Adam, his back to Phil, a bottle of beer in front of him. Tamar held a glass of champagne. An impulse ordered Phil to turn around. It wasn't too late to discreetly disappear.

But her feet were glued to the ground. Half hidden behind a potted palm tree, she watched Tamar's hand come to settle on Adam's leg. The silver snake bracelet around her wrist looked ready to bite. Adam's leg flinched, was crossed with the other, and Tamar's hand dropped.

In undeterred self-confidence she smiled. A necklace of blue stones glittered around her neck. An open gift box was on the table. How come Adam had gotten so close to Tamar in such a short time as to buy her a gift?

Tamar adjusted the blink on her cleavage. "You'll get used to it," Phil heard her purr in the voice of a TV sex channel promoter. "Think of Oedipus reversed, all happy-go-lucky. I bet in a while you will actually like it."

She took Adam's hand and kissed his fingertips, even nibbled at his thumb. The tourists gawked. A scooter rattling across the square swallowed her next words. So Phil was shocked when Adam bent forward, grabbed Tamar's wrist, and forcefully pushed her arm on the table. That must hurt. What was wrong with him? This way, he would certainly not gain Tamar's confidence.

Should she interfere? Of course. But when she stepped out from behind the plant, Adam jumped up. And Phil realized it wasn't him. It was someone she had never seen before, a man of comparable stature and Adam's brown-grayish hair but no other similarities. He hissed something and stomped off. Tamar only shrugged. Her eyes, full of the tolerance a mother would have for a stubborn child, followed the man. That's when she discovered Phil and beckoned her over.

But when Phil was at the table, Tamar was steaming with fury. The man had left without paying. "Who ordered?" she raged, frantically waving the check in his direction. But without turning back, he disappeared into an alley.

"Asshole." Tamar turned to Phil. "Sit down, have a drink with me. Beer?" She pushed the bottle the man had left towards her.

"No, thanks." Phil pushed the beer back.

"The nerve of this guy. Fucking whiner. Won't be the last

word on this."

"At least he brought you a nice gift." Phil pointed at the jewelry box.

"Phew. From the duty free. Nothing of value."

"Doesn't look cheap to me. And pretty."

This helped to calm Tamar down. Her fingers felt for the necklace, caressing the blue stones. She had a sip of champagne.

"Hey, where did you leave your cute Mr. Ryan?"

"I thought—no idea. He's not my Mr. Ryan."

"Even better." Now Tamar's good mood was restored. Her eyes shone with hunting fever. "Tomorrow we have a date."

"What about him?" Phil nodded in the direction the angry man had taken.

"What *about* him?" Tamar's lips twisted, "He's pissed, obviously."

"Your boyfriend?"

"*A* boyfriend. I'm not into the couple crap. I mean, exclusive relationships."

"Okay? Why not if I may ask?" Phil was genuinely interested.

Instead of answering, Tamar began to sing, "*One man has hands that are tender, one man's incredibly strong/ To which one should I surrender? My choice is bound to be wrong...*" She grinned, "Know that? Friedrich Hollaender. Became a hit by Marlene Dietrich."

"Yeah, I do..."

Tamar had an impressive stage voice. The tourists at the next table directed their smartphones at her.

"*Some say that love is for always, I say that love's always new./ The goddess sent us out in hallways, love's fun but it's never true./ I'm not about to be faithful, life's less disappointing that way...*"

Tamar made a little bow to the applauding tourists. Her smile was mischievous and so radiant Phil had to smile too.

"You should have become a music star."

"Maybe I still will. Some say I look even better than Marlene. But she got it. Love is the simplest deathtrap on Earth"

To be so self-confident, so totally herself. Phil had never met a woman with such a bold attitude.

Tamar topped it, "Plus *I* always get what I want—and who."

"Well, good luck with that." Phil couldn't think of anything else to say.

"Thanks. I'm aware that Adam is a hard nut to crack, but I'll manage. Just have to get into higher gear than usual." Tamar searched Phil's face, "Sure you're okay with it?"

Phil hastened to nod.

"Great. You know, I can be like a bee around the honey pot. Or a mosquito. I buzz around my victim. I patiently look for where he's exposed. Then I attack. Boom!" She giggled, "Always works. Did you know that only the female mosquitoes suck blood? They guarantee the survival of the species."

"Or get swatted."

Tamar laughed out loud, "Not if they know when to fly away."

"Okay." Phil had no idea what to make of this idle talk. Of Tamar. She had a recklessness about her, a headstrong attitude one could only admire. But there also was her supercilious self-glorification. Phil wondered how Adam saw her. Did he fall for her coolness or share Lluis's opinion that she overestimated herself? The truth was that while Tamar boasted, her wrists showed reddish marks where the man had grabbed her—hard.

"But you're not a mosquito," Phil therefore replied, and, before Tamar found another cool answer, "Something else. I don't know if you heard about it. My friend Dorothea..."

"Oh come on, Phil, not your Dorothea again."

"She's dead."

"What?" Tamar gasped. "But...? This can't be true."

All dams broke within Phil. She burst into tears. She hadn't thought there were any tears left, and as far as she knew she had never cried in a public place, exposed to pitiful stares. But she didn't care. She cried.

Tamar overcame her shock quickly and put her arms around Phil. "Let it out—good. Let it all out."

After a while Phil wiggled out of the embrace and sat straight up. She had a thousand questions to ask and better get started.

"Sorry." She faced Tamar. "When we met you said I could always turn to you if I had questions. Right?"

Tamar nodded. "Sure. Go ahead."

Phil could detect a sudden caution in her voice. She decided to be blunt.

"Concerning Scherer. He offers me a lot of money for my burnt-down house. He doesn't give a shit that Doro just died in it. He is—ice cold."

"I see. That's why you assume he lit the fire. As Adam thinks he has to do with Amanda's death. Quite an imagination you two got." Tamar actually sounded amused. "But here's a secret: Scherer isn't that ruthless. Or courageous. He's lacking the *übermensch* gene, if you know what I mean."

"I don't. What is this supposed to mean?"

"Scherer still clung to Amanda like a dog, even though he didn't even like her anymore. I have known him for four years now, and I tell you—he would never have been able to liberate himself."

Liberate? Interesting choice of word. "How would you know that?"

"Because I spend quite some time with the old bloke. You know I work for him, and occasionally, I let him fuck me. So I've been noticing a few things."

Tamar's face was completely neutral, no hint of embarrassment or any other detectable emotion. Before Phil found her voice, her cellphone rang.

She read the display and pushed the button. "Adam?"
Tamar bent closer to Phil, eager to listen.

"What news?" Phil turned away from her, "Why are you...
Sure, I'll be there right away." She leaped up. "Sorry, Tamar."

"I'll come along." Tamar waved for the waitress.

"You can't." Phil pushed her chair back. "I'm expected at
the police headquarters. They have news concerning Doro's
death."

Tamar's eyes followed Phil, who wiggled her way through
the crowd. A cab stopped, and off she was to see Adam. What
the hell did he do at the police station, Tamar wondered.
Doro's death drifted through her mind, but the thought didn't
last. What bothered her more was the fact that she had talked
about Scherer's and her affair. Damn, how stupid. The first
thing Phil would do now was tell Adam about it. Understandable, in a way; Tamar wouldn't skip such a chance either. But
if Adam was only half the prick his sister had been, he would
be pissed.

Tamar was still furious about the fuss Amanda had made
when she surprised her in Scherer's bed. There had been no
reasoning with her, no matter that Tamar swore it didn't
mean a thing. Amanda had yelled like a fucking shrew, then
started snubbing her, even in front of the guests. And Jorg, the
coward, had tried to stay away from her. Tamar wondered
about herself. How long she had put up with it.

Until she hadn't any more. Tamar smiled. But she still was
surprised when Amanda showed up at Can Follet. Suddenly,
the shrew pretended to have experienced enlightenment.
What a show she made, claiming she too yearned to live in the
spirit of the Great Mother. Bullshit! Tamar knew fake when
she saw it. Inside, Amanda had remained the stuck-up, conservative wife, devoted to her husband so he would fulfill her
materialistic needs.

Tamar applauded her own cleverness when she snatched

the—thing. Great fast reactions she had. How could anyone leave such an expensive piece just lying around? Theft? Phew. Amanda wouldn't need it anymore, and Scherer probably never noticed it was gone. As soon as all the dust was settled, she would sell it. How much would it bring? Twenty? Thirty thousand? It was so unfair that Tamar had to deal with duty-free-shit while someone like Amanda owned something like that. Nothing but show this woman had been.

Okay, one wasn't supposed to talk bad about the dead. Why not, actually? Did death turn people into better beings? Impatiently, Tamar pushed the silver bracelet up her arm. Sure, she did acknowledge that Amanda had tried. And failed. In the end, her death was no one's but her own damn fault.

Tamar wondered how Adam would react to her affair with his brother-in-law. Would he snub her too? So what, take it or leave it, she thought. There were enough other guys in the world.

Tamar smiled at the tourists who still couldn't take their eyes off her. She, the crown princess, played the game according to her own rules. Maybe be a bit more careful in the future, okay, but she had everything under control.

Tamar picked up the check, furious again. What did this whiner think? That he could show up with a cheap necklace, whistle and she'd jump? Well, he obviously hadn't understood a thing either. While Scherer, despite his deficiencies, played in a different league.

CHAPTER 26

When Phil jumped out of the cab, Adam was waiting at the entrance of the police station. He took her arm and led her to Dziri's office.

Phil's stomach fluttered. "What is it? What happened?"

Inspector Dziri's shirt collar was unbuttoned, his hair-do consisted of oily streaks, his mustache hung down like exhausted. He was terribly excited.

"Please do excuse me," he trumpeted, "I just got back from 'Espalmador. The plane crash. We know now that it was the pilot's own doing. But why—no idea. Drives me crazy." He gesticulated. "Please sit down, *señora* Mann. Back at my desk, I found the report. Thought I should let you know immediately."

Phil collapsed in the visitor's chair, while Dziri bent over and petted her hand—clap, clap, clap. Phil pulled her hand back and crossed her arms.

"What is it, Inspector? Please don't beat around the bush."

"Never. Dr. Santos from CSI says he had a suspicion right away. I mean, when he first saw the corpse, as charred as it was. The pelvic bones, you know."

Inspector Dziri, incredibly but true, grinned at Phil. That

was torture.

"We sent them, I mean we sent everything, to forensics in Palma, and what you see here is the result. The analysis. Can you imagine!" A theatrical pause.

Phil heard her heart beat wildly. "What?"

"Our victim cannot be your friend. Because the corpse is male. A man."

"What?" Her mouth fell open. Could this be? Had she heard right?

"Analysis via gender marker?" Adam asked as incomprehensibly, "STRs?"

"Correct," Dziri nodded. "What we have is an elder male person, defective dental status, fragile bone substance, osteoporosis due to decade-long alcohol abuse, the doc assumes."

Phil only had to know one thing, "You are sure it's not Doro?"

"One hundred percent sure. Awesome how forensics work these days. There are only a few bones left of a human being, a square inch of fiber and skin. They take it to the lab and soon enough can confirm it was a man. They also made a comparative analysis. And guess what: They even found the matching DNA profile. The deceased is Otto Niemer, born 1945 in Simmern, Germany."

"Ninguno." Phil and Adam said simultaneously.

The inspector nodded. "Amanda's buddy Ninguno. When we had to deal with the rape of his daughter and the Dutch girl, he among others voluntarily submitted a saliva sample. Other than the gentlemen of the TAB." Dziri looked at Phil, "Seems like Mr. Niemer had been living in your house."

Something hot swept through Phil and left her shaking. She was dizzy, nauseated. Tears of relief ran down her cheeks. For a moment she knew that her massive relief contained some heartlessness against the old man who had died a horrible death. But the feeling couldn't outweigh the miracle: Doro lived.

Now it was Phil who put her hand on Dziri's arm and patted it, pressed it, clutched it. She wanted to hug him but was too weak to get up. How thankful she was that he had informed her right away. Again, tears ran. They had to think she was a crybaby. So? Phil didn't care.

"Oh man," she said, wiping the tears. "Oh heavens. Hallelujah. Incredible. That's crazy. Wonderful."

Adam coughed his emotions away. Something shiny was in Dziri's eyes.

"The question is why Ninguno was in your house," he said, striving for factuality. "Would you, *señora* Mann, have an idea?"

Phil tried to focus. She could only imagine that Doro had met Ninguno in an unfortunate situation and tried to help by offering him a place to stay. Because that's how Doro was: she always had a heart for the less lucky in life.

But, to be honest, the scenario here wasn't realistic as they were talking about a man. Doro, as far as Phil knew, had never gone out with a man or had a male friend. After twenty-five years, Phil had no idea if she was gay or just not interested in a partner. Maybe she knew Ninguno from earlier times? Quite unlikely too, as he was from a small town in West Germany while Doro had grown up in the East, behind the Wall. Most likely, she had met Ninguno through Amanda. Which still didn't explain why he had been in Can Philanton and not she.

"I just don't know," Phil said.

Dziri's eyes took their time to scan her face. "Sometimes one doesn't have a clue what one's own friends are up to, right? Pretty sad."

But at the moment, 'sad' was not available in Phil's range of emotions. "There'll be an explanation. As soon as we can get a hold of Doro."

Which triggered the next question: Where *was* she? Well, eventually she would resurface, Phil thought. She didn't worry anymore; Doro was alive.

"I'm feeling downright sick," she said, surprised by the sensation.

"Oh no. We gotta do something about that."

Whereas Inspector Dziri started to rummage through his desk drawer, and presented a bottle of 'Carlos Primero.' He also found three glasses, poured the brandy and reached one to Phil with the words, "Cheers. To life."

The other glass went to Adam, "Mr. Colleague."

"Call me Adam, will ya?"

"Love to," Dziri slapped a hand against his chest, "Bartolo."

"Philine. Phil."

Three brandy glass clicked against each other.

"Es para mi un placer," the policeman said. A pleasure.

After two more rounds of Carlos Primero, Phil and Adam had to hurry to get to Plaça des Seus where the bus was already waiting. Phil was tipsy, sailing on a happy cloud. Soon they were back at the west coast, the spectacular rock appeared, the monster hotels. To Phil's eyes, not even they looked as ugly as before. She was eager to let Tamar know the news but didn't see her anywhere.

Phil went up to her room to refresh and change into her favorite dress. It was of a bright emerald green, like a symbol for life and hope. When she texted Anton her daily message, she couldn't help spinning some happy and cheerful phrases that probably didn't make much sense. "What's up with you, Mama?" was her son's immediate mocking answer. "Drunk? Stoned? New guy? Hope he's rich so we can keep Can Philanton." Anton was such a teaser. Grinning, Phil fired some emojis back at him. Then she saw a new voicemail on her phone; from her bank, on a Saturday. A somber voice asked her to call back. But how could she bear to have her happiness destroyed right now? Monday she would deal with it.

Phil returned to the patio, but felt too restless to sit down. She had to move, get rid of the leftover stress, not allow the money fears to seize her.

"I'll go for a walk," she said.

"Okay." Adam dumped a piece of bread into aioli creme.

But when Phil was at the stairs, he was behind her. She smiled. All negative thoughts were chased off again; only one fact remained: Doro was alive. Floating on a cloud of pure endorphins, Phil couldn't but smile.

"How would you feel about dinner?" Adam asked, "My treat."

"Oh..." but Phil's stomach growled. Her lunch had consisted of three glasses of brandy. So she nodded, smiling.

In Adam's car, they headed for the beach restaurant Ca na Vergera in Cala d'Hort. Again, they only found a parking space up the bay in the track that led to Can Follet. Taxi cabs lined up at the resort's entrance. New guests were spilling out, women who looked as if they just came from a haute-couture show in Paris. There were fur-lined capes, Chanel-suits, designer-monogrammed luggage. The Can Follet-staff in their Marvel comics- and fantasy goddess-outfits welcomed their guests with the triangular gesture and smiles.

Amused, Phil and Adam watched a chubby blonde lady of middle age struggle out of a taxi. Panting hard, she dropped what she held, a purse, a fur coat, and a Louis-Vuitton bag, into the dust. In pure euphoria, she spread her arms to the sky, shaking both fists like a boxer who had just won his match.

"Wait. Who's that?" Adam asked. "Looks somehow familiar to me."

But Phil had no idea. They walked back to the road and down to the restaurant on the bay, and their lucky star kept shining, as they found a table on the terrace. Phil ordered her favorite shrimp dish, *gambas al ajillo*, and Adam decided for a *lenguado*, sole with vegetables and potatoes in a sea salt crust. The waiter brought a carafe of white house wine and a bottle of sparkling water. When Adam lifted the carafe invitingly,

Phil asked him to pour her a *weinschorle*. She once had taught him the right proportional mix, forty percent water, sixty percent wine, and he seemed to remember, or it was pure luck again.

Phil thought she could sit here forever with Adam and be happy. Every time their eyes met, there were only smiles; she must look like the Cheshire cat. She glanced at Adam's familiar strong hand, holding his glass, his curly hairs growing down to his wrist. "Your hairy beast," he had called himself self-ironically sixteen years ago. But when he held Phil, his paws had proven to be the sensitive hands of a piano player, making every tune in her resound.

Crazy to think of this when they had so much else to deal with. Phil pulled herself together and described her encounter with Tamar. Searching for a considerate way to let Adam know Tamar's affair with his brother-in-law, she stumbled across her words, and ended up simply repeating what she'd been told: Scherer was Tamar's lover. Didn't this allow for a classical motif for murder? "Husband kills wife to be free for mistress?"

Adam kept a straight face. "Scherer had affairs, not only one; he admitted to it. But I've been thinking about Tamar myself."

"She told me she can get whatever she wants. And whoever," Phil grinned, "Looking forward to your date with the *überfrau?*"

Adam didn't understand.

"Tomorrow. That's when you see her, right?"

A nonchalant shrug. "Scherer has money and power. So, a lot to offer Tamar since Amanda is no longer in her way. Maybe he had been waiting for someone to help him break free from his wife."

"So you do think Tamar killed Amanda?" A bit hard to swallow, but, admitted, a possibility. Phil frowned. "Wait a minute. Was she even on the island when Amanda died? I mean:

I met her on the ferry from Barcelona."

"Bartolo checked. She left Ibiza for Frankfurt the morning after Amanda's death. Quite a coincidence, right?"

Plus there was the method of death: poisoning, a typical female killing method. Adam pointed out that this was more a murder mystery-idea than a statistic truth, but still: Tamar had grown up on Ibiza, so she must have been here before this pharmacy that sold the poisonous silver polish closed down. Tamar was greedy for money and completely amoral. She was convinced that no laws applied to her and boasted that not even Scherer was ruthless enough for her. Everywhere one looked, Tamar appeared.

"This would explain Scherer's honest grief," Adam said, "Tamar did what he didn't dare to do, and now he's trapped. Tamar holds sway over him."

"And Ninguno was somehow in her way. Be careful when you see her tomorrow. I mean it, okay?"

Again, Adam only shrugged. Meanwhile, the sun had sunken into the sea. The waiter cleared their table and put a burning wind light on it. People got up and watched, arm in arm, the spectacle of the moon rising behind the magical rock. A single boat steered towards the bay, still too far away to have its engine disrupt the dreamlike atmosphere. Music came out of loudspeakers, a reggae song Phil had known forever: Bob Marley & The Wailers 'No Woman No Cry.' Pure heartbeat-music. Some couples started to dance.

Adam's hand touched Phil's. A tiny caress. She felt his pianist's fingers.

"Let's be done with that tonight. Want to?"

He pulled Phil up, pulled her close and started to sway in the rhythm of the reggae. A movement that started in his hips while his legs remained almost static. He leaned a little bit back so Phil's cheek found a place on his chest.

'I remember when we used to sit,' Bob Marley sang, and Phil remembered everything too. Her body found the rhythm to which Adam moved, her cheek rubbed softly against his shirt, and she thought she heard a little crackle underneath it, like an electric spark. Adam's arms held her in a paradox of feather-light and hard muscle. Incredible, how one could immediately feel at home in the arms of someone, while in a hundred others one first had to overcome obstacles. Through his shirt and skin, Phil could hear Adam's heartbeat. His right hand moved between her shoulder blades above the low-cut back of her dress, his fingers on her skin, his left hand on her hip. Phil could feel its warmth radiating through the fabric. She didn't remember when she had last been so acutely aware of these parts of her body. Her whole body, actually.

'*You can't forget your past, so dry your tears, I say*,' Bob Marley sang. Electricity seemed to pour out of Adam's fingers, pulling Phil even closer until the two of them were one, not a hint of air between them, skin to skin.

Phil lifted her head, and they were two again, but only so she could pull his chin down a bit. Then his lips were on hers. A kiss like a time machine back into the familiar, their intimate past, at the same time utterly new, on this terrace, to Bob Marley's 'Say say say.' A journey at the speed of light into the Big Unknown.

Until the noise of an engine blended with the music and they were back in the here and now. The heartbeat music ended and was replaced by a silly disco hit. They let go of each other and returned to their table. The question was how to act, what to say now.

Phil's eyes fell on the motorboat that had entered the bay and, by virtue of a last wave, slid onto the sand. The woman in it pulled up the outboard engine as if it was a toy and secured it. A tall woman, her long limbs under her dress revealed in the backlight of the moon. She jumped on shore and pulled the boat farther up the beach. She stretched, both arms straight up, locked fingers, palms turned up. A yoga pose. A posture Phil would have recognized among thousands.

CHAPTER 27

Phil had no idea how long she had been clinging to Doro, frantically leaning against her muscular frame to feel with every part of her own body that this really was her. Doro petted Phil's back, trying to calm her down, "It's okay, hey, it's okay." Gently, she wiggled out of the embrace and held Phil at arm's length.

"Phil, what's wrong? What are you doing here?"

"Me? Where were *you*, Doro? I thought you were dead."

"What? Why should I be dead? Calm down, Phil, what the hell?"

Doro sat down in the sand and, grabbing Phil's arm, pulled her down, too. Phil tried to catch her breath.

"Since when are you on the island?" Doro asked, "Why didn't you let me know the date? Man, here I go away for a few days and you show up."

"But I did let you know. I think. This is crazy."

Phil fell back into the sand, dizzy from confusion and happiness. She tried to explain. That she hadn't met Doro in Can Philanton. That the next thing she knew was the *finca* burnt down, that she thought Doro had died in the flames.

"Burnt down?" Suddenly, Doro's face looked haggard, like

a much older woman's face. Petrified in shock.

"So where the hell were you?" Phil insisted

"The *finca*? Where I was?" Doro was confused. "That's a sad story too. A friend of mine died. Suicide. I feel terrible because I should have seen the signs of her depression. I could have saved her but didn't. I needed to get away from it all." She nodded towards Es Vedrà, glittering in the moonlight. "So I went to meditate, say goodbye to my friend in thoughts."

"You're talking about Amanda?"

Doro nodded. "You knew her?"

Now Phil had to mention Adam. That he was Amanda's brother.

This confused Doro even more. "*The* Adam?"

"Yes. He's staying in the same hotel as I am. Imagine how shocked I was to run into him. We—he believes his sister was murdered and suspects Amanda's husband. And his mistress."

Something kept Phil from saying Tamar's name.

"How crazy is this? The cowboy! Amanda's brother." Doro rubbed her eyes. "Honestly: I also think Scherer is guilty. Guilty for making her kill herself."

"So you believe she committed suicide?"

"Unfortunately, yes. That's why we can't hold the sonofabitch legally accountable. I tried to do that for a while, started some investigation on him..."

"I get it, the file... But why was it torn out of the folder?"

"What?" For a moment, Doro looked alarmed. "Yes, the file. Only we couldn't find anything, a complete waste of time. But Scherer is a criminal, if you ask me. He's at least morally guilty for Amanda's miserable life. For him, she was only a burden, an old, undesirable woman. She had lost all self-respect."

"But—criminal. What of?" Phil's thoughts raced in all directions.

"As I said, we couldn't find anything graspable. I wish Amanda had just left the jerk and sued the shit out of him."

Doro sighed. "But let's be happy now. I am happy you are here."

She hugged Phil, quickly let go again and stepped back. Doro with her distance-closeness issue, the reluctant hugger and cheek kisser. Exactly how Phil knew her. At the same time, she seemed a different woman.

First her outer appearance: for twenty-five years, Doro had been in a no-nonsense jeans-and-sweater uniform. Now she was wearing a long, fluttering dress like a *girl*. Jewelry had neither been Doro's style, but here she was, decorated with a bunch of dangling necklaces and bracelets and a clip that looked like a crescent moon in her hair. Had Doro turned into a hippie chick like these women of Can Follet? Did she have something to do with them after all?

Obviously, she did, as she pointed towards the illuminated patio. Female figures moved around, music floated down to them. 'Doll Parts' by Hole began to play: *I fake it so real I am beyond fake*, Courtney Love sang.

"Come to my place, let's celebrate," Doro said.

"Your place? Wait—that's where you live now?"

"Most of the time." Doro explained that some months ago she had joined the women of Can Follet. They all had left their old identities behind to be the woman they always wanted to be. For the first time in her life, Doro said, she experienced happiness in being female.

Phil stared at her open-mouthed, but Doro kept on, "A woman I am close to, Jezebel, created this circle called the Daughters of Tanit. I stumbled upon them when I did research for my book. What the Daughters want is to create a better life for women around the globe, extinguish violence, sexism, and all the taboos women have to suffer. The most necessary task in the world, don't you agree?"

"Sure. Of course."

"And now I'm one of them, a Daughter of Tanit. Here I am, useful. My life makes much more sense than before, even though I do about the same: I teach classes on female history, our matriarchal past, our future options. But here, no asshole of a dean cuts down my resources because he thinks my work is bullshit."

Doro chuckled at the bewilderment in Phil's face. "It's not like I turned into a Martian. Hello, Earth. Phil, It's me."

"Yeah. But I asked for you up there." Phil pointed at the patio. "I asked Tamar and Jezebel, but both claim to not know you. Why would they lie to me?"

Doro uttered an uncharacteristic girlish giggle. "They didn't lie. The secret is that they don't know me by my old name. For them, I am Anat."

"What? Why would you change your name?"

"Because the new name is the expression of my new life. Nothing less, nothing more. Most Tanit Daughters got rid of their old identity. And name."

Doro got up, wiped sand off her dress, and offered her hand, "Come on."

Phil was stunned. Could it really be that easy? You move somewhere, get rid of your name and start a new life. Your old friends can't find you anymore, but you are happy. Why had Doro never mentioned these big changes in her life? Not that she flew back to Germany twice, not even that she didn't live in Phil's *finca* anymore. And now, only because they had accidentally run into each other, Doro presented her with a *fait accompli*.

A pang of frustration hit Phil, a feeling of being left out. But she pulled herself together: the important thing was that Doro was alive. She grabbed her hand to be pulled up and explained that Adam was waiting for her in the restaurant. She at least had to let him know where she was going. Doro raised her eyebrows as if she didn't approve, but she didn't say a word.

When Phil came back, Doro had unloaded the boat: a backpack with a rolled-up sleeping mat, an ice chest.

"Of course, I understand," Adam had said. He had paid for dinner and was ready to go. For a moment, Phil had held him back at his sleeve. He gave her a tiny peck on the cheek, muttered "Bye," and gently withdrew from her.

Phil grabbed the ice chest. "So what will happen to your book now?"

"It's almost done and will be published by Can Follet publishing."

"What about your academic career? You just turn your back on it all?"

"Water under the bridge. Honestly, I won't even bother to submit my resignation. They deserve it, those idiots."

There was such fierce determination in her voice. Phil had not been aware how much Doro must hate her peers. Again, an almost painful irritation seized her. What was *she* now to her old friend? Also someone from the past she would delete from her life? But Doro smiled at her with such genuine affection.

And she had said she was happy to see Phil again. She wanted to celebrate with her. She had hugged her. True. Still, there were so many things she had not said. Where was the closeness of their long years together?

Doro didn't seem to realize Phil's feelings. Or she didn't care.

"I want you to do me a favor, Phil." she said instead. "Please also call me Anat. That's the name I identify with."

"I can try. But after so many years of Doro... Well, I'll try."

Doro tapped Phil's shoulder. "Great. But don't stress; I imagine it may take a while." How sweet she sounded. "Now come on, let's join the others. After dinner, you must tell me the whole story, in every detail. Oh, and this fire. How it could happen and all."

Phil came to an abrupt halt. Somehow the *finca* had been lost in the whirlwind of news. Until now, Doro had not asked about it; she'd probably been too confused as well. Phil hadn't even mentioned Ninguno's death.

"Wait, Doro. Anat. Yes, Can Philanton is gone. And something even more terrible happened."

Doro was so shocked, she couldn't face the partying women of Can Follet right away. Without a word, she walked by them and only motioned Jezebel to come along. The wheelchair followed them into the studio with the two big TV-screens, which were shut off now.

Doro wanted to know everything about Ninguno's death. She had met him a few times at Amanda's, she said, and now, both of them were dead. She couldn't believe it. It was also news to her that Ninguno had been living in Phil's *finca*. He probably took the chance after learning that she had moved to Can Follet, as he didn't have anywhere else to go. He must have been desperate. Doro's distress was obvious. She was so sorry.

"You're not to blame," said Jezebel, but she was also shocked, having known Ninguno for ages. "Since I came to Ibiza and still could walk. And dance. Otto was the best dancer then; no one called him Ninguno. That came later when he drifted off into drugs and booze and started barking at the wrong trees."

"What does this mean?" Phil asked but didn't get an answer.

"Had I taken care of him," Doro mumbled, "this wouldn't have happened. It is my fault. Also that your house burned down."

"Why?" Phil grabbed her arm. "Do... Anat, what is going on? A firebomb was thrown through the window. Weren't you supposed to be there instead of Ninguno? Could they have meant you?"

"Bullshit." A sudden pistol shot of an answer came from Jezebel.

Doro gasped. "You mean someone tried to kill me?" She

shook off Phil's hand, tried to calm down. "Everybody knows I'm staying at Can Follet, even people that may not like me. I appreciate your concern, but Ninguno—he had problems. Alcohol, drugs, money he owed. When I said my fault I meant that I should have tried to help him out of the swamp. But I was too busy. I'm so sorry."

"Oh, don't be," Phil started, but Jezebel took over. "Don't go there, Anat. You couldn't have helped him. Who has to die dies, that's Mother Nature's law." She sounded strangely harsh. "You are not responsible for the whole world."

"Am I not?"

Phil registered a strange exchange of looks between Doro and Jezebel. There was so much here she didn't understand. Maybe the two didn't want to speak ill of a dead man. Or what else was behind this?

"I'm also sorry you had to worry so much about me, Phil. Only now I understand what you went through."

Doro bent down and hugged Phil again, as if she wanted to prove she was able to get close to another person after all. The new Doro, or rather Anat. Tentatively, Jezebel reminded her that their guests were waiting.

"You are right. We better not ruin their homecoming." Anat opened the door to let the wheelchair with Jezebel pass. "Let's show our love."

Still puzzled, Phil followed them.

On the patio, another song by Hole played, 'Nobody's Daughter.' The women got up and welcomed Anat with a standing ovation. A superstar they finally laid eyes on. Anat tapped a shoulder here, returned a hug there, pressed her hands together in the triangular gesture. She even joined in the song's last line. *Don't tell me I've lost when I clearly have won.*

Phil would never have guessed Doro liked alternative rock. In twenty-five years, she had never heard her sing. Not even when drunk!

Music and applause died down. "My sisters, my fabulous sisters," Anat spoke, "We are honored to have you here." She radiated warmth and, at the same time, the dignity of a queen. "Thanks for coming, and love to you all."

"Welcome to happiness," Jezebel said and was applauded a bit too.

The huge patio sat on top of the cliff facing the Balearic Sea like the deck of a cruise ship. Its set-up consisted of two long tables and a shorter one arranged in form of a sharp triangle. On embroidered table-runners sat crystal glasses and pottery in all shades of pink and red, oval plates with voluptuously curled edges. The arrangement reminded Phil of Judy Chicago's *Dinner Party*, the first epic feminist piece of art, a similar triangular table setting dedicated to women who had paved the way for gender equality.

In contrast to Chicago's work, however, the women at this table did not represent only Western civilization. There were Indians in silken saris, Africans with artfully bound turbans, veiled Scheherazades, a Slavic woman with a thick blonde braid, a Mexican with a pink sombrero. Among the Westerners was the chubby lady Adam and Phil had watched arrive, in expensive couture. Others had adapted to the style of the staff, like three teenaged Wonder Women at the blue-haired, star-tattooed Stella's side. In spite of their power outfits, they seemed anxious, and Stella stared at Phil with an obvious frown, before she seemed to force herself to a tormented smile. "Good evening, dear."

Some women looked familiar to Phil. One overly treated face resembled the TV journalist who had interviewed every important politician of this world and ended up co-hosting a daytime talk show. The dark-haired woman next to her looked like the ex-intern of the White House whose affair with a president had ruined her reputation. An elderly redhead, Phil knew for sure: this was Hannah Lukas, a formerly constant presence in German TV.

Anat sat down at the peak of the triangle, and Jezebel rolled her wheelchair to the opposite side. When all the women sat down, the only empty chair was next to Jezebel. With a majestic gesture, Anat motioned Phil to take it.

"But Tamar..." Jezebel protested.

"Who is late will be punished by life. You know this saying, dear? If Tamar honors us with her presence after all, we will add a chair."

"Of course." Jezebel turned to Phil, who was a bit reluctant to take the seat, "Come on, don't be shy. I bet Tamar won't show up anyway."

"I saw her today, in the city."

"I can only guess why she's not here: a ma-a-an."

Jezebel stretched the syllable but smiled to indicate that she didn't mind. Maybe, Phil thought, Tamar had reconciled with her angry friend.

A group of girls appeared, Amaryl among them, and poured champagne into the glasses. Phil toasted with Jezebel and the woman to her left who introduced herself as Bridget from Edinburgh, Scotland, with a loud voice used to giving commands. The girl opposite Phil was only having fruit juice and looked extremely tired. She whispered she was Manasa, from India.

Jezebel knocked a spoon against her glass and welcomed all dear guests, the "disciples of love" in the house of Anat, the Goddess's representative on earth.

Modestly, Doro bowed her head. The women applauded enthusiastically.

What the fuck? was the only thing Phil could think.

Thanks to the genius of Anat, Jezebel went on, they today had profound knowledge of the beginning of their culture, real humanity, in other words: the Matriarchal past. Also thanks to Anat and other inspired prophets, Matriarchy continued to grow back in importance and unite disciples all over the world.

"We know how much more there is to do," Jezebel shouted, "how much we still have to fight. Yet, we've come a long way, and we are not going to cease until love reigns again. Until the world united under the wings of true religion."

Phil threw a glance at Doro and smirked, almost anxiously awaiting her reaction. In her former life, Doro would have been the first to make fun of Jezebel's words. She had researched religion and classified its multiple expressions through history but always kept an intellectual distance, a typical *opium of the people* attitude. The Doro Phil had known was a declared atheist. And now she was supposed to represent an old goddess?

Anat did not respond to Phil's smirk. She sat upright, a benevolent smile plastered on her face, and commented on Jezebel's adulation with the triangular gesture. Jezebel continued with praise of the "priestesses of the Third Circle, the guardians of love and Tanit's sanctuary on Es Vedrà," then thanked all guests for uniting in the spirit of the Great Mother, willing to do their bit for the good of womankind, thus, all humanity. Then she got personal.

"Thanks to Iyolade, the tempest who cuts through the waves," Jezebel greeted the probable ex-intern, "welcome home, dear."

The dark-haired woman blew her a kiss, and Jezebel addressed Hannah Lukas. "Another heartfelt thank you to our Proserpina, the mistress of Acheron."

Doro, no Anat, sent a special smile to the elderly redhead and thanked her in German, *"Wir danken dir sehr, meine Liebe."*

Hannah Lukas, or Proserpina, uttered a heavy sigh. *"Es war so schwer."*

"I know, believe me. But you did the right thing."

"And welcome to our surprise guest next to me," Jezebel went on, "Philine. A name connected to the magical question: *And if I love you what is that to thee?* From Goethe's Wilhelm

Meister, who described his goal as 'making myself into what I am.' Can we not all relate to this wish?"

Applause and cheers. Phil wondered if her mother had thought about this connotation when she chose the name Philine for her illegitimately born daughter. Hard to imagine she would have nourished such subversive humor.

Phil, who had already had dinner—with Adam, she thought, and her heart skipped a beat—stuck to *cava* when the entree was served, roasted vegetables and *conejo a la plancha,* grilled rabbit parts. It made her think of the beheaded rabbit on her gatepost and the sacrifice in Cueva D'es Cuieram. She took a big sip of champagne to chase away the notions.

CHAPTER 28

When Phil woke up, she had no idea where she was. It was pitch dark. A strong wind was howling, waves were beating against the shore. She was lying completely dressed on a bed with a pink duvet.

Now she remembered: she was in Tamar's room. Around two o'clock in the morning, it had seemed unlikely that Tamar would still come home, so Doro, no, Anat insisted that Phil spend the night in Can Follet. Grateful, as she dreaded the hike in the dark, Phil had accepted. If Tamar came home after all, Anat said, she wouldn't die sleeping on the couch for one night.

Phil sat up. She was just as hungover as one could expect after a whole day and night of wine, brandy, *weinschorle*, and champagne.

She looked around. Behind the bed were plastered shelves embedded in the wall, cluttered with books, pictures, and all kinds of knickknacks. Under the window was a couch with a folded blanket. A clothes rack was overflowing with Tamar's flamboyant fashion apparel. High-heels lined up on the floor.

In slow motion, Phil sat one foot after the other on the floor. It seemed to sway for a moment and calmed down. She rubbed her head, thinking back.

The party with the Daughters of Tanit had been an extraordinary experience—amicable, even enthusiastic, shiny happy women holding hands. Phil enjoyed being included and met with genuine interest. Most of the women she talked to loved to share their life stories.

These stories, however, with no exception, were the opposite of the party's atmosphere. They all were dark, disappointing, dangerous. Even cruel.

There was, for instance, the loudmouthed Bridget who used to be Lord Provost of Glasgow. She had given her life for her work, her city, until, after a meaningless one-night-stand, she found herself exposed on social media and was forced to quit office. There was Hannah Lukas, the TV-host who had been replaced by a younger version of herself, while her male co-host of older age remained on screen. The 70-year-old nun who had spoken out against child abuse in her church and got death threats for it. The Mexican lady who lost three daughters to a killer gang in Ciudad Juarez, their mutilated bodies found in the desert and never investigated. Then Stella, the black American with the worried eyes who had been the victim of human trafficking through all her teenage years. When the illegal brothel she was trapped in got busted by police, Stella had to watch her own sister being raped and shot by a white cop.

As heartbreaking was the fate of Manasa, the shy Indian girl. When she, tired from the thirty-four-hour flight from Calcutta, retreated early, Anat told her story.

Manasa was from a West Bengali tribe and had fallen in love with a Muslim man. They wanted to get married, which according to Indian Federal law was perfectly legal, but not for the guardians of tribal traditions. Manasa was brought before an—illegal—tribunal and sentenced to a financial penalty. When her family couldn't raise the money, the so-called judge decided on gang rape as compensatory punishment, executed by himself and other males of her village. Men Manasa had known her whole life as neighbors, fathers of friends, uncles. After that, her family shunned her, and as she was considered impure now, her fiancé moved on as well. Only thanks to Usha, a rich widow from New Delhi and Tanit Daughter, Manasa made it to Ibiza where she had a chance to heal.

Given the backgrounds, the terrible life stories, Phil was impressed by the cheerfulness of the women. They seemed to be dancing on a volcano, but not afraid in their solidarity. And Doro was the one who held them together.

Phil had to accept that her friend had met her destiny. Openhearted like never before, Doro talked about her lifelong yearning for truth. For a while, historical science, this "unbiased and critical" discipline, seemed to offer her a home, but eventually its walls came crashing down. Doro was exasperated at the one-sided narratives, the voluntary blind eyes her faculty turned towards by-gone realities. The science of history, she realized, was nothing but an interpretation of the world by the ones who held the power.

When she met Jezebel, she knew she had found her calling. Her life task. Doro became Anat. And teaching history, female history, finally made sense.

"But..."

"I know what you're thinking." Anat bent close to Phil, confidentially. "All the ado about religion. The Goddess! I know."

Yes, she used to be an atheist. Or rather agnostic. But, Anat said, she always had felt there was something missing. She just couldn't explain social evolution by scientific proof alone. It was her eureka moment when she understood that the missing link, the key component of human thriving, was spirituality. The superstructure of it all, she called it, of highest importance for everyone.

"I understood that we wouldn't save a single one of these wounded souls by scientific ratio alone. What we needed were the most gigantic, most indestructible emotions humans are capable of, faith and love. No one represents these values better than a mother figure: Tanit."

"But a religion..." Phil still couldn't believe that Doro, the former Ms. Ratio, acted as the daughter of a three thousand years old goddess.

"That's right," Anat nodded, "however, none of the existing ones were usable. All male-centric religions had only led to terror over the question whose definition of God is better. What we needed was to go back to the beginnings, to birth. To the one and only honest concept: the Great Mother. Reawakening Matriarchy deletes all the nonsense of the last millennia. It can be considered psychotherapy as well as a political movement. What counts is a real change of the status quo. In the name of Tanit, we are a thousand times more efficient than every pope, imam, or Freud."

"Efficient how? What changed?"

Anat looked proud. "A lot has changed already—radical change has begun. We carry the banner. The #MeToo movement for instance. Guess who started pointing out the Weinsteins of this world? Encouraging sisters to speak out. The women's marches, Time's Up."

"This was... your initiative?"

"Let's say, I was among the sisters. Can Follet is only one hub of a very supportive community. We are skilled networkers. Our ideas are spreading across the globe. We even got someone to introduce the First Lady to the concept... Oh, hello! If you'll excuse me, Phil. How nice to see you, dear."

Anat had turned to a guest who could hardly wait to express her admiration.

Barefooted, Phil went out into the dark hallway. She was so thirsty. There was a bathroom, but the water was too salty; she had to spit it out again. Her throat burning, she went back to Tamar's room and put on her boots, when a framed photo-

graph on the shelves caught her eye: Tamar and Jezebel standing arm in arm, which proved the picture must have been
taken before Jezebel's accident. Two beautiful blonde women
smiling into the camera, flowers in their hair. The photo was
probably taken at a women's march, as Jezebel held up a sign
with the words *Don't play stupid/ Don't play dumb/ Vaginas
where we all come from.*

When Phil put the photo back, she discovered something
else: from a nail on the shelf's back dangled a chain with an
angular remote key and a meanwhile familiar gem in the form
of a brass pendant: the Bes figurine. Two letters were stamped
on the key's face: C S, like Can Salammbo, the clubhouse of
the TAB. Spontaneously, Phil put the keychain in her pocket
and snooped around a bit more, just to make sure there wasn't
anything else relevant. She opened one drawer after the other.
Underwear, shawls, fashion jewelry—and one piece that
looked more expensive than anything else in the room: a time-
less, square ladies wristwatch in pink gold, adorned with dia-
monds. Maybe a Chinese reproduction, but its face bore the
words Cartier and *Swiss made*. Amanda popped into Phil's
mind. Sixteen years ago, when she shook Phil's hand, she had
worn such a watch. Of course, Phil couldn't be sure it was the
same, but still: this watch didn't look like anything Tamar
would wear. But Amanda. Like something Tamar might have
stolen from Amanda. Maybe Adam would recognize it. Phil
took a picture and put the watch back into the drawer. Was
Tamar a thief?

Just a thief or had she robbed the woman she had killed?

Dawn was only heartbeats away when Phil climbed up the
stairs to the coastal trail. The sky spread across the Balearic
sea like a dark comforter about to be pushed aside by energetic
gusts of wind. The sandy bays below the cliffs, besieged by
beach-goers during the day, were still deserted.

Phil concentrated on her steps, her nerves vibrating with

high anxiety. At a sharp curve she noticed how much the cliffs had been nibbled at by the elements, sitting in the air like crumbling balconies. A bit more erosion and they would break off. In the depth of the bay, the tide had carried off most of the sand and left only some pointed skewers of rock.

Phil stuck to the land side when suddenly she heard hurried steps coming towards her. Panting. Before she knew it, Ezra Huber appeared in running gear. Puffing like an asthmatic in spite of his top condition.

"Hey, careful."

But Huber just sprinted by, even jostled Phil with his elbow to the right, the dangerous side of the trail. Phil sent a curse after him, relieved when the trail widened into a rocky field, punctuated by shrub tough enough to survive up here. Out of a round of leaves, a slim, blossomed stalk grew into the sky, an agave's spectacular proof of resistance. But it wouldn't take long till it buckled and died.

Hidden behind a thicket of broom, a dirt track led towards the inner island. But what in the world was that?

In the midst of loneliness, a car was parked. Phil recognized it immediately. This was Scherer's car, the luxury thing that had been standing in his carport.

In the wind, the branches of a broom bush were banging against its silver body. This, however, wasn't the only motion; turmoil was also inside the car. Through the steamed-up windows, Phil could see two human bodies, rocking the limousine so the axis bounced. A moment later, she recognized the bright pink of some familiar overalls.

As if Tamar and Scherer realized they were being watched, all motion froze. Then someone started to tamper with the passenger door. In a panic, Phil leaped behind the bushes and landed right in front of a spider web. Thorn-like hairy legs fidgeted right before her eyes—a huge arachnid, outraged that her thoroughly woven work was now destroyed. Phil suppressed a shriek and crawled back. Trying to wipe the sticky spider webs off her face, she ducked farther down.

Not one second too late, as now the car's door burst open and Tamar's legs appeared. She had to struggle to get out; apparently Scherer tried to hold her back. What kind of violent affairs did this woman have, first the guy in the café and now... Tamar's one hand gripped the door frame while her left elbow shot back. The man wailed, and she jumped out of the car. Her overalls were torn at one shoulder, all buttons open, revealing her breasts over a tattered bra.

Gone as well was Tamar's serenity, the self-assured smile on her lips. Her face was distorted, a grimace, black mascara running down her cheeks. Her elaborate hair-bun had turned into a disheveled web. The whole woman seemed ablaze, out of control furious as she grabbed the outer handle, bending down again to the man in the car. "That's it. You stay the fuck away from me."

Phil couldn't hear Scherer's answer, but Tamar laughed or rather let out an ugly sneer. "You want to threaten *me*? Fuck off, loser."

With these words, she slammed the door shut, adding an extra kick against the metal with her heel.

Phil had seen enough. Crouched down, she retreated even farther back behind the bushes, crawling across rocks and shrub. Out of sight of the fighting couple, she got up. Her whole body was stinging and itching, thistles were clinging to her dress. Across her right palm stretched a painful strip of spines that had belonged to the cactus-ear she accidentally had gripped. She would need her tweezers to get them out. Good it wasn't much farther to the hotel.

Phil hastened on, no longer worried about the steep cliffs, just wanting to get home. At her back, something screeched, a huge bird maybe, almost like a human voice. When it stopped, she again heard footsteps, this time behind her. Ezra Huber running back?

Before she could step aside to let him pass, something

enormous exploded on her head. A rock, a mountain. Phil's legs buckled, her eyesight shut down. *Me too?* were the last words she thought.

CHAPTER 29

Early that morning, only the gay couple were having coffee on the patio. Both looked like they had spent another night in a club with too much booze. That didn't keep Lluis, a thermos in his hand, from giving them a heated lecture.

"...*Los Butanos,* as we call them, the Hare Krishnas. And the witches, necromancers, Ufologists, Voodoo-priests, new Tanitians etc. As a rule, we believe everyone should pursue happiness their own way. That's not what I meant."

"Got it," the older one said, exhausted. "I think we should..."

"I'm talking about hostile takeover," Lluis raged, "can you imagine..."

"Right," the half-naked cowboy yawned, "we really should..."

Adam came to their aid. "Morning, y'all. Lluis, you got a minute?"

"Of course. *Hóla*, Adam." Lluis followed Adam to another table. He held up the thermos, "Coffee? What can I do for you, my friend?"

The questions Adam had were not easy to ask. But meanwhile he suspected more than anything that Lluis's childhood friend, Tamar, must be responsible for Amanda's death. What he and Phil had discussed the evening before only made sense. Tamar had a motive, she more than likely would have had the opportunity, and she seemed ruthless enough. The more Adam thought about it, the more convinced he was that Scherer's insistence that Amanda had not minded his infidelities was a lie. The Amanda Adam had known would have minded.

"Knowing Tamar as you do, Lluis, can you, with absolute certainty, exclude that she poured the poison into Amanda's glass?"

Lluis threw around glances as if trying to find an escape. "I'm not sure how far Tamar would go, ultimately," he finally admitted, "but I'm afraid she is capable of a lot. In all those years—I sometimes thought she was lacking something. In her emotional development. She doesn't know empathy, *eso es.*"

Lluis kept his voice down, "Tamar was five when she was brought here. Her mother Jezebel—then still Isabel—was one of the 'storage wives' as we call them, meaning her husband and, I guess, Tamar's father, had lost interest in family life. He must have been wealthy, so a house was bought, wife and child installed in it, money donated to the international school. Nothing they would miss in their paradisiac exile. Happens quite a lot here. In the first months, the guy typically shows up on the weekends, then maybe once a month, which he blames on his work schedule, and then not at all anymore. No big drama, as meanwhile, the wife has discovered the hippie lifestyle and new men and doesn't miss the old one in the suit. As long as he provides money. The only one left standing in the rain is the kid. In this case Tamar."

Lluis told Adam, as he had told Phil, how often Tamar had been left alone, forced to take care of herself. How the little girl had tried to believe her mostly stoned mother's gibberish about the goddess who would protect and guide her. Eventually, Tamar had swallowed enough of this crap, Lluis said with bitterness. She toughened up and didn't care about anyone anymore, only about herself.

"The crazy thing is that Tamar always stayed with Jezebel. She's in her thirties and still hasn't cut the umbilical cord, not even after..." Lluis stopped short.

"What? After what happened?"

Lluis bit his lips, but went on, "Yesterday at Cueva D'es Cuieram, I mentioned this accident, remember? A woman fell down the cliffs."

"After that, the cave was closed for visitors."

"And again is today. I couldn't believe that Tamar just went in. She of all people! Because she was there, three years ago, with her mother and some others. I can only tell you what I heard: they danced, drank, smoked pot, and some guys joined them. Among them Jezebel's lover of the time who, however—ahm—laid his eyes on Tamar."

Adam understood. "Scherer."

"Yep. Tamar started messing around with him, right in front of her mother, who made a huge scene. Freedom, love and peace, fair enough. But to see her own daughter making out with her lover went too far. I heard they fought like beasts—and that's when it happened. Afterwards Tamar swore that Jezebel slipped and fell. But another girl said she pushed her mother across the edge and just went back lap-dancing with Scherer. It was this girl that called police. An hour later Jezebel was found between the rocks. Since then, she's been paralyzed."

"How did Tamar react to the accusation?"

"She laughed. Said the girl bad-mouthed her because she was jealous. And when Jezebel regained conscience, she confirmed Tamar's version, that she had slipped. So tough luck. No police investigation."

And three years later, Adam thought, Tamar still had an affair with Scherer and still was living under her mother's roof. They would have to find the girl that had made the accusations against Tamar. "Do you remember the name ..."

In sudden shock, Adam jumped up. In a strange zigzag, Phil stumbled up the stairs, barely able to hold herself up. Her dress was covered in mud, her face dark-crusted. With effort, she lifted her hand and crashed against the wall.

"Phil!" Adam caught her before she fell back down the stairs. Lluis shrieked and picked up her purse while Adam carried Phil onto the patio.

She leaned her blood-crusted head against his chest. "Shit."

AN EYE FOR AN EYE

CHAPTER 30

Phil was sitting in her bed wearing a turban of gauze. The doctor had given her two painkillers and said she had been lucky. All the blood came from a laceration at the back of her head, but the wound wasn't deep and would heal in no time. Phil had to promise to stay in bed for at least twenty-four hours and call him if she felt nauseated, dizzy or had visual disturbances. To Lluis, the doctor muttered that it was a crying shame one wasn't safe from the Andalusians, not even in pre-season. A policeman showed up and wrote down that Phil had no idea who had hit her. In the same tone as the doctor, he assured her that generally, Ibiza was a perfectly safe island. "But the Andalusians!"

"Why out of all people should an Andalusian attack me? I didn't even get robbed." Phil had already gone through her purse. "ID, valet, phone, all here."

The answer was a meaningful look. In Ibiza, the people from Andalusia must have a bad reputation.

Lluis accompanied the policeman out. Adam stayed. The pills had turned Phil's headache into an almost agreeable drowsiness. Vaguely, she wondered who had dressed her in the nightgown. She thought about her grandmother who used to sermonize about the importance of always wearing impeccable underwear, as one might get in an accident. Phil giggled—where did this come from?

"I saw Tamar on the cliffs. With Scherer." She told Adam what she had witnessed: the limousine, the fight, Tamar's fury. In return, Adam summarized what Lluis had told him about Jezebel's accident and Tamar's—possible—role in it.

"Then be extra careful at your date with the *überfrau*. As now she is coming after you." Phil countered Adam's frown with dignity, "That's what she said."

"I know how to deal with a suspect. All I'm interested in is a confession."

"Right. After all, there is—what's her name—Lori." The moment she said it, Phil cursed herself.

"Lori is a colleague." Adam's eyes didn't move from her, "An ex, admitted."

Phil pulled the blanket up to her nose. "Okay."

"And Anton?" He tried to sound just as casual. "Boyfriend? Husband?"

"Neither." Phil was light years away from talking to Adam about her son. Quick change of subject. "Doro is convinced that Amanda *did* commit suicide."

She recounted that Doro had gone meditating to deal with her grief over that. That she had joined the Tanit Daughters and called herself Anat now. That instead of merely researching Matriarchy, she was re-introducing it, acting as representative of the Goddess, in order to save the world.

"Sounds rather... outlandish, I know. I had to get used to it too. But for Doro, it's the right life. And the women in Can Follet worship her."

"Are you serious? Is Dorothea now leading a cult?"

Phil tapped her forehead, but Adam wouldn't let go. "It sure sounds like it. How do you define a cult? By sectarianism, a promise of salvation, psychological dependency, a leader. Dorothea surrounded by worshippers? Seriously?"

"Sounds like you're describing the Pope. Just replace God with Goddess."

"So you're saying Dorothea is pope? I thought she was a historian."

"She is like—a good mother. Just leave her alone, all right?"

But Adam had sunken his teeth into the subject. "That's amazingly irrational. Starting with changing her name to a historically important one, which is always meant to ascribe greater significance to oneself. Wasn't Anat an Egyptian Goddess? Reminds me of Waco, Texas, of this self-proclaimed Messiah who upgraded himself as David Koresh. And lead his sect into a deadly massacre."

A lousy comparison, Phil opposed. The new names of the Tanit Daughters, as Doro had pointed out, merely signified their new identities. It had nothing to do with self-upgrading.

Adam sized Phil up as through a lens of disappointment. "I wouldn't have thought you are so easily fooled. Well, I guess, why wouldn't I..."

Something heavy pushed down on her. Here it was, the patronizing tone she hated and would never accept. Of course she knew what Adam was alluding to: to the aftermath of their fight sixteen years ago. He had accused her of hiding behind Dorothea in whose vocabulary "to forgive" didn't exist. But who just proved to be unforgiving?

"Why is it so important to you to badmouth Doro?"

"It isn't. My point is, even the mighty Dorothea isn't omniscient. That she says my sister killed herself doesn't make it true."

"I get it. But Anat and Amanda were close."

"So close she couldn't make it to her burial." Adam's sarcasm was like a sharp knife, "What's wrong with you, Phil?"

"I trust Doro. More than—anyone."

"I trust my instincts."

The instincts of an ex-cop who smelled crime behind every

bush. "What are we really talking about here?" Phil felt exasperated. "About Amanda's death, considering all options, or about your aversion against Doro because of ... *then*?"

Adam seemed to think about it. Then he got up.

"I'm sorry, Phil. This is not where I want to—or can—go back to."

"Me, neither."

He brushed his hair back and muttered something about Phil surely needing to rest. When the door shut behind him, she sank back into her pillows with a curse. Her head did not appreciate the abrupt movement and sent a painful protest.

To be honest, she could somewhat understand Adam. A little. Last night at Can Follet, Phil had also had a hard time swallowing Jezebel's and Anat's—how should she put it?—mythical show. When Jezebel conjured the "divine nature" of the assembled women, for instance, their "Amazonian strength." Or when she called Anat "the world's savior." The term "mumbo jumbo" had popped into Phil's mind. She had to get drunk to be okay with it.

Mostly, she wondered about Doro. Being so offended by the nickname "Fairy Aunt" in academia, she always made sure her papers, no matter how expressively written, were well researched and verifiable. Only to leap, in a matter of months, from science into irrationality. Suddenly, terms like sanctuary and divinity replaced hermeneutics and empirical analysis. And how benevolent Anat, the *priestess*, was towards her *disciples*. Terms that never in a million years would have crossed Phil's mind in regard to Doro. As if she were roleplaying, but without any irony involved.

So, Phil had to admit she could somewhat relate to Adam's skepticism. But to compare Doro to this crazy Waco guy, only because she exaggerated a bit playing Anat, was unfair.

Phil thought about the party. How Doro had radiated. How empathic she was among these women. Really, just like a good mother. What a change from former times when she had been

quite egocentric, not afraid of alienating others, always argu-
ing for life or death.

At Can Follet, the misunderstood lone wolf had turned into
a charismatic alpha animal. Made sense, Phil thought, that
someone who reinvented herself like Doro needed a new
name. If she also needed a goddess, whose business was it, and
to whose disadvantage? Even school medicine had their Ascle-
pius.

Phil woke up in the late afternoon. She took another painkiller and sent her daily message to Anton without mentioning
what had happened. Her head felt okay but for a dull pain and
a pinch where the bandage tugged at her hair. The cactus
spines in her hand, however, burned awfully. She pulled out
as many as she could grasp and turned on the shower. It was
hard to avoid the bandage while washing her hair, and some
single hairs pinched her scalp so badly she took her nail scis-
sors and tried to cut them off in front of the steamed-up mirror. A bigger strand slipped between the scissor blades and
was cut off, too.

Now she looked like a punk, pretty! But she didn't have to
be pretty; she had to find out what was going on here.
Wrapped in a bath towel, Phil dug through her travel bag.
Good, she had brought the black beret...

In the lobby, Trudy Huber was sitting in front of the flickering TV.

"Hi." She gave Phil an insecure smile. "I heard what happened. Awful."

Trudy seemed to have made a quantum leap in communi-
cation.

"Ah, thanks, it's not too bad." Phil poured herself a coffee
and sat down.

"So dangerous with all these Muslim terrorists."

Phil frowned. "What gives you the idea this was a Muslim
attack?"

"Well," Trudy bit her lips, "They always say..."

"They..." Phil felt liking kicking Trudy out of her naiveté. "*They* spread propaganda that messes with people's heads. There is no reason to believe I was attacked by a Muslim, okay?"

"Okay," Trudy squeaked, "I'm... sorry, okay?"

"Okay."

For a while, they sat in silence. On TV, a documentary was running—a CNN report on the opioid crisis that in the last years had killed more people in the U.S. than all other drugs put together. A recent prominent victim was the religious radio host Bud Winslow, who had demanded stronger laws against drug misuse. Only to be found dead with a lethal dose of prescription pills in his digestive tract. OxyContin, the commentator specified, one of the most addictive drugs on the market, which, due to common abuse, was known as "hillbilly heroin."

Abruptly, Trudy shut off the TV. Her eyes sparkled in agitation, her rabbit's teeth bared. "Such a hypocrite," she shouted, "do you know where Reverend Winslow was found dead?"

Surprised by Trudy's vehemence, Phil shook her head. "No idea."

"In a bar for—sickos. Homosexuals, you understand? Even though he condemned them as much as drugs and other evils."

"Muslims and other non-churchgoers too, I fathom."

Trudy reluctantly nodded. When she talked again, it sounded like a resignation. "Bud Winslow pretended to be the most righteous man in the United States, conservative and strong in faith. And then he turns out to be a sicko himself."

Phil tried hard to ignore Trudy's gay bashing. "Seems like this guy was just up to propaganda. Happens all the time."

But that aggravated Trudy even more. "But if things like this just *happen*," she whined, "what can we still believe? Whom shall we trust? It cannot be that the world is full of lies, lies, lies..."

CHAPTER 31

Adam strolled through the harbor district of Ibiza-city called *La Marina*. It must have been renovated lately. The promenade's tiles shone like fresh lacquer, the young palm trees still had to grow used to their new home. An elegant obelisk was dedicated to the Corsairs, Adam read on an attached sign, who through centuries had protected Ibiza from the attacks of hostile pirates.

To the west of the harbor district, on Paseo Vara del Rey, was the Gran Hotel Montesol Tamar had described to him. It was the oldest hotel on Ibiza, a pastel yellow building in Colonial style with white-framed balconies and window arches. To Adam's American eyes, it looked like a gigantic key lime pie with whipped cream. Opposite it was the café Mar y Sol, their meeting place. It had an inviting patio shaded by palm trees and sun umbrellas with a San Miguel beer advertisement. The same as on the beach pub's patio, he recalled from the night before.

Of course, Adam thought, he only noticed the stupid umbrellas because of the night before. When he had dinner with Phil and danced with her. And kissed her. Holy shit, what in the world had gotten into him? Later he would check on her and make sure she didn't think too much of it. He also would apologize for judging Dorothea so harshly when Phil was just happy to have found her. Not very sensitive of him, either. Let sleeping dogs lie.

However, recalling how Dorothea had judged *him* sixteen years ago, still made Adam furious. How helpless this bitch had made him feel. How he had almost begged... Forcefully, he shook the memory off and checked his phone. Already a quarter past seven.

Just then, Adam's phone buzzed. It wasn't Tamar, though, but Bartolo. In his excitement, he squeaked like a Texan crackle bird.

"Is she with you?"

"Tamar? Not yet."

"Adam, you won't believe what I found out..."

Earlier, Adam had contacted him for details on Jezebel's critical fall three years ago. So Bartolo had spoken to a colleague who had shown up at the cave.

"He confirmed the incident just as Lluis told you. There was a party, Jezebel fell into the abyss, and this girl said Tamar had pushed her. True also, this lead wasn't followed by police because Jezebel insisted she was the only one to blame as she had stumbled and fell. But now listen: this girl that called police and accused Tamar was—Neves Niemer."

Adam was electrified. "Ninguno's daughter. Holy shit."

"Right." Bartolo's excitement literally flew out of the phone. "And not even two weeks after the incident, she was dead."

Adam let out a long, low whistle. Suddenly, everything appeared in a new light again. Until now, they had assumed Neves's death had to do with the allegations of rape against the TAB. But this, of course, did not have to be true. Again, Tamar was involved. Had she pushed her mother into the abyss and then got rid of the only witness? A reasonable suspicion.

"Nobody but me and my father connected Neves's death to anyone, and we concentrated on the TAB," Bartolo affirmed Adam's thought. "This may have been a mistake. Adam, what would you say if I came by the Mar y Sol in, let's say, half an hour? And interfere a bit in your date with Tamar. With some questions I'm burning to ask her. For instance, if she really was innocently sleeping in her bed the night Amanda died—as so far only her mother confirmed. And where she was when Neves's father Ninguno burned to death."

"I think that's a damn good idea."

While Adam was waiting for Tamar, Phil had a tortilla on the patio. Lluis fluttered around her like a mother hen and advised her not to drink alcohol with the painkiller pills, let alone smoke. As soon as she could without being impolite, Phil withdrew to a lounge chair in the front yard, taking along the cup of melissa tea Lluis had forced upon her, but also her tobacco pouch. Another maternal character, Trudy, brought her a blanket. When Phil said thanks, Trudy ran back on the patio, as if embarrassed by her own kind gesture.

Thankful indeed as a chilly wind had come up, Phil wrapped herself in the blanket. In front of her inner eyes, images kept showing up: Tamar in the morning, furious, in her half-torn overalls. Now all prettied up again, with perfectly painted lips and sexy eyes. Their suspect, the likely killer toasting to Adam, beguiling him, trapping him.

Stop it, Phil told herself. Adam was a pro... But this only brought the movie *Basic Instinct* to her mind, in which the detective was seduced by the ice-cold blonde he interrogated... Stop it, for hell's sake. For the hundredth time, Phil's fingers felt for the bandage on her head and the stubbles of hair from which her vanity suffered more than from the wound.

Vigorously, Phil pulled her beret back down. She must get in touch with Doro, explain why she had left in the morning without saying goodbye and what had happened to her. But her phone rang and rang to no answer.

The Ibizan flash-twilight came and went, and darkness spread out. In spite of the waxing moon and the light that fell from the patio into the yard, Phil suddenly felt uneasy. What if her attacker was hiding in the shadows, ready to strike again? Nonsense. There were plenty of people only a few yards away. Still, Phil decided to go back to the patio. It was getting colder by the minute, anyway.

She struggled out of the chair, keeping the blanket wrapped around her, when a bright light blinded her. Alarmed, she ducked back down, but it was only the headlights of a car turning into the parking lot. A rental SEAT. Adam's car? How could this be? It was barely nine o'clock. But it sure was Adam.

"Mr. Ryan, huh, already back. How come?"

"Hey. How is your head?"

"As good as new. Now tell me, is Tamar our killer? What besides the latest flirting techniques did you get out of her?"

Adam pulled a wry face. "Nothing, sorry. She didn't show up. Instead, Bartolo came and had something to say."

Adam summarized the news about Jezebel's fall and Neves Niemer. Around seven-thirty, the inspector had appeared in the Mar y Sol, but Tamar still wasn't there, so he sat down in the back of the café. At eight o'clock he joined Adam at his table. Still no Tamar. Adam tried to reach her on the phone without success. At eight-thirty, they gave up.

"She either forgot about you," Phil said without believing it, "or she realized she's in danger to be uncovered. Which would mean we're right with our suspicion. So how shall we proceed?"

"Nothing we can do right now but wait. Tomorrow morning, Bartolo will officially try to nail her. Then we'll see."

Overwhelmed by what they suspected of the apparently nice, helpful woman she had met on the ferry, Phil dropped back into the lounge chair. If Tamar really was ruthless enough to push her mother over a precipice, she likely also had the guts to kill Neves, Amanda, and Ninguno for being in her way. Was a murderous psychopath hiding behind the cliché blonde sex bomb?

"I'll get myself a drink." Adam stretched his legs. "Need something?"

A contemptuous glance hit the Melissa tea. "A wine, please, and a lighter."

Adam grinned. "On my way."

He stopped short when a light beam flared up and Ezra Huber came flying across the drywall.

Huber was wearing his running gear and a headband with an attached LED-torch. Stunned, Phil and Adam watched him land in the succulent bed, struggle back on his feet and run towards them. He stumbled across a sun lounger set up here with the view of Es Vedrà, which bounced up and hugged him with its extended armrests. Frantically, he shook it off.

"Police," Huber howled, "someone get the police."

Lluis came sprinting down the stairs, Trudy behind him, shrieking in panic. Phil jumped up, ignoring the sharp pain in her skull. Adam grabbed Huber's arm.

"What happened? Calm down, man, tell me."

Huber literally drooled. "The... the... blonde lady's lying down there..."

Trudy shrieked again and fell down on her knees. "Dear God, no." With both fists she hit the ground. "That's doom, Ezra. Doom."

The other guests realized something was wrong and came running too.

Phil trembled in shock. "The blonde... Tamar?"

"She's dead," Huber croaked.

A collective gasp was the answer. Huber had gone for a run, he stuttered. He didn't mind the lonely trail as the moon shone bright, and he also had a light. His fingers tapped the

LED torch on his head.

"Another run," escaped Phil's mouth.

"Right. And?"

Huber almost choked, but when Adam gently repeated, "Please tell us what happened," he calmed down. He had run for about two miles, he said, then turned around. When he looked out over the bay, he noticed something down there, a big fish or bird, he first thought. Way down, between those sharp needle-rocks. He directed his light at it. And saw it was the dead body of a woman in pink overalls.

Lluis had already dialed the emergency number. His eternal Ibiza tan had turned ghostly pale. "Police are on their way," he said after finishing his call. "Mr. Huber, would you please show me where exactly—it happened?"

When Huber nodded weakly, Lluis asked the others to stay behind, but neither Phil and Adam nor anyone else listened. In a silent parade, they followed him and Huber towards the sea, along the coastal trail, passing the spot where Phil had been attacked. When she woke up, she had been lying on the outer edge of the cliff. One wrong move and she would have fallen to her death.

Just behind the turn where the trail was so narrow its ridge hung over the abyss, Phil had seen Scherer's car. And Tamar. There was the broom-bush behind which she had hidden. Huber pointed down where the earth was visibly broken up, the brush battered. Dragging traces led to the cliff. These tracks, he said, had caught his attention. That's why he looked down and saw—it.

"Careful. Don't get closer," Lluis warned, "The overhang can break off."

"Careful," Adam echoed, "Everyone go back on the trail. You are about to destroy evidence the police will need. Y'all, stay away."

But they had already seen: the cliff fell maybe a hundred feet straight down into the bay with the rock needles and the agitated sea gushing around them. With the flow, the water had partly retreated and left the rocks exposed, shells and seaweed sticking to them, looking eerie in the cold moonlight. But most shocking was the female body between the rocks, her head rammed into a gap, one arm reaching out. With every approaching and retreating wave, the body weltered upwards as if she tried to free herself.

Inspector Dziri arrived, followed by three police cars. Policemen cordoned off the area with barrier tape so the gawkers had to retreat into the field. A coast guard boat appeared in the bay. Her fingers clutching the worthless good luck-charms of her necklace, Phil watched two frogmen jump into the wild waters. With a rope, they tried to pull Tamar's body out of the clef. But in vain, as they kept being pulled back by the strong surf, in danger of being smashed against the rocks themselves. After a while, they had to give up.

Then, the sharp noise of rotor blades announced the arrival of a rescue helicopter. It came to a stop in mid-air. The rotation whirled up the water in a torrential gush, engulfing the bay in a spooky mist. In the strong spotlight, another frogman was hoisted down until he reached the body and attached a rope to it.

Tamar was lifted up in the air. Water pearled from her in silver sprays, the shreds of her overalls whirling around in the vortex the rotors created. An agonizing moment later, Phil realized it wasn't the torn overalls blowing in the wind, but Tamar's skin. Sliced on the sharp rocks, it hung from her body in scraps, her limbs chafed down to the bones.

Adam grabbed Phil's arm, "Don't look." But it was too late.

A collective shriek pierced the night. People screamed and clung together in horror. And with them, Phil screamed like never before. Because she had seen Tamar's face. It was illuminated by the searchlights, surrounded by waving blonde hair. Nothing was left of it but crushed matter.

CHAPTER 32

The helicopter with its searing lights had caught the attention of the monster hotels' tourists who came tramping up from the northern bay. Possibly for the first time in their all-inclusive vacations, they noticed the Esperanza, so much more authentic than their own faceless lodgings. Out of breath from the climb, they trampled the pretty succulents in the front yard and tried to push their way into the lobby. Excited chatter filled the air.

"So who was the woman... wow, isn't it romantic here? Want a beer, babe?"

"Waiter, do you know who... *Hello?* What the... can you believe this guy?"

"What? Are you saying I'm not allowed to ask...?"

"My ID? Why? In my hotel room."

The policemen tried to separate potential witnesses from sensation-seeking rubbernecks who hadn't seen or heard anything but wanted to know everything. Adam was standing with Dziri, their heads stuck together. Bartolo looked worn out, his chin longing for the second shave a day that his testosterone required. With nervous fingers, Phil rolled a cigarette.

After a while, the chaos was organized. The guests of the Esperanza found themselves in the lobby, while two policemen at the entrance kept the nosy others out. The pandemonium was over. Dziri got people's attention by knocking on the reception desk.

"Listen, everybody," he said, "I now will ask you a few questions. Please consider carefully if you may have something to say about what happened here. Anything you may have seen or heard concerning Tamar Stettin. Even if it seems unimportant to you now, every detail may be a potential lead." His thumb pointed to the door behind him, leading to Lluis's private tract. "In there, please. The first, if you may," he nodded at Huber, "is you, Mr. Huber. Would you be so kind..."

"Ahm. Sure." Misery personified, Huber shuffled to Dziri who held the door open for him. But before he was through, Trudy jumped up. With a raw energy no one would have suspected from her, she cut her husband's way.

"Did you do it?" she hissed, "because she wouldn't play along?"

The demure wife had lost it. She spat right into Ezra's face. A shockwave rolled through the lobby.

Ezra was too stunned to react. He dabbed at the spit and babbled something like "Wh...wh... wha..."

Trudy lifted her hand to slap him, but Dziri grabbed her wrist. "Easy, Mrs. Huber." He steered Trudy back to her chair. "No need for violence. Take a deep breath. Good. And now tell me why you think your husband may have anything to do with Ms. Stettin's death."

Trudy stared at him like a maniac. "*Why?* Isn't that obvious? Because he was all over her. That's why we had to do this stupid tour to the cave. And then the cliffs... Since we arrived, he keeps going there. Because he suddenly needs to run three times a day? Ha! Sex is what he's looking for."

"Trudy! Shut the fuck up." Huber remembered his marital dominance. "I forbid you..." He made a menacing step towards his wife, but again Inspector Dziri stepped between them.

"Mr. Huber, stay where you are." With a nod, he ordered one of the uniformed men to take charge of him. Huber almost disappeared behind the bulky officer who kept him in check.

While Trudy metamorphosed. Suddenly, the submissive woman, the female coward, was a person of the past. "He thought I wouldn't say a thing," she screamed, "because when we got married I had to swear to obey him. But I have eyes in my head. As if I could have missed it. Ezra is the biggest womanizer in the world, he just pretends..."

"This is totally not true. Are you out of your mind?" Huber was heard yapping behind the policeman.

"*Thou shalt not commit adultery. Thou shalt not kill.*" Trudy screeched like possessed. "*Thou shalt not covet thy neighbor's wife nor thy...* whatever. *But I say unto you, that whosoever looketh at a woman lustfully hath already committed adultery with her in his heart.* Matthew something."

"Calm down, Mrs. Huber."

"For Christ's sake, woman." Huber reappeared at the policeman's side, now ready to counterattack. "Always the same! Inspector, you must know. My wife is eaten up by jealousy. She hates every decent-looking woman. Especially the blonde lady. Since she first laid eyes on her. My, it was unbearable ..." Huber wrung his hands. "Dear God... woman. What have you done?"

People, still flabbergasted by Trudy's outburst, started to stir again. "What's he suggesting?" someone asked.

Phil couldn't believe it. Was Huber really trying to insinuate that Trudy had pushed Tamar across the cliff out of jealousy? That was nothing less than ridiculous. The idea alone: short, chubby Trudy pushing Tamar! Tall and strong like an amazon, Tamar could have crushed her with one finger! Ezra Huber, however, was physically quite fit. Phil thought about him doing one-arm push-ups. And how nimbly he had hiked up to the cave, whistling a sexy song...

"What a jerk," someone said.

Lluis lifted his finger like a school kid, "Ah, Bartolo... *comisario*. To me, honestly, it was obvious that Mr. Huber was quite attracted to Tamar."

"He was ogling," one of the Danes said, "remember? In the cave."

"Lecherous," someone else agreed.

"Sex. He wanted to have sex," Trudy whined.

A woman put her hand tenderly on her shoulder. "Always the same old story. I'm so, so sorry for you."

Trudy glimpsed at her, surprised to meet pitying eyes. "Me, he never touches anymore," she tested frankness, "even though I'm his wife."

"Defamations," Huber gasped, "Dear God, be with me." He glared around. "I never committed adultery."

"One can believe this or not." Shaking heads showed what people believed.

Dziri raised both hands. "Come on now, people, what are you doing, *por dios*? No prejudgments here, all right?"

His words brought people back to reality. Phil bit her lip. How easy it was to go one direction. Sure, Huber was a prick, a lecherous creep. But that didn't mean he was a murderer. So far, they only knew that he had found Tamar dead. *In dubio pro reo*, the laws of fairness must count for everyone.

But then, so must the truth. Phil cleared her throat. "This morning, on the cliffs, I encountered Mr. Huber. Right after I saw Tamar."

She knew Adam had told Bartolo about Scherer's car on the cliff and the fight with Tamar she had witnessed.

"You didn't mention you saw Mr. Huber, Phil."

"True." Phil tried to remember how much she had told Adam. "I didn't make the connection then, I guess."

"There is no connection," Huber yelled. "I was only running. I didn't see anyone."

"Well, *that's* definitely not true. You almost ran me over."

"Throw him into the blazing furnace," came again from Trudy's biblical ranting, *"where there will be weeping and gnashing of teeth."*

Dziri had his hands full dealing with all the commotion. He motioned the bulky policeman to lead Huber into Lluis's office and asked Phil to come too.

Huber flopped down in a chair.

"So what is the story of this morning?" Dziri asked him softly. "Did you run into Tamar Stettin by chance or had you planned to meet her?"

"No... no."

"Looking for a little distraction out of the marriage routine?"

Huber's chin was as trembling as his voice, but he still clung to the lie, "I didn't see anyone. True, I saw her," he nodded at Phil, "but not the blonde..."

Dziri looked at Phil, who vehemently shook her head. "He must have seen her." She described how Huber had come towards her on the trail, only one curve away from Scherer's car. It was impossible that he could have overlooked it—and Tamar in her pink overalls—when he ran by.

Dziri nodded. "Between Hostal Esperanza and the villas on the cliffs, there is only this one trail leading from the inland to the coast. You did not run along the road for ten miles to take it, Mr. Huber, right? And even if, you still couldn't have missed the car." Again he spoke softly. "If you saw Tamar Stettin with Mr. Scherer, you should admit it, Mr. Huber. I'm sure you don't want to unnecessarily incriminate yourself."

The American was clearly struggling. He didn't want to be the one who had to *admit* anything. His ego crashed against reason. But in the end, reason won.

"All right." His face was a burning red, "I did see her. They were screwing."

"They were fighting," Phil opposed.

Huber turned to her. How close set his eyes were, how

pointed his nose, like a possum—but no, that wasn't fair to possums, Phil corrected her thought.

"Later they fought," Huber snarled in a last attempt at superiority. "First they had sex. I saw it with my own eyes."

"So you lied to us." Dziri was getting impatient with the man. "You did watch Tamar Stettin and Scherer. What time was that? How long did you peep?"

"I didn't..."

"What time?"

"Don't know."

"He came towards me when it was just getting daylight," Phil said.

"So you left the hotel when it was still dark. Is it your habit to run so early?"

"Early to bed, early to rise makes a man ..."

"I wouldn't call it wise to watch other people having sex. Or decent. Okay, you peeped till they started to fight. What was that about?"

"Don't know. They yelled at each other in German, I guess. So I left."

Huber buried his face in his hands. All superiority had left him. "I sinned," he admitted, "I'm only human. God, I ask for forgiveness."

Dziri ignored the whining. "How much farther did you run from there?"

"To the next bay." Huber described how he had stopped for a water in Cala d'Hort. The waiter at this beach bar would surely remember him because they had gotten into an argument about two euros fifty for a little bottle of water without even ice cubes.

"You went back the same way, right? Were they still there? And the car?"

"Yes. And no, the car was gone with both of them." Huber sat up. "Why do you ask me all this? I found the dead woman tonight. Who cares what I was doing in the morning?"

"I do." Dziri said, "Because we know Tamar Stettin's life ended at least twelve hours ago. Right about when you watched her."

Huber had to digest this. His finger pointed at Phil, "She was there, too."

"So when you came back along the trail, you saw Ms. Mann lying there? Unconscious and bleeding?"

"What?" Huber seemed genuinely baffled. "What are you talking about? No, I didn't, I swear on my father's grave." The sun had blinded him, he said, maybe that's why he didn't see anything. No injured person, and not what he saw at night, with his flashlight: the torn-out brush, the traces. The body. He swallowed hard. Phil couldn't tell whether he lied or told the truth.

Dziri ordered Huber to the police station next morning to sign his statement. And he might consider calling his embassy for a lawyer. Which would only be necessary if the DNA test he would have to agree to showed a positive result.

"And if I don't agree?"

"We would have to take you into custody for now. But if you are innocent, you've got nothing to fear."

"Okay. I'll do it."

The door closed behind Huber. Phil and Bartolo exchanged a look.

"Do you believe him?" she asked.

"Well, yes. That he found Tamar speaks for him. And that he agreed on the test. I'm glad you got off relatively lightly. How is your head?"

"Better." Her head was the last thing Phil had been thinking about. Now she realized what Bartolo meant. "Oh shit."

"Right. With you, Tamar, Scherer and Huber on the cliffs there was either another person who attacked you—which seems unlikely..."

Or, after killing Tamar, Scherer had tried to eliminate a potential witness. Phil had been extremely lucky.

Out in the lobby, the Hubers had disappeared. The other guests stared at her expectantly. Adam sat at the bar, an empty stool beside him. As promised what felt like eternities ago, he had ordered a red wine for her and one for himself. Next to Phil's glass was a lighter. She rolled two cigarettes and had a sip of wine. They went out on the patio to smoke. Not one word had been said when Phil stubbed out her cigarette.

"I don't want to be alone tonight."

"Neither do I," Adam replied.

CHAPTER 33

It was early in the morning, the room still bathed in twilight. Phil's face lay in front of Adam like a dream apparition, one eye half-hidden in the pillow, the other one directed at him with a maybe wondering look. The eye's iris was astonishingly green like the color of a deep natural pool, a *cenote* in Yucatan or Hamilton Pool in Texas. The color of underground waters. Phil's lashes, in contrast, were rather light and stuck together with some leftover mascara. Black crumbs dotted her cheekbone. Adam didn't stir because he didn't want to wake up.

The night before, they had stretched out on Phil's bed, stunned by what had happened. At the same time overwhelmed by being so close again. For quite a while neither of them had moved a muscle, until Adam slipped his arm around Phil and pulled her head on his shoulder. Then, they had begun to forget the world and all of its tragedies. Phil uttered a profound purr, and Adam breathed the faint scent of her hair brushing his chin. The scent of Phil. She snuggled even closer to him in a way he had missed for so long it almost broke his heart.

After a night of whispers and wonderful wordlessness,

they now had to find their way back into reality. Adam gave Phil a tiny, careful kiss. She sat up, still with this questioning look in her eyes. Sometimes in the past, Phil had also had this expression, and Adam never understood what it meant.

"Morning." He didn't know what else to say.

"Hi." Phil's hand went to her head. "Damn."

"Does it still hurt?"

"Barely. I mean *damn* as I can't believe we were so wrong. I seriously thought Tamar was a crazy psycho-killer, and now she is dead. I wish... I don't know. I feel horrible about that."

"That she's dead doesn't necessarily mean she didn't have anything to do with it all." Adam was kind of relieved to talk about the case. "She may have known more than Scherer wanted her to know. Maybe she blackmailed him."

Phil thought more in terms of relationship problems. She saw Tamar in front of her, singing the Marlene Dietrich song: "I belong to myself/ I'll be fine on my own." Her self-assured smile. Her rage after making it out of Scherer's car. The word *loser* was the last Phil had heard her yell.

"Or Scherer did kill Amanda to be free for Tamar, but she didn't want to play wife replacement. And he flipped out."

"Possibly. Anyway. Here we have Scherer! Concerning him, we have been on the right track from the very start. Now, Bartolo should have enough ammunition for the prosecutor to nail him."

The night before, at the crime scene, Bartolo's team had meticulously gathered samples, footprints, tire tracks, every bit of fiber they could find. After that, he had ordered his men to drive by Scherer's villa, confiscate every pair of shoes they could find and take imprints of his Bentley's tire tracks for comparison. Bartolo had been excited: if they could prove it was Scherer's car on the cliff—and of course it was; Phil had seen it with her own eyes—no prosecutor, no matter how bribed or blind, would be able to deny the fact. If the seawater had not washed away all proof, the coroner might find further evidence on Tamar's body.

Phil sat straight up. "Shit, I have to call Doro. I can't even imagine how she must feel. After all, Tamar was one of them, even though I don't think Doro liked her much. And poor Jezebel. Oh damn."

"I know." Adam put his arms around her.

A bit later, when the door closed behind him, Phil buried her face in the pillow his head had been lying on, inhaling the faint scent. She had loved it from the first moment she met Adam, even before she fell in love with him. Senses are older than consciousness, she had read, and the instinctive sense of smell is the oldest of them all. If you don't like someone's smell, that person, for mere biochemical reasons, doesn't stand a chance.

The thought that she had to call her bank crossed Phil's mind. Instead she pushed Doro's cell phone number but couldn't reach her. Did she never answer it anymore? On the Can Follet landline, she reached an audibly shaken-up Stella.

"It's horrific. You okay, honey? You must leave this rotten island as quickly as you can. Believe me. All the horror is here."

"What? I mean, yes..." Phil was confused. What was it with Stella?

But before she could organize her thoughts, the phone clicked and Anat was on the line. She also sounded genuinely distraught in face of the tragedy, but said she had to be strong for everyone, especially for Jezebel. After two "insensitive male cops" stepped across their threshold and brutally confronted her with news of Tamar's death, she had collapsed.

"The poor thing. I'm so glad she has you."

"I know, right." At the moment, Anat continued, she was busy organizing a three-hour mantra recitation for all Daughters of Tanit to help Jezebel find the noble path into solace. "Come join us. As long as you don't get impatient."

An unexpected feeling of frustration flooded over Phil. "Thanks, but no thanks," she said brusquely, "instead of chanting *ohms* or whatever, I'd rather help find Tamar's murderer."

"You? That's what the police are for, don't you think?"

"Well—can you trust those insensitive male cops?"

"We can only do what lies within our power."

That was true. Phil thought she shouldn't judge how others dealt with death.

When Phil and Adam entered the police station, Ezra Huber emerged from Dziri's office and, ignoring them, ran to the exit. Phil thought about Trudy's spitting attack and his insinuating that she pushed Tamar. How could the couple spend another minute with each other?

Bartolo welcomed them with news. The night before, he had only reached Scherer on the phone. He was on Mallorca, on a business trip, but the Bentley was parked in the carport of Villa Éscorpion. So Bartolo talked the prosecutor into signing a court order, an expert disarmed the alarm, and the forensic team compared the tire profile of Scherer's limousine with the traces on the cliff. Bartolo almost drooled with excitement; half an hour ago the results came in. Without any doubt, both tire treads were identical.

Bartolo was ecstatic. "I sent an officer to the airport to welcome Mr. Scherer back home. They will be here any minute."

As if on cue, a policeman in uniform brought Scherer in. Irritated, he gave Adam and Phil a nod and plopped down in a chair opposite Dziri.

"Please do sit down, *señor*."

Irony was lost on Scherer. "What's up, *comisário*?"

Drumming his fingers of one hand on the back of the other, he made it clear he didn't want to waste his time with senseless banter. In wordless response, Dziri took his time, slowly digging through the papers in front of him, stapling them accurately, opening a file. He read through it, shook his head, frowned. Only then he looked at Scherer with an innocent smile.

"First, *estimado señor* Scherer, I have a question of rather general interest concerning the property Can Salammbo in the bay of Benirras. Is it right that it has recently been sold to you?"

Scherer nodded without bothering to answer and kept on drumming. Only to the effect that Dziri turned even more tedious. He pulled out an abstract from the land registry of Can Salammbo, read it aloud, word by word, including every incomprehensible number, square footage, dates of a former selling and so on. Meticulously, he put paper after paper back into the folder. Phil could physically grasp Scherer's impatience.

"You don't have to answer my question," Dziri said, falsely demure, "but is it true that, for this mansion, you only paid 800 thousand euros?"

Scherer snapped. "You just read it out aloud."

"A small sum, *señor* Scherer."

"The American didn't have a clue about the prices on the island. I would have been a fool to reject his offer."

"But how could Colonel Cruz be so oblivious? As he himself paid more than two million just three years ago?"

"A friendship price; he wanted to sell quickly. When I get a good offer, I take it. Wouldn't you?" Arrogantly the realtor added, "If you dealt with this kind of dough."

But arrogance couldn't hide his irritation. That's what Bartolo was aiming at. Adam jumped to his aid.

"So Cruz is a friend of yours. A TAB Brother, right? I guess he sold your clubhouse in such a haste to cover up the connection."

Scherer ignored him. "*Comisário*, I didn't deem it necessary to ask the gentleman for his motive to sell. If that'd be all, I have work to do..."

"Easy, *señor,* we still have..."

Scherer jumped up. "And I wonder what fucking authority Mr. Ryan has to ask me questions?"

"*Oye*, sorry. He will be quiet." Suddenly, the inspector's voice was as sharp as a blade. "But *I* ask you: What did you do to Tamar Stettin?"

"Wh... what are you talking about?"

"You heard me. Tamar Stettin. With whom you had a fight yesterday morning. On the cliff between Cala'Hort and Cala Cabó. From where she was pushed to her death."

All color had left Scherer's face. He seemed as shocked as one could get. Either he is an extremely talented actor, Adam thought not for the first time, or his shock is genuine. Maybe he's shocked to hear that Tamar didn't disappear in the ocean's depth.

"I want to talk to my lawyer," Scherer said. "Now."

On his insistence, Dziri asked Phil and Adam to leave, so they waited in the lobby. When he followed them ten minutes later, he was in best spirits. Scherer had to wait for his lawyer who had just gone to *siesta*. Enough time for them to eat at Tia Maria.

The aunt welcomed them like long-lost family members and the food was as delicious as before, as was the inevitable wine. Scherer, Bartolo said, had given him an alibi which was even weaker than the one before. He had been on Mallorca for a real estate deal, he said. On a Sunday. Sure, his client confirmed she met with Scherer. But this didn't have to mean a thing.

"Tamar was killed at dawn; the flight to Palma Scherer claims he took left after eight. Unfortunately, he can't find his boarding card. A colleague is checking the airline right now." Bartolo lifted one finger after the other. "Even if he was on the flight, he could have done it. We've got the tire tracks, we will compare the footprints, plus we have one asset Scherer doesn't know about: our Peeping Tom, *señor* Huber. I ordered an identity parade for tomorrow morning. Until then, Scherer can relax in his cell for the legally justifiable twenty-four hours."

Bartolo giggled smugly. "I got him when I confronted him with the sale of the mansion, didn't I?"

"A brilliant idea," Adam admitted.

"The only thing that pisses me off is that we still haven't come closer to the TAB. But maybe we can take advantage of the stir that will be caused by Scherer's arrest. And maybe," Bartolo nudged Adam with his elbow, "you can use your Big Brother contacts and find out more about this colonel and his hasty sale of the villa. What do you say?"

"Do you have a landline I can use?"

CHAPTER 34

Back in the police station, Scherer's attorney had arrived. Before taking him to the interrogation room, Bartolo opened his office for Phil and Adam to use his phone. Adam checked the time: Two-thirty p.m.—eight-thirty a.m. in Washington D.C. If he was lucky, someone was already at work.

He was lucky. "McCullen. How can I help you?" a voice said. Adam pushed the loudspeaker button so Phil could listen. Andy McCullen, Lori's top connection to the information office, was exactly the man he needed.

"Mr. McCullen. Adam Ryan speaking."

One could literally feel how, thousands of miles away, McCullen sat straight up. "What's the problem, Mr. Ryan?"

Adam got right to the point. "You know who I'm talking about when I say T-A-B, McCullen, right? No PR firm in South Carolina..."

The eloquent silence on the other side of the line was his answer.

"Okay. Then you also know that Colonel Cruz, our new ISAF commander-in-chief, is a member."

He was sharply interrupted. "You have no authority to investigate Colonel Cruz. Your specific interest, Mr. Ryan, is met by a serious lack of comprehension in the Office..."

Adam did not beat around the bush. "I know I was told to stop digging up dirt. But as an investigator, I'm especially interested in dirt that may be dug up."

Before McCullen could answer he went on, "So, Cruz is or was a member of the TAB and took part in some really hot parties, to say the least." Now, Adam had to improvise. He needed McCullen to think he knew a lot more than he did. "Or should we talk about orgies, drugs, and rape? Suspicion of murder?"

"Cool it, Adam." The voice on the other end of the line had lost its sharp edge. Suddenly McCullen sounded nervous. "Come on, what are you talking about? Colonel Cruz is a man of integrity beyond doubt. You are one of us. You know we would never..."

"... allow the news about the good colonel's bad company be leaked?" Neither would Adam be lured into fake solidarity. "What if the media caught wind of it, right?"

Silence, interrupted by hesitant hm-hm-hms. McCullen was thinking hard.

"Sorry, man," Adam said kindly, "that stinks."

"Okay." The Pentagon's PR man changed his strategy. After all, he might think, Adam *was* one of them.

"You are absolutely right." How confidential he suddenly sounded. "There was a time when Colonel Cruz was closer to this brotherhood than he should have been. Not that he did anything illegal, don't get me wrong. He just wanted to party a little, have some fun. Understandable, right, after spending so much time in crisis regions where women are veiled and going to a pub means risking your life. But now we have a problem that could turn into a PR disaster."

"A *PR* disaster?" Adam almost laughed.

"You bet."

In his new buddy voice, McCullen summarized the staggering increase of sex scandals worldwide. "Remember how it started? Suddenly the press was full of *rape culture* in India and Brazil. *Bunga bunga* parties in Italy. France's Strauss-Kahn. The sex trips of those German business elites. And so on."

An avalanche of allegations had been set off, McCullen complained, resulting in a loss of trust in the most important leadership countries. That's what he meant by PR disaster. When the frenzy swept over to the US motherland, the real tragedy began.

"The fall of CIA Director Petraeus. The best of the best and has to resign because of this idiotic affair with his biographer. Anthony Weiner's dick on Twitter. And instead of calming down after a while, the media has gotten into a sex frenzy. All those trusted politicians, ministers, priests, and Academy Award–winning actors. The Stormy Daniels bullshit, Weinstein and Epstein. The media is full of accusations by women who never cared before about men's behavior and suddenly are stirred up like a bunch of crazy hornets."

"To not dare at some point doesn't mean to not care..."

McCullen ignored this. "And who knows better than you the many sexual charges in our military. Like a rampant tumor!" He seemed beside himself with worries. "Grown at a raise of 38%. These times, our no-tolerance policies have to be applied to every aspect of public life. Even if it concerns nothing more than a villa on Ibiza and the membership of an elite boys' club. Got it, Adam?"

"I get it: it doesn't matter what happened. As long as it stays out of the public eye."

"Let's be realistic: the Pentagon can't afford another scandal. But, of course, we looked into the brotherhood. The TAB. We screened them thoroughly."

"So, the death of Neves Niemer..."

"Who is that supposed to be?"

"I thought you screened them thoroughly. Now her father is dead, too..."

"I have no idea what you are talking about." Andy McCullen was indignant again. "Listen, Adam, every single suspicion against the TAB has been proven to be unfounded. Fake news, understand? Nothing illegal. The TAB is a private club of some prominent guys who like to be among themselves. All allegations can be traced back to fake news writers, jealous wives, greedy prostitutes, and envious neighbors that won't grant these guys a little fun. Our only problem is that we are at that crazy point in history where the mere connection of Colonel Cruz and a little fun may do harm."

"The problem *I* see is that the TAB's little fun may have led to the death of several people," Adam snapped, "crimes that are not looked into but covered up to save someone's ass. How can you justify that?" Thoroughly disgusted by the hypocrisy, he added, "From you and the Office I expect every possible support in my investigation." He hung up.

Phil looked at him with big eyes. "Wow."

"Let's see how they are going to react. And react they will."

"Aren't you afraid to lose your job?"

Adam reflected on the question. Was he afraid? If the Office avoided looking into the TAB for the sake of the Colonel's reputation, his questions must have irritated them, to say the least. But Adam was sick of all the hush-hush.

"I didn't drop out of the Army to stay in the swamp. I'd rather drain it."

"I thought you liked being a military cop."

"I couldn't go on."

"What happened?"

Only after a while Adam talked, in a low voice Phil barely understood.

"In 2003, a few months after we—after I returned to the U.S., my unit was transferred to Bagdad to help install the new Iraqi police forces..."

Over there, Adam was sent to the military prison of Abu

Ghraib to support the understaffed American security personal. At this time, the White House was of the opinion that endless interrogations, sleep-depravity and waterboarding did not collide with the prohibition of torture in the U.S. Constitution's eighth amendment. If this wasn't enough to question humane standards, Adam was about to experience the abolition of all morality in Abu Ghraib. He saw an MP private nonchalantly holding a leash, tightened around the neck of a naked and blindfolded Iraqi prisoner. The combat booted foot of her peer on the neck of another prisoner, like a big game hunter showing off his prey. The abuse, torture, rape, sodomy, even murder.

A soldier with a conscience handed in photos but nothing happened. It took the international press to reveal the crimes and cause worldwide outrage. But besides sparking a wave of retaliatory beheadings by radical Islamists, there were no consequences but a few trials, a little jail time for the *primary torturers*. And then the nonchalant appeal to get over it.

"When I was back in the States," Adam said, "I was done with the Army."

But he needed a job and was actually grateful when he got the offer to work as civil investigator for the Pentagon. Thanks to his expertise, they said, he could help eliminate the wrongdoings within the military. Adam believed he had found a meaningful task. He was ready to separate the wheat from the chaff.

Reality caught up with him when he investigated one of the ex-torturers of Abu Ghraib who had served a short prison time, paid a fine, but was still able to pursue his military career. When he was charged with raping a subordinate, a military court acquitted him in spite of numerous witnesses supporting her claim.

Adam resurfaced from the past when Phil squeezed his hand. "It's a crying shame," she said.

"A decision." Adam brought her hand to his lips and kissed it.

CHAPTER 35

Back at the Esperanza, Adam immediately disappeared into his room. Phil understood he needed time alone. She called her son Anton, who had decided to only speak English as long as he was in England, and sent virtual hugs. Then she was alone again with her anxiety.

Still, she had not called her bank, a torturing thought, but it was past five, so it'd be closed now anyway. Phil opened a newspaper. The headline, of course, was Tamar's gruesome death. The plane crash had been moved to page 2. But there was an update in that case: *Poison*, the article's header screamed. They knew now that Maurer, the pilot, had fainted before crashing. Possibly the result of food poisoning or a third party's responsibility. Which would mean murder.

In the advertisement section of the newspaper were some ads of local real estate agents. Phil dialed the first number, but the agent on the phone was not interested in a burnt-down ruin. The second one offered her eighty thousand flat and was not willing to negotiate. The third asked Phil for the address and wanted to take a look before making an offer. Damn. The clock was ticking.

Phil jumped up. She couldn't bear to sit around any longer.

Her beret pulled tightly down, Phil rode the scooter to Santa Eulalia. As it was getting close to Easter, the number of tourists had noticeably risen. On a stage at the sea promenade, a rock band was getting ready for their gig. A crowd of teenagers had already gathered in front, applauding wildly whenever one of the longhaired musicians appeared. It was hot, like in summer. Sweat ran into the wool of Phil's beret.

The door to the *Insular*'s office was open. From the editor-in-chief's office Phil heard Nia's voice, risen to a high pitch, yelling something about her rights. Hans insisted he had rights too. "Maybe not even yours," Nia screamed. Abrupt silence set in. Phil knocked at the door, which immediately opened to Nia's furious face.

"You again!"

"Sorry. I need to talk to Hans one more time."

Behind Nia, Hans was trying hard to recover his composure.

"Phil, sorry, bad timing. We are about to leave. Call me tomorrow, all right."

"You heard it." Nia shut the door right into Phil's face.

"Okay, no problem. Bye." She stomped to the entrance door, opened it and smashed it shut with a bang. Then she tiptoed back to another door that she knew led to a little kitchen. Silently Phil closed it behind her. She could only hope that neither Hans nor Nia needed caffeine before they left.

Voices were heard again, in the hallway now, Nia's theatrically scornful. "Don't freak out, it was you. Which still doesn't make it *yours*. Just keep on doing this shit. I don't care anymore. Right after the birth, I'll be gone anyway."

The doorknob turned. Panicked, Phil pressed herself against the wall behind the door that swung open, right into her face. Through the crack of the door, she could see Nia put a cup into the sink. Her voluminous batik shirt, Phil realized, did not cover excess weight but a baby belly.

From the hallway, Hans pleaded, "Come on, Nia. If they wanna sell Es Vedrà, I can't stop them. I'm only a journalist."

Nia's voice dripped with sarcasm. "Yeah, sure: journalist. Someone who spits on paper what has been dictated to him."

"What a bitch you've become. Vedrà doesn't belong to you guys either."

A spoon smashed into the sink, and the kitchen door closed violently behind the pregnant woman. Phil dared to breathe again and rubbed her nose. Hans could be heard begging Nia to come along. After all, her name was on the guest list. Nia wondered why he didn't get the simple fact that prenatal yoga was more important to her than dinner with, of all people, these jerks.

The entrance door opened and was locked from outside. Damn. Well, Phil would have to deal with that later.

First, she searched the Bisley file cabinets containing Hans's archive—and found nothing. Nothing in the magazine issues sorted by publication dates or in the hanging files with the text material. Nowhere any information on the TAB. One folder contained photos with Scherer: on a construction side, shaking someone's hand, cutting a red ribbon, in the center of people in festive attire. *Oct. 16, 2012,* it read on the back. *Thanks to the generous donation of Jorg Scherer, the Phoenician Museum could be expanded by a new tract.*

Phil studied the photo: there was Amanda in an elegant dress. With a watch that looked like the one in Tamar's drawer, and an absent-minded face. There was her generous husband, grinning his pompous Scherer grin. Next to him was a younger man with a tousled mop of hair and a sour look on his face. Everyone else was smiling. Something in the photo had caught Phil's attention, but what?

She sat down at Hans's desk. His laptop, of course, was secured with a password. On a dog-eared notepad, he had jotted down some keywords: *Pos. perception: sale to Ibiza lover w. relevant resources. Sensitive development. Ensuring ecolog.*

balance. Nat. reserve. Visitor center. Generate jobs. There were also question marks. Hans didn't seem overly convinced of the article he had to write about the sale of Es Vedrà. Spat down on paper what others dictated, Nia had said.

Phil leaned back in the chair, wondering what the hell she was doing. Going through someone's stuff without even a plan. How stupid to be locked in here. Typical. When would she learn to think first and act later? How could she get out now? Jump out the window and break her neck?

Outside on the *ramblas*, the band began to play. The sunlight faded, and when the song ended in a cacophony of guitars and percussion, the Ibizan dusk was over. The audience cheered while Phil, frustrated, turned on the Tolomedo-desk lamp. It threw a perfectly round beam on the blotting pad with the ad of a printing shop and a calendar. Tonight, Hans and Nia were invited to a restaurant uptown. *8 p.m., Amadéo, Plaça de Sol (O. Máral, Cll. Ins.).* "Cll. Ins." probably meant *Consell Insular,* the highest organ of government in Ibiza.

But what was that? Phil took a closer look. Below the entry, the pad was covered with numbers and abbreviations. Also some drawings, probably jotted down while on the phone, absent-minded... Hans had artistic skills. The teased-up hair, the cleavage, the cool expression were of high recognition value. And this number? Phil opened her phone on contacts and saw: it was Tamar's phone number below her portrait. And an ink-line went from there to two letters: R and W. The initials of the guy who had promised Hans a story about the TAB.

Phil took a picture of the pad while the band's next song ended. It was replaced by a noise behind the door. A key in the keyhole. The key turning.

"*Hóla,*" a voice said, "*señor* von Brolow? *Puedo limpiar?*"

When the cleaning lady, armed with a vacuum cleaner, entered, Phil was on the floor, leaning against the open file cabinet. The boss's new assistant who had been organizing the files but fell asleep.

"While *el jefe* already called it a day." Phil yawned. Well, her first day in the office. She'd wanted to show her work ethics. "First impressions count, right?" She closed the cabinet. "I'll be out of your hair. *Buenas noches, señora.*"

"*Buenas noches.*" The vacuum cleaner was switched on. It got loud, and the door was open.

CHAPTER 36

The scooter chugged towards Ibiza City, passing the brightly lit Phoenician Museum on top of Puig de Molins. The mountain's belly was dark, hollowed out by an enormous necropolis. Almost three thousand years ago it was built by the Phoenicians who came to bury their dead here where Tanit would grant them a good afterlife. The Carthaginians still kept the custom when in most parts of the world, the Great Mother had been replaced by all kinds of Gods and Baals.

The city was bustling. All the shops in downtown Sa Penya were open now, offering their arts and crafts and the legendary "ad lib" fashion of Ibiza. The ancestral Phoenician trading genes were fired up, and tourism abided, flocking in droves to spend their money.

Phil parked the scooter in a dark corner below a stone-walled bridge that led to Portal de Ses Taures, the entrance to uptown. The tunnel through the meter-thick Renaissance wall opened up to Plaça de Vila, a romantic, cobblestoned square swarming with tourists, framed by art galleries, souvenir shops and restaurants. The next square, Plaça del Sol, was quieter and had only a handful of exquisite restaurants. An age-old facade conquered by ivy and hydrangea bore the discreetly illuminated name "Amadéo." Hans sat in a group of men in suits and low cut, dressed up women. The chair next to him was empty. Phil sat down.

"Nia couldn't make it. I substitute, okay."

Hans swallowed. "Well..."

"Absolutely." Her neighbor on the other side, a heavyset, middle-aged guy poured red wine into the empty glass in front of Phil. "Onofré Maral. *Encantado, señora.*"

This had to be the guy from the *Consell Insular*. Phil smiled. On the table were dishes with seafood salad and tapas. She was dying with hunger.

"*Salud, amor y dinero.*" Onofré Maral raised his glass. "And you are...?"

"Philine Mann. *Salud.*"

Everyone raised their glass. Phil could feel something exciting in the air, a note of accomplishment. She wondered if it had to do with the selling of Es Vedrà. Was this the celebratory dinner? Hans didn't seem quite sober anymore.

"What are you doing here?" he whispered, emptying his glass in one gulp.

"Oh Hans, I'm sure you know," she said as softly, hoping *señor* Maral didn't understand German. "Tamar. She was the cute girl that introduced you to R. W. Right? She knew a lot about the TAB. And now she is dead."

All blood drained from Hans's face. Hectically, he looked around, but no one at the table had paid attention to Phil's words. *Señor* Maral was busy shuffling seafood onto his plate.

"Not now, okay?" Hans said under his breath. "Wait till we're done here."

The dinner went on for two hours. Phil understood that the important people around the table were not only from the *Consell Insular* but also representatives of the *Escuela Universitaria de Turismo*. Yet, no one mentioned if they celebrated the Es Vedrà deal or something else. Phil had to fend off *señor*

Maral's attentions, while Hans sat there in silence and so solemn Maral asked if he was lovesick or what.

Finally, the evening came to an end. The drunken women were put into cars, the drivers ordered to drop them off at home. The gentlemen who still had things to discuss decided to go for a nightcap. Phil endured Maral's cheek kisses, then followed Hans down Carrer de Sa Creu to a pub where the wine was cheap and smoking only officially prohibited.

"Okay." Suddenly Hans didn't seem drunk anymore. "You are right. Tamar approached me, and R. W. was her boyfriend or a friend. She called him Rob, and from all I could tell he was crazy about her."

He lit a cigarette. Phil waited silently.

"No question, R. W. knew a lot about the TAB. He not only pretended. And he despised them, that was crystal clear. He had a whole data file of photos."

Hans sighed, then hastily kept on talking as if he feared his courage would leave him. "Photos of the Bes Brothers having their orgies, as you suspected. Really decadent stuff. And the Brothers themselves—guys you find on cover pictures of business magazines or in the news. Also local VIPs. Onofré Maral, for instance. He's head of the *Consell Insular* and just received a big chunk of money from the EU for the tourism school of Ibiza. Funds he will fiddle with as usual, so a good percentage ends up in his own pockets. He was on a number of snapshots, in group sex and some other disgusting, kind of occult stuff. Also *Herr* Scherer. And girls that look no older than twelve. Had this been published, it would have been the biggest scandal the island had ever seen."

"So you had the evidence and proof you needed."

"Right. I *had*." Hans nervously ran his fingers through his hair. "But all of the sudden, they disappeared. The photos, the whole file on my hard drive, the backup and R. W. himself—vanished into thin air. And sweet Tamar suddenly didn't know of a Rob, had no idea who and what I was talking about. You should have seen her: she lied without batting an eye. I was so mad I published the article without photos; after all I had seen them with my very eyes. 'Bunga Bunga on Ibiza,' I titled it. Immediately the TAB's lawyers showed up. You know the rest."

"But who could have fiddled with your PC? Who in your office..." Phil's eyes widened. "Nia?"

Hans's crestfallen expression confirmed it. He feared the mother of his unborn child was the traitor.

"But this doesn't make sense," he desperately said. "Why should Nia, out of all people, protect the TAB brothers? She hates them. No, it can't be Nia. Could Tamar have broken into your office? I mean since she obviously changed her mind about the whole thing."

"She was there only once, didn't have a key, and how would she have figured out my password? It's a real hard one."

"I know—I mean, I imagine."

"It must have been a professional hacker."

Or Nia after all, Phil thought. But how could this make sense? And why would Tamar approach Hans and initiate a scandal and then drop him without getting what she came for? Because someone paid her to keep her mouth shut?

"Did Tamar work for Scherer at the time she came to you?"

Hans shrugged. "Guess she knew him. But work for him? I don't know. When I asked her how R. W. had gotten hold of the photos, she said she was like Mata Hari and had infiltrated him into the TAB. Only to pretend later I had dreamt it all up. She was the most ruthless woman I have ever met."

So, bribery seemed the most logical explanation. Phil could well see Tamar accepting money and possibly a job from Scherer in exchange for ditching Hans. And R. W. either played along, or Tamar ditched him, too, so she alone could profit from the hush money. And then? Maybe she had wanted more and threatened Scherer to make her knowledge of the

TAB public after all. So he had to get rid of her. But how could Tamar be a Daughter of Tanit, a feminist, and at the same time work for and sleep with Scherer who had orgies with minors? A confusing scenario. Everything seemed to be connected, yet nothing made sense.

"Another thing I don't understand: Why is Scherer so keen on buying Es Vedrà? What of interest is there? I mean, is there more than just rocks?"

Hans looked at her in surprise. "What are you thinking of?"

"Maybe an old treasure? Something valuable."

Hans let out a shrill laugh. "Oh, come on. No, it's just a rich client who wants his own island. That's how they are."

Still there was something new in his eyes. *They* weren't good liars.

The waiter started to heave chairs on tables; it was time to go. Down in Sa Penya, Hans offered to give Phil a ride home. "This time of the night, there are only drunk drivers on the roads."

Phil wasn't sure how much less drunk than other potential drivers Hans was. However, not to ride the Vespa across Ibiza in the pitch dark was a tempting idea.

It was past one o'clock when they arrived at the Esperanza. Only one light fell through a window on the second floor—Adam's room. Phil could hardly wait to tell him what she had found out.

"Thanks, Hans," she said when they had unloaded the scooter. "So what are you going to do now?"

"Don't know. Sell my business and get the hell out of here. Maybe Mallorca, or back north." Hans sighed profoundly. "There was a time when I decided what was published in the *Insular* or not. Now, it's like living under Mafia rule, controlled by the Marals and Scherers and such. Nia accused me of being their slave, not a journalist, and she's right. I've had it."

"But we can't just leave it at that. I mean: the TAB. The girls. Tamar. Someone killed her."

"I don't care. The bitch ruined me. And I don't want to end up like her."

And like Amanda. And Ninguno and his daughter. In a way, Phil could understand Hans's fear as well as his humiliation.

"In the good old days, Nia would have followed me everywhere. Do you remember how jealous she was of you?" Hans smiled nostalgically. Then his face turned grim, "Now she's expecting my child and intends to raise it without me. Because only the mother counts or some bullshit. So there's nothing left for me here. You are leaving Ibiza too, right? What do you say? Let's go together."

Suddenly Hans's arms were around Phil, pulling her close. Pressing his lips on hers. Right when the door to the Esperanza opened, and Adam appeared.

"Stop it!" With both hands, Phil pushed Hans away. "What the hell, Hans?"

"Oh come on, Phil—didn't we have a great time together?"

Ages ago, for two nights, yes. But it never meant a thing. Only a fling. Phil pushed harder, and reluctantly, Hans let go.

"No chance, Hans, sorry."

She looked over to Adam who already turned around. "Hey, Adam, wait."

Only now, Hans realized the other man. He jerked back. "I get it. Shit. Sorry." He almost ran back to his Jeep.

Adam sat down on the patio, his face like stone. Phil plunged down next to him, rolled a cigarette, reached it to him and rolled another one for herself. Already kind of a ritual between them.

"That was Hans von Brolow, the editor of this German magazine I told you about. I once worked there for a few weeks. No idea what he was thinking just now, but—well, but tonight I learned some really interesting things from him."

She told him.

"Wow," Adam said when she was finished. "Good work, Miss Smilla."

"Huh?"

He broke out in a grin. "And I thought I was the pro." The awkwardness between them was gone. "We need these photos. That Bartolo is after Scherer for killing Tamar is good, but not enough. I also want justice for Amanda. And Ninguno and his daughter."

"Exactly what I want too."

"So first we have to find R. W. What do we know about him?"

"He's German, and Tamar called him Rob, Hans said."

"This Hans, are you two...?" The very moment those words involuntarily slipped Adam's lips, his phone rang.

"Hell no. Admitted: an ex."

Adam parked his cigarette on the edge of the patio railing and put the phone to his ear. "This is Adam—oh, hello, General Kearns. Yessir. I'm listening."

Phil remembered that his colleague and ex, this flirty Lori with her "Adam baby" had mentioned General Kearns. His voice barked out of the phone, reminding Adam of his patriotic duty. He strictly forbade him to disclose any connection between Colonel Cruz, Ibiza, and this gentleman's club to anyone, in any circumstance, ever. This, the general bellowed, was a high-priority official order.

"Sir..."

But the man in Washington kept on barking until Adam interrupted him, determined. "Sorry, sir, I'm an investigator, not a cover-upper."

A moment of silence followed. Adam looked surprised by his own words. Then Kearns's rhetoric storm started anew.

"No sir," Adam repeated firmly, "I'm sorry, but I cannot and will not do this. So yes, I accept the consequences. Goodbye." The phone went dead.

"What?" Phil asked.

Adam took a last drag and threw the butt into an ashtray. "The Office is worried that I, due to my personal situation—meaning my sister's death—am not impartial enough these days to do my job. I'm told to immediately return to the U.S. or bear the consequences. Which, you heard me, I accept."

Phil could think of only one word, "Bravo!"

CHAPTER 37

It had happened, he lost his job. Adam was lying on his bed trying to figure out what this meant to him. Probably relief, at least in parts, as he had been questioning his task for a while. Now it was done.

All right, then. He would bring this mess to a conclusion and then think about the future. He had some savings, his military pension and the five-bedroom villa his father had left him, a veritable McMansion in Plano. He would sell the monster, should have done it long ago. Then he could think about moving to the prairie. He imagined a farmhouse with a barn he would convert into a garage, a few cars to work on, a dog to pet. Peace and quiet.

But suddenly, there was Phil's face in front of Adam, when he wished her a good night. He was not sure what her expression had meant. Relief or disappointment? He had never been able to read Phil's mind. Well, why should it matter? It didn't make sense to spark off a fire that would only burn them again and leave nothing but scorched earth. Phil, Adam thought, must think the same. How hard she tried to keep her distance. How she turned quiet every time he asked about her life. This one night, a mere twenty-four hours ago, was already a thing of the past. A memory he would store way back in his mind and eventually forget.

Only he knew it wasn't true. Not even an option. For Adam, the night before had been like coming home. He had to admit he still had feelings for Phil, whether he liked it or not. Feelings that had infected him and could not be killed, like malaria or Lyme disease. Dangerous.

What the hell was he doing? Adam sat up. He had to take his mind off these things. Now. He opened his MacBook, googled Colonel Andrew Cruz and learned that the man on top of the military elite had just been proposed as successor for the ousted CIA Director. Of course his hands had to be immaculately clean.

Next, Adam googled the other American who had owned a villa on Ibiza and whom Dziri had mentioned in connection with the TAB: Bud Winslow, the ultra-conservative radio host. He had used his microphone to keep people in sync with his belligerent idea of God, rant against refugees, liberated women, blacks, gays, and drugs. And was found, full of opioids and dead, in a gay strip club known for their extra-juicy decadence. What a hypocrite.

Adam tried to sleep, only to realize that General Kearns's attempt to put him in his place still pricked his pride. He again opened his MacBook and formulated his resignation from the Office, in the end quoting himself: *I have always been an investigator in the service of truth and will not be reduced to a cover-upper of it, even if it concerns a Colonel's reputation. For less than the truth, I am no longer willing to serve my country.*

Without further hesitation, Adam hit the send button.

In the morning, Bartolo's police car, recognizable by its purple reflex foam cushion on the driver's seat, was parked in front of the hotel. It was almost ten, so Huber must already have faced Scherer in the identity parade. This time, Adam knocked at Phil's door and opened it when he heard her "Come in."

"Morning." She smiled at him. "Ready? Let's go!"

Obviously, she had not been yearning for him through the night. "Sure."

"You think Scherer confessed?" She nodded towards an old backpack on a chair. "After breakfast I will bring Doro her stuff and ask about this Rob. She or Jezebel may know of a German friend of Tamar's."

"Good idea. I bet Bartolo questioned Scherer about him too. They must have known each other, if Rob really is an insider in the TAB. Bartolo is here."

They sat down on the patio and waited, but no Bartolo showed up. Not even Lluis. Strange. After breakfast, they knocked at the door to his office.

"Lluis? It's Adam and Phil."

"Come in," a muffled voice answered, "all the way through."

With hanging arms, Lluis was standing in his living room. Bartolo was crouched on the sofa, his face buried in a cushion.

"Bartolo?" Adam asked in astonishment.

The inspector seemed to have a hard time lifting his head. "It wasn't him."

"What?" Phil and Adam asked in unison.

"Scherer. *Porca miseria.* It wasn't him on the cliffs." Bartolo exhaled a mighty sigh. "For once, the airline confirmed he was on the plane. But worse: Ezra Huber didn't recognize him. He says the guy in the car was way younger than Scherer, with brown hair and only some wisps of gray."

"Damn." Adam punched the doorframe. "How many Bentley Mulsannes are on this island? I thought you had his tire tracks."

"We do. This is inexplicable to Scherer. He swears his car was in the carport when he left for Mallorca."

"And in the car..."

"Besides his and Tamar's fingerprints we've got tons of

samples we can't attribute to anyone specific yet. Scherer says, of course Tamar was in his car on occasions, as well as a lot of other people. We also have the statement of the cab driver who picked him up at seven. Scherer doesn't like to leave the Bentley at the airport. He took the 8:25 flight. As much as we'd like it—it wasn't him."

"But the time frame," Phil threw in, "I saw the Bentley on the cliffs right after sunrise. When does the sun rise? Around 6:30?"

"6:20. Scherer says someone must have stolen his car."

"And brought her back afterwards? Friendly thief." Adam was frustrated.

"How can this even be possible?" Phil was stubborn. "So, someone stole the car in the night without Scherer noticing it. What about the alarm system? The engine-noise? Then the thief got Tamar into the car, killed her, knocked me out and brought the car back after sunrise. Again without Scherer noticing anything, right around the time he was waiting for his cab. Is the man deaf, dumb and blind? Give me a break."

Adam and Bartolo agreed. It didn't make sense.

"But," Bartolo sighed again, "we have Mr. Huber's statement. He swears it was a younger man. But who?"

CHAPTER 38

The next hours seemed like inert mass. Phil felt the pressure like a migraine, but couldn't make her fingers dial the number of her bank. Tomorrow, she swore, she'd deal with it. In the afternoon, she shouldered Doro's backpack and set out for Can Follet. But when she was on the coastal trail, she spun around and ran back for the scooter key. The memory of being knocked out, right here on the cliff, was still too fresh.

The sun was standing high when Phil arrived. Sounds of happiness drifted up from Cala d'Hort, screaming kids, laughter, and music that contrasted sharply the solemn atmosphere at the resort. The woman in the guardhouse, wrapped in a white robe and veil, looked like an abandoned bride.

Only in the yard, the yoga-group doing *asanas* created an illusion of normality. Inside Can Follet, an eerie silence reigned. The female fantasy world seemed frozen in a state of shock. Manasa, the young Indian, sat crouched in a chair. When Phil gently said hello, she stared at her like a trapped cat. Tamar's murder must have conjured the horror she had had to endure.

Suddenly, one pure, exclusive emotion swept over Phil: hatred. Hatred against those who, simply because of physical strength, were able to destroy other human beings. Hatred against traditions and social systems that enabled it.

Almost shocked by the extent of her feeling, Phil, a declared pacifist, realized she wanted to see the men who had abused Manasa suffer. They should hurt like they had hurt her. *An eye for an eye, a tooth for a tooth.* Also Tamar's murderer: Phil wished she could force him to stare into the abyss, knowing these were the last moments of his life.

She took a deep breath to get a hold of herself, while Bridget, the Scottish woman, brought Manasa a cup of tea. As brash and loud-mouthed as she had acted before, she now was all empathy and motherly care. Phil felt a bit comforted knowing that among the Daughters of Tanit, human compassion still reigned.

Stella, the black woman with the star tattoo around her eye, was watching her from behind her desk. Phil went over to her.

"Stella, it's so cruel." Then she blurted out, "Is this why you call Ibiza a rotten island? With all the horror?"

Stella seemed to hesitate, then she sighed and merely nodded. "Isn't it reason enough?"

"Absolutely. But..." Phil just couldn't put her finger on this strange feeling she had about Stella. Neither could she put it in words. So she gave up and only asked, "How does Jezebel cope?"

"Don't ask. She's a complete wreck."

In the morning, Stella said, Jezebel had consulted the oracle of the *hadas*, the fairies of wisdom. She implored them to show her how Tamar was doing in the otherworld. But the wise women remained silent, no matter how Jezebel begged. After this, she suffered a breakdown. She hadn't stopped crying yet.

Phil could only imagine how Tamar's mother must feel. Sadly, she asked for Anat who, Stella said, was on the roof patio, where she tried to get in contact with Tamar through meditative immersion. Phil could go check if she was done meditating, but to leave her alone if not.

Anat was sitting cross-legged on a yoga mat, exposed to the glistening afternoon sun. Her hands were resting on her knees, palms opened up towards the sky, eyes closed. On the stairhead, Phil hesitated. But when Anat opened her eyes and stretched, she approached on tiptoes.

"Phil."

"I hope I don't bother you..."

"No. I've spent enough time begging the goddamn cosmos to react."

With a sigh of relief, Anat unwound her legs and got up. She gave Phil a hug, smelling a bit sweaty from sitting in the sun for long. They stepped into the shadow.

"So," Phil wasn't sure if she was asking in earnest, "it didn't work then, your heavenly request?"

Doro snorted. "For a moment, I thought I was getting a signal. But I guess I just nodded off, and the shape of the Goddess was only in my dream."

"Do you seriously believe this stuff?" Phil asked in honest wonder, "I mean that you can get in contact with the cosmos, and a Goddess will speak to you?"

Anat gave her a stern glance. "Well, of course I do." But then, a grin spread over her face, and Phil saw good, old Doro emerging. This one scratched her butt and yawned with her mouth wide open.

"Frankly," she said, "it doesn't matter if I personally believe in the Goddess's appearance—or even existence—or not. What counts is the power of faith. Jezebel believes Tamar's death is only a transformation and that she's now living with the Great Mother. This gives her comfort and hope. By no means is her faith more absurd than the one of millions of people who believe in someone's resurrection, or that his body materializes in a chip of white bread. Or that dead bodies are selected to either go to heaven or hell."

"Okay, but you..." Phil didn't know how to formulate her question.

"I've made a decision." Doro looked at the rock standing in the sea like a solemn, atavistic cathedral. "If there is faith, we can change the world. To the better or worse. Have you ever heard about the hunt of billy goats on Es Vedrà?"

"Yeah. Awful."

"Right, that's what it is. A sadistic tradition based on a pre-Christian ritual. A male goat, or Capricorn, has always been the cultic companion of the Great Mother. So when men brought her down and replaced her by a male fake god, they started the goat hunt. A symbolic murderous act."

Phil decided to be open. "Are you suggesting that Tamar's murder has something to do with this? With male aggression against women?"

The answer was firm. "Without any doubt."

"Scherer?"

Doro wiped sweat off her forehead. "An obvious assumption, isn't it?"

"But then—I just don't get it. Why in the world did Tamar work for him?"

"I know, right? I asked her about it, and she pretended to do it for a good reason. For us. Infiltration, she called it, as if she was Mata Hari. I think it was more about her personal profit." Doro sighed, "Tamar was stupid. She underestimated men. That's always dangerous." She bent down to roll up her yoga mat.

"You didn't like her, did you?"

"I tried," Doro admitted, "but I couldn't. Tamar confused our philosophy with a dumb power game. She was greedy and wanted to dominate, be the tamer. She was so convinced of herself she didn't realize males, even weak men like Scherer, are beasts that can only be tamed when well fed."

"But now we know Scherer has an alibi."

"What? For real? An official alibi?"

Phil summarized what Bartolo had found out. She could see how Doro's brain worked feverishly. If not Scherer—who else?

"Maybe her murder has to do with the TAB, this men's club," Phil said. "As far as we know, Tamar organized some— events for them."

"I can't imagine. Who is this man Tamar was in the car with?"

"If we only knew. But why can't you imagine?"

Doro only shrugged, averting Phil's eyes.

"One more thing: Do you know a friend of Tamar called Rob? A German?"

"Rob?" Doro tried to remember, "There was a Robert, I think. But wasn't he American? Tamar had many boyfriends, so I lost track."

"I thought I could ask Jezebel about him..."

"No way. Not now. She's devastated and must be spared every extra stress."

Of course, Doro was right. Silence fell between them as they looked across the bay, bathed in sunlight. Beautiful, how it glittered on the water and dressed the waves with silver linings. *El sol* came to Phil's mind, the bringer of light, *Phoibos Apollon,* the most handsome of Gods.

They walked down the staircase. Thinking about the sun had brought back the little tune Tamar had sung the last time Phil saw her: "The sun and stars don't only shine on one man/ They shine on whomever is their pleasure..."

She stopped so abruptly, Doro bumped into her. In all clarity, Phil saw the man in front of her who had grabbed Tamar's wrist so hard it had left red marks. He perfectly matched Huber's description of the man in the car: a lot younger than Scherer, tall, brown-haired. The man Phil had taken for Adam.

Doro had no idea who that might be. She had hardly left Can Follet in the last months, she said as they entered the quiet lobby, only when she went to meditate on Es Vedrà.

Phil frowned in surprise. The last months?

Just then, Jezebel's wheelchair came buzzing towards them. Her face was swollen from all the tears she had shed. Even more heartbreaking was the glimmer of hope in her eyes at the sight of Anat.

"Anat. Did you see her? Could you get in contact with my daughter?"

Like a chameleon, Doro had already changed her colors and was the motherly priestess. She raised her hands as if she wanted to bless the poor woman.

"I think I did see our dear Tamar," she lied, her voice carrying a dignified tone, "and she is at peace. But she first has to settle into afterlife before she can contact us mortals. It was a rather weak connection, I admit, but enough to know that the Goddess is watching over her."

"That's wonderful." Jezebel broke out in tears.

Anat bent down and took her into her arms. Hot tears dripped on her sunburned shoulder while she rocked Jezebel to and fro, again and again repeating some strange words, *"Kadoish, kadoish kadoish, Schechina Aschtarot."*

Phil was overcome by pity. Of course Doro was right to give all the comfort she could to the grieving mother, and if it meant mumbling strange magical words. Especially since it worked. After a while, Jezebel lifted her head from Anat's shoulder, wiped her eyes and didn't seem quite as desperate anymore. A heartfelt "thank you" went to her priestess, a nod to Phil, and the wheelchair rolled off.

"See, Phil," Doro said, "that's how religion works." She smiled melancholically. "And I'm looking forward to a shower. Then I have to take care of our guests. But I'd love to have dinner with you. Tomorrow—what do you say?"

"Sure. Just you and me?"

"Just us. You know, I love my responsibilities here, but sometimes it can get a bit much to always be the mother. The alpha animal. Then I actually start to miss university and even those fruitless discussions with my ex-colleagues." Doro pulled a face. "Did I really just say this? If it even crosses my mind to miss these jerks, I guess I need a little time-out from being the great Anat."

She tugged at her embroidered silk tunic, "And from all that. What about San José? You still like Can Manyanet?"

When Doro moved to the island, Phil had recommended her this genuine Ibizan restaurant, loved by locals and foreign *residentes* alike.

"Yes. Let's do it."

They agreed to meet at nine p.m., hugged, and when Doro had disappeared down the hallway, Phil flitted by the exit into Tamar's room.

In there, everything looked heartbreakingly alive. Phil was taken aback by Tamar's presence emanating from her chaotic cloth rack, her now orphaned high-heeled shoes, the squadron of cosmetic tubes. Tamar's face with all that make-up appeared in Phil's mind, her provocative giggle, quoting Shakespeare: "Hell is empty, and all the devils are here."

Phil had planned to sneak in here, put back the remote key she had taken last time and disappear again. But now she hesitated: Was this really a good idea? Tamar would never know anymore. Hadn't Adam mentioned a forthcoming party of the TAB Brothers? With the key, they had a chance to check what was going on in Can Salammbo. And while she was here...

Instead of putting back the key, Phil started to rummage through the desk drawer. It was almost ridiculously easy to find what she was looking for: a well-thumbed address book. Under the letter R was a Robert Wendling, Christoph-Knips Street 17, in 60435 Frankfurt. The German R. W! Phil typed address and phone number into her phone. A quick check in another drawer: the probably stolen Cartier watch was still there. Phil had to tell Adam about it.

Back at the door, she heard steps coming down the hall. A

voice. Shit. Phil froze. Amy's voice.

"It's confirmed," she said with audible pride. "Fourth month."

"Oh my God." This now was Trudy, her voice a bit shrill and muddled at the same time. "But—how? I mean by whom? I didn't know you were with someone. Oh, Ezra will be delighted. His first grandchild. You're going to get married now, right, Amy? Who is the father?"

"Wrong questions, mother." Amy sounded as if she was talking to a moronic child. "Have you still not gotten it? My baby is none of Ezra's business, nor from whom I got the semen."

"But, honey—that's not how it works."

"Yes, mother, it works only this way." Amy laughed. "And you know it."

The voices faded away. Phil slipped out of Tamar's room and headed towards the main door.

When she arrived at the Esperanza, she realized that Adam's car was not there. Neither did he answer his phone. Phil called Bartolo Dziri, who praised her investigative skills and immediately wanted to call a colleague in Frankfurt about Robert Wendling. He had no idea where Adam was.

Okay. She could have a glass of wine and wait until he got back. But should she? Patience was not Phil's forte. She studied the map of Ibiza hanging in the lobby. Five kilometers behind San Miguel was the turn to Cala Benirras, the bay Bartolo had mentioned where the TAB Brothers' meeting place was, Can Salammbo. She only would take a look. Phil restarted the scooter.

CHAPTER 39

The traffic through Sant Antoni de Portmany was pure hell, crammed with rental cars. For this harbor town with its history of wild drinking parties, the always inventive Ibizans had created the name "Tanga City." San Antonio's charms were not as obvious as the ones of Ibiza City, but it also had things to offer: a sea promenade lined by lush caoutchouc plants and palm trees, the best views of the dramatic sunsets, and the *Ou de Colom*, an egg-shaped sculpture displaying a model of the *Santa Maria*, the flagship on which Columbus sailed to America. The bay also offered a scenic view of *La Conejera*, the "rabbit island," believed to be the legendary Tricuarda, birthplace of the Carthaginian Hannibal.

Phil almost missed the tiny sign to Cala Benirras. The scooter stuttered up a steep track, smoothly paved and lined by oleander bushes. Here, the lots and villas were of enormous proportions, vacation homes of Big Money folks. Up the hill, a half-moon-shaped ramp led to a massive portal that bore two metal letters: C S. Through the iron bars Phil got a glimpse at an impressive mansion in the Moorish style of the Alhambra: Can Salammbo.

She turned the scooter off, and things went quiet. The air

seemed paralyzed by the afternoon heat. Then somewhere behind the gate, a lawn mover started to chug. Phil mumbled
"shit," as it meant someone was at home. So? She wondered
about herself. Had she, even for a moment, considered using
the key? Seriously, she told herself, she had come to throw a
glance. Only a glance.

The chugging got louder. Through the bars, Phil saw a
huge lawnmower move into the front yard. On it sat a giant
man in green gardener's pants and an undershirt that showed
incredibly muscular arms. Phil squatted down to not be seen.
Suddenly, there was a wet snout right in her face.

"*Guapo*," someone called. "Come here, Guapo. Leash."

The dog, a typical Ibizan black and white Podenco-mix,
gave Phil another slobbery dog kiss. An elderly man with a chic
straw hat came closer, waving a leash. Phil pretended a screw
at her scooter had to be adjusted.

"So sorry," the man said, "Guapo still has to learn. I just
got him from the shelter."

"Oh, don't worry." Phil patted the dog's head. "Guapo,
what a fitting name. He is very pretty. For me, you don't need
to put him on the leash."

But the man had already attached it at Guapo's collar,
causing ear-whirling protest. "Thank you, miss. But this one
would mind." He nodded towards the giant on the tractor. "If
my Guapo sets one paw on the lot, Martí Blasco freaks out."

"Why in the world? Is he crazy?"

"Indeed he is. Deaf-mute and crazy." But the man grinned
in good humor. "At least he listens better to his master than
my boy." He pulled at the leash. "Now, Guapo, let's go home.
You have a wonderful day, miss."

"Just a second, please." Phil pointed at the mansion. "This
is Can Salammbo, isn't it?" When the man nodded, she added
as nonchalantly as if she could afford such a mansion, "I heard
it's up for sale. We, my family and I, are looking for a vacation
home, quiet and big enough for all of us."

"I had no idea the villa was on the market."

"TAB real estate is offering it. Mr. Scherer. You know him?"

A shrug was the answer. And, if Phil wasn't mistaken, a hint of contempt.

"As I said, we need something quiet. You live close by?"

"Two houses down." The man pointed to the left. "And we would love if someone seeking peace and quiet bought Can Salammbo. So please do."

"Is there a problem?"

"Rather a disgrace. But I don't want to gossip."

He made a goodbye gesture with two fingers at his hat. "Guapo, we have to tell this to the Missus. Goodbye, miss; I hope to welcome you soon in the hood." He smiled when Phil gave Guapo another pet, then they were gone.

And now? What was she supposed to do? Turn around without anything? Phil felt for the remote key. Or was there a way to snoop a bit without getting caught by the crazy giant on the tractor? Who, shit, seemed to have taken notice of her. She jumped on the scooter and cranked up the engine.

The wall around Can Salammbo extended some hundred meters parallel to the track before it gave way to wasteland. An idyllic field lined by rosemary and Aleppo pines looked as if it had been painted on a canvas of blue. Phil turned into a trail along the western side of the castle-like wall. Thorny ground cover scratched her ankles, loose gravel made it hard to steer the scooter. After a while she gave up, hid it behind a scooped-down pine trunk and walked.

The trail ended on top of a cliff, at a staircase. Below it, a small bay nestled to the overhang that cast long shadows across the beach. Only a few bathers still lay in its still sunny far corner. Over there, the sand was coarse and spiked by jagged rocks; below Can Salammbo it was pristine, golden sugar. A wooden pier cutting right through the bay stressed the social injustice of this world: on the public side some old fishing boats were knotted to its posts. On the sugar beach side, two exclusive yachts were gently rocked by the waters.

On the wall's massive back door a sign warned: *Atencion perros peligrosos*. But if there were any dangerous dogs, wouldn't they bark?

What now? This Martí Blasco, Phil thought, would be busy for a while mowing the park-sized yard. So maybe it wouldn't hurt to throw a glance into the villa. Only through the windows. Too bad the remote key wasn't of any use; the back door had an old-fashioned lock. But a pine tree leaned against the wall, one branch touching the metal roof of a shed with set up solar panels. A climbable tree. So of course Phil climbed. She slid along the branch, pulled herself up onto the roof, hiding behind one of the panels, just in case. What a noise her boots made on the metal. An idiotic idea of her shoemaker to strengthen the heels with iron. In the yard, the blind spot between shed and wall stored some propane cylinders, easy to be used as a slide. Now Phil was on the villa's premises.

The back facade was in the same Moorish style as the front with elegant columns, chiseled brickwork and arched windows. The shutters in the first floor were open, but the windows were too high to peek in. Phil prowled around the eastern corner of the villa where the architect had foregone all decor. The wall, only a few feet away, kept this side in eternal semi-darkness. There were four wooden doors. The first two were locked, but the rusty handle of the third one screeched and moved down.

Without wasting a thought on reason, Phil stepped into the stinking darkness of a stable. On the floor, rabbits were huddled together in way too small cages. Some that had made it through torn wire mash hopped around her feet. Poor things. Phil knelt down and petted a white buck's trembling snout.

What in the world was she doing? Just taking a look, she comforted herself. Trespassing, a stern voice in her head said. She should get the hell out. Liberate the rabbits to do one good deed and disappear. Or she could try to find out what was going on here.

She opened all the cages, then the door to the yard. Mesmerized, the rabbits turned their long-eared heads towards the faint strip of daylight. The white one gave Phil a look as if asking whether he should dare.

"Run," Phil whispered, and the little beast took off, triggering an exodus of runaways. If they ran in the right direction, they could easily crawl out under the wooden gate. Phil, however, didn't follow the rabbits, but switched off her brain and opened the other door in the stall. It led to the villa's back entrance, kept open by a bucket and mop.

She stepped across it and was in Can Salammbo.

A swing door with panels of black leather opened up to an extensive lounge with a bar full of high-spirit bottles. A beverage fridge was stocked with wine and champagne of sinfully expensive brands. On the counter paraded a troop of ice buckets in spotless shiny silver. Suddenly, Phil gasped. Someone was standing there—no, only a life-sized but lifeless figure wrapped in a cardinal red cloth. Its shape identified it as Bes, the god with the enormous dick.

Elegant French doors allowed a view into the extensive courtyard, shaded by palm trees and furnished by table groups and loungers around an oval swimming pool. In the hallway, large windows opened the view to the front yard—where the noise of the lawn mower suddenly died down. Alarmed, Phil peeked out, but the gardener only got off his machine to rake the mowed grass. He pushed it towards an ancient cistern in the far corner of the park. As if dealing with a pastry fork, he lifted the big wooden rake and threw one pile of grass after the other into the shaft. Not even a third of the lawn was done mowing and raking, so he still had a lot to do.

Phil tiptoed up a wide staircase to the second floor. A thick carpet swallowed every noise of her steps. There were doors to the right and left, some standing open, leading to pompously decorated bedrooms with chandeliers and polished brass candle holders. Curtains in dark velvet, pornographic oil paintings and big TV screens. In front of mirrored walls were gold-framed whirlpools and the hugest beds Phil had ever seen. At the end of the hallway was an abandoned trolley with piles of bed linen and a door with a sign: *Privado.*

Phil pressed an ear against the door but didn't hear a thing. She moved the handle and was in an office. Its walls were covered with shelves holding long rows of folders, a safe in one corner. An enormous black desk hosted an Apple-Retina-iMac, a phone, piles of papers.

Tamar must have been here: Next to the phone lay the big silver bracelet in form of a self-entwined snake that Phil had admired when she met her on the ferry. Here maybe absentmindedly taken off while its owner was talking on the phone, and then forgotten. So, Tamar had worked in the clubhouse of the TAB! And must have been here after Phil saw her the last time. In the café, with the man who probably was her murderer, she had also worn her snake.

On a roll-top desk next to the big one was a pile of slit open letters and a silver opening blade. The phone's display was blinking a red 13, the number of messages received. Without thinking twice, Phil pushed the button, and an automatic voice said, "Message One. March 8, 9:33 p.m." The announcement was followed by a female voice talking in German with an obvious American accent.

"Honey, I don't want to fight anymore either. So sure, let's meet tonight at home and talk. I'm looking forward to you bringing champagne. Please don't be too late, okay? I'll be waiting for you."

Kind of macabre to listen to a deceased person's voice. It sounded tense, as if Amanda had tried to encourage herself. March 8th. Was this the night she died from poisoned champagne? Scherer had promised to bring champagne...

Phil went through the next messages, mostly informative stuff, confirmations of a registration, questions concerning accommodations or cars. A subcontractor announcing a delivery with a complicated technical name. Then Tamar, chirping, "Hey, I'm back, call me." The last message from this morning was by a bossy voice yapping into the phone.

"Listen, Scherer, that's not how it works. We get the impression that you are lacking the necessary control over the organization and especially the bitches. What the fuck, Scherer? You have to solve this, and I mean: right now! You and no one else, *capisce*! If you do not provide an immediate replacement and proceed exactly as you were told, we will have to consider consequences."

Replacement. A shiver ran down Phil's spine. No thirty-six hours after Tamar was killed, Scherer was ordered to replace someone. Her?

Phil picked up the first letter on the roll-box desk. It was addressed to TAB, c/o Jorg Scherer, San Miguel, *en lista de correos,* a post office box. The sender's address was Frankfurt; the name: K. Maurer.

Suddenly, there was a sound at Phil's back. She instinctively let the letter slide into her waistband and pulled her shirt down. The sound was like the panting of a huge dog. *Perros peligrosos*—dangerous dogs after all? Shit shit shit. Phil whirled around. And froze. A dog would have been the better option.

From close, the gardener looked even more gigantic and violent. Fattened up like a Sumo-wrestler, with a burly, bald head and sagging tits under his dirty tank top. He grunted. Deep-set eyes stared at Phil, blank rounds like metal bullets, without any expression or intellect. He was blocking the door.

Martí Blasco's mouth, wide like a barn door, ejected another grunt that had nothing to do with words. Deaf-mute and crazy, the neighbor had said. With shovel-like hands Blasco

pushed himself off the doorframe. Despite his massive appearance he moved fast, a steamroller, ready to overrun whatever
was in his way. But to reach Phil, he moved away from the
door. Her only chance.

She took it. With a desperate jump, she was around the
desk and seemed to run right into the man. But instead, she
kicked the roll-top desk into his way. A tsunami of letters
poured over his feet, while Phil made a rabbit-change to the
door. Blasco howled and grabbed for her but at the same time
tried not to trample the letters. Phil ducked under his paw,
was out of the door, in the hallway. A ferocious kick catapulted
the trolley with the bed linen into the door, blocking her
chaser.

She raced to the staircase. A clattering noise. Blasco had
just overrun the trolley. Again this panting behind her. Phil
darted down the stairs, through the back hallway, across the
yard. On her way, she kicked over the bucket with the mop.
Water spilled, while she disappeared in the pitch black of the
stable. But wait, where were the rabbit cages, the door she'd
kept open? When her eyes got used to the dark, Phil realized
she had run into the wrong shed.

It contained a strange construction, a massive rack with a
car on top and a metal slide in the back. But it wasn't a car; it
didn't have wheels but some kind of metallic thrusters and a
turbine, a belly like a whale's and two Plexiglas cupolas. Behind it, the door to the backyard was locked. Desperately, Phil
ran back out to the next shed. The stinking one, with the
empty cages and the bit of daylight falling through the open
back door. The rabbits had made it out, but there was the
panting again and Martí Blasco's massive presence. Phil
kicked the metal cages into his way. He stumbled, got up
again, just waltzed over them.

But now Phil was at the right door and banged it shut behind her. Only to hear splintering wood. Blasco didn't even
bother to push down the handle, just went through the

wooden panel as if it was air. She swooped down the alley to the shed at the wall. No way to make it back up across the slick gas bottles. But the empty wicker basket. Phil turned it upside down; yes, it was stable enough to climb and, balancing on its base, she tried to pull herself up to the roof. The sharp metal edge cut into her palms; and then Blasco was right behind her. Howling in triumph, he kicked over the wicker basket so Phil was left dangling, her palm cutting even deeper into the metal, blood dripping. Her legs kicked the air. Her muscles gave way. Not one second longer...

"Your hand."

The moment Blasco managed to grab her right ankle, a strong hand from the other side seized her wrists. With her free foot, Phil kicked back, right into Blasco's face and heard something snap. A cry of pain; the grip released, and her ankle was free. Immediately, Phil was pulled up. Her body stretched like a rubber band while she slid on her belly across the metal roof. Her jeans ripped. With merry clanks, the remote key toppled across the roof, into the yard.

"Have you gained weight? Jump."

Hormones of fear roared through Phil's system. Adam pulled her across the roof and down the tree. She jumped and landed safely on the ground.

"No more than three pounds. Or four. Maybe you lost muscle mass?"

"Hell, Phil."

Her toes hurt from the collision with Blasco's nose. On the other side of the wall, the gardener was rattling at the door. Luckily, the bolts sounded stuck, rusty from the rains and salty air. Still, no time to lose. Side by side, they ran down the stairs. Happy rabbits jumped in all directions while they stormed across the beach, passed under the wooden pier to the west side of the bay. Only two young men were still lying in the sand, lost in love and kisses.

Phil looked back. Blasco came speeding down the stairs

from the villa.

"Faster."

Adam ran ahead, up to the trail that lined the bay where his car was parked. He shoved Phil through the passenger door, ran to the driver's side and gave the engine such a hasty start it protested with a shriek. Gravel hit the car's body like hail. In a cloud of sandy dust, they raced off.

Phil held her injured palm straight up so the blood would drip into her sleeve and not on the car seat. She knew too, she'd better shut up. While Adam rumbled like a furious weather god.

"Damn, Phil, I can't believe you are crazy enough to break into this house. Isn't a smashed skull enough? Only you can be such an idiot."

Phil pulled her black beret over both ears. "Thank you, Adam."

"Do you think you'll always be lucky enough to have someone save your ass? Hell, I'm not made to be a guardian angel."

"Thank you anyway. Thanks for saving my ass."

"The guy could've killed you. Would have. To break in, for Christ's sake! And typical: to get caught. Medical kit is in the glove box."

"Thank you."

Phil took out a bandage and plastered it over the deepest cut on her right palm. At least the blood stopped running.

A gruff side glance hit her, "That's how one risks blood poisoning."

"I will clean it as soon as I can. Thank you."

"What's it with all these thank yous? There should be iodine in the kit."

"Thanks. And you?" Phil asked in a sweet voice that didn't sound anything like her own. "Why again were you there?"

"Isn't that obvious? To help a crazy burglar get away." Another glance met Phil, sharp as a steak knife. "Really, Phil, you must be out of your fucking mind."

She tried to think of a reasonable, eloquent answer without expletives, but, of course, Adam was right. Blasco would have crushed her like a fly. And then, she realized in shock, Anton would have been left alone in this world. What an irresponsible mother she was. Phil felt like kicking herself. She only got away because Adam had been there.

"Thank you," she repeated as she couldn't think of anything else. Suddenly, she felt extremely nauseated, "Th... thanks."

The shock came late, but reliably.

CHAPTER 40

Only when they passed the town sign of Santa Gertrudis de Fruitera was Phil able to talk again. "The scooter. I forgot about the scooter."

Adam parked close to the pedestrian zone around the old fortified church, the little town's center.

"Of course," he said, "but first I need a schnapps." He got out of the car and opened the right door for Phil. "We'll go to this bar, there. You wash your hands and put the iodine on the cut, then a new bandage. I'll order drinks."

His voice sounded harsh, but in his eyes Phil could see how worried he had been for her. She put a still trembling hand on his arm and pulled it back before he could shake it off.

"Sure, Adam. I'm really very sorry."

They walked across the church square and into the Bar Costas where enormous legs of Serrano ham were dangling from the ceiling. The air was full of their aroma. Phil had no idea if drying ham in the open of a bar was merely a touristy show, or if there was a good reason behind it.

Some elder Ibizans and tourists of all ages sat around the bar. Adam ordered two *hierbas* and a bottle of water and went to the furthest back table. When Phil came back from the bathroom with a freshly bandaged hand, she first didn't see him. For a moment, she thought he had abandoned her.

"Here." Adam pulled a chair out from under the table and pushed a *hierbas* in front of her. "Drink!"

Alcohol as shock treatment. Phil swallowed the liquor like bitter medicine.

"Okay, Adam." She cleared her throat "You are right. I'm a bloody idiot, and this was one of my most idiotic ideas."

Her little lopsided grimace contained the fear she had gone through. It made Adam also empty his *hierbas* in one go. The idea alone that this guy could have laid his hands on her.

"Fault confessed is half redressed." He still sounded grumpy but had a smile in his eyes. Phil smiled back. For a while they sat in silence, recovering.

Then Adam questioned Phil about Can Salammbo and wanted to know every detail she could remember. His interest made, in her eyes, a little sense of her break-in after all. She tried to be as accurate as possible. The most important detail she saved for the last.

"When exactly did Amanda die?"

"The night of March 8th. Why?"

So it was true! Excited, Phil told Adam about Amanda's phone message. That very night, Scherer must have been on his way to her—with a bottle of champagne.

Adam banged the table with his fist. "That's it! Where is the phone with the answering machine?"

"In an office on the second floor."

"We need to get the recording before Scherer deletes it. This is evidence. Much better evidence than his alibi by some wasted guys. Wow, Phil." Then he remembered, "Still doesn't justify your..."

Phil waved it off. "So how do you want to get it?"

"The legal way. Bartolo must get a search order."

"Which the prosecutor will provide? I doubt it."

"We will see. Anything else?"

Phil thought about it. Maybe there was one more thing: the strange vehicle with the thrusters in the shed. "A bizarre-looking machine. Like a—what do submarines look like? I mean small ones, not warcraft?"

Adam pulled out his phone and googled small submarines. They were a new trend among the super-rich: first they had needed private helicopters, now it was U-boats. He went through photos with machines for sale, until Phil pointed to a yellow one. The Perry submarine, it read, had room for five passengers, enabled commercial and scientific applications and could be modified to go three thousand meters underwater. On sale for a mere one and a half million euros. An expensive toy for the shallow waters around Ibiza.

"You're sure that's it?"

"I remember the name on the machine's belly. Maybe it was even a bit bigger than this one."

"Hm." Adam would get back to this later. First he needed to call Bartolo, even though he shared Phil's skepticism. The chances of getting a search warrant for Can Salammbo were minimal. Bartolo didn't answer his phone anyway. But Adam needed the tape. He would have to think of something else. After he went to find the scooter. "Alone," he pointed out, when Phil jumped up.

"You wait here. Don't move a muscle. Or do you want to risk running into this guy again? He hasn't really seen me, but he would recognize you."

True. Relieved, Phil sank back into her chair and described where she had hidden the scooter. She only hoped it hadn't been stolen.

And then she waited. She ordered wine, rolled cigarettes. An hour passed, another half. Phil took turns silently cursing herself and Adam. She kept walking out to the patio to smoke, hoping Adam was all right, wondering if he played a stupid punishing game with her. The Bar Costas got crowded. The male guests kept looking over to the pretty redhead who drank alone, fidgeting on her chair, but never made eye contact with anyone.

The wound on Phil's head hurt again. The hammering and throbbing drove her crazy. She had to stop drinking and smoking, it only made things worse. But again she was on her way out and rolled a cigarette with aching hands.

When she looked up, Adam was walking towards her. Hallelujah.

"Did you get lost? Got it?"

Adam pointed to his car parked next to the church. The scooter's butt was sticking out of the trunk. Phil uttered some more heartfelt thanks, and they went back inside to their table. Disappointed at the sight of Adam, the men at the bar concentrated on their drinks.

"So? What happened?"

First, Adam had tried to sneak into the villa, only to find every door and window hermetically locked, and the alarm system turned on. This, however, he didn't intend to let Phil know.

"You were gone for quite a while."

"When I had the scooter in the trunk and drove by the mansion, the door opened, and this giant came out. He was in a Jeep, windows rolled down."

"Oh, shit."

"I gave him a friendly nod."

"Are you crazy?" And he gave her hell for being reckless!

"Why? He can't have seen more of me than my hand on the shed's roof. And someone running away with you in a far distance. I asked him for the way to the next beach. He only kinda growled."

Remembering those growls still sent shivers down Phil's spine.

"I followed him in a little distance to San Miguel. To the

bar Santa Lucia."

"While I'm growing roots here..."

Adam grinned. He had ordered a beer and watched the giant go to the bar's back wall that held a number of mailboxes. He opened one, took out a heap of letters and left again. Adam talked to the girl behind the bar and learned that in Ibiza's countryside with its long distances between neighbors, the mail was usually brought to the next village's central pub. People picked it up and took the chance to have a glass and a chat. But this guy who the girl called El Sordo didn't get a drink.

"Meaning the deaf guy. His name is Martí Blasco."

"Okay. The barkeeper said only people who've known him forever can understand his growls. But they're all jealous of him, because he has a steady job in this villa and always enough money in his pockets."

"You sure are good at making bargirls talk."

"And what are you doing?"

To Adam's amazement, Phil was rustling with the waistband of her jeans. She totally had forgotten. The expensive paper of the letter was moist and shaped in the form of her belly, as, in the last hours, Phil had sweated a bit.

"Adam, I really appreciate that you got the scooter. Thanks, okay."

"Is this a new obsession of yours? I heard enough thanks for a year. What's that?" He pointed at the letter.

A bit embarrassed, Phil put it on the table. "What does it look like?"

Both starred at the crumbled address: TAB. Can Salammbo, San Miguel II/17, Ibiza, *en lista de correos.*

"Wow." Adam was impressed. "Trespassing, personal injury and now even theft. Quite some criminal tendencies."

"Personal injury?" Phil again felt her foot smash into Blasco's face. "That was pure self-defense."

"You should see his nose."

Phil tapped the letter. "Should we not...?"

"Sure. I guess with your criminal record, a ridiculous secrecy of correspondence won't make much of a difference."

"Very funny."

The letter contained an invitation:

Dear Brothers, disciples of BES,

After our last reunion at Can Salammbo turned out to be a huge success with 67 participants and 44 new members worldwide, we are excited to invite you to our Rites of Spring party under this magical March's full moon. In the name of Bes, our divine patron, and with great joy, we and our novias want to welcome you to a very special event. We promise you, once again, ecstatic pleasures.

You will find the grandiose program on the website only we Bes brothers can access. As always, privacy is our utmost priority. Binding commitments are expected up to March 7 (see reverse.) Participants of the event last fall are welcome to commit again.

We are also happy to announce that our prices have remained stable, to be paid in Euros (6000) or US Dollars (7500). They include board and lodgings for three nights. There may be extra fees for drinks and equipment on special request in the suites. Besides the exclusive accommodations in our center, we provide equal standard lodgings in the following residencies: Can Caliban, Casa Negrita, Villa Candida, Villa Escorpión, Can d'Arxiduc, Can Viscosa Serpiente and Casa del Chivo (see reverse) Please let us know your preferences. If you have questions or requests of any kind, you may contact us under one of the secret numbers.

As always, we will indulge you with the most exquisite and eccentric delights. We are confident that every one of your expectations will be met. So please come and join us for a weekend in the spirit of our divine patron and our brotherhood. Love to all.

An unreadable signature followed.

"Next full moon." Phil was excited, "We have to be back in

Can Salammbo, take photos and snatch the phone with Scherer's message." She raised her hand against Adam's protest. "Come on, you know this is our only chance to find proof against the TAB. When is full moon?"

Adam swallowed what was on the tip of his tongue, checked his iPhone and said, "Tomorrow." He would not allow Phil to put herself in danger again.

In the RSVP line of the letter, Kai Maurer had signed and added that he wished to be accommodated in Can Salammbo, preferably in a first-floor suite. He had completed the form March 6th.

Phil pointed at the signature, but Adam was faster, "Kai Maurer will not join the party after all. This brother is gone."

"Right. His death is the other case that drives Bartolo crazy because he's not getting anywhere. The plane crash on S'Espalmador."

Adam called the inspector. They agreed to meet at Tia Maria's bodega.

CHAPTER 41

Bartolo was stunned by Phil's appearance. While he, as usual, was immaculately dressed in a designer shirt and tight black jeans, she seemed to have crawled out of a crashed car. Besides the patched-up mess on her head, she now also had a bandaged hand. Her amazingly dirty jeans had cuts that ran from her knee up to her thigh, too much for a fashion tear. But politely, Bartolo ignored the derangement and blew a kiss on Phil's left hand.

While he ordered drinks and tapas, Adam gave him an account of her adventure in Can Salammbo. In quite exaggerated words, she thought. Bartolo, however, didn't seem to mind her break-in or the letter she had taken.

"So Maurer was a Bes brother, and on his way to this full moon party..."

"Any new insights there?" Adam asked, "About why he crashed?"

Bartolo rubbed his chin, adorned by black stubble. "The examiner thinks food poisoning. Happens, I guess." He didn't sound all too convinced.

Adam nodded to Phil, "Tell him about Amanda's call."

She did, and Bartolo got newly jazzed. To police, Scherer

hadn't mentioned his plan to meet Amanda with a bottle of champagne the night she died. But how could he have entered Villa Éscorpion without being seen?

"Rosenda said Amanda told her to go home around eight," Adam said. "The surveillance cameras were turned on, right?" As Bartolo nodded, he wondered, "so why wasn't he seen on there? Strange."

"Very strange. We must get the tape with her voicemail. That might be our only chance to break Scherer's alibi." Bartolo gave a little girlish shriek. Adam had kicked him under the table.

"I will take care of it," he said sotto voce, with a meaningful glance at Phil who was just ordering more water and didn't seem to listen. Bartolo understood.

He tapped her forearm. "I've got news, too. Two hours ago, the colleague in Frankfurt called me back. Nice guy—well, a Robert Wendling used to work for a travel magazine called *Globo*. He quit, it seems, right when the TAB lawyers reacted to this article in the *Insular*. Three months later, he took a job in the press office of a chemical plant. Could you call him, Phil?"

Of course, as Bartolo didn't speak German. He handed her his phone with the saved numbers.

"Claudia here," a voice at the other end said.

Phil introduced herself and asked for Robert, but was disappointed.

"Gone again," the woman said with audible disdain, "But he said he'd be back in a couple of days, and I say: hopefully alone."

"Oh! Are you his..."

"No, no, no." Claudia clarified that she shared a flat with Robert and two other guys, and that they all were fed up with his girlfriend drama.

"Ah—sorry, but who are you?" she asked, suddenly suspicious.

Phil explained that she was trying to reach Wendling on behalf of Inspector Dziri of the Guardia Civil. That she only translated his request.

"Is Robert in trouble?"

"Don't worry, police only need some information. I'm calling from Ibiza."

"I figured. That's were he is. Hotel El Puerto. When you talk to him, please tell him to leave the diva where she is."

"Tamar Stettin?"

"Right, Tamar. We're sick of their fights. Of her."

Phil swallowed hard. "Don't worry. Tamar will not come back again."

She pushed the button and translated for the others what Claudia had said.

"Hotel Puerto," Bartolo said, "that's in the city, Carrer de Carlos III."

Adam jumped up. "We better hurry. If he's involved in Tamar's death, he may already be packing."

Not even Bartolo insisted on having dinner at Tia Maria first. He drove his police car so aggressively into town that Adam had a hard time keeping up. Traffic was insane. Bartolo kept his finger on the horn until, with squealing breaks, they came to a stop in front of the Hotel Puerto.

At the front desk, they learned that Robert Wendling had already checked out, even though he had paid for two more nights. The clerk said they had been pretty worried about this guest who hadn't left his room for the last thirty hours, and in all that time merely ordered two bottles of brandy from room service. When he returned the key, *señor* Wendling looked accordingly horrible.

Bartolo was already on the phone alerting his staff to check all ferries and planes that had left or were scheduled to leave Ibiza this evening.

"Do you have an idea where Mr. Wendling may have gone?" Adam tried.

"Sorry, no," the clerk said. "He was met by a woman and left with her."

"Can you describe her?"

"Let's see: In her fifties or sixties, probably a local, in an apron dress. She waited in front of the hotel, and they walked to a car that was parked over there—no, I don't remember the license plate—a small, dusty thing."

"What about video surveillance?"

The clerk admitted, a little embarrassed, that El Puerto would upgrade to CCTV only after this year's season, when a major renovation was due.

"So this woman's car, you said, was parked over there? In front of the bank?" Phil pointed to a La Caixa building across the street. Both sides of the entrance were flanked by an ATM, each with a camera on top.

When the clerk nodded, Bartolo lifted both thumbs. He would take care of it first thing tomorrow. Suddenly he was in a hurry to get away. A date, he said.

The sun had set when Phil and Adam unloaded the scooter at the Esperanza. Phil wondered—and wasn't surprised when, on the stairs, Adam yawned dramatically and mumbled something about being dead tired. At nine.

"Bye now, I'll get some sleep. See ya tomorrow." He hurried off.

What a lousy actor he was. Phil went to her own room and took a hot shower. She hadn't brought black jeans, so a black hoodie, black skirt, and tights would have to do. She opened her door a crack and waited.

CHAPTER 42

She had known. Only half an hour later, Adam's door opened again very carefully. When Phil stepped out of hers, he jumped.

"Dead tired, right? As if I didn't know the full moon's tonight."

Just like her, Adam was dressed in black and carried a black leather jacket over his arm. Phil stuffed her unruly curls under the beret while he ran down the stairs, trying to escape. In vain, of course. When he was close to his car and pushed the remote key, she was right behind him.

Adam was mad as hell. "Go back. I will absolutely not take you along."

"All right. I'll follow you on the scooter."

He let out a deep sigh. "Damn, Phil, haven't you had enough for today? Blasco will eat you alive if he sees you one more time."

"That goes for you as well."

"Do I hear concern? About me?"

"Idiot."

"I'm more cautious than you. I know what to do. After all, this is—was my job." He even used a John Wayne voice, "It ain't my first rodeo."

"Then don't lollygag."

Even now she could beat him at his game. "Really, Phil, that's not funny."

But she just opened the right door—damn, he should have locked it— and plopped into the seat.

"Get out. I'll take care of it and be back in no time."

"Let's go."

Stubborn as a mule, this woman. Adam was fuming. But as there was nothing else he could do, he started the engine. Phil gave him a smile.

He returned a frown. "You sure can worry the horns off a billy goat."

"That's a new one. Meaning?"

"You're annoying."

Phil's smile was openly smug. "Well, doggone it."

They drove across the island. Phil turned on the radio where—what could be more fitting?—the old CCR song 'Bad Moon Rising' was playing. A shiver ran down her spine. In spite of her brash attitude, she was getting more nervous as with every kilometer they came closer to Can Salammbo. But to have Adam go there alone was not an option.

As if to show her, he hummed along, "Don't go around tonight, it's bound to take your life. Hey, there's a bad moon on the rise..."

Abruptly he turned off the radio. "We'll have to be extremely careful. You know that, Phil."

"I do. We will."

Cala Benirras was in the grips of a perfect full moon. Adam drove by a line of high-end cars—Mercedes, Audi, BMW, Porsches, a Ferrari, some expensive SUVs. Patrolling security guards eyed them suspiciously when they passed.

Out of sight at the very end of the field, Adam parked under a low pine tree that looked like a black paper cut against the bright sky. When the engine was turned off, they heard music and voices loud enough to drive every neighbor crazy. Faint lights crawled through the mansion's window slits. Along the wall, above head height, tar torches in heavy metal cramps increased the impression of an old Moorish castle. Adam put on his jacket.

"Move over to the steering wheel and start the engine as soon as you see me come back," he tried.

"Forget it."

Phil took the lead, and they walked towards the cliff, careful to stay in the shadow of the trees. The music got louder the closer they came to the villa's back, an intense tune-mix of funk, jazz and a throbbing, oriental beat. One torch shone dimly on either side of the back door, leaving everything else in darkness. A good starting point. But the branch of the tree Phil had climbed in the afternoon had been sawed off, as well as all the other lower branches. Adam tried to pull himself up across a stump and, thanks to his physical size, succeeded.

Phil balanced on the stump. Her damn 5'2" were not enough to follow him.

"Adam!"

"Sssh! Wanna let them know we're here and bust us?"

"Help me, damn."

He grinned, "You're too short. What can I do?"

"Please. Two are always better than one."

She hated her pleading voice, but Adam was already crawling across the wall to the shed's metal roof. He sighed like a parent who couldn't withstand his kid's pleas.

"All right. Get off the tree."

"No way."

Adam had his leather jacket in one hand. "Just do it, man."

"I'm not..." Phil shut up when she realized what he was doing. Lying flat on the wall, he let one sleeve of his jacket dangle down.

Quick as lightning, she was down and grabbed it. Her

shoulder joints overstretched, her cut hands throbbed in protest. The seams of Adam's leather jacket made dangerous cracking noises, but weathered her weight. With only a few extra scrapes and a run in her tights, Phil was on the wall.

"Thanks."

"A burglar in a skirt. I can't believe it."

"Then don't." Keeping a straight face, Phil took off her boots. Adam rolled his eyes.

"Experience," she snapped. "These make too much noise on a metal roof."

"Oh. Just leave them here."

"My favorites?"

Perplexed, Adam watched Phil unzip the pocket of her hoodie, take a plastic bag out and stuff the boots in. He couldn't suppress a grin.

"You are full of clichés, Adam Ryan. Let me tell you something: There are things in this world one may feel attached to. Surprised?"

"Not at all, my dear."

She glared at him, then pointed her black-clad toes to the left. "Over there are some gas bottles we can slide down on. But we'll have to find another way back up."

Like a special unit, they wriggled across the roof. They didn't have to worry about being heard, as the party music below them boomed. The gas bottles were still there. Phil put her boots back on. The backdoor to the mansion, however, was locked. Sticking close to the wall, they crept around one corner and the next. There wasn't even a mouse hole to sneak in.

"Wait." Adam pointed at the balcony framing the building's front. "I guess that's my only chance. You, in the meantime..."

"What about this?"

A wooden trellis supported a huge Bougainvillea that grew rampant up one side of the balcony. All the security guards seemed to be on the other side of the wall, keeping watch on the cars. And the party people were all inside.

Phil started to climb, giving Adam a vindictive smirk. "I don't think it's strong enough for you."

But that was lost on Adam, as he was already climbing up a vertical water pipe at the balcony's other side. Half hidden under another Bougainvillea, it went up to the rain gutter under the roof. The clay pipe was attached to the wall with iron clamps where Adam could set his feet. Surprisingly easy.

A nanosecond before Adam, Phil arrived on the balcony, which was decorated with potted plants and lined by French windows. All were locked and the curtains closed. Only from under the last door, a reddish light crept out. Their only chance was across the roof.

Phil mustered all her courage, tried not to look down, and made it safely up. But when Adam followed her, one of the iron clamps got loose and fell on the balcony, smashing a huge rose pot. Chunks of loose cement rained down.

"Fuck." Adam pressed his body against the roof like a giant spider.

Underneath them, a door opened. "What the hell was that?" said a male voice, "Look at this mess."

"Probably a cat," a female voice answered from inside, "they always freak out with the moon." The door closed again.

Phil rolled up and gave Adam a little kick with her boot that hurt her because she had forgotten about her bruised toes.

"That was close, man."

On hands and knees they crawled across the roof to the side of the courtyard from where the music and the voices rose up. They peeked across the edge. What in hell was that?

Down in the yard, in oval-shaped copper bowls, lay dead animals. Bodies with wrenched heads and slit-open throats, blood dripping over the rims. It ran in rivulets across the terracotta tiles, trickled into the foam-filled pool, turning its water dark. The rabbits Phil had set free had been replaced and killed. Probably sacrifices to this pervert wannabe god, Bes. She felt nauseated.

Adam murmured, "Yuck."

The Bes worshippers, however, didn't seem to mind the perversion. They were partying hard. To the rhythm of a fast oriental beat, red flashes twitched through the yard, colliding with the bluish rays of tube heaters lining the walls. Their heat would be highly welcomed as the night was chilly, and the party folks were all more or less naked. Some men were wrapped in white cloth like at a frat toga party, but most of them only wore golden masks over elderly bulging bellies and sagging skin. A few showed off a lifetime of workout with their toned torsos.

The women were in the majority. They all were pretty and young; some had transparent veils knotted around their hips, but most of them were stark naked. Their sight reminded Phil of the Fellini movie *La Dolce Vita,* which a critic had called "three hours of explicitness." Down in the yard, worse than explicit was one haggard old guy who walked two girls on a leash, they on all fours with spiked harnesses around their naked breasts. A scene more like out of Pasolini's *Salò, or the 120 Days of Sodom*, which Phil had barely been able to watch—an appalling display of man's perverse desire for dominance.

The party folks were dancing to the lashing rhythm. Arms and legs whirled around, sweaty, slick skin everywhere. Coolers with champagne bottles and hard liquor bottles sat on the tables. The smell of cannabis and other substances drifted up to the roof.

Adam got his phone out. "Bunga Bunga on Ibiza."

In the middle of the foam-filled pool, on a pedestal, was a life-sized statue of Bes. Probably the figure under the red veil that, in the afternoon, Phil had first taken for a real person. How long ago this afternoon seemed!

Now, the veil was gone. Bes's stocky body was golden from head to toe; his huge, erect penis glittered in the flashing lights. Around the statue, naked people danced ecstatically in the foamy water. A lot of grabbing, kissing, licking, rubbing and even spanking was going on. Phil watched a scene in which a young black girl and a silver-ager with a fat ass were the protagonists. The man chased the girl through the pool, slashing the foam with what looked like a rubber whip, enjoying her screams. He looked somewhat familiar—had Phil seen his face on TV? Right: this was a German politician, member of the Council of Europe, Secretary of Health and Human Services. Günter Minz—now the name popped into Phil's head—a well-known conservative.

Adam was already trying to get a picture of the scene, but due to the flashing lights, his camera struggled to focus.

The politician grabbed the girl at her neck and forced her to go down on him. For a mere second, her face was in frontal view before it was pressed into the man's groin. But the short sight startled Phil, as the girl also looked familiar to her. Where from? Then she had it: the group of girls in the hallway of Can Follet, later doing yoga in the yard. The old man's sex kitten looked exactly like one of them.

But—this wasn't possible, was it? How could one and the same girl stay in Can Follet, the sisterhood of feminism, and at the same time take part in an orgy, allowing a man to humiliate her? If Doro knew about this, she'd freak out. What happened down there contradicted everything she and the women's resort stood for: female solidarity, pride, even the Goddess rigmarole. No, it could only be a random similarity; Phil must be wrong. Or not? Tamar had been a Tanit Daughter and worked for the TAB.

The sound level was so high, Adam cursed loudly. But through all the wires, flashes and blinding lights, his camera lens still wasn't able to adjust and take a decent picture of what was going on in the yard.

"We have to get closer."

He wriggled his way along the roof's edge to find a better position. Phil followed him, totally irritated now. When the girl had finished her job on the man, she looked up, and Phil got a good view of her. It *was* the girl from Can Follet. Without any doubt.

CHAPTER 43

Suddenly the music stopped, people got out of the pool. The dancers calmed down, bodies separated. To a dark, resonating gong, girls in short tunics came out of the building carrying water bowls and towels so the bathers could dry themselves. Other girls filled up champagne glasses.

Then a chubby elder man, wearing a golden toga and a pompous mask, stepped in front of the Bes statue. He raised his hands and began to speak. His English had an accent: Swedish, perhaps. His voice carried forcefully.

"Brothers," he said, "my friends of kindred spirit who have come from all over the world. Let's now say our heartfelt thanks to Bes, our beloved God."

Now, you could hear a pin drop in the yard. All men took a devotional pose.

"In the name of the greatest power on earth, Desire, we faithful brothers, we chosen few, have worshipped Bes and offered him our *molkmors*. With thankful hearts and full of love, we sacrificed to the Master of Scorpio, commander of all creatures wriggling under him. Our Lord over Tanit, the star from Lebanon, Venus of the tides. Our Master who sets right what so often is wronged in our times: the acceptance of our natural superiority. Our male dominance. With our offerings accepted, we have become the great Bes's manifestation on Earth, the phallic dominators of all other beings, Bes's own image. *Erimus sicut Deus.*"

"*Erimus sicut Deus,*" the men responded.

We are like God, Phil translated in silence. The what? Phallic dominators?

The men in the yard had no problem with the hybrid claim, listening to the laudation with obvious pride.

"As token of her appreciation, Bes's passionate mistress Tanit, curator of our lust and lasciviousness, sent her daughters to us, the rightfully chosen few. Tanit, whose empire reaches from Indus to Eidanus, from north to south and east to west. Goddess of sex, we thank you for entrusting your children to us. As we are the Masters. As we are like God. *Erimus sicut Deus.*"

"*Erimus sicut Deus.*"

Phil and Adam exchanged a glance while the man kept on blustering about the greatness of man. No, not *man* but only the men down there, the Bes Brothers.

"The chosen few?" Phil whispered, but Adam hushed her.

"I'm recording."

Great idea, she thought. Natural superiority, what was this supposed to mean? The Masters, for fuck's sake? No wonder the Bes guys had to hide in a secret brotherhood to play their chauvinist role games. In the real world, the public would demonize, or at least ridicule them for their idiotic claims. *Phallic dominators*, what an outrage these words would evoke.

Phil thought about the man she had recognized, Günter Minz. His boss, the Prime minister of State, was a woman. The country's chancellor was a woman, and there was a women's quota in political positions. If Minz's colleagues and voters knew he only pretended to be a good German democrat, and in reality saw himself as a phallic dominator, he could forget his career. It would make him look even worse than being caught at an orgy.

Down in the yard, the strange laudation was replaced by collective mumbling, something like a litany. Then, a fanfare resounded, and everyone shut up. While the women stayed back, the men formed a passage. Two of the servant girls opened a double-winged door, and out of it came a procession. Seven girls in transparent body veils, headed by a black woman with a glittering crescent moon on her veiled head. Very young girls, Phil realized in horror, seven childlike silhouettes. They stopped at the pool opposite the Bes statue.

"We welcome our novices," the speaker started anew, "our carefully selected debutantes, the youngest Daughters of Tanit. Tonight, under the full moon of the Phoenician *Month of KRR,* they will be introduced to the world's greatest enigma. By you," his arms opened wide, "the fortunate winners drawn by divine providence. They will not hesitate to serve the gods ad libitum. *Erimus...*"

"*...sicut Deus,*" the male crowd yelled along. The atmosphere had become palpably dense, full of tension.

"*Eritis sicut Deus,*" seven timid voices answered from under the veils. Very young voices, Phil thought with growing horror.

Adam was also shocked. His "Oh my God," sounded strangely out of place. "Oh hell, these fuckers," he clarified, his fists clenched. "We have to do something."

The woman with the crescent moon on her head turned to the girls and gave them an inaudible instruction.

"I know. But what?" Please, don't let it be, Phil silently begged.

But in vain: when the woman turned back into Phil's view, she had lifted the veil off her face. And Phil saw her suspicion justified. Right in front of her eyes, a world of trust came tumbling down.

Without any doubt, the black woman was Stella, the receptionist of Can Follet with her blue hair and the tattoo around one eye. Stella, who only a few nights ago had sat at the triangular table, two chairs down from Doro. Stella who had so sweetly comforted Manasa, Trudy, and then Jezebel, who had an easy smile, liked to crochet, and smelled of pot. Stella who kept sending Phil strange warning messages she couldn't understand, alluding to horrors. It was Stella who was leading girls into this mob of Weinsteins to be humiliated, raped, destroyed.

Phil could hardly breathe. She thought of Doro who had given up everything to live her dream in Can Follet. The female dream. Doro who worked incessantly, teaching, guiding, trying to make the world a better place. The newly opened up, charismatic mother figure Doro, or rather Anat. Phil could only imagine how devastated she would be to learn that Stella was a traitor.

Only when Adam started crawling on all fours to a glass cupola on the other side of the roof did she snap out of her shock-induced paralysis.

"We have to find a way to take pictures," he whispered. "We need proof."

Down in the yard, the music was blasting again. Up on the roof, something snapped, Adam cursed, and the blade of his Swiss Army knife was broken. As were three of Phil's fingernails. Still, the operation had not been completely senseless: the frame of the skylight had gotten loose.

"Damn," Adam knocked the broken knife against the last rusty screw.

Phil blew air on her chapped thumb. "This won't do."

"If we had a hammer or something..."

Again, Phil took off one of her boots. One well-aimed hit, with its iron-shot heel, and the screw catapulted into the night. "Here you go."

A lifted thumb was Adam's answer, and Phil put her boot back on. Together they heaved the skylight's glass cupola off its frame. Below them was an elegant bathroom with a round tub and some leftover foam bubbles. The strong scent of Patchouli floated up to them. Adam made sure his iPhone was standing in his shirt pocket, ready to shoot. He lowered his long legs into the opening and, with one jump, landed in the foam.

"On my shoulders. But quiet."

Phil slid across Adam's shoulder, down his back, into the tub. The party music was only faint in this bathroom. Through an open door, however, came a roaring snore. With utmost care, Adam stepped out of the tub and tiptoed towards another door that must lead to the hallway. But when Phil followed him, her foot touched an empty bottle standing on the tub's edge. The crash was buffered by the fluffy bath rug, but then the bottle rolled across the tiles, picked up speed and, with an ugly bang, slammed into the ceramic base of the sink.

The snoring came to an abrupt hold. With one jump, Adam was behind the bathroom door, pulling Phil with him. She flew against his chest. A bed frame creaked. Both stood paralyzed, holding their breath. Only when the snoring started again did Adam let go of Phil, and together they tiptoed out. Behind the open door, they got a glimpse at a naked old man sprawled out across the bed. His wide-open mouth puffed drunken growls. A half-empty glass of whisky, a staple of papers and an open box of Viagra lay on the nightstand, some pills missing. The man wore a golden mask marking him as one of the phallic dominators, as he was lying here in a drunken stupor with his tiny, limp dick kinked. Obviously, the Viagra had failed him. Oh, *schadenfreude*. Thousands of euros, only to be drunk and impotent and missing the orgy.

Carefully, Phil pushed the mask upon the man's head and signaled Adam to take a picture, but he shook his head. Irritated, she pulled out her own phone and let the camera click a few times. No sound was coming from the hallway. They slipped out.

"An unknown man with a golden mask," Adam whispered. "No informative value. We have to get a better shot."

The staircase was empty as well, dipped in a reddish light. Here, the noise and music from the courtyard were louder again. Somewhere a door clicked. Water running could be heard and some banging action behind closed doors. The thick carpet muffled the sound of steps, so the masked, toga-wearing man walking up the stairs came as a surprise. No time to think.

Behind Adam, Phil disappeared through one of the long window curtains while he picked up a tray that was sitting next to a door, ready to be cleared away. Glasses clanked against an empty bottle. An overflowing ashtray held golden cigarette butts.

"*Buenas tardes, señor,*" Adam mumbled with his head bowed, stepping aside to let the man pass who dragged two naked girls along. With one hand he held both of them gripped around their skinny wrists. The girls were way too young to be here. One didn't look older than twelve, probably belonged to the so-called debutants. A kid that should build sandcastles on the beach.

The man opened a door, pushed the girls in and turned around again.

"Hey, *hombre*, wait a minute."

He entered the suite, leaving the door open, so Adam got another glimpse at the young girls standing in front of a huge four-poster bed. They were holding each other by the hands; their heads bowed. Then the man was back with a bundle of bills.

"*Más* booze." His voice was used to commanding. "But the *Gran Reserva* again, this one." His enormous, square chin nodded at the bottle on Adam's tray, "not this cheap Carlos stuff." A good-humored slap with the bills hit Adam's arm. "Keep the rest, will ya. And *pronto, hombre*. Also get me some more stardust."

"*Si, señor, gracias.*"

With an exaggerated bow, Adam took the money and stepped back. When the door to the suite was closed, he joined Phil behind the curtain.

"That's him," he whispered, his voice tense, "Colonel Cruz, I'm pretty sure, he's got this chin. Unbelievable. Guess he's not scared of being uncovered here."

On the windowsill of the niche, half-hidden behind the curtain, was a vase with a bouquet of spring flowers. Adam poured some of the water into the empty brandy bottle. Then he wiped the bottle and a glass with a corner of the curtain so they looked untouched.

"We'll wait a few minutes until they've started—whatever. Then I go in with the tray and leave the door open, so you can take photos. With mine, okay?"

Adam handed Phil his iPhone. "When you hear me say, 'the brandy, *señor*,' push the button. But make sure the guy's face is in the picture. And of course the girls. In there, he will hopefully take off his mask."

"Okay."

"If not, I'll somehow manage to pull it off him. If we don't get his face to prove it's Cruz, we'll have nothing. Even if it's not him but another big shot. How old do you think these girls are? Shall we let him go on with this?"

"You're preaching to the choir."

"We need him in full action. With the photos we'll get him sacked. We'll immediately go public."

"Yes, we will."

CHAPTER 44

A few minutes can be an eternity. At one point, Adam took his phone to take some pictures through the window. From here, he could only catch a glimpse of the hustle in the yard, but nevertheless. When he handed the phone back to Phil he saw that her fingers were trembling. He wanted to squeeze them. Wanted to tell Phil how courageous she was; wanted this part of the night to be over, so he could take her in his arms. All kinds of things Adam wanted. But here they were, standing in this niche, extremely tense. They heard voices, laughter, a shrill squeak that made them flinch. Doors were opened and closed. Not only Colonel Cruz seemed to continue the party behind closed doors.

"Are you ready?"

Phil's voice was clear and steady, "I am."

"Try to keep your hand still. If necessary, run."

Adam took the tray, rapped against the door and immediately pushed it wide open. The man was sitting on the bed's long side with spread legs, the mask pulled up on his forehead. Now Adam was sure: It was Colonel Cruz! Half behind him, on the bedspread of dark silk, the younger girl was lying on her back, naked and beautiful like an odalisque. Her apathetic eyes were directed at the bed's baldachin, one little foot dangling down. The other girl was kneeling between the colonel's legs, trying to give him pleasure. Behind him, Adam heard a succession of clicks. Phil had already started to photograph the scene with the man's face in frontal view. Bravo to her!

The colonel didn't seem to realize what was going on around him. Strangely enough, though, his distraction wasn't due to the girl's blowjob. He was starring at the huge TV screen in front of the bed. His mouth was gaping wide open, his prominent chin almost down to his chest.

It wasn't a porn movie that had the colonel's attention, but a CNN news report. The alarmed face of a female reporter filled the screen. Adam could hear her excited voice, but the sound was too low to understand what she was talking about. Something shocking, for sure, something tragic. Onscreen, a wooded hill came into view, a Mediterranean landscape. A whitish, round hut like a jelly bag cap. Three men wearing white overalls. A hearse.

The kneeling girl gave up on the colonel. The girl on the bed didn't move. Adam approached the man, his tray in front of him like a shield.

"*El* brandy, *señor*," he yelled.

Colonel Cruz jumped up, pushing the kneeling girl so she fell on her back. She winced. Without as much as a glance at her, Cruz pulled the toga over his lap.

Adam had to gasp at the ugly reality: here he was, face to face with one of the highest-ranking officers of his country who just had his cock sucked by an underage girl. He wanted to spit into Cruz's face.

The colonel was clearly upset too. "What the fuck, man." He pushed the girl further out of his way. "Off with y'all. Now."

The girl crept away on all fours, while Cruz leaned across the other one on the bed. She gave a shriek, but he ignored her, grabbed a remote control, and turned the TV louder.

Adam signaled her to get away. Obediently, she slid across the bed to the door. Cruz looked over his shoulder and saw Adam was still there.

"You too. Out."

He turned back to the TV, while Phil peeked through the open door, Adam's phone in her hand still clicking away. She lifted her thumb, while the reporter said something about a horrific accident in Italy, "for what we know now..." The last word Adam heard was "death." Then he closed the door behind them.

The hallway was still empty, but from the first floor and courtyard anxious voices rose up. A command was yelled, the music stopped. Something huge had ruined not only Colonel Cruz's pedophile sex games, but the Bes Brothers' complete full moon party.

Through the window they saw that all the flashing red lights had been turned off. Only the blue rays of the heaters and a flickering TV screen were left, throwing eerie lights on toga-wearing men that stood together, upset, perplexed.

Phil gave Adam a little push and pointed at the door with the sign *Privado*. They still needed to find the phone with Amanda's message before getting the hell out of here. But there were voices behind the door. Adam bent down and peeped through the keyhole—directly at Jorg Scherer. His brother-in-law was behind the desk, his face buried in his hands. A flickering light showed that a TV was on here, too. In front of Scherer stood another man, his back to the door.

"Let me see." Phil pushed Adam aside. The guy in front of Scherer was as upset as the men in the courtyard. His voice was cranked up to an angry pitch; "... completely out of control," he yelled. And then in pure shock, "Fuck! It *is* him! That's beyond damage control."

Phil could see Scherer jump up. She flinched back, stumbling into Adam.

"They're coming!"

In a flash, they ducked behind one of the long curtains. A moment later, the door flew open, and Scherer and his companion raced down the hall. Phil and Adam waited, but just when they were about to leave their hiding place, another door crashed open. Colonel Cruz's came running out, pulling up the zipper of his pants. And then more and more doors opened, and men in togas or partly dressed, some carrying hastily packed bags, rushed to the stairs. All clearly in panic, as if a fire had broken out.

Something indeed had ruined the party. Men who had come to indulge in their sex fantasies now were driven by only one instinct—flight. Spontaneously, Adam stepped out into the hallway and addressed one who had stopped to put his lost shoe back on.

"Hey man, what happened? What's the uproar?"

The man was frantic. "Haven't you heard? It happened again. They just confirmed on TV—it's Brother Sandro."

"Sandro? Who's...?" But the man was already gone.

Phil came out behind the curtain. "No idea. We must get out, too."

But first, they had to get what they came for. They slipped into the now-abandoned office. On TV, a commercial was hyping an addictive painkiller. The phone was on the desk, a red 27 blinking. As it would take ages to find the right message and copy it on the iPhone, Adam unplugged the whole thing. Phil got her plastic bag ready. Then they were back in the hall, hallelujah, without having been caught by Scherer or his hellhound, *El Sordo*. The floor was empty again. All Bes Brothers must have fled their suites.

"Damn, Adam," Phil hissed when he headed towards the stairs and not to the bathroom through which they had come. But, of course, he had to find out what was going on here. She followed him, keeping close to the inner wall. The voices downstairs got loud again.

Peeking around the last turn of the staircase, they counted

about forty men and a few women gathered in the lobby. More men pushed in from the yard. Jorg Scherer was standing right in front of Adam and Phil, with his back to the staircase, both hands lifted like a preacher. To his right, the double-winged entrance door was wide open. The faces in the crowd reflected pure horror.

"From all we know so far, a heart attack." Scherer tried to keep his voice calm, even though it quivered. "Brothers, it's another sad night for us, but we all know Sandro had major health issues."

"That's bullshit, and you know it," someone in the crowd snapped.

"He was killed," came from someone else.

"Murdered," a third person said, "we all know it."

"Now, let's not jump to conclusions..."

That very moment, Martí Blasco, *El Sordo*, appeared. In his mighty paws, he carried a tray with cognac bottles and stacks of clinking glasses. Grunting softly, he trotted towards Scherer, coming close to the stairs' turn from where Adam and Phil were watching. Way too close.

Both made a hasty step back, but too late. Blasco had registered the motion. His furious growl interrupted Scherer's attempts at appeasement.

"Run," Adam whispered.

The moment Blasco needed to deposit his tray on a sideboard gave them a tiny lead. They used it to race by the stunned crowd, through the open entrance, into the front yard, towards the main gate...

Scherer barked a command, "Get them."

Blasco had the stature of a sumo wrestler, but he was incredibly fast on his feet. No chance to outrun him. When he was close, Adam abruptly stopped, let Phil pass, and whirled the bag that held the phone like a catapult above his head. He aimed at Blasco's solar plexus, but the man saw it coming, ducked down, and was immediately back on his feet. He plunged towards Phil. She cried out, blindly kicked him with her boot's iron heel. Lucky enough, she hit the region where even the toughest men are vulnerable. Blasco gave a yelp and buckled. Again, Phil kicked him as hard as she could into his private parts, which took increased effect. Blasco slumped down, whining like a kid.

Adam and Phil ran. But where to? If they climbed the front gate, they would fall right into the arms of the security guys. The way back was also cut off as the partygoers came flooding out of the building. Blasco was already struggling back up. In wordless agreement, Phil and Adam ran to the wall, behind bushes, trees, and the cars that were parked here. They had to make it to the shed.

But Blasco was tenacious. His whining had turned into a crazy roar as he resumed the chase. Phil and Adam were running for their lives.

Strangely enough, Phil wasn't afraid. It seemed unreal, almost annoying, to be running again from the same guy, through the same park as just some hours ago. Compared to the naked panic that had engulfed her then, she now felt oddly uninvolved. As if she watched someone else running. She was under shock.

Blasco might be crazy, but he knew what he was doing. Suddenly, the yard was bathed in a glaring light. Adam and Phil ducked behind a car before the light beam hit them. A door crashed open. Heavy steps crushed the gravel. A protracted whistle followed, a one-syllable command. Then panting, barking. *Atención perros peligrosos*, flashed through Phil's mind. Blasco had let the dogs out. Now, like a smack in her face, panic set in after all.

In the dazzling light, two long-stretched shapes sped across the yard. Quick moving muscle, trained for attack and fight, that belonged to two Doberman hounds. Both Adam and Phil screamed. With one parallel jump, they were on the hood of a parked car, then on the roof. One hell hound pressed his paws against the car's body. By a tiny margin, teeth like daggers missed Phil's ankle. The other dog snapped at Adam who again lashed out with the plastic bag holding the phone and banged it on the growling snout, loosening one of the bag's straps. The whole thing flew across the dog's head and dropped on the gravel. The dog jumped for it, shredded it. The other dog came running to help him.

"Fuck, fuck, fuck."

With the torn-off strap, Adam tried to lash out against the dogs, and they turned back at him. Hard claws scratched the car's body, scraped down the metallic paint in ugly screeches. Two men advanced, one holding a flashlight.

"Adam! This way." Phil leapt over to the next car.

He followed Phil, and they jumped from hood to hood and tried not to fall from the sleek metal. Plunging from the last car's hood, they disappeared out of the light beam. For a moment, the dogs didn't know how to react and instinctively tried to follow them across the hoods, but were pulled off by the men with vigorous commands. Pitiful yelps. But the Dobermans had picked up their scent.

Phil was in panic. She knew they couldn't make it to the shed. In the open yard, the dogs would tear them apart. But here, close enough, was the ancient Phoenician cistern. An image flashed through her mind: Blasco depositing the mown grass in it. The cistern would be filled up with grass.

"Up here, Adam."

Phil jumped onto the stonewalled circle. Only to look into an eternally black depth. High anxiety flooded her system. She was ready to give up. But to what? The dogs would maul her. Them. Dagger teeth snapped for her, brushing her boot. Adam was right next to her on the cistern's wall. He kicked the hound's nose so hard, its head spun sideways with a howl. It shook in bewilderment, ears whirling. But for those muscles, the well's wall was a piece of cake...

Phil had moved closer to the inner edge. "Adam, jump! We

must."

Her blow hit him between the shoulder blades. More out of surprise than the hit, Adam fell. Phil's screams accompanied them down into the darkness.

CHAPTER 45

Phil had read that people falling from great heights go into a coma, so they don't consciously experience the deadly collision with earth.

Their fall through the well shaft, however, was surprisingly short. And neither did they go into a coma nor smash their bones. They bumped against the wall, suffered a bit of skin abrasion. Phil's skirt flapped around her like a parachute. Then they landed smoothly, next to each other, in a moist heap of grass. Phil's arithmetic had worked.

"Are you okay?" Adam's voice came from very close.

"Yep. You?"

"All good. Shit. Let's calm down, and I'll think of a way out."

Phil felt calm enough, happy to be alive. She pulled her skirt down and lay back in the soft grass, feeling Adam's arm right next to her. Gently, she scooted a bit closer to him, and the arm was under her neck. Still a bit closer, and her head was lying on Adam's shoulder.

How romantically the stars shone through the circular frame above them, how perfect the moon—until two Dober-

man heads appeared and ruined the atmosphere. They slob-
bered and barked wildly, which sent a creepy echo through the
shaft. Then there was a sharp whistle. The dogs' heads disappeared and were replaced by Martí Blasco's. He jabbered
something unintelligible. Then something heavy scraped on
stone. The full moon turned into a half-moon, a crescent
moon. A few last stars, then a lunar eclipse. Blasco had put a
cover on the well.

"Okay, let's stay calm," Adam repeated, even though Phil
hadn't said a word. His fingers felt for her face, caressed her
cheek.

"We are still alive, and for now we are safe down here."

Phil grabbed his strong hand. Now, it was so dark in the
well, she couldn't even see any contours. Adam's fingers trembled slightly.

"Safe until we rot." She was shocked by her own brutal
words.

Even when her eyes got used to the dark, there was nothing to see but vague shadows. Adam turned on his iPhone's
flashlight. The Phoenician builders had done a good job, grout-
ing the walls in perfection. Even the natural rock had been
sanded to an insurmountable polish.

"Bartolo," Adam pushed a button of his phone. But of
course there was no cell phone reception down here.

"They have to get us out of here. Right? I mean, they can't
just..."

Phil choked on her words as three people came to her
mind, people who had been killed. Of *course* they could do
that. Adam only patted her hand.

"How long, do you think, can we survive down here?" Phil
grabbed a bundle of the moist blades of grass and sniffed at
them. "I mean: without water."

This very moment, the well's cover above them was
slightly pushed aside again, and something was stuck through
the gap.

"A rope. Adam, he's letting down a rope!"

"That may be—holy shit."

The rope was a hose. A super wide commercial one. Somewhere above, a water tap was opened. The sudden pressure whipped the hose to and fro, then it calmed down. The water started to run more evenly, like a sudden waterfall. Phil was soaked and gasped for air. Adam pulled her even closer, both pressing against the wall to avoid the cold jet. While the water started to climb up their feet.

"We still have time," Adam said, "we'll find a way out."

Phil's feet were already numb from the cold, but when Adam built a leg-up with his hands, she climbed it. Standing on his shoulders, she scanned the wall with her fingers, inch by inch. But there was nothing but smooth stone. Only farther up, close to the edge of the well, she thought she saw something. A ledge, maybe. But the cellphone light didn't reach far enough to really see it.

"Damn."

Phil tried hard to suppress a sob. *Don't cry.* When she slid down Adam's back, the water was already playing around her knees. *Don't panic.* She held her breath. Would they really just drown here?

Adam took her in his arms. "I'm so sorry, Phil. So sorry—for it all."

He didn't need to see her. His arms enfolded her with blind certainty. His lips found her forehead, kissed her eyes, not knowing if the wet was tears or the deadly water that would drown them.

"Phil, I wished—I was such an idiot. I mean: then."

"Me too. There was no way to turn it around, somehow."

"True. But I should never have—I should never have slapped you."

"True. But I shouldn't have been so unforgiving. After all it wasn't exactly—I mean: a cardinal sin."

"But awful. I'm sorry."

"Me too."

They held each other as the water was steadily rising.

"I think I'll cry," Phil said and cried. The water was now up to her thighs. This can't be, she thought. They couldn't just wait to drown here.

"Okay," Adam said as if he had heard her thought. "Plan B. We do it like in the military."

"What?"

"Like two soldiers would do if they fell in a well."

"Right time for a rhyme."

"Saw it on TV. A documentary on military bravado. The kind of film my father loved. Come on."

Gently, Adam directed Phil towards the center of the shaft, her face to the wall. The water rushed down her back, splashed around her hips.

"Just ignore it. The hose, too. Don't move."

Keeping his hands on her, her waist, her arms, her shoulders, he moved around her and suddenly had his back to her. Pressing his back against hers.

"Now push against me as hard as you can and link your arms to mine. Like that, right—as tight as you can. Keep them close to your sides. Flex your muscles, make them like steel. Don't let go, never. Okay?"

"Okay."

"Now press your feet against the wall. Don't forget: your back tight against mine. Like that. We have to be Siamese twins, all attached. One body. Got it?"

"One body," Phil said, tensing up.

"It may be twelve, fifteen feet up. We have to get there, before the water hits the cover. So listen: When I start counting one, you lift your right foot against the wall, one length up. When I count two, you lift your left foot. I'll do the same, only half-length. That's how we'll walk up the wall. Then we'll push off the lid."

"That'll never work."

But it did. Foot length by foot length they crawled up the shaft. Phil's muscles were so tense they vibrated as she tried to keep steady against Adam's back, to withstand his heavier weight. But it was easier than she would have thought. She only had to follow his commands, one—two—three, and they moved in perfect sync. Feet against the wall, his pressure against her back, the counter-pressure of her body, both aligning as well as they could. Like a four-legged insect, skilled by evolution, they crawled up the completely vertical wall. Two feet or so below the lid, they reached the ledge Phil had seen from far down. From here, it looked more like a niche, a concave indention. They had to stay away from it to not break step. The water was rising with them, the lid was near, not perfectly closed with the gap for the hose.

"Now." Adam pushed the crown of his head against the cover and tensed his neck muscles. Pushed and pushed. But the lid wouldn't budge.

"I have to get my fingers in the gap. Keep your back strong against mine."

"Don't let go." Phil panicked. "When you let go of my arms, we'll fall."

"Have to. Now. Concentrate."

Phil's legs started to shake even more when Adam released his arms from hers. She tried to press her fingertips against the wall like suction cups. She needed even more strength in her back to keep up with Adam's pressure, but where should it come from? Adam's fingers slid through the gap and pushed the lip.

With a desperate yelp, Phil fell. Her body crashed into the water, dived deep, water shooting against her stomach. She popped back up like a cork.

"Swim." Adam held on to the lid with four fingers. Phil paddled frantically. Swallowed water, choked, her arms flailing.

"Swim."

Adam couldn't hold on to the lid any longer and fell too. He tried to grab the hose, but in vain. He sank deep and reappeared next to Phil. The well's diameter was not wide enough for both to make real swimming strokes. They crashed into each other, had to tread water on the spot which was extremely exhausting. Phil couldn't feel her arms anymore, her legs got lame, she bruised them against the wall, against Adam; every movement was an unbearable effort. She tried with all that was left in her, but her arms were like iron. She sank.

"Hang in there. Phil, please."

But how? Adam was stronger; maybe he would make it. Pure Darwinism, those with the muscles survived, the others drowned. The water was cold, but Phil was sweating. Anton, Anton, Anton. Her son's face passed by her in the dark. Oh, Anton. No more strength.

"Adam," Phil fought to draw a breath, "please listen. Important..." She spat out water, tried as hard as she could. "It is—Anton. I was pregnant when—when we—he is your son. Please take care of him. Please."

"*What?*"

"Your son. Anton." One more stroke. One more. A last one. "Promise."

Phil tried to keep her head up, tried to catch a bit more air, but the water was in her mouth, her nose. It had risen far up the shaft. She drowned...

That's when the unimaginable happened: The wall opened. The concave indenture below the well's mouth turned out to be the entrance to a drain channel, not a niche, but a hole, sucking the water in. Instead of rising farther, it gushed off, into a channel. And then the suction caught Phil and carried her along, down into a black depth without air. Only the channel got wider, which accelerated the water's flow, whirling her around like a puppet, like in a tsunami. She suffocated, she knew this was her last breath, her last thought was Anton.

Anton.

Then the channel spat Phil out.

Suddenly there was water and air. She sank, came up again, and there was more air than she could ever remember. It was like waking up from a nightmare—she was free. Easily, she turned on her back and drifted in the cool but not ice-cold water, salty water now that burned in her throat but not in a scary way. She gasped, could swim again, her body feather-light on soft waves. She was alive.

"Adam," Phil yelled with her first long breath. Had he made it? He must have, please. She heard water rippling, getting closer. Then Adam was at her side, without a word. He also floated on his back, on water that carried him gently. They drifted, exhausted. When Phil lifted her head, she saw Adam was already scanning the area. There was the dock with the yachts on one side and the fishing boats on the other, the half-moon-shaped bay and Can Salammbo on top. But for the murmur of the waves, all was quiet. And Adam and Phil were alive. The drain channel had swept them right into the Mediterranean.

With powerful crawling strokes, Adam swam towards the dock. He pulled himself up and reached his hand out to Phil. When she was up too, he dropped her hand as if it was poisonous.

"To the car."

She ran behind him, up the stairs to the mansion's back wall. They crossed the wasteland with its wind-beaten pine trees, right under the bright full moon. Phil couldn't believe how careless Adam was. What if Blasco or one of the security guys patrolled around the lot? But there was no one. Meager light rays crept out under some windows, but only the wind and the waves could be heard. The torches were blown out. The cars that had parked along the track had disappeared.

Adam's rental was still where they had left it, dangerously obvious and alone in the field. He gestured Phil to stop. They had to make sure that no one was lying in wait for them. After some long minutes, uncomfortably crouching side by side behind a bush, he pulled the remote key out of his drenched jeans pocket. The beep that opened the car sounded like a fire alarm in the night. Lights flashed and Phil's heart skipped a beat, but still no one came running out or pointed a gun at them. Adam ran to the driver's side, and she raced behind him and dropped down in the passenger seat. Only when they were on the main road, Adam turned the headlights on. In tortured silence they rode on.

It took Phil all the way to Santa Gertrudis—the lovely old town with the Bar Costas, where half a day ago they had been allies—to find the courage to speak. Timidly, she put her hand on Adam's arm.

"Adam, about Anton—I know this must be..."

He brusquely shook of her hand, sounding heartrendingly disillusioned. "Phil, don't. Just be quiet."

"Adam."

"Shut up, for fuck's sake." He raced the car furiously into a turn, causing it to skid. Phil fell back in her seat, uttering a little cry.

Adam brought it back under his control. "Sorry," he mumbled.

Despite the late hour, Lluis was still sitting behind his desk. Open-mouthed, he stared at the two walking in, dripping wet, with hanging heads.

"Evening." And Phil was already on her way up the stairs.

Before Lluis could react, Adam asked for a pack of rice, making clear it was, at this moment, the most urgent thing in the world.

CHAPTER 46

Adam had taken his iPhone apart and turned it carefully in all directions. Water dripped out from everywhere. He knew it was unlikely to save any data but he had to try. When no more water leaked, he stuffed the phone into a plastic bag filled up with the dry rice Lluis had brought. Now Adam could do nothing but wait until the rice had soaked up all the fluids. He needed tons of luck to restore at least some of the photos, but it was still quite unlikely.

Adam was frustrated. First he had lost the phone with Amanda's voicemail that would have been evidence against Scherer's version of the story, and now they might not even have any proof of the orgy and Colonel Cruz's involvement. How should they proceed? They? He, Adam corrected himself, or he and Bartolo.

Adam finally got out of his wet clothes and took a hot shower. He contemplated driving back to Can Salammbo to try to find the phone in the courtyard. But the way the dogs had mauled it, there could hardly be anything left. Plus there were Blasco and the security men. Adam was not suicidal.

When he stretched out on his bed, the other issue he had stubbornly avoided thinking about attacked him. He knew he needed to confront it.

He had a child. A son. No, he didn't have it, Phil had hidden it from him for almost sixteen years. Never before had Adam felt so bewildered, so helpless. All these years, his child had grown up without him, without knowing his own father. Probably had to live with some damn lie about why this father had never taken an interest in him. Adam clenched his fists. He tried to imagine what it felt like to have a child. A little creature, undeformed yet by the rules of society, whom he could help grow up. He had no idea how children ticked, when they had their first teeth or started to walk or said *Daddy* for the first time, or what one should read to them. But he could have learned, couldn't he? He knew he would have loved seeing his child grow up to a sixteen-year-old boy with a mind of his own. Anton—with the same capital 'A' like his own name, and his genes. That he had never heard Anton say *Daddy*, never read something to him, gave Adam an overwhelming feeling of loss. He ached all over, not only in his heart but in every single cell. How could Phil have done this to him?

Adam got up again and opened the bottle of red wine from his minibar. He filled up a glass, gushed the wine down in two gulps and refilled it. Had he and Phil ever talked about kids? Of course not. In those months together they had not even exchanged the words "I love you." Adam once told Phil that his sister Amanda had badly wanted a child, but then could not even get along with the one Scherer brought into their marriage, a defiant little punk from a former relationship. Amanda hadn't liked the boy, and the dislike seemed to be mutual.

"Who even wants to put a child in this world, the state it's in?" Adam remembered Phil saying, and he had agreed with her.

He poured himself more wine and wondered how the bottle could already be empty. Was there more, somewhere? He lay down again, only to toss and turn, as sleep tonight was definitely not an option.

Phil couldn't sleep either. She knew that everything was over—again. Everything that had to do with her newfound whatever it even was with Adam. Probably for the best, but it hurt. Why had she, idiot that she was, opened her mouth? Because she had thought she would die in that well and didn't want to leave Anton alone, without knowing who his father was. That's why. Phil had told herself that one day she would tell him, but so far she never had. When Anton started asking about his father, she had mumbled something about a one-night-stand; that she didn't really know the man.

And she really didn't, right? Phil also remembered that, once the subject came up, both Adam and she had agreed that one shouldn't put more children into this world. So what should she have done? Fight with him, split from him, and then—surprise!—announce she was expecting his child? A child he didn't even want? Well, she had changed her mind about this, right? Since the first moment Phil felt the tiniest of movements in her belly, unborn Anton kicking, he had always been the most precious being in her life.

Okay. Or not okay how she had treated Adam. But she couldn't turn the clock back. If only they had not met again!

The whole night seemed like a surreal nightmare. The Bes Brothers, the underage girls—girls from Can Follet, for heaven's sake. The brothers' panic because of someone's death. Their escape from Blasco and the dogs. The well. Almost drowning. The agony. Talking about Anton. The end.

Phil tried hard to sleep, but what had she expected? At three in the morning, she was still wide awake, and her thoughts wandered to the other horror: Stella's outrageous betrayal of the values Doro and the Daughters of Tanit stood for. They needed to know as soon as possible that a Judas was living among them.

Suddenly, there was a knock at Phil's door. She jumped up and pushed the curtain aside: Adam. Apparently dead drunk.

When she opened the door, he swayed slightly, supporting himself with one hand against the doorframe. He didn't speak, just looked at her, with bloodshot eyes.

"Listen, Adam." Nervous chills ran down Phil's back. "Concerning my son. You know I only talked about Anton because—in this situation. Can you please just forget it? You do not bear any responsibility. I didn't want to impose a child on you then, and I have no intention to do it now."

"You have been hiding my child from me for sixteen years," he stated with an amazingly steady voice.

Did he want to make demands? Phil got even more nervous. "You never wanted a child. It's hard enough to get along with yourself, you said..."

"Neither did you, *you* said."

"But we had been together for only three months. How could I—wouldn't you have felt trapped?"

Phil was painfully aware that she shone a pretty self-righteous light on herself. Because sixteen years ago, in this night that got so terribly out of control, she had wanted to tell Adam. She had not hidden her pregnancy from him because she feared he might feel trapped, but because of the girl and their fight. With a kind of revengeful pride, she had decided that she didn't need him. Didn't want a man who kept her waiting with a stupid self-cooked dinner like a stupid pregnant *hausfrau* while he kissed another girl. Hell no. Also, Adam had slapped her. A man who beats women should never be a father, Doro and Phil had decided.

Now, Phil badly needed to be honest. "I wanted to tell you that night. I really did. But then I got so angry with you. This girl. And you were so drunk. Somehow I couldn't. It was all so fucked up. Please talk to me."

"I will, of course, pay for my son. Just let me know what I have to do."

"Adam, I thought I would die. I mean, it's not about duties. I manage."

Between his bloodshot eyes was a deep vertical crease. Phil bit her lips when he turned away to stare at the dark sea in front of them, so calm and normal like nothing else the entire night.

"You would never have told me," Adam said matter-of-factly, "not even after we slept together again."

There was only one honest answer. "You're right. I wouldn't have."

He nodded. "I don't hate you for it," he said and knew it was true. "And I won't do anything concerning my son if you don't want me to. But I will never get over it. Never."

"I am so sorry."

His hand combed through his hair with this characteristic gesture of his. "I am too," he said. "I will try to go on, try to forget that there is a son, my son living on the other side of the world, and I don't know him."

"Adam." But Phil couldn't go on. Tears blinded her, as he walked down the balcony and his door closed behind him.

CHAPTER 47

The next morning when Phil came down the stairs, Bartolo waved her over to the table where he was sitting with Adam. She nodded, relieved. She had wondered whether she would dare to go to Adam's table and risk being rebuffed.

Chivalrously, Bartolo pulled out a chair for her.

Phil felt like shit. She thought she must not have slept another second after Adam left. But a while ago she woke up, soaked in sweat. She who woke up must have slept, right?

"Morning," she mumbled, got a short nod from Adam, and a lot of patting on the arm from Bartolo. His cheerfulness, though, turned into irritation when it dawned on him that something was not right between his friends. He made a face like a worried father, knitting his brows.

"So, spit it out. What have you gotten yourselves into, now?"

In unemotional words, Adam informed him about their adventure in Can Salammbo. Again, Bartolo didn't seem to mind that they had broken the law he was supposed to represent.

"You two are a super team," he said, shooting meaningful glances. Phil hid her hands under the table, afraid he might take them and join them with Adam's.

"Sex with underage girls, now we'll get them. And we definitely will take another look into Mr. Scherer's alibi. Maybe someone we haven't talked to yet saw him drive up to Villa Éscorpion the evening of March 8th. Or someone remembers him buying the champagne. Additional great evidence is the voicemail. And when the photos go public, the Bes Brothers' lawyers can lament their, well, their illegal origin all they want. Great job, guys, I can't wait to let the prosecutor know. Show me the photos, all right?"

All the more frustrated was Bartolo when Adam continued that the phone with the voicemail had been chewed up by the dogs and that his own soaked phone with photos of the orgy and Colonel Cruz gave little hope to be restored.

"*Qué leche.* Fucking shit. I can't believe it."

"There is something else..." But Phil hesitated.

Should she tell Bartolo about Stella's part in the orgy? Have him be the one to confront the already traumatized women of Can Follet with this ugly truth? No way. She would talk to Doro first. And Doro would deal with the problem and prepare the women for the encounter with police. Doro would also know what to do with Stella. She needed to be kicked out of Can Follet. And Doro was the only one to take care of the abused girls and convince them to testify against the Bes Brothers. So this time, these bastards would get what they deserved, a criminal conviction. Not an easy way out like in the case of Neves and the Dutch girl. Stella had to be brought to court, as she obviously was the girls' pimp. When Phil thought about Stella's easy smile, her sweet empathy, she still had a hard time believing what she had seen.

Then she had another idea: "I also took photos, of this sleeping guy and Colonel Cruz. My phone was zipped in the pocket of my rain jacket. It's drenched, of course, but maybe— it's drying now."

"Hopefully." Bartolo sighed. "I also need to talk to Martí

Blasco. After all, he tried to kill you guys. The problem is that I'll need our sign language expert for this, and he will put on record that you broke in and stole the phone. Damn."

"Do it anyway." Adam shrugged, "I don't care."

Phil only nodded.

"Okay." Then Bartolo remembered why he had arrived so cheerfully. After requesting the information of the Caixa bank's IP cameras opposite hotel El Puerto, he learned that they were set on continuous monitoring. So it hadn't been a problem to look into the eligible half hour.

Bartolo pulled out his smartphone. The video he had taken from the surveillance monitor showed a number of people withdrawing money. A leashed dog setting a giant turd on the sidewalk was pulled away. A backpacker who seemed to conjure his card before inserting it in the ATM, which swallowed it immediately. They watched him throw up his hands in desperation and step back, right into the turd the dog had left.

Then a dusty SEAT showed up. Too bad the camera's perspective didn't allow them to read its license plate or see the driver. But it showed a tall man who opened the back door, threw a traveling bag in, and dropped down on the passenger seat. The camera had captured his profile precisely.

"This is Robert Wendling," Bartolo said. "We sent the info to the airport and ferry terminals. He didn't get a last minute-ticket for last night, so now we're prepared. Whenever he tries to leave, we're on him."

Phil had immediately recognized the man. "Robert Wendling was in the café with Tamar. He first gave her a necklace, and then they started to fight."

"And his description fits perfectly the man Mr. Huber saw in Scherer's car, shortly before Tamar's death."

"So he did come back." Remembering the scene on the cliff sent a shiver down Phil's spine: Tamar struggling to get out of the car, her distorted face, her spiteful words.

"I guess Tamar and Wendling were partners—partners in

crime, so to say—when they approached the *Insular* editor, Hans von Brolow, and then chickened out. Now, Wendling came back, but this time Tamar rebuffed him."

And Wendling hadn't put up with it. Phil thought about the bruises his grip had left on Tamar's arm. So was he her murderer, not Scherer? But why had he been in Scherer's car? And what did the drama between him and Tamar have to do with Amanda, Ninguno, and Neves? Maybe there wasn't a connection after all. Maybe the big thing they imagined was a succession of unrelated occurrences.

Bartolo focused on Adam who stared at the video. Now, he put his reading glasses on, rewound it, watched it again, and finally looked up. Four eyes with question marks in them met his gaze.

"I'm pretty sure," Adam said, "even though I only met him once, a long time ago. But still, I'm quite sure: Wendling is Scherer's son."

Two mouths formed a perplexed "O."

Phil reacted first, "But the Scherers don't have children."

Adam addressed Bartolo. "My sister didn't, but he has a son with an ex." He frowned, "I met him at Amanda's and Scherer's wedding, twenty-five years ago. Nobody bothered to introduce him to me, but Scherer called him Junior. He was quite a punk, dark and moody, and he gave my sister the cold shoulder at her own wedding while Scherer kept throwing commands at him—Junior, get the cognac, take a picture, Junior... He and I talked a bit about music."

Adam again studied the recording, "Yes, I'm sure that's Junior."

"*Carajo*, can it get even crazier?"

The inspector glued the phone to his ear and ordered someone to immediately contact the colleagues in Frankfurt for the confirmation that Scherer really was Wendling's father.

"If you are right, Adam," he shook his head, "we have to

assume that Scherer and his son had a relationship with the same girl. Sick."

"I guess it was okay for her," Phil said, "Tamar told me she wasn't into the one-and-only love interest thing."

"But at least one of the gentlemen was not willing to handle this. Or not able. Probably the son." Bartolo's sigh came from the bottom of his heart. "Which may mean that her death has nothing to do with the TAB after all, but originates in—how shall I say—a varied Oedipal complex. There is the father who doesn't marry Junior's mother but another woman, and doesn't even introduce his son to his wedding guests. That's how much he cares about him. And later he even starts an affair with his girlfriend. Jeez!"

"Okay." Adam started to march around the table to think. "So first, Junior tries to harm his father by contacting a local journalist, this..." He looked at Phil. For the moment, his aversion seemed forgotten.

"Hans von Brolow."

"...with explosive proof of the TAB orgies that he or Tamar collected."

"But wait. Tamar had an affair with the father and worked for him. Why would she of all people try to harm her employer slash lover?" Bartolo asked.

Exactly what Phil wondered about.

"Maybe something happened between them." Adam kept circling around the table. "Maybe this had to do with Amanda. Even though Scherer told me she didn't care about his affairs."

"Maybe she did at the time." Bartolo shrugged. "Anyway, Tamar introduced Wendling to von Brolow and wanted him to go public with the scandal. Then they turned around and fed him to the sharks."

"According to Hans," Phil said, "Wendling was in love with Tamar. She must have convinced him to pull out. Ibiza is a small island, so I imagine that she ultimately decided not to mess with Scherer, the island's king. I mean: she kept working for him, right? And she kept on having an affair with him."

She occasionally let him fuck her, had been Tamar's words.

Adam sat back down. "Finding out his father's affair with the woman he loved, must have been a shock for Wendling. How he must have hated Scherer."

In thought, Adam and Phil locked their eyes and hastily looked away.

Bartolo took over. "And in his hatred, Wendling kills his father's wife, Ninguno and Tamar, the woman he loves... Why not just kill the father and *basta ya?* Does this make sense?"

Hell no, Phil thought, and Adam also shook his head.

"*Exacto.* That's why I think the murders don't have anything to do with each other. There is something else behind it all." Bartolo jumped up. "We have to find Wendling. If we only knew who that woman was who picked him up."

Adam came to a stop. "A middle-aged Ibizenca. I think I know who she is."

CHAPTER 48

Bartolo's police car raced along the road, direction San Rafael. The inspector had immediately shared Adam's presumption that Rosenda Marí Torres, Scherer's long-time housekeeper, had come to pick up Wendling at his hotel. They must know each other, and she was no fan of Scherer either. So they decided to pay Rosenda a surprise visit. All three went to the parking lot, but while Adam got into Bartolo's car, Phil hesitated, gave a short wave, and turned back.

"What?"

Bartolo looked at Adam for an explanation, but he only said, "Let's go."

Approaching San Rafael, they passed the biggest discotheque in the world, the Privilege, which sat in the tranquil landscape like an abandoned UFO. Opposite it, the smaller but as showy Amnesia also seemed to have landed here from another galaxy. While Adam wasn't a fan of discotheques, Bartolo proudly boasted that in the Amnesia, that opened only one year after the Franco terror ended, dance music had been invented to start its triumph around the world.

San Rafael was a small village with a large number of stylishly restored restaurants and pottery studios, organized around an old fortified church. The romantic churchyard opened the view on D'Alt Vila and the medieval castle above Ibiza city. The Phoenician harbor below was dotted with boats. A huge ferry was just leaving with a goodbye wave of steam.

Rosenda lived in an outskirt of the village, in a white-washed square *finca* constructed in the unique Ibizan way that looks like a combination of oriental tradition and Bauhaus. A ladder was leaning against the front. Rosenda was up on the flat roof, sweeping the clay tiles with a besom broom. When Bartolo got out of his car, she pretended not to have expected him.

He pointed at the cloudless blue sky. "*Hola*, Rosenda. Chasing away the *barraguets*, or does it look like rain?"

Rosenda poked with her broom in the roof's gutter that led to a cistern.

"Rain, *qué si no*," she snarled, immediately defensive. "What you want?"

"Is he with you? Robert Wendling?"

Rosenda only shrugged, watching Bartolo out of the corner of her eye. But when Adam got out of the car, she recognized the inevitable, threw the broom down to the ground, and followed it across the ladder.

"*Señor* Ryan," she said sternly, "*Fue un'accidente*. He didn't mean to..."

"Did you really mean to hide him?" Bartolo spoke Spanish, but Adam could guess what he was saying. "Damn, Rosenda, we are the law. You should have brought him to us."

"*Ah, la ley. Como su padre, verdad*?" Rosenda looked at Adam and turned to broken English. "The father destroy him. The poor *niño se siente devastado*."

Adam was far from allying himself with her. "Robert is no *niño*," he said coldly, "and how could you just stand by and ignore what Scherer and the TAB have been doing to others? To the little *niñas*."

Rosenda uttered a tortured yelp and covered her eyes with

her hands.

She knows it, Adam thought, still shocked even though he had suspected it.

"You worked for Scherer and saw what the TAB guys do. And how it drove Amanda into desperation. And sure, you felt uncomfortable, but you didn't speak up. So much could have been avoided."

Rosetta rubbed her weather-worn face with both hands, as if trying to wipe off her guilt. "*Ninguno puede*... Evil not be avoided, *no possible*. We can only try to contain it, but it's a *pandemia*, always break out again."

Ignorance and fatalism going hand in hand! Adam had no tolerance for this kind of jabbering, had heard it too often from people who tried to explain why they had ignored a crime. It's always the sheep that keep the wolves alive.

Bartolo's phone rang. He took it, and his eyes widened in surprise. "What are you saying?" He went back to the car, mumbling over his shoulder, "One moment please" and closed the car's door behind him.

Rosenda glared at Adam, suddenly furious. "Amanda, she can go away, she no prisoner." She held her hand up in front of his face and rubbed thumb and index finger against each other. "But she stay for Scherer's money and comfortable life. Always *lamentarse*, but always stay."

"Who poisoned her? Was it Scherer...?"

"*No lo se.* Don't know."

"...or Tamar?"

Rosenda gasped in shock, while Bartolo came back out of the car and walked by her to the *finca*. "Now, I need to talk to Wendling," he said and pushed the door to Rosenda's house open. Adam followed him. At his back, the woman protested meekly.

Their eyes had to get used to the darkness. The air in here smelled delightfully of fresh herbs and garlic and the fire burning in a charcoal oven. In front of it, on a wooden stool, sat

Robert Wendling. His face was turned towards the wall like a disobedient pupil's, put there for punishment.

When he turned around, they looked into the unhappiest face on Earth: ash gray, eyes swollen from crying, stubble on the unshaved chin, and a long, crusted scratch down one cheek. Next to him on the floor was the travel bag they had seen in the surveillance video, and a jacket on it.

Wendling got up and tried to put on the jacket, but was swaying as if he was too exhausted to stand. He sat back down, struggled with the jacket, and when he finally had it on, got up again and shuffled towards the door with insecure steps.

"Let's go. I'm ready."

"*No, Roberto, no,*" Rosenda helplessly tried to block the door. To Bartolo, "Don't you see? *Está cansado, todavia enfermo.*"

Dziri laid his hand on Wendling's arm. "Wait. Do you need a doctor?"

"I'm only tired. Haven't slept for three nights. Ever since Tamar is gone..."

At the door, he gently pushed Rosenda aside—and noticed Adam. He stared in surprise. "Adam? Adam Ryan?"

"Oh man, Junior. Robert. What in the world have you done?"

Wendling began to sob, "I'm so sorry. About Amanda. And Tamar."

"Your father..."

Adam was interrupted by Bartolo. "Adam, wait."

The inspector's eyes were glued to Wendling's face' "Your father, Mr. Wendling, has just turned himself in. He confessed that he pushed Tamar Stettin to her death."

Wendling froze. "What the fuck?"

Rosenda was the first to recollect herself. "*De veras? Por fin!* Finally he does a right thing." She hugged Wendling. "*Cariño*, it *is* only right..."

"A confession?" Adam frowned. "Scherer confessed? And

what's with Amanda? And Ninguno?"

"Nothing, he's very clear about that. He says he pushed Tamar, and she fell to her death. I wonder how the dragging traces fit in. Can't be related, he says."

The inspector kept looking at Wendling, who seemed nothing but stunned.

"Did Scherer explain why?" Adam asked.

"He says he was frustrated by Tamar's constant demands. That she kept nagging him to commit to her while he only saw her as an affair."

"I don't believe one word of that, sorry."

"Neither do I." Bartolo didn't take his eyes off Wending, "Tamar didn't like commitments. She was for open relationships, not possessive ones. Right, Mr. Wendling? She was annoyed by your jealousy."

Rosenda stepped between the inspector and her protégé. "*Dejaté*, Dziri, will you? Scherer confessed. That's all you need."

"Plus, he has an alibi," he said nevertheless.

"Leave the boy alone."

Rosenda again hugged Wendling, which brought him out of his paralyzed state. He started to laugh, shrill, desperately, ending in a sob.

"That's funny," he said. "For once in his life my father admits to being guilty of something, and then it's not true." With a contemptuous grin, he nodded to Adam, "You're right, Adam, confessions don't suit the old bloke. He's only saying this now because I'm the only one left."

"Ssh, ssh, Roberto, be quiet, no more..."

"Nobody but me, the unwanted bastard who owes his life to a ripped condom. Only fit to be the underling in the old man's hierarchy."

"Scherer admitted to his guilt," Rosenda screamed, "and he is guilty."

"True, he is." Almost pitifully, Wendling looked at the

woman who wanted to protect him, "but it was me who dragged Tamar to the cliff and pushed her."

He turned to Dziri, pointing to the scratch on his cheek, "That was Tamar, with her nails. I'm sure you can easily verify it."

"Sure, we can." The policeman sighed as if he regretted this.

"She fought like a lioness. She was in a panic."

Tears were running down Rosenda's cheeks, "Please, *mi niño,* stop it. *Fue un'accidente.* An accident."

But Wendling was not to be stopped anymore. "I met Tamar at one of the few occasions I was granted the mercy to visit my father on Ibiza. And Amanda." A burning glare met Adam. "This woman couldn't stand me. Oh man, she let me know that whenever she had a chance. At the same time, she was also under his thumb and very unhappy."

"I'm sorry," Adam mumbled, but Wendling only shrugged, "Well, yeah, guess that's why she made her way out."

"What do you know..."

But Wendling was somewhere else. "I immediately fell in love with Tamar. The old bloke had something going with her mother, that's how we met. A tour around the island, something a father would do with his visiting son, he made Amanda believe. But in reality he went to see his lover, and Tamar and I were left on our own." He giggled cynically, "In the end, Amanda found out anyway and, man, was she pissed. But I was happy because I found Tamar. I was never like—I really let her be herself. I closed both eyes, no matter how it made me feel. The other men, I swallowed everything. I understood that she needed to be free. But my own father! She swore she had ended it, that she only worked for him. That he had seduced her and she hadn't been able to defend herself. A big fat lie."

"But you had everything in your hand, didn't you? The evidence against your father and the TAB," Dziri said. "You could have had them thrown in jail."

Wendling nodded miserably. "I know. But suddenly, Tamar urged me to give it up or, she said, we would end up being the ones screwed. Then Hans called, in panic, and said all the photos I had given him had disappeared, and all the data deleted. I guess Tamar was behind this, too. In the end, she convinced me to let it all be. She said she hadn't been aware that the pictures would hurt everybody, also the innocent ones like her and me and the women of Can Follet."

"Leave them out of it, *comprende*," said Rosenda, who had just been sobbing, with a coldness Adam couldn't understand.

Wendling lifted both hands. "*Vale*, Rosenda," he mumbled, quite the disciplined kid that had been sitting on the stool, his face to the wall.

"Why would this hurt the women of Can Follet?" Adam probed, "I'd think they would be happy to have these predators exposed."

Wendling shrugged. "I only know what Tamar wanted. Or not." He turned to the inspector. "Guess you know that Hans published the article after all, and the TAB lawyers came after him like bloodhounds. I only got off the hook because I went back to Germany to work in the press office of a chemical plant, whitewashing environmental crimes. I couldn't reach Tamar for a long time, until two weeks ago, she suddenly showed up in Frankfurt and pretended she had missed me. She also said she was staying away from my father and the TAB. Another lie, as I found out when I followed her one day and realized that even over there she met one of the Brothers. But when I confronted her, she denied it. She is—was such a liar. Anyway, we fought, and she left. And when I came to Ibiza to make up, I learned she was still fucking my father. So that was it."

After this outburst, Wendling picked up his bag.

"*Señor* Wendling, you need to come with us." Bartolo's words were not necessary, as Wendling was already headed to the police car. Adam felt nothing but pity.

"Roberto," Rosenda called after Wendling, "Roberto, *cuídate!*"

He lifted his hand and made the peace sign. Then he plunged into the back seat. Rosenda dabbed her eyes with her sleeve, but her expression, to Adam, was inscrutable. "*Qué?*" she asked aggressively when she realized he was watching her. Without bothering to answer, Adam followed Bartolo to his car.

Not one word was spoken until they arrived at the police station in Ibiza city. When Bartolo escorted Wendling up the stairs, the entrance door flew open, and Scherer came running out. More than ever did he look like a ghost with his disheveled hair and fluttering shirt.

"Junior," he panted, "Don't say a word. Not one word." He pointed at the inspector, "You stay away from my son, Dziri. My lawyers will deal with you."

His trembling hand grasped Wendling's sleeve—but was shaken off immediately. "Wow," Wendling said, addressing Adam, "does he suddenly display father feelings? When I wasn't a murderer yet, this never happened."

"Listen to me, Junior..."

Wendling ignored Scherer and turned to Dziri. "I want to make my statement now." As if to torture his father even more, "Just to be clear: It wasn't a spontaneous emotional act. I dragged Tamar to the cliff. She tried to defend herself, pleaded to be spared, but I kept dragging her. Then I pushed her down."

"Junior. Robert, please don't."

"Okay," Dziri said, "that's what we figured. And the second woman?"

Wendling looked puzzled, then remembered. "Oh, right. I really didn't mean that. She just happened to be in the wrong place at the wrong time, and I panicked. I thought she'd be a witness, which seemed to matter at the time. So," he bit his lip, "I grabbed this rock and ran after her and hit her on the head. She made a few more steps, staggering, and I couldn't watch anymore. I'm afraid she fell off the cliff, too. I'm sorry."

He gasped as Adam grabbed his shirt collar and pulled him close, almost spit into his face. "You are lucky she's still alive, or you'd really be sorry."

He pushed Wendling, who stumbled backwards and fell on his butt. He struggled back up and rubbed his throat. "I'm honestly glad about this."

Scherer uttered a cry of protest. "Junior!" Now he sobbed, "You weren't of sound mind. You're not accountable for your actions. I'll call my lawyers."

He already had his phone in his hand, but Wendling gave him a sneer. "Rejected, old man. I don't give a damn."

With a cynical grin, he pushed by his father and disappeared with Dziri into the building. Scherer lifted both hands as if this could somehow stem the tide, then dropped them helplessly. Without another word, he walked down the stairs, with his head hanging, his shoulders drooping. The king of Ibiza, the Bes Brother, was a lonely, broken man.

CHAPTER 49

While Adam and Bartolo were at the police station, Phil was stretched out on her bed trying to think about her next steps. Strategic withdrawal, she thought cynically, that was all left for her to do. Of course, Bartolo had noticed the tension between Adam and her, and by now would know why. And Adam was the professional investigator. She'd better start dealing with her financial drama and go home as quickly as she could. She still had to talk to Doro, though, this night when they would meet for dinner. The thought alone made Phil's stomach churn. But after that, she would be gone and never see Adam again.

Phil called the one real estate agent who had shown a vague interest in her burnt-down house to ask whether she had taken a look at it. An automated voice told her she was calling outside business hours. In desperate determination, she called the other agent who, without seeing the property, had offered her a dumping price. When again she only reached the answering machine she realized it was a Sunday. Phil had lost track of the days. Nothing she could do right now. Next morning she would take care of her problem and be gone.

Phil got up. In the lobby was Trudy in a travel suit, a suitcase at her side.

"Gosh, the time a cab takes," she complained to Lluis who was behind his reception desk, "could you call them again?"

"I just did, Mrs. Huber. It will be here any minute now."

Nervously, Trudy's eyes kept darting towards the staircase. She cringed when Ezra appeared on it. At the sight of her, he uttered an owlish cry that had Trudy flee behind the desk. Like a little girl she hid in Lluis's back.

"Don't," she warned Ezra. "Leave me alone."

Clasping the stair rail, Ezra came stumbling down. When he landed on the lowest step, he tripped over the rug and fell on his knees. Nothing was left of his superior attitude; the whole guy a complete mess. His sweat pants hung down to his knees like a neglected giant child's jumpsuit.

"Trudy," he whined, "You can't leave. I haven't done anything."

"Yes, you have."

"I only looked. I only threw a glance..."

"Marginal difference," Trudy hissed from her safe place behind Lluis. "Amy is totally right about you. And *I say unto you, that whosoever looketh at a woman lustfully hath already committed adultery with her in his heart.*"

"Trudy," Ezra wailed, "stop it..."

Lluis tried to step away from her, "Mrs. Huber, please calm down."

"Matthew 5:27. As you, Ezra, should know."

When Trudy reappeared from behind Lluis, it was apparent that Ezra's misery had redeemed her from all fears. There was piercing cold triumph in her voice. "Amy was always right. You have no right or ownership over us. I'm moving in with her and hope to never see you again, Ezra. Oh, and as the money on our shared bank account belongs in half to me, I withdrew my part this morning."

"Wha—what?"

"You can keep the Bible, but half of the house belongs to me as well. Amy will help me find a good divorce lawyer."

That moment, a man appeared in the entrance. "Taxi?" he asked.

"For me, please." Trudy marched around the desk, picked up her suitcase and handed it to the driver. "Thank you." She gave Phil and Lluis a happy little wave. "Goodbye, dears. It was nice to meet you."

Ezra received another, quite theatrical wave, "Have a great future, Ezra, and don't forget to pray for your sins."

Her heels banged on the tiles like pistol shots. Then Trudy was gone.

Ezra fell down on a chair and started to wail. He was a broken man. The patriarch had turned into a discontinued model, discarded to collect dust.

Phil had agreed to meet Doro at the road junction. It wasn't more than half a kilometer to walk from the Esperanza, but she felt a strange tension in her neck and kept looking back. When Doro's car appeared, Phil came shooting out from behind the cistus bush where she had been hiding.

"Phew, hi, Doro. There you are."

Doro knocked against the clock on the dashboard. "Hi. I'm not late, am I?"

"No, it's just—after the attack on the cliffs, I feel uncomfortable standing here alone in the dark."

"Shit, I should've picked you up at the hotel. Sorry, how insensitive of me."

Phil shrugged it off. "No worries, really. You're here now."

"But I should have known. An act of violence always provokes trauma, for the victim as well as the violator. Everyone involved is left with a mark."

Doro petted Phil's knee, her other hand on the steering wheel. "The good news, however, is: the trauma doesn't need to last. You'll be fine, eventually."

"I surely don't intend to live my life like a rabbit caught in a headlight."

"That's my girl." With a smile, Doro hit the gas pedal.

Phil watched her out of the corner of her eye. For the first time since they reconnected, Doro looked like the person she had known. Like her best friend. In jeans, a sweater and her old hiking sandals instead of the fluttery dress that seemed to be the trademark style of the Tanit Daughters. Also without the jewelry, her dark hair kept together with a simple rubber band. Exactly how Doro had looked in her former life: unpretentious, un-made-up. A queen *incognita*.

But, Phil bore in mind, for the women of Can Follet, Doro was much more than a queen. Or a friend. She was Anat, the representative of a Goddess on Earth, the Great Mother, believe it or not. Doro herself didn't seem to believe in this role but thought it necessary for the greater good. She played Anat to such perfection the Daughters of Tanit believed her, adored her, even worshipped her.

As if she heard her thoughts, Doro smiled at Phil and gave her a little nudge with the elbow as if to say, *hey, it's me.* And Phil felt at home again.

They turned into the road to San Josep de sa Talaia, as the village was called in *Eivissenc,* named after the island's highest mountain in its back. Doro chatted about a hike up the peak she once organized for the Tanit girls, and how awestruck they had been by the breathtaking view. Since then she had been dreaming of a sanctuary for the Goddess on Sa Talaia, she said, a mountain temple in the old Phoenician style. She had to find a way to realize it. Phil decided to use this as a hook for what she had to say.

"In the sanctuary of D'es Cuieram, I saw that these Bes Brothers have some kind of altar too. A real pervert one right behind yours."

"Well, the sanctuary is not only ours. You wouldn't believe

how many Ibizans still worship Tanit. While running to Catholic churches on Sunday."

"Okay, but what do you, I mean the Daughters of Tanit, have to do with the Bes Brothers?"

Doro gave a disgusted snort. "As little as possible! There are, of course, cross-connections like Scherer and Amanda. But all those rich jerks are totally awful, not spiritual but greedy, all about money and themselves. They'd love to take over everything. Es Vedrà and basically the whole island."

"So all your marches have been in vain?"

"Admittedly, we haven't been very successful yet. But I believe our mission will eventually sink in. Our biggest obstacle—and the TAB's best help—is the Ibizans' ignorance regarding their own history. This and *their* greed. They may pray to Tanit when they want something from her like rain or love. But the moment one of the Brothers waves with a bundle of bills..."

Doro sighed profoundly, and Phil thought how hard it would be to let her know that even some Tanit women had been corrupted by the TAB's money.

"I learned the hard way," Doro went on, "that all the tolerance and happy-go-lucky-attitude the world identifies with Ibiza is nothing but ignorance."

They drove into San José and found a parking lot close to the parish. Of all the villages on Ibiza, Phil liked this one the most because through decades of tourism it had remained authentic. The little owner-run shops, the grocery *tiendas*, the modest restaurants and bars were all real. Tour buses on their way to the western beaches might stop at the old fortified church, a simple, dignified building, but by no means an architectonic highlight. The tourists might stroll around a bit and buy a souvenir, some pottery or an original Ibiza raffia-bag, maybe have a drink. But in the evening, one could count them on one hand. At the same time, San José was one of the places where foreigners and locals lived side by side all year round. People from all parts of the world had settled here and adapted to the Ibizan rhythm, not the other way around.

Doro hadn't made a reservation at Can Manyanet, a long-established restaurant known for its traditional cuisine, but they were lucky. A couple was just done eating and handed them over a table at a window with a view of the lush flower garden. They ordered water and wine, and Doro chose the dish Can Manyanet was most famous for, *Sofrit Pagès*, a casserole of lamb, chicken and saffron-potatoes. Phil chose a vegetable soup. Listlessly, she poked her spoon through it, while Doro dug into her food as if she hadn't eaten in days.

Their conversation was slow, hesitant, a bit about Anton, about Mainz. Soon, there were only trivialities left. What had happened to their old, self-understood closeness? Phil could read the disappointment in Doro's eyes.

"Phil, what is wrong?" she finally asked.

Phil took a deep breath, prepared herself. But first things first. "Doro. I just don't know what to think anymore. You know why I came here, right? I came to sell the *finca*. Not because I want to but because I have to. I'm bankrupt."

Doro took a sip of wine. "Oh, don't you worry about it."

What? Of course, Phil worried. She had debts, a burned-down house, no job, and a son to bring up. All of the sudden, things spilled out, unsorted.

"Tamar recommended agent Scherer to me whose wife just died and who was her lover. Tamar's, I mean. Now she's also dead, probably killed by Scherer's son, also her lover, out of jealousy..."

"What? Tamar's lover? And what son?"

"...And it's proven that Ninguno's death was no accident but murder."

"Oh heavens." Doro was perplexed. "No! Under these circumstances, how can you even consider working with Scherer?"

"I know, right? I don't, of course. But I need money or I'm

screwed."

"Don't worry, as I said. I can give you money."

Phil stared at her friend, irritated. "What... you?"

Doro had always been financially tight. She owned her apartment, the one she had so generously offered Phil and Anton to stay in, but apart from that? Of course, she had—or used to have—the job at the historical institute, but spent all her earnings on research.

"Yes, me. I can, believe me," Doro said.

Phil felt like crying. "Doro. There is so much I don't understand."

"Ask me." Doro leaned back and smiled. "If I have an answer, I'll answer."

"Ninguno, for instance. He hadn't been staying in my house for just this week you went to meditate. Right?"

Doro bent forward again and took Phil's hands. "Shit. Right. Six weeks, maybe eight. I offered him to stay there. I should have been honest with you from the beginning. But I was afraid you would take it as a breach of trust."

"But why?"

"Please try to understand: I had found the Daughters of Tanit, and they welcomed me with open arms. At the same time, Ninguno had lost his home—one dark, miserable room he called home—because he couldn't pay the rent any longer. For a while, Amanda allowed him to sleep in her garden shed, but only secretly as Scherer couldn't know about it. This was such a miserable life. I got the most beautiful room in Can Follet, with a view to the sea, while Ninguno..."

Now Phil grabbed Doro's hands, while a tear ran down her cheek. "Doro, you are right. Had you told me then, I probably would—I wouldn't have understood. A homeless alcoholic in my precious *finca*! One can be so petty-minded." She wiped off the tear, lifted her glass and toasted to Doro. "Don't you worry. You did everything right."

They drank, relieved, and smiled at each other like in the

old times. Almost like in the old, closer-than-family times.

"And then: Scherer and the TAB. I don't understand this either. Why did Tamar work for him considering he is what he is? She even had an affair with him. And with his son. After she lured Scherer away from her own mother, whose lover he was first. I even heard she pushed Jezebel so hard she broke her spine. How in the world does one deal with that? I mean..."

"That's nonsense," Doro interrupted, "mean gossip. I know, I wasn't with the Daughters yet when it happened. And, as you know, I did have my problems with Tamar, but she and Jezebel were very close. I was shocked when I first heard this rumor, but Jezebel assured me it was an accident. Why else would she have wanted to have Tamar around her all the time?"

"But..."

"And the sex, the affairs—true, in the beginning I also had my problems with that. But Jezebel brought up Tamar in the spirit of free love. She always encouraged her to act out her sexual needs and wants, no matter with whom. Jezebel doesn't believe in any claim of ownership. She's a very strong person."

Lost in thought, Doro looked out of the window and twirled the end of her ponytail. "You know, I personally never had an interest in sex."

Phil did know. In all those years, she had not once seen Doro with a partner, or even a date. People thought she was a closet lesbian, but she had never said a word about this to Phil, either. One single allusion Doro had made to sex, many years ago, had to do with an uncle she hated because he hadn't kept his fingers off her as a kid. Phil remembered the bitterness in Doro's voice when she added that her parents had always looked the other way. The one time she complained, they even blamed her for the uncle's abusive behavior. After this, Doro turned her back on her family as soon as she legally could.

"Everything physical I kept away from me," she now said in her new frankness, "the slightest hint of lust. I didn't even realize how I reduced myself to a pure cerebral idiot, living out only half of my being, not even half of it. I couldn't accept that sex is the biggest need as well as the biggest power in the world."

Was this Doro talking? "And now you live out your— need?"

Doro smiled. "I learned a lot from Jezebel. Taboos only harm us."

That's when the most terrible idea hit Phil. A never heard of, never imagined suspicion that had her heart race, made her sick to her core. But before she could ask her question, the waiter approached with the check. Doro rummaged through her purse for some bills and waved off the return of change. The waiter thanked her enthusiastically and left. Phil bent forward.

"Doro, what exactly do you have to do with the TAB?"

"Why do you ask?" A question full of caution.

"Why? That's what I want to know. Do you know about Tanit Daughters taking part in their orgies?"

Phil's heart was throbbing up to her throat. This couldn't be true. It took a while until Doro answered.

"Among others," she admitted, "there are some Daughters of Tanit."

Phil felt like fainting. "And you accept it? I can't believe it."

"When I first heard about it, I was shocked, just like you. Then, with time, I gradually learned to understand."

"You can't be serious. You just can't be. I saw her, Stella, your so-called sister, the one who was a victim of sex trafficking in her teens. Leading underage girls to these men…"

"The girls are all older than fourteen."

Speechless, Phil only shook her head. Doro pushed her chair back.

"Come on," she said gently. "Calm down. Let's have one for the road at Bernat Vinya, and I'll explain. You must listen to me before you judge."

"I'm anxious to hear what you've got to say. Damn, Doro!"

They went out into the night, the air smooth like satin, passed the church, and crossed the main road. At this time, 11 p.m., the village already lay in nightly peace. But the traditional bar Bernat Vinya was still busy. All tables were occupied by mostly black-clad men absorbed in their games of cards or dominoes. Doro and Phil found two stools at the bar.

"So?" Phil asked brusquely.

But first, Doro ordered wine. When the barman put a glass in front of her, Phil felt literally reluctant to pick it up. But she had to hear Doro out.

"You must know," Doro began, "the Tanit Daughters have always wanted to live in harmony with men without accepting their claims for dominance."

"Sounds reasonable."

"For that, we have to comply with some of their—in this case, the TAB Brothers'—wishes to show our goodwill. Just as the Goddess Tanit made a point of being on good terms with Bes, this little demigod of obscure descent."

"And that means?"

Doro seemed to consider her next words carefully. "That means we, for instance, share the celebration of the spring rites with them."

"An orgy!"

"An ancient ritual in honor of the Goddess."

"So—the TAB guys also worship Tanit?"

"Well, they may not be there yet. But we do everything we can to integrate them in the greater good."

"What good?" Phil didn't find any more words.

"The greater good, let me explain. You know, Phil, in many ancient cultures, body and mind were seen as a unit. The perfect unit that makes humans strive. Nothing physical was considered sinful. On the contrary, lust was used as a motivation for spiritual and intellectual growth. It connected the human being with everything there is, fellow humans, nature and the divine. In these times, a demigod like Bes who only through modern eyes looks like a ridiculous pervert, was quite content with his role as companion of the Great Goddess. Only since the split, the separation of the two halves of our being—which is a result of monotheism—everyone is confused. Unsettled, uncertain of their role, needy. Men compensate this feeling of incompleteness with exaggerated claims of power, women usually with adaptation or even submission."

Phil felt sick to the core. "What the hell are you talking about?"

"About fulfillment," Doro said while at the same time Phil continued to ask, "About sex?"

"Not about sex as entertainment or acting out domination fantasies. I'm talking about spiritual transformation. About the fusion of energies and healing. In many ancient cultures, sexual and mental energies were equally ranked, and to bring them into balance was understood to be the integrating female power. Have you heard of the Harimtu? Aphrodite's Foals? The Hierodules, the Hetaeras?"

Phil was only familiar with the last term. "Hetaeras were prostitutes."

Doro adjoined her fingertips in a kind of Angela Merkel gesture.

"They dedicated themselves to men," she said gravely, "to have them act out their sexual needs and, at the same time, stimulate their mental capacities. They showed them that the male and female principle are opposites, but belong together in an intrinsic way. That both are dependent on each other. The Hetaeras taught man the art of devotion and re-integrated him in the only true creation myth. The Tanit Daughters follow this tradition."

Phil felt herself scooting away from Doro, even though she didn't move an inch. "So, do they also get paid for their wonderful integration work?"

Doro pretended to not hear the cynicism. "Sacred prostitution was rewarded to finance the temples, just as we need money for our project. In former times, no one considered this disreputable. In the contrary, the work of the priestesses was highly esteemed. They were the ones who ensured gender equilibrium."

"What equilibrium? I only hear you trying to justify prostitution of minors."

"Come on, Phil, nobody forces them. Show me one fourteen-year-old that hasn't had sex yet. And domination games don't mean dominance."

"And what equilibrium are you talking about, when Amanda and Ninguno and Neves and Tamar are dead?"

"What does that have to do with anything?" An audible edge had snuck into Doro's words. "Don't you get it? Amanda committed suicide. Ninguno was an old drunk who messed with who knows what wrong people. Neves was a drug-addict. And Tamar, as so many women before her, was the victim of a violent male."

Doro replaced the sharpness of her voice with a gentle, soothing tone. "I know, Phil, I really know how hard it is to accept all this: sex, prostitution, devotion. Believe me, I was there, and it took me a while. It's never easy to see the big picture through other eyes beyond one's own socialization."

Doro waved to the barman, and both of their glasses were refilled.

"Most feminists have problems with this concept," she said, "as I had, and as you are having now. That's the result of dissociating sexuality from the fight for equality. Before I realized this I, for instance, thought that Madonna—the pop singer, I mean—was not much more than a sex doll sputtering trivialities. When she showed her tits on stage in Istanbul, for example, and declared she supported the 'My body belongs to me' campaign of liberal Turkish women. I thought she only added fuel to the fire of male assholes who deem themselves in the right to suppress women. What I didn't understand then was that my rejection of Madonna's act only showed how much I myself had internalized male thinking. Female sexuality is not allowed to be shown, the patriarchs say. But why not? I tell you why not: because it demonstrates freedom."

"The freedom to be fucked for money? Openly shown female sexuality, I'd say, must be something better than that."

The more irritated Phil was, the more gentle Doro became. "Well, the human being, by all means, is a spiritual *and* sexual creature; we can't change that. When our girls decide they want to party with the Bes Brothers they, indeed, are doing an integrative job. A highly important one, actually. They show those males the power of love and devotion. Stella gets it... I think. She has been exposed to racism, subjected, diminished as a human being..."

"Right. She has been abused by men. And now she helps abuse others?"

"Don't you understand? Now she is in charge, and she doesn't—we don't—force any girl to do anything they don't want to do. We merely try to change the world, change men, with our most powerful weapon."

Phil tried to think clearly. She wondered whether there was a single idea in Doro's talk she could accept. She couldn't find one. "And this *works*?" she finally asked, "Do the Bes Brothers, the phallic dominators they think they are, learn something by your—intentions?"

That was still a problem, Doro had to admit. "They cling pretty hard to their power fantasies. But we can't give up, as this is the only way to prevent the human race from self-destruction. When the first Bes Brother heals, the effect will multiply. These guys are really influential, you know. People all over the world listen to them. When they start to rethink their gender policies, the world will change for the better."

"And if not?"

"Then we're all lost."

Phil fell silent. She almost jumped when Doro's hand fondly brushed her arm. "Take your time, Phil. Think about it and come visit our library. We have a huge archive on this subject I'd be happy for you to use. It will open your eyes."

"We'll see. Excuse me."

Phil went to the restroom. In the stall, she opened the window, sat down on the sill and, with shaking fingers, rolled a cigarette.

CHAPTER 50

The same evening, Adam was waiting in the Tia Maria restaurant for Bartolo. The inspector had brought Wendling to
court for a statutory hearing, and then had to write the report
on the arrest. While waiting, Adam opened the MacBook he
was carrying while his phone—hopefully—dried out in the rice
bag. He was restless. He couldn't help thinking that the arrest,
that everything they had found out, hadn't really brought
them anywhere. They were still poking in the dark.

What exactly did they have? A self-confessed murderer in
the last case, Tamar's death. But concerning Ninguno? Neves?
Nothing. And Amanda? Adam had to admit there was some
evidence pointing at suicide after all: her loneliness, her unhappy marriage. Maybe depression, maybe her knowing about
the orgies and not being able to do anything about it. Was this
the cause of her fight with Scherer she mentioned in her last
voicemail?

But then: Scherer had wanted to meet her at home and
bring a bottle of champagne. And that night, Amanda had died
of poisoned champagne. So, evidently—but in the core of his
heart, Adam didn't believe anymore that Scherer was the vil-
lain. How could someone who falsely admitted to murder to

save his guilty son be a murderer himself?

Tomorrow, Adam decided, he would visit his brother-in-law and ask him about the phone message. Also about Tamar, her eventual involvement in Amanda's death. And again, about the TAB—with not much hope, though, that Scherer would tell him the truth. What else was there? Adam was sure they had only just glimpsed at the tip of the iceberg. Not even that. They hardly knew anything about the TAB. Another death came to his mind: Kai Maurer, who died in the plane wreck off the Ibizan coast, had been a Bes Brother. Adam opened his MacBook to search for information about this. Maybe it would give him new ideas.

When his laptop lit up, the headline of the news site announced the death of the former Italian Prime Minister Alessandro Barracchi. The part media tycoon, part politician had been found lifeless on the island of Sardinia.

Adam recognized it immediately: the southern landscape, the round stone hut, the men in white overalls. He had seen it on TV in General Cruz's suite, the news that had shocked the Bes Brothers so much they forget about their orgy. "It happened again—it's Brother Sandro," one guy had said. Alessandro Barracchi, Sandro, must have been one of them. Another dead member of the TAB.

Barracchi had died under strange circumstances. In the early hours of the previous day, Adam read, two hunters had found his mortal remains on a remote strip off the Sardinian coast. Apparently, he had died of a heart attack before being half devoured by a herd of the island-typical wild boars. What Barracchi had been doing there, in one of the *pinnettus*, the—also island-typical—round stone huts that nowadays only serve touristic purposes, was unknown. His wife said she had no idea. But as Barracchi was said to have links to the Italian Neo-Fascists and the Mafia and had been involved in an impressive number of public scandals, speculations went wild. It had to do with a secret political encounter, some said. With sex games in the *pinnettu* that were too much for his heart, said others. With a lone hike along the coast that ended with a heart attack, the right-wing press wanted to make their readers believe. It was still unclear if Barracchi's breath had stopped for good when the boars' tusks tore him apart.

Adam googled everything he could find about the incident, but there was not much more, yet. In Barracchi's lifetime, however, the media had found fodder in his czarist lifestyle, his constant tweets about his own genius, his bashing of opponents he called enemies, his derogatory remarks about boat refugees dying off the Mediterranean coasts. The yellow press also loved to wallow in rumors about prostitutes, way too young mistresses, Bunga Bunga parties. In the last months, most articles were about Barracchi's unprecedented war of roses with his soon-to-be ex-wife about money, mansions, and their kids.

Adam typed in the name of the other dead Bes Brother, Kai Maurer, and found some similarities: Maurer, the head of a big German insurance company, had been a philanthropist and active member of the conservative party when about a year ago, he found himself in the center of a huge scandal. As an incentive treat, Maurer had invited his high-ranking employees to a brothel in Palermo, Sicily. No one would probably have cared much, had he not been blatant enough to deduct the trip as business expense from his tax return. The tax authorities reported him, the press got interested. Women threw raw eggs at him in front of his office in downtown Frankfurt. After that, Maurer disappeared out of the public eye until he crashed his plane off the Ibizan coast.

Adam looked up when Bartolo greeted him with a slap on the shoulder and the words, "Googling Maurer? You're smart. But on water alone?"

He hailed a waiter. "*Una jarra de tinto*," and plunged into a chair.

A second later, the waiter was back with the carafe of red

wine. Bartolo took a long sip before he was able to speak.

"Kai Maurer," he said, "had a date before he took off to Ibiza. In a bar of the airport hotel in Émpuriabrava. The date was a blonde woman in her thirties who spoke excellent Spanish and German and whom the bartender described in a—aah—quite unambiguous way." With an expansive gesture in front of his chest, Bartolo imitated the barkeeper. "He had never seen her before and assumed she would take the plane with Maurer. But they started to bicker in German, which the barkeeper unfortunately doesn't understand. Next thing he knew, she smashed her glass on the counter and left Maurer where he was. He paid, boarded his plane and flew to his death."

Bartolo nudged Adam. "Blonde, German, with a TAB guy and..." He repeated the expansive gesture.

"Tamar."

"We mailed her photo to the bartender, and just now got an answer. He's pretty sure it's Tamar; just not a hundred percent, as she didn't take off her sunglasses. The day before the encounter, March 12th, her name was on the passenger list of the Iberia flight from Frankfurt to Barcelona."

Two weeks ago, Wendling had stated, Tamar came to see him in Frankfurt totally unexpectedly. He also said she met a Bes Brother there, even though she denied it. Maurer's office was downtown.

"Which makes it quite probable," Bartolo continued, "that she met him in Frankfurt, then flew into Barcelona and from there went to Émpuriabrava to see him again at this private airport where he kept his plane in a rented hangar."

"So she was lucky not to board with him, or—fuck! When exactly did Maurer take off?"

"March 13th, 6:30 p.m."

The day Adam arrived on Ibiza. The morning after Phil boarded the ferry in Barcelona where she met Tamar.

"How far is it from Émpuriabrava to Barcelona?"

Just some hundred and sixty kilometers, Bartolo explained. Enough time for Tamar, after she left the bar, to return there, embark and be in Ibiza the next morning. If it had been her intention to begin with or not. This was the crucial question: Had Tamar planned to fly with Maurer? Had she escaped death because of their argument—or had it all been a perfidious plan to kill the man?

"I'll have the ferry company check," Bartolo pulled out his phone, "when Tamar bought her ticket to Ibiza. Only on the evening of the 13th or before. Why didn't she fly directly from Frankfurt to Ibiza? Because she planned to go with Maurer from Émpuriabrava? But if she bought her ferry ticket from Barcelona before she met him there, we can assume her plan was a different one."

They waited until Tia Maria had served their dinner—*conejo a la plancha* with roasted potatoes and a vegetable sauce—in her usual ceremonious manner.

"What about Maurer's death?" Adam asked after she left. "The poison. Do you know more about it by now?"

"We do, and that's as strange as it can get. The doc found Tetrodotoxin in his body, a neuronic poison. It occurs in all kinds of sea creatures, the best known would be the blowfish, but also in the blue-ringed octopus and even certain marine snails. When swallowed, this toxin creeps into every part of the organism and paralyzes it. This takes a while, but is, in the end, invariably fatal."

Bartolo snapped one finger, and a waiter with another carafe of wine appeared, apologizing for the delay. When he was gone, the inspector continued, "*Señor* Maurer was just above the island of S'Éspalmador when the poison took effect. Can you imagine what a horrible death this must be: You try to steer, but can't move your hands. You see your crash coming."

"So definitely death by outside influence."

"Likely, but we can't say yet with absolute certainty. In rare cases divers are stung by cone snails, right through their neoprene suits. But Maurer didn't go diving. Neither is there a Japanese restaurant anywhere close to Émpuriabrava that serves *fugu*, nor do we have blue-ringed octopus in our waters. What we know is that the blonde woman ordered *tapas*, among them a seafood salad. Nobody would have noticed a few added cone snails."

But how should Tamar have gotten hold of such a rare poison? It seemed so far-fetched. However, fact was that Maurer had been with her and was poisoned.

Bartolo and Adam finished their meal and went to have their digestif at the bar. The news about the Italian ex-Prime Minister's death flickered across TV for the umpteenth time. Adam told Bartolo that Barracchi must be the Bes Brother Sandro whose death had ruined the TAB orgy. Bartolo got excited, but a moment later, his palm slapped his forehead. Adam knew he realized as well: If Tamar was Maurer's murderer, where was the connection between his and Barracchi's deaths? Tamar herself had been dead when Barracchi suffered his fate.

"Still strange that two guys of the same club die so shortly one after the other," Bartolo said, "and neither in bed, after the last rites."

"Guess the TAB Brothers are not very well-liked. Wait a minute!"

Adam imitated Bartolo's gesture by slapping his own forehead. What about the Texan who had owned property on Ibiza, had been associated with the TAB, and now was dead too? Bud Winslow, the radio moderator, a big fan of the Alt-Right movement and every concept that leaned toward fascism, racism, misogyny. A while ago, his death had been all over American media.

"Confusing," Bartolo summed up, "so Wendling killed Tamar. Tamar possibly poisoned Maurer, and may also have killed Neves and Ninguno, but she can't have poisoned

Amanda as she wasn't on Ibiza that night. Barracchi died under strange circumstances in Sardinia and this other one, what's his name..."

"Bud Winslow."

"...and Winslow died in America. What caused his death?"

"An overdose of OxyContin. He died in a gay bar, even though he was the biggest homophobe you've ever seen."

"Figures. And all of these deaths are connected to the *Tertulia de los Amigos de Bes*. A very confusing situation indeed."

Adam agreed.

They called it a night and went to their separate cars. On the way back to the hotel, Adam passed the village of San José. It was only around eleven-thirty, but most houses lay in nocturnal darkness. Only one bar was still open. In a whiff of melancholy, he thought about this Hemingway story; a clean, well-lighted place where he could spend some time, before spending another lonely night.

He immediately recognized Dorothea. She was sitting at the bar, an empty stool next to her, a glass in her hand. She looked just as she had the last time Adam had tried to talk to her sixteen years ago—gorgeous, tall, strong as a horse. Maybe a bit more haggard now and with some gray in her hair. Phil's best friend, the forever unforgiving Doro, the big manipulator, the fucking bitch, as Adam had called her in thought ever since she came to his place to pick up Phil's things.

He had swallowed his pride, then, almost choking on it, to explain his sin to Dorothea even though it was none of her business. He stupidly hoped she would forgive him and put a good word for him in so Phil would too. But the bitch brushed him off like a speck of dust. She was ice cold when she said, "Sorry, Adam, but I don't talk to men who beat women." Beat women. Fucking bitch.

Dorothea sat very upright on her stool, radiating an aura of courtly froideur. None of the men at the bar would ever dare to talk to her, let alone make a pass at her, Adam thought, not even if they were completely wasted. She did have the attitude of a cult leader, an imperious but also charismatic alpha animal.

When Dorothea recognized him, her posture turned even more rigid. A warning sign flashed in her dark eyes. But Adam wouldn't be intimidated.

"Hi, Dorothea," he said. "Can we talk for a moment?"

"You are quite impertinent, Mr. Ryan."

"I'm sorry you think so, Dorothea. But I need your help."

Dorothea's voice was like ice. "If you could call me by my name: Anat."

"You knew my sister, Anat, didn't you?" He tried to say the name naturally, without irony. She didn't nod or deny. "I have to understand why she died."

Dorothea made a movement as if she wanted to get up and leave. Her voice, however, was less cold when she answered, "I would like to understand too."

"First, I was convinced Scherer killed her." Adam tried to say it matter-of-factly. "I had the theory that Amanda had something in her hand against him and the TAB and threatened to go public with it."

"Why should she have blackmailed her husband?"

"To keep him from buying the rock you are, or your society is, so keen on."

"What do you think Amanda had to do with our—society?"

"I know what my sister wrote me in her last letter," Adam said, consciously vague. He could see something light up in Dorothea's eyes, an increased alertness. Or alarm. "I also know she confided in you," he kept probing.

With that, he had hit the bull's eye. Dorothea nodded. The temperature of her voice had risen several more degrees. "Amanda was such a lost soul. Scherer dominated and humiliated her whenever he could. When she told him she wanted to lead a self-determined life in the name of Tanit, he called her ridiculous."

"But what could she have used against him? Was it the orgies? Did she know about them? The underage girls?" He ignored the sharp breath Dorothea drew. "Did she have proof? Photos? There must have been something specific."

"So being dominated and humiliated isn't specific enough for you?" Dorothea's voice was back to ice, but her evasive answer did not even make sense. "Amanda wanted to live a life of love and peace without violence, but this was denied to her. But how, out of all people, should you know what that means."

Adam flinched as if something had bitten him. "One mistake," he said slowly, looking Dorothea right in the eyes, "one damn mistake sixteen years ago that makes you judge me for the rest of my life. You think that's fair?"

"That's not the point. I think you have no idea what you did to Phil."

"Oh yes, I think I do. I also know what I did to myself."

"All right, at least that."

"I was drunk. Tired. Outraged. Does the term 'to forgive' not exist in your vocabulary? Only the Old Testament's *An eye for an eye, a tooth for a tooth*?"

Dorothea's eyes flashed over Adam's shoulder and came back. "Bullshit. Why would I ever refer to, of all myths, the fairy tales of patriarchy?"

"Don't you think I've been punished enough? Of course you know about my son." This wasn't a question. "The kid I never got to know."

All of the sudden, there was dismay in Dorothea's eyes. Or pity?

"Adam," she said, "Phil was totally confused. She didn't mean to punish you. And I—I was so worried about her. She was a mess. And pregnant."

"And it never occurred to you that I may have wanted to assume my responsibilities for my kid. Because I'm only a man. If the father." Adam grinned melancholically. "Old Saul at least had the chance to transform into Paul."

He was surprised when Dorothea returned the tiniest of smiles. "Leave me alone with that jerk. He wasn't a tad better as Paul. Only more eloquent."

Adam decided to take a direct foray. "Dorothea, what was it with Tamar?"

"Tamar?" The smile vanished. "Tamar is the victim of a violent man."

"But was she *only* a victim? Do you know a Kai Maurer who's also dead?"

Perplexed, Dorothea stared at him, but then her eyes again flitted across his shoulder. Before he could check what it was, she nodded, suddenly conspiratorial, "And I have a suspicion. There's something—very puzzling I have to show you. Let's meet in an hour at Phil's *finca*. You know where that is, Adam, right?"

"Yeah, but..."

"Till then not one word. To no one. You'll understand soon enough." In a louder, sharp tone she added, "By the way, Adam, you are sitting in Phil's chair."

Automatically he got up, looked across his shoulder and saw it was Phil Dorothea had noticed at his back. He could smell she had just had a smoke.

"Adam," she said wearily.

"He's just leaving." Dorothea said. "Right, Adam? Bye, Adam."

Adam had no idea what this was about. All he could say was "Phil."

But she wouldn't look him in the eye or say another word. So he gave Dorothea a nod, repeated "bye" and left. He would wait for her.

CHAPTER 51

In the early morning, Phil was lying in bed and watched the sunbeams cross the windowsill. Words, sentences, images tortured her: body and mind a unit, love and devotion, sacred prostitution. Words! Behind which stood nothing less than the fact that the Daughters of Tanit sold themselves to the Bes Brothers. Sex against money. Bunga Bunga on Ibiza. And Doro went along with it.

The night before, she had brought Phil back to the Esperanza and said goodbye with an affectionate hug, oblivious that Phil stood stiff as a poker.

"I know you are completely confused now, Phil. This is all new to you, and it really isn't adequate to have third-level knowledge without instruction on the first. But I promise I'll teach you, step by step. In the end, it will all make sense."

"We'll see," Phil had muttered, "Or rather, I don't want to know anything more right now. I just want to go home."

"I understand. Anton. Then another time. Give him a hug from me."

Phil had only one more question: What had Adam wanted in the pub?

"Nothing. Pure coincidence. He made some stupid remarks and left. Forget him, sweetie, better not to see this one
again."

Exactly. Just like sixteen years ago when Doro knew what
Phil should do, and Phil followed her lead. She wished she had
reacted differently, more approachable when Adam said "Phil"
in such a tentative way. But she had been in shock. Doro—Phil
just couldn't put her head around what Doro had told her. She
thought about the welcoming party at Can Follet, Doro as the
much-admired Anat on her throne. Anat, the mother figure.
The women who had come to find refuge in Can Follet after
going through hell. The Indian girl, Manasa. And Stella.
Women who wanted to draw new strength from each other,
learn to be free, start a new life. Can Follet was a spiritual,
political, therapeutic institution for women, Phil had thought.
How did this go together with prostitution?

She needed to do something. In a hurry, she got dressed
and went over to Adam's room. She knocked against the door.
No reaction. The curtains were closed, no sound was heard.
With both fists, Phil banged against the door. Even if Adam
had still been sleeping, this must have woken him up. Phil ran
back to her room and locked the door. She probably had imagined this tentative "Phil."

At ten o'clock sharp, she was standing in front of another
door in Ibiza City. The real estate agent offered her a coffee
and admitted that she hadn't found the time yet to visit Phil's
finca as it was *Semana Santa*.

Phil hadn't thought about the 'Holy Week' before Easter,
which was a big deal on Ibiza. Nobody seemed to be working
for their jobs then, but for the processions the *cofradías*, the
church brotherhoods, organized. They carried every single
statue of Jesus, the Virgin or whatever saint through the
streets, hiding their faces under pointed hoods with slits for
eyes. This inevitably reminded one of the Ku Klux Klan, but
Phil had read that the disguise was only meant to protect the

penitents' anonymity. Still, to her, the hooded figures carrying burning torches and the sinister music with its lashing rhythms were spooky.

When she explained that she just couldn't stay on Ibiza any longer, the friendly real estate agent offered to look at the house right after Easter and mail her offer. In the next agency, Phil was neither offered a coffee, nor did the *Semana Santa* seem to interfere with business. An overactive salesman fired off a bullet storm of terms like 'sensible buying habits' and 'nowadays' low interest rate environment,' which meant he could unfortunately not keep his offer of eighty thousand. But sixty.

Phil turned around and slammed the door shut.

And now? She decided to contact every single agency in the city. At one p.m., when the church bells reminded her of *siesta*, she was exhausted and disheartened. Most agents kept their doors shut for *Semana Santa,* others put her on hold until after Easter or didn't show any interest at all. Frustrated, Phil returned to the *hostal* and again knocked at Adam's door. To the same result: silence.

"He has left," a voice said behind her. Lluis.

"What?" Phil spun around. "That's not possible."

"He texted that he had to return to the U.S. immediately."

"Could you show me the message?"

Adam wrote he was sorry he had to leave in such a rush and without goodbye, but unforeseen circumstances forced him to. He would wire the rent and was already at the airport for the next flight to Barcelona. *'Best wishes, Adam.'*

"I don't know what happened between you," Lluis said, "but I am sorry."

Phil bit her lip. Obviously, Adam hadn't been able to deal with the news of his fatherhood. Guess he couldn't stand running into her again, so he left. Understandable—and heartbreaking. She felt like screaming.

"He even left all his stuff but his laptop. What in the world happened?"

"That's—an old story."

Phil fled to her room. After half an hour of sobbing into her pillow, she started to pack. When she zipped her travel bag shut, there was a tentative knock at her door. A jet flame of hope darted up in her heart, and she raced to the door. It wasn't Adam, though, but Doro. She was in her Anat outfit with her old backpack dangling from one shoulder. The triadic hand gesture and the soft-spoken "Love to you" now sounded so crude to Phil that she flinched.

"Oh please, Phil, come on," Doro said, "We two—we still must be able to talk with each other."

But Phil wasn't there yet. She nodded at the only chair in the room and sat down on the edge of the bed, in maximal distance, behind her packed bag. Doro shoved it aside and sat down beside her. Carefully, she put one arm around Phil's shoulder. The arm felt like a ton of weight.

"I know exactly how you're feeling, Phil. I've been there. It's difficult."

Phil risked a glance. Doro, usually bursting with self-confidence, looked just like herself. Weary, sad, visibly shaken.

"Tomorrow is Tamar's burial. I really would appreciate if you could..."

"Tomorrow I'll be gone. Please give my condolences to Jezebel."

"Of course." Doro sighed, "I'm worried about her. She's devastated. Scherer's son has confessed to killing Tamar out of jealousy. It never stops."

An imploring look met Phil. "Imagined male entitlement turned another decent guy into a murderer. Can't you understand that we desperately need a new—and at the same time age-old—culture of togetherness? We have to break the power structures."

Preposterous words. "Culture of togetherness? What I saw was sex abuse of minors, no matter what mumbo jumbo you knit around it."

"As I said: it's completely voluntary, no one is under fourteen, and it's an ancient mythical tradition to show men the path to love and devotion."

"That's bullshit. A fucking cliché, and you know it."

"Cliché happens to be the simplest variety of myth," Doro said so smoothly Phil could have kicked her.

"Whatever words you wrap it in. How can you out of all people accept it?"

Doro closed her eyes like she was in pain. "What could I do? I out of all people? When there is no other way to go."

"I'm sure you don't believe this shit yourself."

"But I do. How else shall we deal with man? With reason? Force him to be fair? With sweet loving words? With violence? Sex is the only invariable in evolution, the most powerful engine of mankind. If we keep ignoring it and leave the steering wheel to man, we will never be able to go where we can."

"But..."

"I don't like it either, Phil. Actually, I hate it. I wish this idea had never come up. I would love to believe in reason. And love. Not in sex. Stella is like me, she resisted for a long time, but eventually we both got it. It's a fact: sex is the strongest power on earth. The strongest female weapon. It was so damn hard to understand. We're not like Tamar or Jezebel. But it is historically proven that sacred prostitution existed and served its purpose. *The* purpose."

Doro's eyes were so full of pain, Phil had an idea of her struggle. Of course she must have rejected the concept. How torn she must feel. Tamar, on the other hand, had identified with the idea of an only sex-driven world. She had not even believed in love. What had she called love? "The simplest deathtrap on earth" and "the continuance of war with different means." Or maybe that last sentence Phil had read somewhere. Whatever: in comparison to Tamar, Doro almost sounded like a romantic trying to conjure love when there was only war.

Doro rubbed her eyes. "I did get it, but the concept was developed by others. I love Jezebel, but she and Tamar—well, I myself am on another road. You know that, right? My task as a historian is a fair examination of history. To crucially recollect and re-examine women's past. What has been lost."

Now, Phil managed to agree with the tiniest of nods. Doro seemed so relieved, she hugged her for a moment, but that was too much. Phil froze.

Doro got up. "Tomorrow then. Oh, girl! What's with your *finca*? Have you been able to sell it for a good price?"

Phil gave a tortured groan. "No. If I'm lucky, I get an offer after Easter. I only hope my bank will be patient. When I'm home, I'll immediately look for a job. Whatever job as long as it pays to survive. Your apartment..."

"I don't need it anymore."

Doro placed the backpack between her feet and took out a large envelope. In it was a printed document filled out in her handwriting. Phil read: *Gift Agreement*. And below it: *Contract between Dorothea Bartholdy—hereinafter referred to as the donor—and Philine Mann—hereinafter referred to as the recipient.*

"I transferred the ownership to you. This is the first copy of confirmation; you just have to sign." Doro pointed to a line where, underneath "Ibiza, March 25th, 2019," she had already signed as donor. The line above *recipient* was empty.

Doro gave Phil a pen. "With your signature, the contract is legally valid. Just get an appointment with notary Seitz to pick up the final version of the document and sign this one, too. The apartment is paid off; you'll be eligible for every credit you need to get back on your feet. Also keep the furniture, or sell it."

Phil's mouth was a pure O. "But—why?" she finally managed to ask.

"Why? Because it's my fault the *finca* burned down. If I

hadn't allowed Ninguno to stay there, this wouldn't have happened. And..." Doro smiled a little sheepish smile, "and because I love you. You and Anton. You are the only ones I considered my family before the Daughters of Tanit."

Doro's face had turned bright red; she still didn't find it easy to talk about her feelings. But she had come a long way. "You must always know this, Phil, okay? I love you. No matter how unhappy you may be with my choices."

She again hugged Phil and mumbled into her neck, "I so hope that one day you will be able to came back to me. I'm waiting for you."

A few minutes later, Phil was standing on the balcony watching Doro get in her car. A last wave, then the red pickup Tamar had driven disappeared.

Phil returned to her room like in trance. She picked up the document and still couldn't believe what she read. There was the address; the floor number, 4th; the square footage, 150 qm²; and the apartment's value, 500 thousand euros. Underneath was Doro's signature. And her own.

Phil's emotions were running amok. There was shock, incredulity, a dreamlike feeling, overwhelming gratefulness. With her gift, Doro had saved her from bankruptcy, subsidized living, unemployment benefits. At the same time, there was a huge sadness: Phil was mourning Tamar, Amanda, and also Ninguno and Neves, whom she had never known. She was mourning Can Philanton, the good times on Ibiza and that she would never see Adam again. And she was grieving over her friendship with Doro that, in spite of the generous gift, was gone. Phil had accepted the apartment—she had signed the paper as it would have been financial suicide to reject grasping the sheet anchor for Anton and herself.

Yes, Phil had taken Doro's gift. But she never wanted to see Anat again.

DEAD GODS

CHAPTER 52

Lluis insisted on bringing Phil to the harbor, and said he would return the Vespa. Her head leaning against the window of his car, she wished goodbye to the hotel with the misleading name 'Hope.' Goodbye to the rocks Es Vedrà and Vedranell, to the azure-blue sky above the White Island and the open horizon where dark clouds were building up.

One last time, Phil was on the winding country road, lined by blooming almond trees. They passed San José with Sa Talaia towering above it. In the orchards, the peach trees had blossomed overnight to a thousand shades of pink. The lemon and orange trees waved farewell with their arms full of fruit.

In Ibiza City, Lluis stopped at the obelisk on Plaça d'Antoni Riquer. Gently, he laid his hand on Phil's cheek and caressed it. Then they exchanged a long hug.

"Bartolo says goodbye too. He wished he could do it in person."

"Thanks. I really got to like him."

"And Adam? Will you see him again?"

"No. You know, we—it's over." Phil bit her tongue.

Lluis didn't press her, just mumbled "too bad," and that in his opinion, they had made a wonderful—team.

"When you hear from him, please tell him I'm sorry. Okay?"

"Absolutely."

They hugged one last time, then Phil got out of the car and walked straight across the square to the ferry building. She had to wait in line, and when she finally got her boarding pass, Lluis's car had disappeared.

The ferry company announced that due to technical problems, boarding would start an hour late. Which meant one and a half hour's extension of Phil's goodbye Ibiza pain. She stowed her bag in a locker. A rain front was approaching, but it would still take a while until it hit the island. Enough time to stroll one last time across the *pista*, the so-called 'Mile,' stretching from the harbor to the old quarter of Sa Penya, the beating heart of Ibiza's nightlife.

Phil wondered why the German truism "offense is the best defense" kept popping into her mind. Because of the corsair Antoni Riquer's monument? Because the platitude comprised the whole politics of piracy? She climbed up the steep alley, trying to sort out this last, awful week with the rhythm of her steps. It didn't work one bit. Instead, step by step, a strange anxiety took over.

The higher Phil climbed, the narrower the alley became, full of sudden corners, labyrinth-like. The typical Ibizan cube buildings got shabbier, with loopholes instead of windows and flaking whitewashed walls. One open door revealed a dark *sala*, decorated with family photos, a crucifix and a TV, broadcasting loudly the death of the former Italian Prime minister Barracchi.

Phil arrived at a square with a view across the harbor bay. The Balearia ferry that would bring her to Barcelona was sitting in it like a giant in Lilliput-land. Cars were parked in front of the still folded-up boarding ramp. Below the square was a maze of chimneys and patios, tiny vegetable gardens and clotheslines with laundry drying in the breeze. Phil fumbled for the prepaid phone Bartolo had given her in exchange for her own phone. He hoped his technicians would be able to restore her photos of Can Salammbo, as Adam's data didn't look promising.

Wait a minute, Phil thought. How could Adam have sent a message to Lluis when his phone didn't work? Well, maybe Bartolo had given him one of these prepaid things too, or he had bought one himself. She wished she could have said goodbye to the inspector—and to Adam. Somehow it just didn't feel right...

Phil sat down on a little wall. Nothing about Adam felt right. It didn't make sense that he would have left Ibiza without solving his sister's death. Even if a real emergency had happened at home—wouldn't he have told Bartolo he'd be back as soon as possible? Maybe he had, and Bartolo hadn't told her. Or Adam hadn't left after all, only pretended to, so he wouldn't have to see her anymore. Did this make sense? In a way it did, but Phil had never known Adam to be a coward. No, it just didn't feel right.

Phone booths with valid directories didn't exist anymore, and Phil wasn't online. Fortunately, she remembered the number of the magazine *Insular*. She called Hans and had him give her the number of the police headquarters.

"Thanks, Hans, and the best of luck to you. Also to Nia and the baby."

"The same to you, Phil, big hug." In a pained voice Hans added, "But Nia left me with my unborn child. She doesn't want to be with me anymore, only with these goddamn women in this resort."

"Can Follet?" Phil asked in surprise.

Hans gave an affirmative grunt. "Well, I won't hold her back. But what the fuck am I supposed to do now? If I go back to Germany, I'll never get to know my child. An unbearable idea."

Phil felt a stab in her heart. "So you're staying?"

"For now. I'll try to get my magazine back on her feet."

Another urgent question had to be asked. "Hans, you know that Robert Wendling killed Tamar, right? Because of her affair with his father."

No doubt he knew; it had been the headline of every Ibizan media.

"I need to ask you, Hans. Nothing that may get you in trouble, I swear. I still don't understand why Tamar was trying to harm the TAB with this article. I mean, I know that Robert hated his father. But Tamar? Why did she give you all the evidence only to pull out again?"

Why had Tamar turned to Hans in the first place? What did she think she could achieve biting the hand that fed her? That fed the Tanit Daughters. Doro had suggested—and this Phil fully believed—that Tamar and Jezebel were the masterminds behind this sacred prostitution bullshit.

"Was it about the rock? Es Vedrà?"

She heard Hans take a sharp breath. "You know it, don't you?"

"But I don't understand. Did she try to put pressure on the TAB? Bribe them? Hans, come on. Tamar is dead." Phil tried to stay calm, "I swear this will stay between us. I'm leaving Ibiza in less than an hour, the ferry is already here."

"Well, okay." He sounded only half-convinced, but went on, "Listen. I think it was like that..."

Hans knew some facts and had tried to piece the rest together. He believed that Tamar, with the help of Wendling, wanted to intimidate the TAB in order to keep them off Es Vedrà. She had given out only part of the information she had, just some embarrassing orgy-snapshots with no real proof of crime, but her message was clear: She had more in her hands and could create a scandal of massive proportions. stay away from Es Vedrà, was her warning to the TAB, and your real dirty secrets are safe with me.

But once again, Tamar had overestimated herself. She

hadn't understood that she was about to shoot herself in the foot. Because as much as Robert's article focused on the TAB, it also gave attention to the Daughters of Tanit.

Phil could only imagine Tamar's dilemma. She wanted to protect her community and didn't realize they weren't in the least interested into going public, either. Like Phil, every woman of the so-called first circle would be shocked by the Tanit Daughters' sexual services and turn away. Because, according to Anat, they didn't understand the concept of sacred prostitution yet. Doro—no, Anat—didn't yet live on Ibiza when Tamar contacted Hans, and the article was written. So it must have been Jezebel who opened her daughter's eyes.

Amanda also warned the TAB—via Scherer—to stay away from Es Vedrà. She and Doro demonstrated side by side. Phil frantically tried to think the whole thing through: neither Jezebel nor Anat had mentioned what kind of threat the TAB actually posed to their sanctuary. As they had orgies together, could they not share the stupid rock? Why exactly was it so important to them? And why for the TAB? Why didn't the Daughters of Tanit just move on, for instance concentrate on the mountain peak Doro had talked about? And couldn't the TAB brothers find something better to purchase than an uninhabitable piece of rock?

Suddenly, Phil knew they had just barely scratched the surface. She remembered the story Jezebel had told her about the sunken Levantine ship. Did this have to do with treasure hunting after all?

Hans gave a cynical snort. "Some old wedding gifts? These guys are way too rich to bother with that. But..." He hesitated.

"Yes, Hans, what is it?"

"According to Tamar, Ninguno started the rumor about something much bigger. Scherer, he said, had purchased a submarine. Not for underwater sightseeing but a heavy-duty one for scientific explorations. Ninguno swore he saw it when he was gardening at Can Salammbo."

The engine with the turbines in the shed. Phil got excited. "I saw it too."

"There you go. Tamar said she innocently asked Scherer about it—what he needed a submarine for—and he got really mad. He denied owning one, accused Ninguno of snooping and kicked him out. But Tamar started digging and found some papers. Have you ever heard of rare earths?"

"Ahm. Wait. Something to do with magnets?"

"Right, the strongest magnets in the world. Neodymium, for instance, called the 'gold of technological times,' is needed in wind turbines and electric car motors, in smartphones or military missiles. In the last decades, over 95% of the element had been coming from China and was sold to the West for pretty low prices. But since the U.S. started the trade war, the Chinese government imposed more and more strategic material control. This not only sky-rocketed the prices, but also raised concerns as to economic dependence and embargoes. So now, the whole world is digging like crazy for neodymium, on land and especially in the waters of the Seven Seas."

Phil had an immediate idea what this had to do with Es Vedrà. The rock was known to be one of the most magnetic spots on Earth.

Hans confirmed her thought. "So far, Es Vedrà has not been officially inspected for neodymium. But the papers Tamar found in Scherer's office contained lists of mining and drilling equipment, such as compass clinometers, hydraulic grinds and waterproof sampling bags. I've seen them with my own eyes—until the emails disappeared."

Nia, Phil thought, and again Hans confirmed, "Thanks to my ex, Nia, I guess." He sighed, "Well, long story short: if the magnetism of Es Vedrà can be attributed to neodymium, there must be a large amount of it in the rock. So mining it would be worth a fortune. Billions. It would also destroy it."

"Wow! That's..."

"That's all I know—or rather, assume. I don't want to have

anything to do with it, though. Scares the shit out of me."

"I understand."

Phil and Hans exchanged goodbyes and promised to stay in touch.

Down in the harbor, the ferry's ramp had been opened. Not much longer, and the cars would drive up, and the passengers would climb the stairs. How much time did Phil have left? An hour, half an hour? With trembling fingers, she pushed in the police station's number and asked for Inspector Dziri.

Bartolo had received the same text message from Adam as Lluis, in the exact same words. And he was as irritated as Phil.

"Why now? We're not done with the TAB yet. Last night, Adam asked me to find out something about the Brothers for him. Why would he leave without waiting for the result?"

Phil wondered whether she should explain that it might be because of her and Adam's fall-out. But meanwhile, this didn't seem plausible anymore.

"Adam seemed quite excited," Bartolo went on. "He asked me to inquire on the death of the Italian ex-Prime Minister, Alessandro Barracchi. And man, this is just as strange as Kai Maurer's death."

"What is with Barracchi?"

"The latest report has just been released: cause of death is asphyxiation. Barracchi choked to death. Precisely: death by bolus. This happens when a big bite of food gets stuck in the larynx and can't be coughed out. Looks like no one was with *señor* Barracchi to apply the Heimlich maneuver."

"Tragic. But why strange?"

"Because Barracchi had not eaten anything when he choked." The inspector hesitated, maybe had to remind himself that Phil still belonged to the insiders. "There were only some liquids in his stomach. I talked to my Italian colleagues, and when I referred to the TAB, they immediately got alarmed.

At this point, however, they are reluctant to give out confidential information. Understandable, considering who Barracchi was." Bartolo hesitated again. "What I tell you now will have to stay *entre nous.*"

"Of course."

"In Barracchi's gullet and stuck in his throat were some super boilies." Bartolo made "hm" at the obvious question mark in Phil's silence. "I didn't know what that is either: air-dried dumplings made of fishmeal and egg rolled around a worm, a European nightcrawler. Can you imagine it actually is a hermaphrodite, I looked it up. It has both male and female reproductive organs."

Bartolo giggled and became serious again. "This worm also contains something called LiquiVerm, that anglers say is the best bait for fishing. It also attracts boars like an aphrodisiac. No one in their right mind would ever eat something like that voluntarily."

"Oh shit." Phil felt goosebumps crawling up her body.

"Right. Which means someone must have forced Barracchi to swallow the boilies. And then the boars were all over him. Let's hope he was dead before they started chewing him up."

"Pure horror."

"Nothing less. We have some bizarre causes of death here: neuronic toxin, probably in seafood, paralyzed and killed Kai Maurer. Fish boilies with this worm for Barracchi. OxyContin in the case of Bud Winslow that may or may not have been an accidental overdose. *The New York Times* pondered if someone set an example of him, maybe revenge for his public defamation of gays. I mean, Winslow died in the yard of a gay bar. Only an assumption. But we have three dead TAB Brothers. And then the cyanide that killed Amanda and kerosene that burned Ninguno—it's crazy."

Phil felt dizzy. "Holy crap. Maybe Ninguno's death has nothing to do with them after all, and the poison that killed Amanda was intended for Scherer. Which would have made four dead Brothers: Winslow, Maurer, Barracchi, and Scherer."

"Smart." Bartolo drew a hard breath. "That's an option. But who hates these lovely gentlemen that much?"

"Do you know more about the rock they want to buy, Es Vedrà? About Neodymium?" When Phil repeated what Hans told her, the inspector was stunned. "Hans has to be kept out of it. You must promise, Bartolo. He's scared to death."

"He has nothing to be afraid of. Nothing concerning me. I wonder who else knows about this."

"If there is rare earth in the rock, Hans said, it'll be worth billions."

Bartolo now was hyper-excited. "We have to find out who exactly wants to buy Es Vedrà. The TAB or some individual? And does the *Consell Insular* know about this? Probably not if they still consider the sale. Anyway: potential billions make a lot of enemies."

Phil had a seemingly unrelated question, "What's with Adam's phone? You didn't give it back to him, right?"

Bartolo knew immediately what she meant. "No, we're still trying to save his pics. Adam must have gotten another phone. Not from me, though. I keep trying to reach him under the number he texted me from, but no response. Because he's on the plane? You're right, it is strange: He doesn't find the time to pack, tell Lluis he's leaving, or pay for his room! But then he goes to a store to buy a phone, and doesn't even call us but writes a text message."

"Maybe he borrowed someone else's phone."

"Then why doesn't this someone answer my calls?" Bartolo sounded genuinely worried. "Adam did bring his car back to the rental at the airport, though. Or someone else did. *Puta madre*, gotta check this. I'll call you back."

"Bartolo, wait, I..."

But he was already gone. Damn.

In Calle Barcelona, Phil found an internet café and first

googled the name of the American Bes Brother Adam had recognized in Can Salammbo: Colonel Cruz. Just a few days ago he had received a military award in Washington D.C. and must be in good health, otherwise it would be mentioned here. The photo of the distinguished-looking guy with the shiny medals on his uniform made Phil's stomach churn. She remembered him naked on this bed in Can Salammbo, with the girl kneeling in front of him. Next, Phil googled the German politician, Günter Minz, who had dragged another girl around on a leash. A Wikipedia entry and a whole list of articles praised his achievements in the EU as Secretary of Health and Human Services. Another stomach churn.

Phil thought about her first encounter with Scherer. When he saw this graffito on his wall: *Tu, lleno de toda maldad, hijo del diablo*... You, full of malice, son of the devil. Scherer's reaction had been a curse, "Those goddamn crazy..."

Her brain worked feverishly: Tamar was the main suspect in Maurer's case. She was linked to Scherer and must have known at least some of the other TAB guys. But what about the rest of the Tanit Daughters? Had any other suspicious deaths occurred in their surroundings? Could any of those women be associated with Bud Winslow or Barracchi? Phil sighed in frustration: if only she knew the real names of the Tanit Daughters. She could hardly remember some of the self-chosen ones: Jezebel, Elisha, Proserpina. She tried Jezebel, then Isabel, then Isabelle Stettin—to no result. Under Dorothea Bartholdy, a lot of entries popped up, scientific publications, articles, gender studies lectures and colloquia, nothing personal. One latest entry mentioned that Dr. Bartholdy had taken a sabbatical from the History department of Johannes Gutenberg University, Mainz.

Now, Phil remembered one other real name and typed it in: Hannah Lukas. In most entries, the former TV celebrity was mentioned along with her years-long partner on screen, show master Will Koenig. Photos showed him grinning into the camera with gleaming false teeth under a rug-like hair-piece. First with Hannah Lukas at his side, then with a perfect replica of her, the same stunning figure and signature red hair, only thirty years younger. Some articles mentioned Lukas's humiliation about being replaced like an old toy. After that, her name showed up less and less, then not at all anymore. Until, shortly after Koenig's death, a sobbing Hannah Lukas was quoted, "Of course, I had forgiven him long ago."

Koenig's death! About two months ago, Phil read, he had attended the German Television Prize ceremonies to accept a lifetime achievement award. But he didn't show up on stage and was soon found dead on a urinal with dilated pupils, an open fly and priapism, a permanent erection. Koenig's heart, the article explained, had failed him: too much Viagra. Hannah Lukas had also been invited to celebrate Will Koenig's achievements from a back-row seat.

Phil launched another test balloon, typing 'India', 'tribal traditions', 'illegal tribunal', and 'gang rape.' Immediately, the heartbreaking story of the girl from the Adivasi tribe showed up who had fallen in love with the wrong boy and been condemned to gang rape by a self-proclaimed village judge. For about fifteen minutes, Manasa's case had triggered global outrage, and some adjustments were made in the Indian criminal law. Then the media moved on. Half a year later, only one British newspaper reported that the tribal judge and three of his 'colleagues' had been found with their penises and testicles torn off, left to die a slow death by bleeding dry. The assumed motif? A tribal feud, the article suggested.

Phil's heart was banging wildly. One only had to look for correlations, and they seemed to be everywhere. Bud Winslow, for instance, was described in the net as an unwavering fighter for the conservative cause. He had publicly defamed women who took the pill as whores. He had said women didn't deserve equal pay because they couldn't work as well as men. A YouTube video showed Winslow with his wife, a demure, middle-aged blonde. Phil recognized her immediately. In front of Can Follet, she had posed like a victorious boxer, both fists up in the air.

Bartolo had wondered who killed the Bes Brothers. A profit in the billions produced a lot of enemies, he said. But what else might do that?

In shock, Phil left the café. In the harbor, a caravan of cars queued up on the ramp. On deck, passengers were getting their paper rolls ready to throw. Doro—no, Anat—had sermonized about teaching the Bes Brothers love and devotion. For the goal she described as re-installing the lost balance between women and men, she tried to justify the prostitution of underage girls. But what if the Brothers, if men, proved to be resistant against this higher purpose and still wanted to dominate? A quote Phil had found in Doro's papers appeared in her mind. The author Claire Goll had appealed to women in World War I to defend themselves by all means against warmongering men. *If not with love, then with violence.*

How far would Doro go?

Down in the harbor, the ferry's horn blew. Whoever wasn't on board yet had to hurry up. Phil started to run.

CHAPTER 54

Adam wanted to slap himself, but his hands were tied behind his back. How could he have fallen for Dorothea's sudden confidentiality? Stupid ass, Adam Ryan, ex-cop and investigator, had stumbled into the fucking bitch's trap like a bloody amateur. He had walked in front of her towards Phil's burned-down house, his back to her. Idiot. He barely felt the puncture in his neck.

When he came back to his senses, he was lying face down in a boat, his bound arms and legs bound, gliding through the night. Out of the corner of his eye, he saw Dorothea at the wheel and another woman at the bow. Directly in front of his eyes were two broad feet in running shoes, stocky legs disappearing in a dripping wet skirt. The sea roared and lashed splatters of ice-cold water into Adam's face. Saltwater burned in his eyes that he couldn't wipe off.

"Careful, Elisha," he heard Dorothea's warning. "I think he woke up."

"What? Bastard."

One of the feet moved and hit Adam right in the face. Pain `pierced him like a hot needle. Blood squirted out his nose and dripped down to his chin until the next splash of seawater

381

burned it off. Instinctively, he rolled to the side, while the foot kicked him again, this time against the ear. He gave a tortured gasp.

"Stop it, Elisha. This isn't necessary," Dorothea, at his back, said sharply.

"That'll teach him," the woman hissed in a familiar tone. Texas twang. With effort, he lifted his head and tried to look into the woman's face. "If he doesn't learn to respect us," she said, "he'll outsmart us the moment he can."

"Come on, how in the world should he do that?"

Indeed, how should he as he was tied up like a goddamn piece of ham. Adam tried to focus on the woman in front of him. Her crazy glare, fake-blonde hair frizzing around her face in the sea spray. The last time he had seen this plump-featured face, it had been smiling triumphantly. That was when the woman got out of a cab at Can Follet.

For a while, Bud Winslow's demure wife, Elvira, had been on every American TV screen. Like a lioness she fought for her late husband's reputation, after his body was found full of hill-billy heroin behind the wildest gay bar in town. "My Bud was a straight man without malice or vice," Mrs. Winslow had yelped from the screens as if there wasn't proof of the opposite. Then she disappeared out of the public eye.

With great difficulty, Adam rolled around so he could sit halfway up against the boat hull. With his bound hands he felt along the wall, trying to reach the oarlock that had to be some-where there. Maybe he could find a metal edge, something sharp enough to tear through the rope. At the same time, Adam tried to talk to the crazy woman in front of him.

"I can understand that you would have liked to kick your husband, Mrs. Winslow. But what have I done to you?"

The woman made a hasty movement backwards that caused the boat to wobble. "My name is Elisha."

"He was a real piece of shit, wasn't he, such a hypocrite. But why didn't you just divorce him?"

The truth hit him: this woman had killed her husband, just as Tamar had killed Maurer. "I mean, to pump him up with drugs and kill him! How did you even manage to bring him there, into the yard of this bar?"

The woman glared at him with hate-filled eyes. "You'll never know, dickhead. That was a piece of art. And he got exactly what he deserved."

She seemed to enjoy her hatred. Her first murder had given her a kick, Adam thought, the next would be a pleasure. The power to decide about a life could be intoxicating.

Other than the widow Winslow, Dorothea—no, Anat—seemed uncomfortable with the demonstration of hatred. When the foot now kicked against Adam's throat, her voice intervened like thunder. "Stop it, Elisha. Now. That's not worthy of you or us. Enough is enough."

To Adam, "Normally, Elisha is the sweetest thing on earth. What you see is what an abusive man has turned her into. We're trying to deprogram her."

Mrs. Winslow was used to being obedient. "I'm sorry, Anat. My apologies."

One hand at the wheel, Anat turned to Adam, who was gasping for air. In a conversational tone she said, "To answer your question: if it only was that easy. To get a divorce and start anew. We would love to live in a world like that. But in the world we are living in, with types like Winslow, women will always be the victim, even when they dare to leave. They get screwed over by divorce attorneys, get cut-off from social life, lose every security. They always lose. So we have to react. It's like a growing cancer, you understand? You have to cut out the biggest tumors, so the smaller ones can be treated therapeutically."

Adam understood perfectly well. "It was you in all the cases: Winslow, Maurer, Barracchi..."

"And a few more, yes." There was a perverted pride in

Anat's words. "We liberated the world from some real monsters. You should not feel sorry for them. When the biggest tumors are gone, the body finds relief, and life goes on. In a better way. We have become pretty good at networking. We are inventive as hell, we are clever, and we sure can cover up our tracks. Which, of course, has to stay this way. You do understand that, Adam, don't you?"

Again, Adam understood. They couldn't keep him alive even if they wanted to; he was a witness to their crimes. He just wondered why they hadn't thrown him overboard yet. Maybe because of the currents, so his body wouldn't be washed ashore. Further out on the high seas they would rid themselves off him.

He had to stay calm. "Okay. So you have killed some real assholes..."

"The time will come when people will be thankful to us. Cherish us for saving the world, women and men."

"But Ninguno? What has he ever done to you? And Amanda." In spite of the situation, Adam could hardly control his fury. "How do they meet your concept of the bogeyman? Was Amanda one of your monsters, Dorothea? My sad, lonely sister? Shouldn't she have been one of the women you saved?"

Anat's expression was pained. There was even a tear on her cheek—or a splash of seawater. "I know, Adam, that should never have happened. That's really tragic. Amanda was..."

Elisha interrupted her. "Collateral damage. You know it, Anat. Amanda was a fucking coward. She said she'd do it, and then she was too weak. Had she given the poison to him, she could be free. Like me."

"That exactly was the problem, Adam." Anat gave a profound sigh. "We prepared Amanda so well. We went through it again and again. She wanted to put the poison in his glass and in her own. We instructed her how much exactly she should sip, so she'd be unconscious but would survive. It was supposed to look like someone was after both of them, and only Amanda was lucky enough to survive. We even prepared a great suspect. But then, Scherer didn't come home that night. Even though he had promised."

"The asshole," Elisha raved, "preferred to party with other assholes."

"And Amanda lost her nerve." Anat rubbed her eyes. The memory seemed to burden her. "We counted on her. Scherer is the worst danger for our sanctuary."

"And we make short work of assholes like him," Elisha boasted.

"Amanda—that was awful." Anat admitted, "But we didn't have a choice. I came to her, that night, to see if everything went according to plan. There is a way through the cistern, so the cameras didn't get me. Had Scherer been taken care of, she would have been fine. But he wasn't even there, and suddenly Amanda attacked me in the most irrational way. She was so naïve. She believed she was safe because she had told Ninguno about our plan to get rid of Scherer. As if this would cover her back. Then the old idiot stole my backpack with our strategy papers. I had allowed a traitor to stay in my house."

"Phil's house," Adam said.

"Right. So in the end, that makes Amanda responsible for Ninguno's death. We still warned him, with the rabbit's head. We didn't want to kill him."

"But," Elisha said, "we had to make sure."

"I guess. Because he didn't know better than to call Scherer. He wanted to give him the papers and get his protection. Fortunately, Scherer ignored him. So we took care of Ninguno. We had to burn the papers. Which meant him as well."

Anat looked at Adam, almost deploringly, "We should have prepared Amanda better. We thought we had. You can plan things in perfection, and occasionally, it still doesn't work out. But we can't allow the whole building to crash because of one weak post."

Anat concentrated on the wheel. She steered the boat around some rocks that stood out of the water like needles. The boat wiggled through a narrow tunnel towards a shore where she turned off the engine. "Here we are. Adam, I'm sorry but we have to sedate you once more. In spite of the situation, honestly, it was a pleasure to get to know you a little better."

CHAPTER 55

Phil steered the car she had rented with one hand, trying to reach Bartolo with the other. The operator assured her the call would be transferred to the inspector as soon as possible. That didn't help. Why hadn't she asked Bartolo for his mobile number? The operator wouldn't give it to her.

"Tell him, it's Phil. Philine Mann. Tell him Adam is in great danger."

"Have you called 112?"

"I need Bartolo Dziri. Now."

"I'll let him know."

In a risky maneuver, Phil passed a car. How slow traffic moved. Damn tourists. She pressed the accelerator down. In San José, a policeman was standing in front of Bernat Vinya, enjoying his coffee. Phil honked, hoping he would jump into his car and come after her. He would have to follow her all the way to Can Follet, because she wouldn't stop before. Come on, man! But the policeman couldn't be convinced to interrupt his *siesta* and let the speedster go unpunished.

At Can Follet, Phil left the car right in front of the barrier and ran. The woman in the guardhouse jumped up, "Hey, what in the world are you doing?" Recognizing Phil, the woman let her go with a, "Love to you—but you have to move your car." Phil just ran.

Behind her desk, Stella jumped up in shock, "Wait!"

But Phil just ran by her. From behind a door, she could hear Amaryl's voice. Another lecture on Elisha's Voyage, the legend of the Phoenician queen who wanted to save Matriarchy with her escape to Carthage. Phil pushed the door open. All heads turned towards her. But no Anat.

"What the..." said Amaryl.

In the kitchen, Trudy was bustling around like a multi-armed Indian goddess. She had no idea where Anat was, but wanted to rhapsodize about her wonderful new life. Phil ran back into the entrance hall, where Stella grabbed her arm.

"Phil, please don't. I beg you..."

But without a word, Phil broke free and ran on the patio, where she almost stumbled into Jezebel's wheelchair. Tamar's mother was staring at the horizon.

"Jezebel, where is Adam? What has Anat done to him?"

Jezebel didn't turn her head. "Leave me alone," she said. "My daughter is dead. For all I care, these monsters can all go screw themselves."

Phil's eyes followed hers. Far out behind Es Vedrà, the rain was falling like a curtain of strings, but above the rock it was still dry. Only a delicate line curled skywards. A trail of smoke. There was someone.

A woman in a fantasy queen's robe came out and sat under the overlapping roof. "I love me a cozy rain with a glass of wine." She lifted a glass. "Cheers."

Probably no Daughter of the so-called First circle, Phil thought, knew murders were committed in the name of Tanit. They thought they were safe here.

There was a little rubber boat lying on the beach, right in front of the patio, the outboard engine tilted upwards. When Phil slammed the patio door open, Jezebel woke up from her lethargy.

"You stay here," she screeched, "you have no right..."

Phil ran. How difficult could it be to start such an engine? She pushed the boat into the water, glad it was light like a toy, jumped in and pushed the engine back which obediently snapped into its bracket. How did it work? A pull starter. Couldn't be much different than a lawnmower.

Jezebel screamed something from the patio. Fortunately, she was bound to her wheelchair, but the other woman appeared on the stairs, her arms flailing. On the public side of the beach, a waiter of the Mar y Sol restaurant cleared the patio tables as it started to sprinkle. He looked over and decided not to get involved.

With power born of desperation, Phil pulled at the cable and screamed in relief when the motor started to stutter. One more try, and it puttered in a regular rhythm. The hand gear was easy to deal with. She maneuvered the boat out of the bay and fiddled for her phone. The rain intensified.

Lluis answered immediately. "Phil, for heaven's sake..."

"I'm in a boat..."

Reception broke off. Phil had read that the rock's magnetism was so strong it could interfere with all kinds of devices and compass needles. Due to neodymium? Were the Daughters also after the neodymium, or had they chosen Es Vedrà to plot their murders? A sanctuary. Bullshit. Phil tried to keep the boat on a steady track. Jezebel had mentioned wild shallows, causing boats to capsize.

Phil tried to remember from which side of the rock the smoke had risen. The sea side. The northern cape was even less accessible than the Cala d'Hort side, only steep cliffs and walls of eroding limestone. But behind a sharp cut ledge was a tiny bay, only to be reached if she maneuvered the boat right through a narrow alley of rock needles. The rubber wall of the boat scraped against the rocks but hopefully wouldn't leak. Then sand was grating underneath the boat.

This part of Es Vedrà looked as if no living creature had

ever set foot on it. But when Phil threw her head back, she detected the column of smoke. It seemed to come straight out of the rock massif's pinnacle, unbothered by the rain that had gotten stronger. And then, Phil detected the almost unrecognizable trace of a trail, just some crushed leaves of grass and pebbles. It led away from the bay and disappeared in the crevice between two vertical rocks, standing steep and repellent.

Phil slipped through the crack and was in front of a high wall of reeds, standing densely side by side. But part of the green canes had been kicked over. It took a few minutes until she found the entrance to the cave. The iron-barred gate was way more stable than the one of Es Cuieram, and well oiled. And open.

Phil entered a pitch dark. With outstretched hands, she found her way along the uneven rock wall, in the direction of something burning. There was a diffuse light, a crackling. Something heavy and dull brushed against her face, smelling like mold. A curtain. She pulled it aside, and the Tanit sanctuary of Es Vedrà opened up in front of her. A high arched cave, dominated by a huge blazing fire. A metal wreath, containing neatly stacked branches controlled the flames. On a slab of rock, lit by the fire's surreal halo, lay a motionless body.

Phil forgot all caution and ran to Adam. For one terrible moment she thought he was already dead. His face was waxen, the closed lids gray. But, very subtly, his chest was moving up and down. Adam was naked but for a loincloth, his skin gleaming in the fire's glow, like oiled. Phil gasped in horror. The Daughters of Tanit had chosen him to be a *molk*, a human sacrifice.

Desperately, she pulled at his ears, hit him in the face with flat palms, tried to lift him up. "Wake up, Adam, please, wake up."

Nothing. But she had to get him out of here. Again, she slapped his cheeks as hard as she could. He had to wake up. Her fingers clawed his shoulders, shook him frantically. Nothing. She took one of Adam's arms lying with folded hands on his solar plexus, put it around her shoulder, and grabbed his wrist with one hand. Put the other under his shoulder and pulled. Got him a few inches up. He fell back like a limp puppet. She drummed his chest with both fists, slapped his face, forced his mouth open to blow air in. A first tiny reaction, a faint wheeze.

"You have to get up, hear me, we have to get out of here."

Again Phil's fists beat down on Adam's chest, and indeed, the tiny sign of life in him, the wheeze, seemed to be getting a bit stronger. But he was far from waking up. Again, Phil blew air into his mouth, shook him...

"He can't hear you," a voice behind her said.

Phil whirled around. In front of the velvet curtain, Anat appeared, followed by Elisha and Proserpina, aka Hannah Lukas. All three were in long white togas, white flower wreaths in their hair. Anat was carrying a silver tray with a carafe and three chalices. Phil was so furious she didn't feel a bit of fear.

"Damn, Doro, that's what you have become. To turn into a pimp of little girls and kill rabbits for your fucking mumbo jumbo—that's bad enough. But a human being. To kill human beings. You are so fucking sick, Doro."

"You should not have come here." Without batting an eyelid, Anat set the tray on a low table with some velvet cushions around it. As if she were preparing a cozy tea ceremony in front of the crackling fire. The other women didn't move a muscle. When Anat straightened up again, the ridiculous cute flower wreath slid to the side of her head. She eyed Phil with a punitive look, no other visible emotion. "I gave you my flat. You are safe. What else do you want?"

"Do you think I could allow you to kill Adam? You are crazy. All of you."

Anat sighed deeply, "No, Phil, we are not. We didn't want this, we *don't*, but there's no other way. We had to accept that it doesn't make sense to count on love. To make men see the value of love. Or reason. *If not with love, then with violence—*

remember? You even wrote it in your thesis."

"That was a quote. About World War One..."

"Do you think this is any less horrific? On the contrary: many more women and girls have died through male violence than soldiers in any world war. And there are millions of battlefields. Open today's newspaper: a three-year-old raped in India. A gang rape in Chicago. A so-called honor killing of an Afghan girl in Berlin. A dead twelve-year-old in Ohio who wasn't allowed abortion after being raped. And, and, and. The author you researched about, Claire Goll, was an insightful woman. She got it: *If not with love, then with violence.* We have been in this global war for a long, long time. Do you think we do what we do for fun? If someone had managed to kill Hitler, millions of lives would have been spared."

"Let's get it over with," Elisha said in Anat's back. "She's just one of the unenlightened. Has no idea what this is about."

"Wait." Anat lifted her hands in an authoritarian gesture, showing she was in charge. But her eyes had a stressed flicker. In reality, she was under pressure.

"What, Phil, shall I do with you?"

"Wanna kill me too?" Phil felt panic growing, "and go on with 'Love to you' and shit? How hypocritical is that, Doro? I didn't do anything to any woman. And Adam—He's working in a department that fights against sexism. He has been on your side the whole time, and you're gonna kill him in cold blood?"

"Stop talking," Elisha said. "Sacrifices have to be made. In every war."

"So you're not any better than men. Warmongering. Innocent people have to die, so you can win. Dominate. Not one bit better than men you are."

Phil hadn't imagined the flickering in Anat's eyes. What a dilemma she must be in. How could she justify murdering Adam? And her old friend Phil?

"We cannot let this mission fail," she said nevertheless,

"Please, Phil, you must understand—all the dead women! We cannot live in danger any longer."

"We *are* the danger," Elisha hissed. Unlike Anat, she seemed to fit perfectly well in the role of the bad guy. Bad woman.

Anat interposed immediately. "No, Elisha. We are only defending ourselves. We are *love*. I hate this." Misery was in her voice. "But don't you see, Phil, what is being done to women? All the uprisings, Times Up, #MeToo, whatever, nothing changed it. Women keep suffering. Mothers, girls keep suffering."

Phil looked Anat straight in the eyes. "I am a mother."

"If there was a drug to make you forget what you've seen, I'd let you go."

Anat lowered her gaze, while Hannah Lukas began to sob. "I can't endure this anymore. It's insane. What are we doing?" She hid her face in her hands.

"Fuck, Proserpina," Elisha yelled, "Don't be a sissy. Let's get it behind us."

She jumped at Phil and gave her a powerful push. Phil staggered to the side, while Elisha lifted Adam up. She panted, but she was strong. In a flash, Phil was behind her and with the metal heel of her boots kicked her calf. Elisha buckled forward. Adam fell back onto the altar. The impact, however, took effect. He steered, shook his head. Phil kicked Elisha hard in the kidney, grabbed one of the erect branches in the stake, and pulled it out. On this end, it wasn't burning yet. Still, the cut on her palm immediately hurt like hell. Like a *Funkenmariechen*, one of the sassy dancers at the Rhineland's carnivals parades, a *Mariechen* gone mad, Phil started to whirl the burning branch in front of her.

Elisha crawled back. The Daughters were forced to back off the whirling, blazing branch. But only as far as they had to, the shortest necessary distance. From there, they were lurking. A pack of predators smelling blood, all senses alert. Not one word was said. Hanna Lukas and Anat were fully concentrated again, all awareness of right or wrong gone, their whole being back to the most ancient instincts. Kill or die. They knew what had to be done. The moment when Phil had to drop the branch, already burning her skin, would be there soon.

"You don't have a chance," Phil yelled, "even if... if you kill Adam and me. You won't have time to get rid of us. Bartolo will find you."

Phil felt her fingers burn, her skin, her palm crack open. She changed the branch to her other hand, close to fainting. She kept whirling the burning stick.

"Phil, I'm so sorry." Anat said gently, "please let go, Phil."

Then Phil had to. Crying out in pain, she dropped the branch. Immediately, Elisha jumped on her with full force, knocking her over, burying her under her heavy body. A bulldozer riding over her.

At that moment, one single word swept through the cave. "Here!"

It was Lluis's voice, followed by an orchestra of moves, breaths, echoes from heavy boots. More voices. Uproar. A glaring light, another word, *"Policia!"*

Elisha was sitting on Phil, both knees rammed into her chest, her fingers clawed around her throat. Fighting for air, Phil saw an apparition above her. Bartolo. Then a howl. The fingers loosened. Suddenly, there was air to breathe. Elisha slumped down, now full body on Phil, crushing her. Crushing her to death. But in the last moment, the heavy body was pulled off her, rolled to the side, and she was free, gasping for air. There were uniforms, policemen, Bartolo. The stone altar. Arms holding Adam, helping him up.

The last thing Phil saw before everything went blank was Anat shaking off a policeman's hand and pushing him away. Jumping right into the blazing fire.

"No, Doro! No!"

CHAPTER 56

When Phil woke up, she was lying in a blinding white field. Afterlife? No, a hospital bed. An IV drip was taped to her left arm; her hands were bound in pressure bandages. Her chest was aching horribly. Every breath of air was pain. And the painful image was immediately back: Doro jumping into the fire.

Phil stared at the ceiling and felt the cracks on it getting bigger while she looked. Doro had known it was over, and she preferred to die than face it. Did she realize, in these last moments of her life, that her fight against the Scherers, Barracchis, Maurers, and Winslows of this world had turned her into a monster also? Did she know that she never had a chance to win without being infected by their poison? Oh, Doro.

The Bes Brothers would lick their wounds and go on. The Hydra would grow a thousand new heads. But Doro was dead. Died in the flames she had sparked for Adam. Phil was shaken to the core: Doro really had planned to kill Adam. And her, Phil, her best friend, the witness. How sick must she have been to justify this? Was Doro aware of it the moment she jumped to her death?

Phil flinched when somebody leaned over her. Bartolo

Dziri.

"Where's Adam?" she asked weakly.

"Like you, safe and sound in Hospital Can Misses. I've come to get you." He waved at someone, "*Señora.*"

A nurse appeared, took the infusion bag off its rack and attached it to the bed's headrest. Phil tried to sit up. A piercing pain shot through her chest.

"Careful," the nurse said, "please try not to move."

She raised the backrest so Phil came into a sitting position and turned to Dziri. "Two broken and two half-cracked ribs. Both palms injured with a two-level incineration." To Phil she said, "I'm afraid there will be some lasting scars." And again to Bartolo, "Moving her at this point is actually prohibited."

"We have to make an exception here, *vale?* Legitimate policing measures."

With the tip of his shoe, Bartolo opened the wheel lock-up of the bed and pushed it out of the room like a giant baby stroller.

Adam was lying in semi-darkness, his arm also connected to an IV drip, Lluis at his side. Lluis jumped up to help Bartolo move Phil's bed parallel to Adam's.

As before in the harbor, what seemed years ago, Lluis caressed Phil's cheek. "I can't believe it. Geez, you two!"

Phil looked at Adam, who had his eyes closed. "What's with him?"

How pale his cheeks were. The stubble of beard on his chin seemed to have turned white overnight.

"He's just pissed off." Lluis shrugged fake-casually. "The doctor wants to keep him here for a couple of nights. He has been sedated for fifteen hours in a row and is completely dehydrated. But our superman doesn't agree."

Adam opened his eyes. "I'm fine." With effort, he heaved himself up to a sitting position and looked at Phil. Holding her gaze.

"Man. Aren't you a sight to see."

"You don't look that hot either."

For a while they just kept their eyes locked. Then Adam grinned. "I felt every single one of your slaps in my face."

"Good. Then we're even."

Smiling together felt better than anything else in a long time. But then, Phil had to ask Bartolo. "Doro. Is she...?"

"Yes. She clung to the burning stakes, wouldn't let go. When we were able to reach her, she was already unconscious. Nothing we could do to save her."

Phil swallowed hard. What was worse: Doro dead—or having to live with Doro, the murderer? She wiped away a tear that ran down her cheek.

"How did you get there so fast? To the cave. I couldn't talk."

"Someone called before you, someone named Stella, and she had a reception. She said she called in your name, we should immediately come to Es Vedrà. Imminent danger of death, she said, and hung up."

Stella! The woman with the star tattoo had saved their lives. Obviously, she was not as convinced of the Tanit Daughters' cause or the need for collateral damage as—Doro. It was hard to even think the name. It was better to think: Stella had saved them.

"And the others?"

"Elvira Winslow was injured by a grazing shot. Later today, she and Hannah Lukas will be brought before the judge. Both swear that no one in Can Follet but the two of them, *señora* Bartholdy, and Tamar Stettin had anything to do with the murders. We think that's what they strategically agreed upon: the ones caught admit to being guilty, everyone else is innocent. Quite honorable, in a way."

"But they can't get away with it, can they?"

"Hell no. They'll be prosecuted. The question is if we can prove who else is involved. My men are scanning the cave. It looks like a scientific laboratory and a control center with all kinds of high-end communicative devices. I've never seen anything like that. No one would have suspected this on Es Vedrà."

"What about this rare earth metal? The magnetism?"

"We're also looking into that. The *Consell Insular* is informed. The sale of the rock is off the table. Not sure what the *Consell* will do in case they really find a profitable deposit of neodymium. Let's hope they won't start mining."

"Have you been to Can Follet?" Adam asked.

Bartolo rolled his eyes. "Yes. Also biting on granite there. Jezebel—Isabel Stettin—maintains she is merely managing a holiday resort for women, nothing else. That it is discriminatory of us to suspect she's involved in a crime, just because one female may have committed one. Her own daughter suddenly is just 'one female' to her. As are her partner, Dorothea Bartholdy, and the two others. She just shrugs it off. How is she supposed to know each of her guests' backgrounds? An ice-cold woman she is. All others swear they have no idea what happened. That they are just vacationing."

"Most of them are probably telling the truth. What about...? Did you see a black woman with a star tattoo around her eye?" Phil asked.

"There was no one like that around."

So Stella had managed to get away. Phil realized she felt relieved about this. She longed for a cigarette. She looked at her bandaged hands and sighed.

"But we met another interesting—visitor in Can Follet." Bartolo hit one fist into his palm. "Just arrived from Italy was the widow Simonetta Barracchi. She is very upset about the stress we are giving her, as she came to recover from her husband's death. They were about to get divorced, she says; so no, she's not really grieving for him. But she needs to calm down and collect herself."

"They are feeling quite untouchable," Adam said.

And maybe they would prove to be, Phil thought. As long

as the Daughters of Tanit stuck together, as long as there wasn't a leak. But now Anat, their leader, was dead. If she really had been that. They didn't know who exactly was the head of the murderous organization. Someone else, somewhere in the world? A multi-headed spider in a gigantic net?

"In the cave of Es Vedrà, we have started to collect data pointing to a global network," Bartolo confirmed her thought, "names over names. Isabel Stettin claims they refer to former, current, or potential guests of Can Follet. Women they approach in their newsletters, advertising the resort and the seminars. There are also names of all kinds of organizations like Lioness Revenge or Globalsis or WeWo and so on. Nothing but basic feminist networking, Stettin insists, manifestations of solidarity, relief programs, aid initiatives for Third World centers, student exchange programs, and so on. Sounds like the UNESCO for women only. All of this has to be analyzed, and the codes have to be cracked. We confiscated everything we could get and sent it to CNI."

Bartolo explained, "*Centro Nacional de Inteligencia*, our Spanish version of the FBI. Our colleagues are just beginning to screen it all, but they already found a number of connections to other unsolved and highly unusual cases of death. Dead men, worldwide, who could rightly be called misogynists. Interpol got involved, but that's it for now. The authorities' task is to prove that those deaths are murders and connected. Ridiculous, Isabel Stettin says in her aloof way, insisting the only connection is that women hurt by men find refuge in Can Follet. And that it's typical for me and all the other defenders of misogyny to blame these poor women for the death of some assholes, instead of blaming the self-destructive male system. This woman can talk! Man, I'm happy to be only a little island cop who can leave it all to the big shots."

For a while, they just sat there, Phil and Adam in their beds, Bartolo and Lluis side by side. Then Bartolo had the urge to go smoke a cigarette with Lluis, before he would wheel Phil back to her room.

The door closed behind them and left an awkward silence. Phil felt tears swelling up in her eyes and only hoped they wouldn't drip down her cheeks.

Adam cleared his throat and, in a coarse voice, whispered, "Anton. Does Anton actually look anything like me?"

Phil swallowed hard, didn't care about dripping tears anymore, and bent over to him. "Don't ask."

With her bandaged hand, she tapped against his chin, his mouth, his cheek, his eyes that were now glittering too. "Here and here and here—and it's not just looks."

Adam waited until something wet had made it down his face.

"Do you think it'd be possible—I mean: Could I eventually get to know my son after all?" he whispered.

Phil only nodded.

THE END

ABOUT ATMOSPHERE PRESS

Atmosphere Press is an independent, full-service publisher for excellent books in all genres and for all audiences. Learn more about what we do at atmospherepress.com.

We encourage you to check out some of Atmosphere's latest releases, which are available at Amazon.com and via order from your local bookstore:

The View From My Window, a novel by Patricia J. Gallegos

Wake Up, a novel by Alejandro Marron

The Dead Life, a novel by Matthew Sprosty

And the Stars Kept Watch, a novel by Peter Friedrichs

Ways and Truths and Lives, a novel by Matt Edwards

The Northern Line, stories by Mike Lee

Madeleine: Last French Casquette Bride in New Orleans, a novel by Wanda Maureen Miller

Ignite, a novel by Marie A. Wishert

Adam's Roads, a novel by Edwin Litts

Heir to the Cross, a novel by Chris Perry

Letters I'll Never Send, a novel by Nicole Zelniker

Somebody's Watching You, a novel by Robin D'Amato

A Gang of Outsiders, a novel by Bobby Williams

The Saint of Lost Causes, a novel by Carly Schorman

Orange City, a novel by Lee Matthew Goldberg

Ulser, a novel by R.J. Deeds

Trace Element, a novel by R.W. Bell

ABOUT THE AUTHOR

Verena Mahlow worked in Germany as a journalist, writer, translator and interpreter and has an MA and Ph.D. in German, American and Italian Studies. She lived in France, Italy, the USA and parts of many years on Ibiza. After some stints in academic Ivory towers, she wrote a large number of scripts for TV-movies and has many short stories and non-fiction published. Her first novel was awarded 1st prize in a female literature competition by the publishing house Lübbe. After she moved to Dallas, TX., she decided to write her second novel in English.

CPSIA information can be obtained
at www.ICGtesting.com
Printed in the USA
LVHW050530210723
752954LV00002B/97

9 781637 528679